The minute the c   l her,
they cleared out,   ippen
that they didn't w   kept
his eyes glued to   Janna
thought. Not a goo

"Ty?"

"Miss MacNeil. What a surprise."

Janna watched him turn slowly toward her, her heartbeat doubling its tempo. She was anxious, yes. But she realized there was more to it than that: clad in sweatpants,
he was shirtless, a twisted white towel casually slung
around his neck, the perfect six-pack of his abs glistening
with hard-earned sweat. He aroused in her a desire that
could only be called primal. She'd never experienced anything so elemental and so *strong*. That the sight of this
man should generate it only made it worse. It was like
being a teenage wallflower and finding yourself attracted
to that one dumb jock in your high school who always
made fun of you at lunch. Her body was betraying her . . .

TY: 1
JANNA: 0

Deirdre Martin

JOVE BOOKS, NEW YORK

BODY CHECK

A Jove Book / published by arrangement with
the author

PRINTING HISTORY
Jove edition / March 2003

For information address: The Berkley Publishing Group,
a division of Penguin Putnam Inc.,
375 Hudson Street, New York, New York 10014.

ISBN: 0-515-13489-9

A JOVE BOOK®
Jove Books are published by The Berkley Publishing Group,
a division of Penguin Putnam Inc.,
375 Hudson Street, New York, New York 10014.
JOVE and the "J" design
are trademarks belonging to Penguin Putnam Inc.

PRINTED IN THE UNITED STATES OF AMERICA

10   9   8   7   6   5   4   3   2

For Mark,
always and forever

ACKNOWLEDGMENTS

I'd like to thank:

My agent, Elaine English, and my editor, Allison McCabe, for their willingness to take a chance.

John Rosasco, vice president of PR for the New York Rangers, for letting me pick his brains.

Jacquie Powers for her gardening expertise.

Meg Janifer, sportswriter and hockey fan, for her insights into what really takes place in the locker room.

My husband, Mark Levine, for his vast knowledge of sports as well as his keen editorial eye.

And last but not least, Mom, Dad, Bill, Allison, Beth, Dave, Tom, and Jane for their unwavering love and support.

CHAPTER
01

Not many women could boast bossing around a locker room full of buff, naked jocks as part of their job description, but then again, there weren't many women with a job like Janna MacNeil's.

A publicist specializing in retooling clients' images as well as damage control, Janna had been hired by Kidco Corporation to help transform the reputation of the New York Blades, the NHL's Manhattan-based hockey franchise. To put it politely, the guys on the team were renowned for playing hard both on and off the ice. Never had this been more obvious than last season, after winning the Stanley Cup for the first time in twenty years. Everyone knows boys will be boys, but *these* boys brought the Cup to a number of strip joints around Manhattan, where they enjoyed the rare and singular pleasure of watching ladies with pasties and very little else "perform" with what many considered the Holy Grail of sports. Worse, rumors abounded that a photo existed of a group of players gathered around the Cup with plastic straws up their noses, heads reverently bowed to snort up a small mountain of cocaine. No wonder Janna's crusty new boss, Lou "the Bull" Capesi, guzzled Mylanta like it was spring water. The team was a PR nightmare.

Janna was being paid big bucks to change all that.

Edging her way through the boisterous cluster of beat writers hovering in the brightly lit, concrete hallway near the locker room door, Janna steeled herself, knowing what awaited her on the other side: naked, sweaty, male bodies. Lots of them. Big, muscled men laughing and joking with each other, flicking towels at each other's butts. Men sauntering off to the shower. Men stretching, massaging their battle-weary bones. She'd met these men—all but their captain, Ty Gallagher, who was a day late to training camp—in these very circumstances yesterday. Lou had introduced her around, and not one of them seemed fazed about parading buck naked or half undressed in front of a petite female publicist. Janna, on the other hand, had had to work hard to avoid the irresistible urge to stare, slack jawed and salivating, at the well-sculpted physiques of these guys. She made doubly sure she kept her eyes north of the equator, too.

Once inside the locker room, the same scene she'd been initiated into yesterday greeted her. Some of the players lounged on the long wooden benches in front of their lockers, chatting, half dressed. Others stood at a large, rectangular table at the far end of the room, gulping down mammoth-sized glasses of Gatorade they'd poured from huge jugs. A few acknowledged her with nods; some, she thought, deliberately looked away. A boom box blasted music. The Who? Pearl Jam? She couldn't tell. The atmosphere was exuberant, almost adolescent in its giddiness. Though it was September, still pre-season, the Blades were clearly psyched about making another run for the Stanley Cup in the year ahead. She took a deep breath, trying hard to ignore the pungent odor of male sweat that was inescapable, and made for the bench closest to the center of the room, climbing up on it. Then, with all the power she could muster, she stuck her fingers in her mouth and whistled. The room fell silent as all eyes trained on her.

"Listen up, guys: Now that I have your attention, I need your help." She looked around the room, carefully making eye contact with each and every player. "As you know, the Blades organization was recently purchased by Kidco Corporation, which prides itself on providing *family* entertainment." Boos and amused chuckles filled the room. "Kidco wants the Blades to be winners both on and off the ice, meaning they'd like each of you to give a little something back to the community you play in." She held the papers aloft in her hand. "This is a schedule of charity events going on all over the city over the course of the next year. I've highlighted those that don't conflict with your playing and travel schedule. I'd like each of you to sign up for at least three."

"And if we don't?" a rogue Canadian voice challenged.

"If you don't, then I kick your butt, and believe me, I can do it. I might be small, but I'm wiry." The players laughed appreciatively, and Janna relaxed somewhat. None of them could tell, but beneath her tailored suit she was a bundle of stomach-churning nerves, something she was a pro at covering up after years of practice.

"Speaking of butt-kicking, I just want to remind you that no one is to talk to the press without clearance from the PR office, understand? I don't care if some reporter stops you outside Zabar's and asks if that's where you shop for groceries. Everything—*everything*—has to go through me or Lou. Not only that, but if God forbid you do find yourself saying or doing something stupid, you're to call me immediately. That's why I gave all of you my cell phone number yesterday. I expect you to use it, day or night, if you have a question about something or if an emergency arises. Now, back to the business at hand." She flashed them a quick, determined look. "Signing up for three events now will save you the aggravation of me following you around and nagging you to death for the rest of the season—which I'm paid *very* handsomely to do." More laughter. "So whaddaya say?"

She didn't expect them to come forward in droves, but she *was* hoping a few might be willing to get the ball rolling. Instead, a stubborn silence filled the room. One second passed. Two, three. Janna's heart began beating just a little bit faster, her palms moistening. She took another deep breath, steadying herself. *You can do this,* she repeated in her mind. As the silence dragged on, she wondered if this was how comedians felt when they "died" on stage.

"Come on, guys, don't make this any harder than it needs to be," she coaxed. "Either you sign up, or I start putting your names down at random. The choice is yours."

She watched as their collective gaze suddenly shifted from studying her to something on her left that was apparently fascinating. She looked. There stood Captain Ty Gallagher, a white towel knotted at his waist, his rock-solid body still glistening with damp from the shower. His blond hair was slicked back, and his deep-set, brown eyes were hard and unwelcoming. Feeling Lilliputian, despite still standing on the bench, Janna struggled not to let herself become overwhelmed by the nausea gathering force and momentum inside her. She smiled at him politely.

"Captain Gallagher?"

"The one and only." The voice was polite but guarded, giving away nothing. Janna gingerly climbed down from the bench and extended her hand to him. Gallagher took it, briefly, for a very firm shake. Her hand grasped in his looked doll-sized; the thought flashed through her mind that with one quick squeeze he could easily ground her bones to powder if he wanted to. Which, thankfully, he didn't. Yet.

"I'm Janna MacNeil."

"I know who you are." He folded his strong arms across

his chest and continued staring at her, challenging, expectant.

"I was just telling your teammates that as part of our effort to improve community relations, Kidco Corporation would like it if every player signed up for at least three charity events. Maybe you could lead the way and sign up first."

"No."

Janna blinked. "But—"

"No." He strode toward his locker and began dressing. She'd heard from Lou that he was an arrogant, uncooperative bastard. Here was her proof. Determined to play his dismissal down, she turned back to the players.

"Moving right along," she continued smoothly, "is there anyone who *would* care to sign up?"

"I'll sign up," a voice called out from the back.

Relieved, Janna stood on tiptoes and peered over the sea of heads to see who had spoken. It was brawny, curly-haired Kevin Gill, one of the team's assistant captains. Janna had met him yesterday and had been utterly charmed by how articulate he was. Truth be told, she hadn't been anticipating too much in the brains department when it came to dealing with these guys. They *were* hockey players, after all. They made a living chasing a little rubber biscuit around an ice rink. How smart could they be?

Kevin came forward, took Janna's list from her, and after skimming it, signed his initials next to three events. "Who's next?" he asked. Janna noticed that he shot Ty Gallagher an annoyed glance, which the captain responded to with an indifferent shrug. When no one moved, Kevin sighed.

"I tried," he said to Janna, heading off in the direction of the shower. Clearly, the guys on the team took their cues from their beloved leader. If the great Ty Gallagher didn't think signing up for charity events was worth it, neither did they. *God help me,* Janna thought. It was going to take a lot more work to polish these guys up than she'd anticipated. Especially if she had to work through Captain Gallagher to do it.

"Well," Janna called out to no one in particular, "if you don't sign up today, I'll be here tomorrow, and the day after that, and the day after that, until you do sign. I'm not going anywhere, guys."

Her threat hanging in the air, she found herself approached by the Russian prodigy, Alexei Lubov, which surprised her. Lou had warned her that many of the foreign players were hesitant about doing PR, because they were unsure about their command of English. They had great trepidation about involving themselves in anything that might embarrass them. Lubov was obviously an exception to the rule.

"Hello," he said carefully in a heavy accent, his innocent baby face serious. "I am Alexei Lubov. You will call me Lex."

Lex? Janna thought, biting her lip. *Lex Lubov? Who was he, one of Superman's archenemies?*

"Hello, Lex," Janna said cordially. "Nice to meet you."

He gestured at her sign-up sheet. "I wish to sign."

"Do you have any idea what kind of events you prefer to be involved with?"

"Girls," he declared, his baby blue eyes lighting up. "Something with many, many girls."

Janna laughed. "There are usually women at all of them. Do you want to participate in a golf outing? A black tie dinner?"

"Yes, dinner." He leaned closer to her, as if he were about to impart a secret. "You will be there, yes?"

"Yes."

"You would like to go out with me?"

It took Janna a moment to realize that what he had meant to say was, "Would you like to go out with me?" At least, she hoped that's what he meant. She patted his arm. "Maybe some other time. But for now, I have work to do."

"Yes, all right," he said somewhat impatiently, and

walked off. He was adorably cute. And God knows Kidco was confident he was destined for stardom. But he seemed a bit . . . boyish. Definitely not her type. And his name! Lex Lubov! She couldn't wait to tell her roommate Theresa that one.

Things began to wind down, and the locker room started emptying out, players departing in groups of two and three. Out of the corner of her eye, Janna caught sight of Ty Gallagher, now dressed, swinging his gym bag onto his shoulder. He donned sunglasses and was about to leave when Janna approached him.

"May I speak with you a minute?"

Lowering his sunglasses ever so slightly, Ty peered down at her with an irritated gaze. "What's on your mind?"

"Well, it's this. Since you're the team's captain, I'll be honest with you. I've been hired to help make over the team's image."

"We don't need a makeover."

"That's debatable. Kidco Corporation, which now owns the team, as you know, was less than pleased with how you guys behaved when you won the Cup last year."

Ty suppressed a smirk. "We shared the Cup with the city. What's wrong with that?"

"You brought it to strip clubs." Janna saw immediately that she'd hit a nerve—the wrong one. The chiseled features of his handsome face stiffened, and she got the distinct impression that he was struggling to keep his infamous temper in check, a temper that once supposedly drove him to threaten to push a player off a moving bus if the guy didn't improve his game. She waited, held deep in the prolonged freeze of what was now, unmistakably, a glare.

"Let me explain something to you, Miss MacNeil." His voice was a low rumble, carefully controlled. "Last year, my guys busted their asses out there on the ice night after night, and for one reason: they wanted to win the Cup.

When they did win, it was their right to do whatever the hell they wanted with it, whether it was take it to a strip club or let their dog eat Alpo from it. You understand?"

"How about snorting cocaine from it?" Janna asked sharply. "Were they free to do that?"

"That story is bull, and you know it."

"I *don't* know it, and neither does Kidco. Ultimately, it really doesn't matter if it's true or not. What matters is that a rumor like that hurts the team's image. It's unacceptable."

"And so your job is to—what? Turn us into choirboys?"

"Kidco doesn't expect the players to go home at night and bake cookies, no. But they *do* expect all of you to give a few hours to do some good old-fashioned PR to help offset the party animal image dogging the team."

"No offense, but none of the guys on this team, especially me, owe Kidco anything."

Janna chuckled, almost a snort. "Oh, really? Who do you think signs your checks now? Who do you think pays that mega salary that makes it possible for you to squire models around? Kidco *owns* the Blades, which means they own you, whether you like or not."

Now it was Ty's turn to laugh, and it was a contemptuous one. "If it wasn't for me, all those soft boys in their suits wouldn't know who the hell the New York Blades *were*. The only reason they bought the team was because we won the Cup, and the only reason we won the Cup is because *I* was brought to New York specifically to turn this club back into a winning franchise, which I did. So don't tell me I owe them. I already *did* my part for the suits upstairs."

Momentarily stunned into silence by his colossal ego, Janna merely blinked in reply. She stared up into his rugged face, which bore small, telltale marks of how he made his living—a tiny scar beneath the chin, another across the bridge of his nose—and then shook her head incredulously. "You don't get it, do you? Kidco Corporation has very deep pockets, captain. Their money could buy the best talent out there come trade time. But there's no way they're going to shell out to build a team that embarrasses them off of the ice. My suggestion to you is that if you want to *keep* winning Stanley Cups, you'd be wise to play it their way."

The icy glare returned. "Are you threatening me?"

"I'm giving you the lay of the land. Your teammates clearly respect you, to the point of asking 'How high?' if you ask them to jump. You do PR, and the rest of the guys will follow suit. I don't think it's too much to ask."

"Yeah? Well, I do." He pushed his sunglasses back up so his eyes were once again obscured. "Do me a favor, will you? Tell *Kidco* to take their 'involvement in the community' and shove it. If I feel like doing a good deed, I will. But in the meantime, my humanitarianism isn't a commodity. You got that?"

"Got it," Janna replied tersely. Against her will, the nausea she'd been keeping at bay began bubbling in the back of her throat.

"Good. Enjoy the rest of your day."

"You, too," Janna returned through gritted teeth as he strode past her. She waited until she couldn't hear his footsteps echoing anymore through the empty concrete hallway. Then, gathering up her papers, she hustled briskly out of the locker room and slammed through the door of the nearest ladies room. Quite unceremoniously, and with a force that frightened her, she threw up her breakfast.

The sheer obstinance! Driving back to Manhattan, Janna mulled over Ty Gallagher. Here she'd been honest with him—downright confiding—and instead of being grateful, he'd behaved like the rich, pampered prima donna he no doubt was. She had clued him in as to how things worked, and he told her to stuff it! This didn't exactly surprise her; but she wished she hadn't let the discussion devolve into a confrontation. Now she'd have to work twice as hard to get the team captain to cooperate. Talk about shooting yourself in the foot.

Well, at least she had fought the sickening insecurity that had flooded her long enough not to have thrown up at his feet. Or on them. On the outside, she knew, she was the picture of confidence and capability. But on the inside, she was a hard-core believer in the old adage, "If you can't make it, fake it." In her mind, she'd spent her entire waking life faking all of it—intelligence, poise, ability—and so far, it seemed to work. Sooner or later, though, she feared someone was going to figure out the truth about her and the jig would be up.

She sighed, as her thoughts wandered to times when the inner Janna had overwhelmed the outer, and she'd wound up saying or doing something stupid. She winced, remembering the time she asked an older actor if his wife was his granddaughter. Thankfully, she was usually able to keep her inner insecurity at bay. She had learned, too, that insecurity could be harnessed toward a productive end. It provided her with raw, nervous energy, energy she used to work harder and reach further. It also gave her drive, and drive had gotten her where she was today.

For two years, she'd been a publicist for the top-rated ABC soap, *The Wild and the Free*. When she'd first arrived, she'd been the low flak on the totem pole, writing bios of the fresh-faced newcomers who'd been hired on the basis of looks alone and who, when asked who their heroes were, would name an MTV VJ. But eventually, she found she excelled at the art of spin. An actor found with a hooker in his dressing room? Let Janna handle it—she'll finesse it with the fans and press. One of the newly hired bumpkins say something out of line in an interview? Let Janna handle it—she'll teach him how to say, "This is off the record," or "No comment."

She was good at it. So good, in fact, that when the spoiled, rambunctious twenty-something cast of the network's highly rated nighttime soap, *Gotham*, started crashing cars and dancing on bars with no panties on, Janna was plucked from the network's daytime division and put in charge of revamping their image. It wasn't easy, but she did it, and kept on doing it for five lucrative years, until one day the phone rang and it was Lou Capesi, head of PR for the New York Blades, on the other end.

She knew why he was calling. Like everyone else in New York, she'd heard about the Stanley Cup shenanigans of the previous spring. Lou Capesi needed her, especially now that the team was a property of Kidco, which prided itself on being unabashedly G-rated. She wasn't a sports fan at all—was a bit of a snob about it, really—but hockey she could tolerate, having caught some of her little brother Wills's games. Lou, on the other hand, clearly adored it.

"In the beginning, God created hockey, ya understand?" he garbled through a pastrami sandwich the first time they met. Sitting on the opposite side of the desk from this passionate, hyperactive troll in his plush office, replete with matching black leather couches and walls crammed with pictures of himself with some of the greatest hockey players in the world, Janna was simultaneously fascinated and repulsed. Here was a man renowned for his PR prowess in the world of sports. Yet he talked with his mouth full, cursed like a trooper, and appeared to be unaware that calling a woman "doll" could land him in court. With his big, fat belly and perpetually stained tie, he didn't exactly cut a professional figure. Yet there was something about him—maybe it was his New York bluntness, or the unconscious way he seemed to pop a Tums every five minutes—that made him kind of endearing. Janna found herself giving him the benefit of the doubt as he multitasked, chewing and talking at the same time.

"Kidco needs these guys to clean up their act. Correction: they demand it. The players aren't bad guys, but the problem is that a lot 'em grew up in East Butthole, Canada, you hear what I'm saying? The big excitement of their life was shooting pucks at their little brother's head and watching reruns of *Three's Company* on the CBC. Now, all of a sudden, they're in the NHL, they're making big money. They start going a little nuts with the wine, women, and song stuff. Kidco wants Blades PR to play up the guys who are married with kids. And they want all of 'em to start going out and doing charity stuff."

"Because the more coverage the players get in the regular press and on TV, the higher the profile of the game, the more tickets we sell, and the richer Kidco becomes," Janna rejoined knowingly.

Lou's caterpillar-size eyebrows shot up. "You got a problem with that?"

"Not at all," Janna assured him. "It's the nature of the beast, I know that."

Lou nodded, wiping his mouth with the back of his shirt sleeve. "Now. I know you can do this job with your eyes closed, and that's why I want you. I've been told you're great at what you do, you got contacts up the wazoo, and if you were able to turn those *Gotham* brats into *Oprah* material, I got no doubt you can spruce up the public's perception of the Blades, most of whom really aren't as wild as the press make them out to be." He frowned. "Only problem might be Gallagher."

That was when he'd explained to Janna about the captain. "Don't get me wrong, he's a great guy, a great hockey player," Lou insisted, stifling a burp. "But he's a huge pain in my ass, a real arrogant SOB. Thinks publicity is a waste of time, a distraction. For him, the only thing that matters is those sixty minutes on the ice, period, end of story. Off the ice, he likes to lead the good life: the best restaurants, the best looking women, you get the picture. He's a bit of a playboy, and Corporate isn't happy with it."

"So you want me to get him to tone it down, is that it?"

"Yeah, because if you can get *him* to keep a lid on it, the rest of the team will follow suit. They'd follow that bastard into the jaws of hell if he asked. Jesus, if you were able to get that anorexic airhead with the silicone chest who plays Treva on your show to do community service—whazzername—?"

"Malo St. John," Janna supplied, stifling a laugh.

"—then I know you can get Gallagher to turn it around. Kidco wants people to see there's more to him than his goddamn obsessive will to win and his never-ending desire to sample the flavor of the month. They want *all* of them to be perceived as caring about Joe Schmoe on the street who pays to see them play. It's important the public thinks they're more than a pack of rowdies with too much money and too little regard for decency, for Chrissakes."

"I'm sure I can do it," Janna asserted confidently, even though she wasn't sure at all. "But you need to make it worth my while to leave *Gotham*."

Lou offhandedly quoted her a salary, and she damn near fell off her chair. She never imagined making money like that in a million years. Still, she played it cool. "And what about stock options? 401(k)? Wardrobe allowance? Vacation time? Assistants?"

Lou sighed, pushing a glossy maroon folder embossed with the word *Kidco* in silver across the front toward her. "This will tell you everything you need to know."

They shot the breeze for a while, and by the time Janna left the interview, she knew she'd take the job. Doing PR for the Blades was just the shot in the arm she needed to get her out of her comfortable rut. Not only that, but the money was simply too good to turn down.

"Why do they call him 'the Bull'?" she asked one of the secretaries on her way out of Capesi's office.

The woman, age sixty or so with a helmet of shellacked hair dyed so garishly red it would make Lucille Ball spin in her grave, looked up at Janna over the half-moon bifocals perched on the end of her nose. " 'Cause way back when he was a boxer, he used to fight like one. Now he just slings it."

Janna had laughed, utterly charmed. A week later, she resigned her job at *Gotham*.

And now here she was, doing ten miles over the speed limit, on her way back to the city to tell the Bull that on her first day out of the blocks, she'd gotten Gill and Lubov to sign off on some events, but Gallagher was unmoved.

Ty, Ty, Ty, she mused. *You have no idea who you're up against, do you?* He won this round, she'd give him that. But come hell or high water, the next would be hers. It had to be.

" *You were a* little rude to her, don't you think?"

Ty glanced up from skimming the sports pages of the *New York Sentinel* to see his teammate and longtime friend, Kevin Gill, looking at him questioningly. The two were sitting at "their" table at Maggie's Grill, waiting for lunch to arrive. Now that the season was about to start, they were getting back into their usual routine: driving upstate to Armonk to practice, grabbing a quick bite afterwards, then driving back to the Big Apple. He should have been in a good mood. Practice had gone well; none of the guys were coasting, saving their real sweat and blood for when the season officially began. They seemed to understand they needed to give it their all, day in and day out, game day or not, if they were serious about winning the Cup in the spring. Plus he had a good feeling about the upcoming year. But then that Janna MacNeil woman had invaded his locker room spouting corporate BS, and his good mood evaporated, replaced by an overwhelming sense of resentment he'd been unable to shake, especially when she'd had the balls to tell him that Kidco owned him.

He took a sip of his beer and returned his friend's look. "She deserved it."

"She did *not* deserve it. She was just trying to do her job."

"Yeah, and do you know what her job *is*, Kev? It's tidying us up so those suits at Kidco can make money off us. Screw them! They don't give a rat's ass about the integrity of the game, or anyone who plays it. We don't owe them a goddamn thing."

"I still don't think it would kill you to sign up for one charity event just to throw the number crunchers a bone. It'd get them off your ass. You keep turning her down, she's just going to keep hocking you."

Ty shrugged. "Let her."

"Jesus Christ." Kevin sat back in his chair, amazed. "You are one stubborn bastard, you know that?"

Ty grinned. "That's why I've won three Stanley Cups so far, buddy. Because I don't give up, and I don't give in."

"Ain't that right."

Ty took another sip of beer. He'd meant what he'd said to *Miss* MacNeil: If, of his own volition, he felt like giving some time to charity, then he'd do it. But he sure as hell wasn't going to do it so some MBA with a cell phone and a trophy wife could fill his coffers. He'd spent fifteen years helping to build a winning franchise in St. Louis. He'd more than earned his right to do what he pleased, and right now, what pleased him was being the best at what he did on the ice and having a damn good time off it. Maybe Kevin was right: maybe it would make his life easier if he played it Kidco's way. But Ty didn't care. It was his way or no way, no ifs, ands, or buts. Too bad if Kidco didn't like it.

He craned his head around, looking for the waitress. Jesus, service in here was slow today. What was the deal?

Kevin, reading his mind, rolled his eyes. "Just cool your jets, okay? She'll be here in a minute."

Ty relaxed. Leave it to Kevin to know just what he was thinking. On the ice, he was right wing to Ty's center, his capacity for speed, power and toughness almost as legendary as Ty's own. The sports press jokingly referred to them as "Batman and Robin." Off the ice, Ty relied on Kevin to tell him the naked, unvarnished truth; he was the

one guy he trusted implicitly. If he was being too much of
a hard-ass, Kevin let him know it. He also let him know
when he thought he was going a little overboard enjoying
the New York nightlife.

Happily married with two kids, Kevin thought Ty
should settle down. "When I retire," was Ty's standard response. But at age thirty-three, fit and strong as an athlete
ten years younger, it looked as if it might be another
decade before Captain Gallagher would even consider
hanging up his skates. Hell, if he had his choice he'd never
retire. One day he would just drop dead on the ice and his
teammates would bear him away, regal as a king—then
they'd continue playing. Because all that mattered was
hockey, pure and simple.

Or maybe not so simple.

Ty had felt a small twinge of desire when he'd loped
out of the showers and found the publicist standing on the
bench giving her rah-rah speech. She was cute—not beautiful, but cute: tiny, pert, with short blond hair, a button
nose, and bright blue eyes that didn't seem to miss a trick.
Energetic, that was it. She seemed energetic. Didn't matter,
though. Janna MacNeil wasn't his type. Not that he really
remembered what his type *was* anymore. It had been years
since he'd been involved in a serious relationship.

The first time, when he was still playing for St. Louis,
one Stanley Cup under his belt and the captaincy right
around the corner, he'd fallen so hard it had affected his
game. St. Louis didn't get anywhere near the Playoffs that
year, the woman wound up dumping him, and that, Ty
thought ruefully, was that. The second time he'd surren-
dered his heart, about two years ago, the relationship went
south when Ty realized she cared more about spending his
money than she did about him. He broke things off, and
she exacted her revenge by telling some cock-and-bull
story to the press about how he ripped his teammates to
shreds in private. Those who knew him well knew it was a
lie, but it still hurt his credibility. He made a vow right

then and there that he wouldn't get seriously involved again until he retired, and he'd stuck to it.

Not coincidentally, he never missed another round of Playoffs again, and he'd gone on to win two more Cups, proof positive that if wanted to win on the ice he couldn't afford to be distracted. For him, hockey was a full-time commitment, and the only thing that mattered was winning. If that meant foregoing a long-term relationship for the time being, so be it. Instead, he concentrated on having a good time.

One of the perks of being a star athlete, he'd discovered, was that beautiful women threw themselves at him all the time. They threw, and he caught, never promising more than he could give, always making sure both parties came away from the encounter satisfied. Sometimes he yearned for more than casual, no-strings-attached sex, but he rode the feelings out, knowing they would pass. What tripped him up was when he encountered someone like Janna MacNeil, who seemed to have the whole package. In fact, all the way over on the drive to the restaurant, he was plagued by unbidden thoughts of that lithe little body of hers, thoughts that made his blood hum and his mind go on the fritz.

"Ty?"

He blinked. The waitress had come and gone, bringing his grilled salmon and Kevin's burger. The small, dark-paneled dining room of Maggie's was filled with regulars, their voices rising and falling with the easy cadence of conversation. And he'd been—where? Off in the recesses of his mind, apparently, thinking about . . . He shook his head, clearing it. "Sorry. I was in the ozone."

"No kidding." Kevin gave a sly smile before popping a fry in his mouth. "Thinking about the publicist?"

Ty flashed his famous scowl, the one meant as a serious warning to the opposing team that he meant business. "Right."

"She was kind of cute."

"I guess. I didn't really notice."

Kevin chuckled. "Liar." He took a big, juicy bite of his burger, washing the food down quickly with a shot of Coke. "Hey, listen. Abby wanted to know if you'd like to come over for dinner Friday night."

"Name the time and I'll be there."

"Let me find out from the chef and I'll get back to you." Kevin paused, drowning a french fry in a pool of ketchup. "You can bring someone if you want."

Ty's gaze was unyielding. "You know I don't date seriously during the season."

"Yeah, well, I just thought . . ." Kevin shrugged. "Whatever."

"You really think I was rude to that publicist?" Ty asked abruptly. He knew what Kevin was driving at.

"Don't you?"

"Yeah," Ty reluctantly admitted, feeling bad as an image of Janna's momentarily stunned expression flashed through his mind. He hated to think she'd come away with a poor first impression of him and would probably be loaded for bear the next time their paths crossed. "I guess I'll talk to her at practice tomorrow," he murmured.

"And say what?"

"That she caught me at a bad time, blah blah blah. "

"Blah blah blah being that you still refuse to do any PR."

Ty raised his glass high to Kevin in mock salute. "To my brilliant teammate, who's finally catching on."

"Bastard," Kevin grumbled affectionately. "Stubborn, ball-busting bastard."

Changing the subject, Ty began talking about Coach "Tubs" Matthias, and who he thought might need a little work on defense. But even as the words flowed effortlessly from his mouth, his mind was elsewhere. He was in the locker room, apologizing to Janna MacNeil, returning that sweet smile of hers that he'd rejected earlier, explaining to her that really, he wasn't a total jerk. He caught his mind wandering and forced his thoughts back to the conversation at hand, while issuing a warning to himself in his head. He was going to have to watch himself and steer clear of Janna MacNeil, or there was going to be big trouble.

And trouble, especially where his heart was concerned, was the one thing he couldn't afford.

CHAPTER
02

Returning to the Blades PR office at "Met Gar," Janna was greeted by the sight of the Bull hunkering down over an open pizza box. On one of the leather couches opposite him sat Jack Cowley. Also an assistant director of PR, Cowley was in charge of gathering the stats, game notes, and other bits of info that the beat writers and network commentators needed each day. Janna wasn't sure she liked Jack, with his perpetual tan, Hugh Grant "do", and lock-jawed way of talking. There was something unctuous about him, insincere, especially in his dealings with Lou. She was willing to suspend judgment until she knew him better, but she got the distinctly creepy feeling that *his* version of getting acquainted might be radically different from hers.

"So, how'd it go?" Lou asked hopefully, holding aloft a slice of pie for her. He'd been thrilled when she came up with the idea of getting each player to sign up for three charity events. Janna waved the pizza slice away and Lou shrugged, biting off the tip before putting it back in the box. "You catch Gallagher?"

"Yup." Janna perched on the arm of the couch opposite Jack's. "He won't do it."

"Keep working on him," Lou instructed. "Pain in the ass," he muttered as an afterthought.

"I got Gill and Lubov," Janna informed him.

"That's a good start. Gill is a good guy, he'll do almost anything. Lubov will need you to hold his hand. His grasp of English isn't too hot."

"I gathered that already," Janna said wryly. "Who else do you think I should go after right now?"

"Hhhmm." Lou tipped so far back in his swivel chair Janna was afraid he was going to topple over backward and crash through the bank of smoky, tinted windows behind him. "Try Michael Dante or Barry Fontaine. They're both single, good-looking guys. You get them to do some charity gigs, get them some ink in a women's mag, that'll help."

Janna nodded. She wasn't completely sure who Dante or Fontaine were, at least not on sight. But she'd learn. "Maybe they'd be willing to be part of a bachelor auction," she suggested, thinking aloud.

"Atta girl." Lou pitched forward, the front legs of his chair hitting the gray carpet with a muffled thump. "That'd be perfect for them. In the meantime, I'm sure you know the drill: Once you get to know the guys, then you'll know who's willing to do what, and the job will be a piece of cake."

"Oh, right." Janna snorted derisively. "Ty Gallagher is a *nightmare*."

"But if anyone can get him to toe the line," Lou crooned, "it's you, baby doll. I got full confidence in your abilities."

I'm glad one of us does, Janna thought. Meanwhile, the Bull prattled on. "We'll talk more tomorrow about who you might want to corral into doing what. In the meantime, maybe you should—" He stopped himself, chuckling. "*Madonn'*, will you listen to me, telling you your job? You know what to do, it's why I hired you." With great effort he rose, stuffing his shirttails into his pants. "And now if you'll excuse me, I gotta run. One of the big boys upstairs wants to see me, Christ only knows what for."

"They probably want your help sticking pins in a Gallagher voodoo doll," Janna offered.

"Probably." Lou couldn't resist one more large bite of the pizza slice he'd offered Janna.

"One other thing before you go," she said.

"Mmm?"

"Do any of the wives ever go to practice?"

"Sometimes," said Lou. "Kevin Gill's wife, Abby, is there pretty regularly. Why?"

"Because I want to feel them out, see if any of them would be willing to do an 'At Home With' feature for a magazine or *E!* or something like that," said Janna. "We need to play up the married players, too, show there *are* some family men on the team."

Lou beamed at Jack Cowley. "What did I tell ya? Is this broad stacked in the brains department or what?" He turned back to Janna. "Sounds great. Now I really gotta run. We can drive up together tomorrow. Be here at nine sharp." Rolling up the rest of the pizza slice, he crammed it into his mouth, waving good-bye to Janna and Jack as he waddled toward the elevators, humming to himself.

"Unbelievable," sighed Jack, rising, his carefully cultivated voice ringing with disapproval. "The man's going to keel over dead one of these days from sheer gluttony."

"At least he'll die happy," Janna noted, trying to ignore the fact that her coworker was eyeing her breasts as if they were long lost friends.

"Care to get some lunch?" he asked smoothly, closing in on her.

Janna forced an appreciative smile. "I'd love to, but

being the new kid on the block, I really have to get up to speed here. Some other time, maybe."

"As you wish," Jack Cowley drawled regally, saunter-ing from Lou's office.

As you wish? Janna thought, watching him go. *Who does he think he is, Patrick Stewart? What a pretentious yutz.* She'd been too charitable in suspending judgment on him. Her first instinct had been right: Jack Cowley *was* creepy, no two ways about it. As for Ty Gallagher, she was glad Lou seemed aware it would take more than one shot to persuade Captain Uncooperative to do some publicity. She'd been worried that the strength of her reputation might work against her, and Lou would expect her to come back with Gallagher's scalp dangling from her belt on her first day out. But he seemed just as aware as anyone of the challenge she faced—a challenge she was determined to rise to. Gathering up her papers, she walked to her own of-fice, her thoughts on Ty and how best to get him to play the Kidco way.

It was close to seven by the time Janna got home—not bad, by PR standards, for a day in the office. She knew that once the season "officially" started in October she'd be re-quired to stick around for games on home ice, which proba-bly meant she'd get in around midnight. Lou wanted her to go on the road with the team a few times, too, just to get a feel for what it was like. And then of course, there were the charity golf tournaments and hockey games and auctions and dances and fund-raising dinners she'd be arranging for and attending with "the guys," as Lou fondly called the players. One day soon, she hoped, she'd think of them as simply the guys, too. But for now, they were still a rare and exotic species, one whose habits and habitat she was still largely unfamiliar with.

She opened the apartment door and was assaulted by a blast of frigid air-conditioning, a sure sign her roommate,

Theresa, was back from the location shoot she'd been on. Closing the door behind her, Janna could hear her warbling in the shower. She poked her head in the bathroom and jokingly shouted, "Honey, I'm home!"

"Be out in a minute!" Theresa trilled back over the din of rushing water. Janna knew "a minute" in Theresa-time meant at least ten in regular time, so she made for the living room, peeling off her navy linen blazer and slinging it over the back of the couch before heading to the kitchen for a Perrier.

She and Theresa had been roommates for close to four years, coworkers on *The Wild and the Free* for two. Janna always thought of Terry as being "real" New York: Brooklyn-born and raised, wisecracking, opinionated, zero-to-low tolerance for BS. She was still doing PR at the soap. By now, the two of them were definitely earning more than enough money to rent apartments of their own, but neither of them really wanted to. Why, they reasoned, live alone when you could live with a friend? Besides, neither wanted to give up the apartment.

A moderately sized two bedroom on First and Fifty-ninth, it boasted high ceilings, polished parquet floors, and a full-size kitchen, which was important to Janna, who loved to cook—not that she was home much to hone her culinary talents. The sunken living room featured a huge Italianate marble fireplace, and a wall of windows looked out onto the 59th Street bridge, a convenient viewing place for the New York Marathon, which Theresa ran in every year. Their decorating style was funky-eclectic, a mix and match of the modern with the antique. A framed Picasso reproduction hung above a rusted Victorian birdcage that was perched on a port table, while a large, overstuffed chintz sofa was offset by a battered old steamer trunk that served as a coffee table. The TV set was hidden away in an antique French armoire, while the CD player was in plain view atop a nicked, old parson's table that Theresa found at a yard sale. The room was always filled with fresh flowers, a passion the two of them shared. Somehow, it all worked.

Janna's favorite room in the whole apartment was her bedroom. Granted, it was the smaller of the two, with barely enough space for her beloved, mahogany sleigh bed, but she'd willingly sacrificed the extra space for French doors that opened out onto a tiny terrace where she kept tidy rows of cracked terra cotta pots filled with aromatic herbs. Lemon balm, lavender, basil, thyme, coriander, oregano, sage, fennel . . . Whenever Janna was feeling stressed, she would simply pluck some leaves, crush them between her fingers, and bring them to her nose, inhaling deeply. It was a calming technique her father had taught her, and it worked every time.

"Hey."

Janna had just finished pouring her Perrier into a wine glass—she'd read somewhere that using fancy glasses for ordinary drinks could elevate one's spirits, although this seemed dubious—and was on her way to the living room when Theresa came scurrying out of the bathroom in her robe, a towel wrapped around her head like a turban, making her look like some sort of exotic Italian princess.

"How was Key West?" Janna asked, kicking off her Blahniks.

"Hot. Whoever had the bright idea to do a location shoot in Key West in early September should be killed." Sighing deeply, Theresa plopped down next to Janna on the couch. "Your not being there really sucked. I had no one to laugh with at the sight of Nicholas Kastley in a Speedo."

Janna shuddered. Nicholas Kastley was one of the older actors; for years he'd been fighting Father Time in a grudge match and was losing badly. "It must have been harrowing."

"No, harrowing was being called to his room to help him apply Just for Men to the hair on his legs."

Janna halted mid-sip. "You're kidding me."

"I wish I was. I'm telling you, the network doesn't pay me enough to do this stuff."

"Yeah, but think of all the good material you're gathering for your tell-all book," Janna teased. "It's a guaranteed best-seller, you know it is."

"Except I'll have to change all their names or wait until they're all dead to write it," Theresa groused, helping herself to Janna's glass, from which she drank deeply. "Mmm, that hits the spot." She handed the glass back to Janna, her expression eager. "Enough about *me*. I want to hear all about those big, manly men on skates you're being paid to hang around with."

"What do you want to know?"

"How many of them are single?"

"Theresa," Janna reproved. She knew this was coming. The minute Janna had told her friend she'd taken the job, Theresa had been on her to get the dirt about which guys were available.

"Well?" Theresa prodded. "Any prospects?"

"I don't know yet," Janna stalled, which was true. "Let me get to know them better and I'll get back to you."

"The captain is good-looking," Theresa observed aloud. She unwound the terrycloth turban from around her head and began vigorously toweling her long, wavy black hair. "What's his name? Tim Gallagher?"

"Ty Gallagher," Janna corrected. She stiffened. "You think he's good-looking?"

"Why, you don't?"

"I haven't really noticed."

"Then open your eyes, girl; he's a hottie."

"I guess," Janna replied mildly. Of course she had *noticed,* but she'd been trying not to think about it. For one thing, Ty Gallagher wasn't her speed. She liked her men a bit more cerebral. For another, she knew she wouldn't stand a chance with him. She wasn't six feet tall, she'd never been on the cover of a magazine, she didn't subsist on air and water, and her boobs—what boobs she had to speak of—were entirely her own. Ty Gallagher would never look at her in a million years.

Theresa, meanwhile, was staring dreamily into space. "What about that new Russian guy?"

"Alexei Lubov? Met him today."

"And . . . ?"

"*And* he's very young and can barely speak English."

"So? He's gorgeous."

Janna eyed Theresa suspiciously. "How do you know?"

Theresa drew herself up, insulted. "I don't live under a rock, you know. There was a huge article on him in the *Sentinel* today. They called him 'the Siberian Express.' " The faraway look returned to her eyes. "I bet his accent makes him sound like one of those sexy spies in an old James Bond film."

"Actually, he sounds more like Boris Badenov."

"You're from hell, you know that?" Dreaminess gave way to mild desperation. "Help me out here, Janna! I haven't been on a date in three months."

"That's not true. You just had lunch with that producer from *Good Morning America.*"

"That doesn't count. All he did was talk about how his ex-girlfriend left him for another woman. By the time lunch was done *I* was ready to turn into a lesbian, okay? He was a nightmare. Look, I'm tired of spending Saturday nights curled up alone watching The Movie Channel. Or playing third wheel to you and Robert."

Janna slumped on the couch. "Robert! Shoot. I was supposed to call him at lunch today."

"Relax, he probably wasn't even home," Theresa muttered, examining her nails. "He was *probably* out reciting his bad poetry to some poor slob who had no means of escape."

Janna was not amused. "Are you done yet?"

"No. Why don't you just dump him, Janna? You know you want to. He's a pretentious mooch! You could do so much better than someone who smokes stinky French ciga-

rettes and thinks that entitles him to the French pronuncia-
tion of his name! 'Call me Ro-bear.' Puh-lease!"

"But how do you really feel?" Janna deadpanned.

"The guy crashed here for six weeks before he found
his own apartment and never once offered to pay for anything!" Theresa fumed. "Not only that, but he had the
nerve to say that the only Italian woman on earth worthy
of adoration is Sophia Lauren! Was that supposed to en-
dear him to me?"

"It could have been worse. He could have said Ma-
donna. He was being poetic."

"He was being an ass."

"Cut him some slack, Theresa. He's had a tough time.
His father bailed on the family when he was ten and his
mother's not wrapped too tightly, okay?"

"I agree, that's sad," Theresa admitted. "But I still think
you could do better."

Janna rolled her eyes. They'd had this conversation so
many times. Theresa just didn't get it. Janna didn't *want* to
do better than Robert, at least not now. After three years,
"the relationship" was comfortable and casual, something
they could both maintain on automatic pilot. A ready-made
date for the weekend if nothing more exciting was on the
slate, a warm body in bed on those nights when one or
both of them craved affection. It wasn't going anywhere,
which was just the way they wanted to keep it. That's what
Theresa didn't understand. For her, every guy was potentially "the one," a concept that Janna refused to buy into.

"Don't you worry about me. When the time is right, I
will ditch *Ro-bear* and throw myself into the arms of my
one true love."

Theresa frowned. "No need to be sarcastic."

"I'm not! When the time is right, I'll know. But right
now, this thing with Robert works fine for me."

"Whatever." She reached again for Janna's glass. "So
tell me all about your first day of work."

She recounted for Theresa what happened in the locker room with Ty Gallagher.

"Sounds like you've got your work cut out for you, honey."

"Oh yeah," Janna roundly agreed, taking back her glass. "But he doesn't realize who he's dealing with."

"The PR piranha."

"You got it." She drained her glass and rose. "Tomorrow I'm going to try using the sweetness and light approach to charm the pants off him."

"Or on him, as the case may be."

The two women laughed.

"Mark my words," Janna called over her shoulder as she headed toward the kitchen to refill her glass. "By the time this season's done, the captain is going to be considered one of the most caring, concerned, and respectable citizens on the planet."

Strength and grace. Those were the two words that sprang to mind as she watched the Blades warming up before practice the next day, the entire team circling around the rink. It was amazing how all of them could make gliding on ice atop steel blades less than a quarter-inch thick seem so effortless. Again and again her attention was drawn to Ty, to his powerful skating stride. Back held erect, he swayed his arms from side to side while pushing off those strong legs renowned for quick acceleration. He seemed focused yet relaxed, his banter with his teammates light and easy. Janna thought she saw his eyes quickly dart in her direction, taking in that she was there, but she couldn't be sure. For the most part, he and the team seemed oblivious to her, Lou, and the rest of the media who sat watching.

Her eyes might be glued to the ice, but her ear was cocked to Lou, who was happily schmoozing the writers. God, he was good, directing spin, fielding interview requests, deftly deflecting questions about players' supposed injuries, dishing dirt on other teams and players in the league. Janna was impressed, and found herself glad once again that she'd taken the job. She could learn a lot from Lou.

The Blades were in the middle of a puck-passing drill when Janna noticed a small, pear-shaped woman with chin-length, light brown hair guiding two small, tow-headed boys toward some rinkside seats near the center of the arena. Before she could even process who it was, Lou's sausage-shaped fingers were poking her in the shoulder.

"There's Abby Gill. Go talk to her about your idea for the family profile. When practice is done, head over to the locker room and see if you can get some more guys to sign up for stuff, 'kay?"

" 'Kay," Janna returned, sliding out of her seat. The arena was virtually empty except for the media and the players, whose raucous shouts echoed off the cavernous, high-domed ceiling. Abby Gill watched her approach, her expression friendly and inviting as her sons excitedly pressed their faces to the Plexiglas framing the ice and tried to get their father's attention.

"Boys, c'mon," she gently chided. "You know Daddy has to concentrate right now." She smiled up at Janna. "Hi, I'm Abby Gill, Kevin's wife. And these two ruffians are Adam and Jacob."

"I'm Janna MacNeil, the new publicist."

"Kevin told me about you," Abby said pleasantly, patting the seat next to her. Janna sat down. "He said Ty was a bit harsh with you yesterday."

Janna grimaced. "I didn't exactly get things between us started on the right foot."

"Don't worry about Ty. His bark is worse than his bite."

"You know him well?"

Abby's eyes drifted to the ice, where her husband was now hustling a puck toward the net. "He's Kevin's best friend. They started out together as rookies in St. Louis."

"How long ago was that?"

"Oh, about a hundred years ago." She laughed. "They've both been in the NHL since they were eighteen."

Janna did some quick math in her head. Fifteen years. Ty Gallagher had been a professional hockey player for fifteen years. He had three Stanley Cups under his belt, and he wasn't even thirty-five yet. Impressive, for an athlete.

"Abby, look, I was wondering—"

"About Ty?" Abby finished for her. "The answer is yes, he's single."

"What? No, no," Janna replied quickly, embarrassed. Why did this woman think she wanted to know Ty's bachelor status? That was something Theresa would ask, not her! "What I was wondering is if you and Kevin would be willing to be interviewed for a magazine about the longevity of your marriage, what it's like to try to raise a family with an athlete's crazy schedule, that kind of stuff."

Abby looked uncomfortable. "Would it involve people wanting to come to the house to take pictures?"

"Yes."

"I don't know. Kevin and I are pretty private people. We really work hard to stay out of the public eye unless it's absolutely necessary. Have you tried asking any of the other married players?"

"Not yet," Janna admitted. "I came to you first because Kevin is both well-known and well respected. And since he agreed to help me out with some charity stuff, I thought you might be willing to help me out with this."

Abby's eyes shone with pride. "He's got a big heart, my husband. But a family profile . . . I don't know, I have to think about it." Her gaze flickered back to the players on the ice. "Is this part of Kidco's big push to reform the Blades' image?"

"You got it." Janna saw little point in candy-coating things, and was pleasantly surprised by Abby's response.

"Personally, I think it's a good thing. So many of these

guys, especially the younger ones, are totally out of control."

"I hear some of the older guys are, too," Janna murmured.

A wry smile creased Abby's mouth. "Are you referring to Ty?"

"Yup."

"Aw, Ty's not out of control," Abby replied affectionately. "He's just enjoying himself."

"A lot."

"Right."

"With a new woman every month."

"Right."

"Corporate hates it."

Abby hooted with laughter. "I can just imagine what Ty has to say about that!"

"If he'd just sign on to do a few appearances for charity, maybe tone down the high-profile dating during the season, they'd be happy. Any advice?"

"About handling Ty?" Janna nodded as sympathy rose up in Abby's tired eyes. "Do you know how many women have asked me that question over the years?"

"Hundreds, I'm sure," Janna replied. "What do you tell them?"

"To forget it. No one 'handles' Ty Gallagher; if anything, he handles them."

"I can't forget it, Abby. It's a huge part of my job."

Abby sighed. "Then all I can say is, try wearing him down. That's the only thing that might work."

"I thought so," said Janna glumly. She rose, smoothing the front of her suede skirt. "Well, thanks for your time. And please think about doing the interview. It would really help improve the team's profile."

"I'll be in touch," Abby promised.

Janna smiled and returned to where Lou was sitting. Practice was coming to an end. One by one, the players began filing off the ice, though the press corps lingered.

She'd barely had time to get resettled in her seat before Lou, ever subtle, pointed in the direction of the locker room. Taking the hint, Janna rose once again, following the players.

Approaching the locker room, she felt like a cowboy in an old western, swaggering toward a showdown. She wanted to stick Ty up, make him yowl for mercy. But that wasn't the right approach. Today she was going to try being cordial. Sweetness and light. She would offer a compromise solution that might help both of them. She put a hand to her stomach briefly to quell the butterflies springing to life there, then plunged inside. *You're a piranha, you're a piranha, you're a piranha* . . .

Some of the guys actually smiled at her; others made a point of deliberately turning away. One or two murmured, "Hey Janna," which pleased her; it seemed a friendly gesture, and it gave her hope. Before going for Gallagher, she made a point of walking around the room and reiterating to the players, as nicely as possible, that if they didn't sign on for at least three charity events, she'd be forced to do it for them. No one budged, although she thought she detected some ambivalence in Michael Dante, one of the young, single players Lou had mentioned the day before. He seemed intrigued by the notion of taking part in a bachelor auction, but in the end stalled, telling Janna he'd get back to her. She knew what *that* meant; he had to go and see if God, aka Captain Gallagher, gave it his seal of approval. Lemmings. Janna wondered if they asked his permission to use the bathroom.

She found Gallagher in the small lounge off the locker room, leaning against one of the cement walls, watching ESPN on the big-screen TV, and drinking a large glass of orange juice, which he'd grabbed from the small banquet table set in the far corner. The table, laden with coffee, muffins, juice and fruit, made Janna's stomach rumble with hunger. Or was it nerves? The minute the other players in the lounge spotted her, they cleared out, obviously expecting *something* to happen that they didn't want to be witness to. Ty, meanwhile, kept his eyes glued to the TV screen—quite deliberately, Janna thought. Not a good sign.

"Ty?"

"Miss MacNeil. What a surprise."

As he turned slowly toward her, her heartbeat began doubling its tempo. She was anxious, yes. But she realized there was more to it than that: clad in sweatpants, he was shirtless, a twisted white towel casually slung around his neck, the perfect six-pack of his abs glistening with hard-earned sweat. He aroused in her a desire that could only be called primal. She'd never experienced anything so elemental and so *strong*. That the sight of this man should generate it only made it worse. It was like being a teenage wallflower and finding yourself attracted to that one dumb jock in your high school who always made fun of you at lunch. Her body was betraying her. She closed her eyes for a moment.

Think piranha!

"Look," she began contritely, "I want to apologize for my behavior yesterday. I fear I may have gone a bit overboard in trying to convey Kidco's expectations to you. I'm sorry."

She braced herself, waiting for him to curse her out. Instead, he responded with an uncomfortable clearing of his throat and a distinct unwillingness to hold eye contact.

"Yeah, well, apology accepted. I had it down on my agenda for today to apologize to you, too. I didn't mean to bite your head off the way I did." His gaze returned to the screen.

"It's okay." Janna glanced at the TV. Some newscaster was talking about the Mets game the night before. "I was thinking . . ." she began.

"Mmm?" Ty tore his eyes from the screen, and took another gulp of juice.

"I have a compromise solution that I think could benefit both of us."

"And that would be?"

"I know you don't want to do any PR. But if you could use your influence to get some of your teammates to cooperate with me, then perhaps I could use mine to persuade Kidco not to be so gung ho about wanting you, specifically, to participate in community events."

Ty nodded thoughtfully, scratching at the stubble on his chin. "Let me make sure I'm getting this straight. You want me to surrender some of my guys to save my own ass."

" 'Surrender'?" Janna repeated incredulously. "What is this, a hostage negotiation?"

"In a way."

"Oh, please." She knew she sounded scornful, and tried to pull back. She was this close to letting inner Janna break loose and ruin everything. "All I'm asking for—"

"Is me to do your job."

"No," Janna replied in an extremely controlled voice, "that is not it at all."

"Janna." His eyes finally met hers and held. For a split second, she could have sworn he was checking her out. "I thought I made it pretty clear yesterday that I don't think any of the Blades owe Kidco anything. I understand you have a certain job to do, and I promise you I'm not going to interfere with your doing it, even though I think it's bull. If one of my guys decides on his own that he wants to put on a penguin suit and go to some three-hundred-bucks-a-plate dinner to raise money for beriberi, that's his business. But there's no way on earth I'm gonna help you out."

"Even if doing so is an investment for the team's future."

"Back to that again, the deep pockets argument?"

Janna held her tongue, trying to keep the rising tide of anger and desperation within her in check.

"Look, I told you. If I feel moved to do something at some point, I will. But in the meantime, I think you're wasting your time and energy trying to change my position. I'm not gonna budge."

Janna looked down at the floor, counted to three, then looked back up. "Can I ask you a question?"

"You can ask me anything."

Janna checked his expression; was he flirting with her? She decided he was not.

"Would it kill you to do *just one* appearance at a hospital or hit a few golf balls for cancer? Would it?"

"Funny, Kevin said the same thing yesterday."

"And what was your response?"

"My response was that Kidco doesn't care about the integrity of the game *or* about anyone playing it, so as far as I can see, I owe them *nothing,* least of all any of my precious free time."

Janna stared at him. "You don't get it, do you?"

"You said that yesterday," Ty pointed out, mildly amused.

"And I'll say it again, because it's true. You're so hung up on sticking to your principles you don't even realize you're shooting yourself in the foot. Fine, refuse to do PR, suit yourself. But understand this: I am not going to give up. I'm being paid to hound you and your teammates, and I will. Every time you turn around, Captain Gallagher, there I'll be, with my dreaded list of community events. I'm going to be the pebble in your shoe you can't get rid of, the annoying song lyric you can't get out of your head. You better get used to me bugging the hell out of you, because it's going to be one of the constants in your life from now until the season ends in June—assuming you make it to the Playoffs, of course."

"Oh, we'll make it to the Playoffs," Ty replied breezily, casually massaging the back of his neck with his towel. "The real question is whether *you'll* last that long."

With a knowing wink, he finished the last of his juice and sauntered away, leaving Janna standing there, a white-hot ball of fury beginning to coalesce in her gut.

Had he just made a veiled threat to see to it that she lost her job? Or was he simply insinuating she didn't have what it took to stay the course? Either way, his parting shot made her furious.

Of course, she was the one who'd taken aim first, she had to admit that.

She had to go and make that jibe about the Playoffs. She couldn't just bite her tongue. And what did it get her? Nothing, with the possible exception of an enemy for life.

She went over to the buffet table, picked up a gleaming red apple, and bit into it, hard. So much for sweetness and light. Ty Gallagher had thrown down the gauntlet. She would pick it up. The battle had officially begun. He might have won the first two rounds, but in the end, she would win the fight. She was expected by Kidco to win. She was being paid to win. She'd fight Ty Gallagher to the bitter end. Not because she wanted to, but because she had to.

CHAPTER
03

"Tyyyyyy. Tyler-Wyler. Wakey, wakey."

Ty cracked open one weary, bloodshot eye. The bodacious redhead he'd brought home the night before was playfully straddling him as if he were her own personal hobbyhorse.

"Could you please get off me," he muttered politely, the jabbing headache behind his eyes surging every time she bounced up and down.

"That's not what you said last night," she teased, leaning forward so her breasts grazed his chest.

"This isn't last night," he replied, closing his eye. His head felt bolted to the pillow, the pain was that heavy and intense. *All play and too much Rémy Martin makes Ty a hungover boy.* The woman whom he'd brought to screaming ecstasy the night before—Laurie? Laura? Lauren?—stopped bouncing, but she made no move to unwrap herself from his torso. In fact, her face was now buried deep in his neck, which she was biting in the hope he would revive and give a command performance. It wasn't gonna happen.

"I mean it," Ty said gently. "I need you to get off me, I'm not feeling too great."

The woman clucked her tongue disappointedly then rolled off, allowing him to feel like he could breathe again. He forced open both eyes, and with what felt like every ounce of strength he had, slowly turned his head toward his night table to see the time. Ten-thirty A.M. *Oh, shi—no wait, wait. Ten-thirty A.M . . . Sunday. Whew.* For a second there he'd been seized with panic that he'd overslept and had missed practice. But then he remembered: Last night had been Saturday, and he'd gone with a couple of the guys to check out some private club down in Noho. The club owner, clearly thrilled to have a sports celebrity in his midst, had told Ty he could drink on the house. And Ty had, the sharp edges of the night growing increasingly fuzzy the more cognac he enjoyed. He remembered ducking into a cab with the redhead now beside him, and could somewhat recall the acrobatics they'd engaged in the night before. But the fact that she was here in his bed was proof he'd had too much drink. Usually, if he was interested in making love to a woman, he made sure they went back to her place. That way, he could leave after a respectable interval of afterglow and not have to spend the night. Now he was stuck.

The redhead was sighing contentedly to herself and snuggling down beneath the covers, clearly intending to go back to sleep. Ty propped himself up on his elbow, and as nicely as he could, gently shook her shoulder.

"I hate to do this, sweetheart, but there's somewhere I need to be."

"That's okay," she mewed in a kittenish voice. "You can just leave me here."

Ty chuckled, surprised to discover that even his face hurt. "No can do, honey. It doesn't work that way at Chateau Gallagher. Why don't you run along to the shower and I'll arrange for a cab to pick you up in a half hour or so?"

The woman sat up, huffing. "Fine." Pulling the sheet to her chest, she rose, Ty's bedding trailing after her as she stomped off into the bathroom. "I know when I'm not wanted."

Thank God for that, Ty said to himself, grabbing his robe from where it hung on the back of the bedroom door. While standing seemed to ease his headache somewhat, he was now acutely aware of the gritty insides of his mouth, which felt as if an invading army had marched through it. Keeping the shades drawn, he made his way into the kitchen, the light from the Sub-Zero fridge blinding him as he opened the door to check what was inside. Bottles of juice. Unused rolls of film. Batteries.

Palm to pounding forehead, he began rustling through the kitchen in search of coffee. His housekeeper, Inez, was always rearranging the damn cabinets, so he never knew where anything was at any given moment. In the freezer, he found the precious ground beans that he hoped would alleviate his headache. Putting up a pot in the Krups, he called the doorman to arrange for a cab for Laura-Laurie-Lauren, fervently praying that she took her time in the shower and didn't emerge in time for a cup of joe and a chat.

For one thing, he wasn't a morning person, especially when he was hungover. For another, he really had nothing to say to her. His mind circled back to the night before—to the sex, specifically. It had been good, no doubt about that. And then he remembered . . . Janna. The bottom dropped out of his already queasy stomach. At some point during foreplay, his imagination had taken over, and he had pretended it was Janna he was kissing deeply on the mouth, Janna's smooth thighs he was parting. *Oh, Jesus.*

Shaken, he went to sit in his huge, glass-walled atelier living room, daylight stabbing him. This is what he needed: to be brutalized by bright morning sun so that he'd come to his senses. Ever since his exchange with Janna in the lounge the day before, he hadn't been able to get her off his mind. She had guts, standing up to him like that, and he admired her for it. Some of his own guys longed to go toe-to-toe with him, but didn't have the balls to do it. But this tiny woman—who would, no doubt, be busting his chops day and night as she threatened to do—she let him have it but good. He *loved* that. It turned him on. Showed she had brains, spirit, and courage—the same stuff needed to make it out on the ice. *I'll be the annoying song lyric you can't get out of your head. Man, she was right about that.* Now he just needed to figure out what to do about it, because there was no way in hell he could let himself fall for this woman, not when she worked for those corporate bastards at Kidco, not when he couldn't afford to divert his attention from winning. He had to expunge her from his thoughts. Avoid her. Ignore her. Whatever it took.

"Can I at least get a cup of coffee before you throw me out?"

The sharp voice of Laurie-Laura-Lauren behind him brought Ty back to himself. He turned from the window to see his playmate from the night before standing by his large, cream-colored leather couch glaring at him, her low-cut emerald dress from the night before looking cheap and incongruous now in the morning light.

"Sure," Ty replied, moving toward the kitchen. A cup of coffee and cab fare was the least he could do. But even as he was politely pouring out the steaming black liquid into a mug, his mind was fixated on one thing: Janna, and how to nip his desire for her in the bud. It wouldn't be easy, but he could do it.

"There's my girl."

Her father's greeting as she pulled into the circular driveway of her parents' Connecticut estate never failed to bring a smile to Janna's face. Ever since she could remember, those had been the first words out of his mouth whenever he'd catch sight of her. He had been bent low over a bed of Japanese anemone, their pale pink blossoms quivering slightly in the September breeze. He straightened up when he saw her, the bright eyes, set deep in his ruddy, weathered face, twinkling with delight. Peeling off his dirt-caked gardening gloves, he let them drop to the ground and came forward to hug her. Janna reveled in the comfort of his crushing embrace as she took in his scent: light sweat mixed with Dial soap, an aroma that took her straight back to childhood, to the happiness of time spent with him.

"How's it going?" she asked, inspecting the beds. Everything she knew about gardening, she'd learned from her father. How many hours had they spent together poring over seed catalogs, planting and digging, weeding and watering? She wasn't sure which had been his greatest gift: his unwavering belief in her, or the love of gardening that he'd passed on. She was certain she never could have survived her crazy childhood without both.

"They're taking over," her father replied in answer to her question. "I'm trying to get them trimmed back before they choke out everything else."

Janna nodded sympathetically. He looked tired; then again, when didn't he? Patrick MacNeil was known as a "workhorse." Back when he'd first started out, working in construction, he was renowned for his sheer brute strength and stubborn endurance. There was no task his squat, square body wouldn't tackle and keep at until it was done, and done properly. It was that same determination that had allowed him to strike out on his own as a builder.

Now, thirty-five years later, he sat at the head of a small building empire, the word *delegate* nonexistent in his vocabulary. He oversaw every detail of every operation from start to finish. Janna knew it was more than a matter of pride. She'd figured out long ago that losing himself in work gave her father a much-needed respite from the battleground that was his marriage.

As if on cue, Janna heard her mother's tinkling laughter float through the open front door. Courtney MacNeil was the *Town & Country* woman come to life: tall, regal, unmistakably WASP. Born with a silver spoon in her mouth, she had never quite forgiven Janna's father for temporarily yanking it out during their early years together, despite the fact that his business now earned more money than she could spend in a lifetime—although God knows she was trying. At fifty-four, she had the body of a woman half her age, and people viewing her from a distance, struck at first by her long mane of ash-blond hair, often mistook Courtney for one of her daughters, usually Petra or Skyler, which pleased her immensely.

Janna loved and hated her mother simultaneously. Loved her because a child doesn't know how to do anything else, and hated her because her mother had always made her feel she was lacking. Sandwiched as she was between her older sister, Petra, who was tall and brilliant, and her younger sister, Skyler, who was tall and gorgeous, Janna was the odd girl out—pint-sized, ordinary, the classic middle child who fought to shine but never even managed a flicker. At least not in her mother's eyes. One of her most painful memories was hearing her mother say to a room full of guests at a party, "Petra's got the brains, Skyler's got the beauty, and Janna"—here she had paused with pursed lips, obviously trying to think of *something* to say—"Janna's got the drive."

The drive. As if that was something lesser. No wonder she had always gravitated toward her father. He understood drive, didn't see it as gauche or somehow grasping the way her mother did. She looked at her father now, and tears began welling in her eyes. He was the one who had encouraged her to start her own business, who believed in her savvy, who told her repeatedly not to give up. So why had she? Why did she work for big corporations, and not for herself? The answer was simple: fear. She was afraid of failing. Afraid that what her mother had said was true—all she had to offer was drive with no talent to back it up. So what if she'd studied at the Wharton School? She was an impostor, always had been. She'd tricked her professors into believing she had a solid head for business, just like she continued tricking everyone into believing she knew how to do PR. Like Lou, for instance, who thought she was MENSA material. Well, her mother knew better.

A blast of rock music coming from an open window on the second floor caught Janna's attention.

"I see the birthday boy is home," she said to her father.

He glanced up at the screened window, a look of unmistakable displeasure crossing his face. "He calls that music."

"Careful," she teased, patting his arm. "Your age is showing." Her father sighed, shaking his head, and returned happily to digging in the dirt.

Janna headed inside to wish her baby brother, Wills, a happy birthday. The last of the MacNeil children, he was twelve today, the age gap between him and his sisters sizable. Janna's mother claimed he'd been "an accident," but Janna and her sisters all concurred that having Wills had been their parents' last-ditch attempt at trying to save their marriage—an attempt that had failed, leaving poor Wills to grow up alone in the big Georgian house with two warring parents. His solo status filled Janna with guilt. At least she, Petra and Skyler all had each other when things got rough. Wills had no one, which was why Janna made an extra effort to call and see him whenever she could. It was her way of letting him know that she was there for him, even if they didn't live under the same roof.

Inside the house, her mother sat in the huge country kitchen chatting away on the portable phone. She gave a distracted wave as Janna popped the cake she'd baked for Wills in the fridge. Before heading upstairs to see her brother, she detoured to the back patio to say hello to her sisters, both of whom she knew were there thanks to the twin Mercedeses parked in the drive. Petra sat poolside in shorts and a T-shirt, engrossed in a book. *Pet and her books,* Janna thought affectionately. *Why did she become a lawyer when what she really should have been was a writer?* Skyler was poolside, too, her tanned, perfect body barely covered in a hot pink, crocheted bikini. Predictably, Skyler was a model. A very successful model, too. Janna loved her big sister Petra, but Skyler was another story. Shallow, vain, judgmental, she reminded Janna of their mother. Janna's fervent hope was that Skyler would wake up the morning of her 30th birthday to find herself the size of Pavarotti. She knew it wasn't nice, but Skyler was so damn gorgeous that Janna had no choice but to occasionally *hate* her for it, certain that every other normal looking woman in America occasionally felt the same way, too.

She chatted with them for a few minutes before leaving to check up on Wills. Her parents' house reminded her of a museum: everything in its place, the climate carefully controlled, all hints of the combative, turbulent lives being lived there artfully concealed. Except for Wills. Though the music blasting from his room *was* earsplittingly loud, at least it signaled some sense of vitality the rest of the house lacked. Janna literally pounded on his bedroom door, knowing there was no way he'd hear her if she knocked politely.

The door flew open, and there he stood, his face breaking into a wide smile revealing two tidy, gleaming rows of braces, his head bopping up and down to the music. Like Janna, he was small, but he had his father's sturdy build and dark coloring. "Hey," he said, playfully punching her arm.

"Hey, yourself," she half shouted at him. "Can I come in?"

He stood aside to let her enter. Janna didn't want to appear uncool in his eyes, but the music was so loud the floor was shaking. She gestured towards the CD player, wincing apologetically. "Could you—?"

"Wuss." Wills turned down the stereo.

"Thanks."

Janna gazed around the four walls of the messy room. Every inch of available space was covered with pictures of either Britney Spears and Christine Aguilera, or posters of Wills's sports heroes. There was Mark McGwire standing at home plate, and Michael Jordan three feet off the ground in the middle of a slam dunk, and—

Ty Gallagher, holding a place of honor above the headboard of Wills's bed.

Janna turned to him. "When did you get that?"

"Last week." Wills flopped down on his stomach on the bed. "Dad said you work with him. Is that true?"

"Yup."

"Can I meet him?" There was no hiding the excitement in his voice.

Janna hesitated.

"Pleeeasse?" Wills begged.

Janna cleared away some dirty laundry and sat down on the edge of the bed. "All right," she promised, images of Ty telling her and her punky brother to take a hike dancing through her head.

"Yes!" Wills pumped his fist in the air. "I knew there was a reason you were my favorite sister."

"I thought it was because I baked you a double chocolate brownie cake for your birthday."

"Double yes!" Wills exclaimed. He looked at his sister with outright adoration. "You rule."

"I try." Janna's eyes kept drifting to the bright color poster of Gallagher on the ice, his expression fierce. He looked so—manly. Intense. Like some kind of warrior, not at all like the arrogant, uncooperative jerk she knew him to be. She tore her eyes away, focusing her attention on her brother.

"So, how does it feel to be twelve?"

Wills shrugged. "Dunno. The same."

"What did Mom and Dad give you?"

"New hockey skates," Wills recited, bored. "New skate-board." He shrugged again. "Stuff."

Stuff, Janna thought, her throat growing thick with words she longed to give voice to but knew she couldn't. That had always been her parents' way: to ply their kids with stuff, a way to assuage their guilt over not being able to give their children the important things, so caught up were they in their own drama.

"How's it been around here lately?" Janna asked quietly. She watched as her brother flipped over on his back and stared up at the ceiling, his hands folded on his stomach in repose.

"The same," he said evasively. "You know."

The same meaning their mother having one cocktail too many before dinner then tearing into their father, telling him she married beneath her. Both of them yelling about working-class this and hoity-toity that. Shanty Irish. Ice Princess. *My God,* Janna despaired. Didn't they care how it affected Wills? Then again, why should they? They didn't care how it affected her and her sisters.

She ruffled his hair, a gesture he obviously thought he was now too old for as he jerked his head away. "Sorry," she apologized. "Look, you know you can come stay with me anytime. I mean it. Or call me."

He turned to her, hopeful. "If I stay with you, can I meet Ty Gallagher?"

"How 'bout this." Janna thought a moment. "How 'bout you come home with me tonight, and tomorrow morning, I take you to a Blades practice with me and you can meet the guys?"

Wills jumped up. "You can do that? Really?"

"Sure I can do that," Janna assured him, her heart filling with happiness as she saw the excited, little boy expression on his face.

"And I can get autographs and stuff?"

"Yup."

"And a picture of me with Ty?"

"We can try."

"You're the best!" He hopped off the bed, impulsively kissing the side of her face. "Wait till I tell the guys about this!" He was halfway out the room to call his friends when he halted, rounding on Janna again. "Can I bring my skates? Can I skate on the same ice as them after they're done?"

"I'll check with my boss," she said carefully. "But I don't think it will be a problem."

Whooping with delight, he tore out into the hallway and down the stairs. Alone now, Janna rose, turning back to the image of Ty above the bed. God, he was handsome, even with sweat dripping from his brow and his body bent forward in an attack position, ready to blast a puck down the ice. But so what? It wasn't his looks she cared about right now. It was his heart. She hoped that beneath his surly exterior, he could find it within himself to be nice to a kid, even if that kid did happen to be her brother. Because if he wasn't . . .

Doing PR had perks, and here was the proof: sitting rinkside, she was watching her baby brother watch the Blades practice. Wills's eyes never left Ty; everything he did was pronounced the best, the greatest, the most amazing. *That's what you think,* Janna thought, knowing she'd have to go into the locker room after practice and try, once again, to talk Captain Stubborn into putting in some face time for a good cause. But when Ty glided past them and flipped a puck over the Plexiglas to Wills, Janna's stance softened ever so slightly. He might not want to deal with her, but he clearly cared about making a young fan happy. The least she could do was give him credit for that.

Watching him, Janna tried to see Ty through the eyes of her brother, the fans, and his teammates. To her brother, he was a sports God whose courage and determination had helped him carve out a spot in athletic history. Fans loved him because he was larger than life, a legendary player and proven winner who had delivered the Stanley Cup to New York and seemed poised to do so again. His teammates loved him for the same reason and more: he was their leader, but he was also their friend, someone who genuinely cared about them individually. Lou had told her a story about a rookie who'd come to the Blades midseason and was being put up in a hotel. Gallagher invited the young player to stay with him instead, and even helped him find an apartment. Janna's jaw had hit the floor when she heard that; she had a hard time reconciling the egotistical jock she'd been dealing with to this softie who supposedly had a heart. Who *was* this guy?

Practice over, Wills began lacing up his skates, eager for the chance to tell his friends that the blades of his Bauers had actually touched the same ice as those of Ty Gallagher. Janna's plan was to let him skate a few laps to get it out of his system, then bring him into the locker room with her and introduce him to the players. Usually, Gallagher was one of the first off the ice and into the shower. Today, however, he was the last, and was in fact skating at an easy pace toward Janna and Wills, prompting Wills's eyes to nearly double in size and Janna's gut to shrivel into a tight, defensive knot.

"Hi," he said through the Plexiglas to Wills. "I'm Ty."

"I—" Wills halted, too dumbfounded to speak. He turned to his sister. *Is this really happening?* his gaze asked.

"It's okay," Janna cooed under her breath, gently redirecting his gaze back to Ty, who seemed unfazed by her brother's sudden dumbness. If anything he looked vaguely sympathetic.

"You must be Janna's brother," Ty continued smoothly, his expression amiable as he took both of them in. "I can see a resemblance."

Wills just swallowed.

"This is Wills," Janna said warmly, putting her arm around her brother and giving his shoulder a quick, reassuring squeeze. "He turned twelve yesterday."

"Happy Birthday," said Ty.

"Thank you," Wills managed in a whisper.

Ty pointed to the skates on Wills's feet. "You play hockey?"

Wills nodded.

Ty's head bobbed in approval. "Good man. It's the only sport that matters. You want to do a few laps with me, pass the puck?"

This time Janna and Wills both went wide-eyed.

"Ty," Janna began, trying to keep the astonishment in her voice at bay, "you don't have to do that."

"I know. But I want to." He flashed Wills an encouraging smile. "You game?"

"Yeah," said Wills, awed.

"There's just one condition."

Of course, thought Janna bitterly. *I knew this was too good to be true.*

"If I miss a pass, you can't tell a soul. I do have a reputation to uphold, after all."

Wills grinned, and looking to Janna once more for reassurance, joined his hero on the ice. He was nervous at first, and seemed unsure of his footing, but gradually he loosened up. Janna couldn't hear what Ty was saying to him, but whatever it was, it was making her brother smile and laugh. Janna was moved. When was the last time she heard her baby brother laugh like that, so carefree and happy? They skated, taking turns at playfully checking each other into the boards, passing the puck back and forth between them. It gradually dawned on Janna that right now, she wasn't seeing Ty Gallagher as his fans saw him, or as her brother saw him, or as his teammates saw him.

She was seeing him as a woman sees a man, one who could, if permitted, cross the line from periphery to potential. She saw a strong man, one who cared and whose convictions ran as deep as his emotions obviously did. Someone willing to take the time to make a young boy happy; a man whom a woman could imagine . . .

She stopped herself right there. What was she thinking?! The man out there charming her brother to death on the ice was the bane of her professional existence. Not only that, but he was a jock—uneducated, egotistical, probably sexist, too, if you scratched his surface, which she certainly didn't want to do! No, she'd stick to Robert, cerebral, pretentious, unmotivated Robert. Safe Robert. At least thinking about him didn't whip up feelings deep inside her that were scary as hell. That had to count for something, right? But exactly *what* it counted for, she wasn't sure she wanted to know.

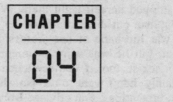

CHAPTER

04

Being nice to her kid brother had been a mistake. Ty could see that now.

It was the end of October, a month into the official season, and ever since he'd made the kid's day by giving him a few minutes of ice time, along with signing an autograph and posing for a picture or two, Janna the Human Terrier had been on him, relentlessly cajoling and wheedling and pleading and begging and bargaining, trying to get him to show his face at an event, *any* event.

Which, of course, he wouldn't.

Much as her constant nagging made him want to snatch a roll of athletic tape from one of the trainers and plaster some over her mouth, deep down he realized she was just doing her job—a job which seemed largely to center around bugging the living hell out of him. It had become something of joke: all she had to do was come within three feet of him and the first words out of his mouth were a swift, emphatic, "No."

It was his own fault, he supposed. If he'd ignored the

kid, just headed on into the locker room that day the way he usually did, then she'd still think he was a hard-ass. But no; he'd gone out of his way to do something nice, and in doing so, had revealed a small chink in his armor, one she was now trying to blast through with that jackhammer approach of hers, obviously thinking that if she pressured him long enough, he'd eventually cave. Too bad she was wrong.

So why had he done it? He pondered the question as he looked out the window of the Amtrak train as it sped toward DC. They were playing Washington that night. So far the Blades were eight and four, three of those losses taking place on the opponents' ice. He hoped the guys could keep their equilibrium and focus tonight, because God knows they would need it. Washington played a hard, aggressive game. They were tough and fast. *But we're tougher and faster,* Ty thought with no small measure of pride. *And if we can maintain our focus, we'll mop the ice with them.*

His thoughts drifted back to his petite nemesis and her little brother. Why had he done it? Easy: he wanted to make the kid's day. He got a kick out of the fact that something as simple as shooting the breeze, along with a few pucks, could make someone happy. It wasn't too much to ask, and he was glad to give it. Plus, the kid—Wills—reminded him of himself at that age. Stocky but shy, afraid to own his own space. He wondered if the kid's father was on his ass constantly to win, win, win the way his own old man had been. Ty figured that if a private audience with one of his heroes helped boost the kid's esteem even a little, or helped ease the possible pressure of trying to be good enough to please his parent, then it was worth it.

But ensuring the kid's birthday was unforgettable was only half the reason, and he knew it. The other reason was that he wanted to impress Janna. Afterwards, when she looked at him with those big, baby blues glistening with gratitude and something else he didn't want to dwell on, it

dawned on him that he'd been waiting for that look, and
had in fact just engineered it. The look that said she knew
there was more to him than his all-encompassing need to
win and stubborn refusals.to cooperate with her. The look
that said—

Desperate to clear his head, he rose from his seat to circulate among his boys, make sure everyone was comfortable, nothing too heavy weighing on their minds. He
always did this as part of his job as captain, even though
the press teased him about it and called him "Pops," a
nickname that stuck in his craw. A handful of guys on the
team were in fact older than he was, and he wasn't that old
himself. As he walked down the aisle, he saw that the Bull
was on a cell phone haranguing someone while depleting a
bag of Skittles the size of a hot water bottle. A few rows
up, Ty could see Janna. The Bull had dragged her along to
help keep everyone in line. She was reading the riot act to
two of his rookies, Guy LaTemp and Barry Fontaine, both
of whom had been stupid enough to let themselves be pho-
tographed coming out of one of the best known topless
bars on the East Side, drunk.

"This is what's going to happen," Janna was barking.
"I'm going to write up a statement for the press telling
them you're both sorry about behaving in a less than professional manner, and that it will never happen again. Because it won't, do you understand? Kidco won't tolerate it,
and neither will I. You want to be bad boys, do it in disguise. Understand?"

Both players nodded.

"Good. One more thing: if anyone from the press asks
you about this, you say, 'No comment.' Period. Not 'We
were just trying to have some fun,' not 'It was harmless,'
not 'The mean lady from PR told us we couldn't talk about
it.' *'No comment.'* I mean it.

"Finally, the two of you are going to take a class in drug
and alcohol abuse awareness. It's called image rehabilita-

tion, and you're going to pretend to love it even if it's your worst nightmare. Am I making myself clear?"

The players nodded again and skulked away. Impressed, Ty watched as she marched back to her seat on the aisle. A second later, Alexei Lubov approached her, bending low to say something. Ty wasn't one for eavesdropping, but the frustration in Janna's voice caught his attention.

"Alexei—Lex—I told you. I don't want to go out with you."

"But I wish it."

Janna rolled her eyes in irritation. "Well, I don't wish it, do you understand? You're a very nice guy, okay? But I'm not going to go out with you. And the sooner you get it through your head—"

Unheeding, Lubov reached for her hand and put it on his bicep. "You feel that? Rock solid, a real man. How can you not want?" His voice dropped down seductively. "Admit it, you do want. You—"

Janna snatched her hand back, flustered. "Alexei, *stop it.*"

That was it. Something reared up inside Ty, which he refused to name but couldn't help acting upon nonetheless. Every nerve in his body thrumming, he strode toward the pair, his brown eyes flashing a warning to his teammate that was unmistakable. If Lubov thought he could behave that way off the ice—if he thought his captain would stand for him harassing a woman—then newsflash, bucko, he had another thing coming. The closer he got, the more Lubov seemed to shrink before him, so that even before Ty grabbed him and pinned him up against an opposing row of seats, he could see Lubov was aware that he'd seriously misstepped.

"What part of her 'no' didn't you understand?" Ty growled.

"I am sorry," said Lubov, his eyes clouding over with shame at seeing his leader's anger and disappointment.

"Don't tell me, tell her." Ty released Lubov and with a small shove, pushed him in Janna's direction.

"Janna." Lubov's eyes were wide as saucers, guileless now. "I am sorry I bother you. I will leave you alone now." He nervously turned to Ty as if to say, "Will that do?" Ty gave a small, almost imperceptible jerk of the head and then Alexei was gone, hustling toward the back of the train car to escape the watchful eyes of his teammates and lick his wounds of humiliation in private. Ty watched him go, then turned back to Janna, who looked mildly shell-shocked.

"You okay?"

"I'm fine," said Janna. "But I could have handled him myself, you know."

"Really? So why didn't you?"

"Because you didn't give me a chance," she replied sharply. Pink flared in her cheeks, charming Ty against his will. How many women really, truly blushed these days?

"Alexei's harmless, you know that," she was saying. "Half his problem is he doesn't understand how things work in this country, least of all interactions between men and women." Her mouth pressed into a thin, disapproving line. "Maybe you could teach him."

"Are you poking fun at me, Miss MacNeil?"

"Never, Captain Gallagher. I'm merely alluding to an off-ice talent I've heard you have."

"What else have you heard about me?"

"You don't want to know."

Ty laughed. He saw the smile in her eyes then, and responded in kind. He liked this, the easy way they bantered back and forth during the few, rare moments she wasn't harassing him. Liked her. Which is why he wanted to deck Lubov: because the thought of him even going near her made his guts churn so badly he couldn't even think straight. Jesus H. Christ. What the hell was wrong with him?

He stepped back—from her and from himself—gesturing at the papers on her lap. "I'll let you get back to it," he said stiffly.

"Okay." His abruptness left Janna looking befuddled. "I suppose I should thank you," she said quietly. "It's nice to know chivalry isn't dead."

Chivalry. Her use of that word pleased him, made his heart swell with pride. But it unnerved him, too, as half remembered feelings from true romances past began drowsily to awaken. He couldn't let it happen. Wouldn't let it.

"Maybe you could write the incident up for the boys at Kidco and pass it off as an act of community service," he quipped, although he wasn't sure she heard him, since he was already half way up the aisle to his seat, where he fully intended to stay put for the rest of the trip.

"*OhmiGod, did* you see that?! What was that thing he just did, that thing with the puck? What was that?"

Janna waited for the savage roar of the crowd at Met Gar to die down before answering Theresa's question. It was a Saturday night, and the Blades were playing their number one rivals, New Jersey, on home ice. Alexei Lubov, number 55, had just scored the first goal only ten minutes into the game. Enthusiasm was high among the sold-out crowd, which was renowned for its loyalty to the team as well as its vociferous voicing of both delight and displeasure. Janna gazed around the overheated arena at the sea of electrified faces and found herself catching a spark or two, excitement surging through her as she felt the crowd's energy.

Maybe it was because she was beginning to understand what happened down there on the ice, or maybe it had to do with knowing the players personally, but she was actually starting to *like* hockey, and to appreciate the consummate skill and talent that went into playing at the professional level. Not that she'd ever tell anyone this, apart from maybe Lou, and her brother and father. She imagined telling her mother and sisters, and could just picture the Amazon trio peering down at her in soul-withering condescension. As for Robert—well, fuggeddaboudit, as Theresa's uncle Carmine would say. Robert would sarcastically ask her if she'd been knocked in the head by a stray puck, or had undergone a lobotomy without telling him. It was one thing to do PR for a hockey team, quite another to care about the sport itself. What was it he always said? "The masses are asses"? *God help me,* Janna thought, mortified. Theresa was right. Comfortable or no, she really had to ditch him.

"What you saw him do is called a 'deke,'" she explained. "It's when the player with the puck kind of fakes to get around the enemy, or else tricks the goalie into moving out of position."

"So that's why he moved the puck to one side and then quick-shifted to the opposite direction," Theresa observed excitedly.

"Right."

She turned to Janna. "How do you know this stuff?"

Janna shrugged. "Oh, you know, just from watching the game."

Theresa nodded solemnly, impressed, and returned to eyeing the action down below. Janna came close to telling her the truth—that she'd gone out and bought a copy of *Hockey for Dummies* which she studied religiously—but decided against it. It was much more fun having Theresa think she was a sports genius who could spout hockey lingo at will.

Janna looked to the ice now, too, her eyes invariably seeking out, as always, the jersey bearing the number 29. Ty was at center ice in face-off position, waiting for the puck to be dropped. She saw his lips moving, and deduced he was probably trying to provoke his opponent in an effort to get him off his game. Janna knew from hanging around the locker room that he could have quite a mouth on him when he thought he needed to; she didn't want to think what he was probably insinuating about the other guy's mother or sister. Ty won the face-off, and then all the bodies on the ice were in motion, a manic, ruthless ballet of might and speed that was nothing short of exhilarating.

It dawned on Janna, as she booed along with the crowd when the ref made a bad call, and cheered when a good, clean hit was made on one of the Jersey players, that she finally thought of the team as "the guys," just like Lou did. Because that's who they were: guys, with personalities, likes and dislikes like everyone else. She pretty much knew now whom she could count on anytime to do PR, and who refused to do a damn thing to help her; who preferred doing hands-on stuff with kids, and who got off on dressing up and hobnobbing with the grandees of New York society intent on demonstrating their noblesse oblige. They were an okay bunch, hardworking and generous, despite the weekend rowdiness so many of them persisted in involving themselves in. But time was on her side here. If she hung in long enough, she had no doubt she could strong-arm most of them into an image-enhancing activity or two.

Except for their sainted captain, of course.

She didn't get it. Didn't get *him*. She knew he had a deep generosity of spirit, because she'd seen it firsthand, both with her brother and with his own players. She knew he was a caring person, too, if his near throttling of "Lex" on the train to DC a few weeks back was any measure. So why was he still so resistant to publicity, especially the kind she did, all of it for a good cause? And why was he avoiding her like the plague lately? Okay, so he always tried to steer clear of her *anyway*, especially when he saw her coming at him with a clipboard. But ever since the train incident, he'd been even more tightlipped than usual, and when he did deign to talk to her, he was monosyllabic and curt, which some people might interpret as rude. What was the deal?

The question lingered in the back of her mind as she and Theresa watched the Blades kick the stuffing out of Jersey, 5–2. When the game was over, Theresa finished her beer, and, plunking the empty plastic cup down on the concrete floor between her feet, turned to Janna expectantly.

"I want to meet them."

"Who?"

"Who," Theresa repeated, exasperated. "You know who! The Blades. Take me down to the locker room."

"Oh, no. No way." Janna tried to picture Theresa walking into that sea of sweaty, muscled flesh and knew instinctively that it was a recipe for disaster. Besides, she was in no mood to watch the entire team turn into blithering dolts at the sight of her gorgeous friend. "Forget it."

"C'mon," Theresa pleaded.

"No."

"Well, can't we meet up with them at a bar or something? I know a bunch of them go out for a brew or two after a home game, and I know you know where. C'mon, Janna." She clasped her hands together as if in prayer, her expression as innocent as a choirgirl. "Please?"

Janna thought. To be honest, the last thing she wanted to do was go out to some smoky bar and watch Theresa search for her soul mate among the players. That's all she'd need—her roommate dating one of the Blades. Plus she'd been out three nights this week at fund-raisers and was exhausted; all she wanted to do was go home, take a shower, and crawl into bed with the latest issue of *People*. Was that too much to ask? Apparently so, if Theresa's expression, which was now morphing into a "You owe me" scowl, was any indication.

"All right," Janna wearily agreed as Theresa clapped with delight. "But on one condition."

"What?"

"*A*, you behave yourself, and *B*, we are out of there by two at the latest."

"Agreed. And since that's *two* conditions, I have one, too."

"What?" Janna asked suspiciously.

"When we get there, you have to tell me which of the guys looks best naked."

Janna rolled her eyes. "I wouldn't know. They all look the same."

Which was a lie. She knew damn well who looked best, but there was no way she was going to tell Theresa, just in case he was there.

Ty was at the bar getting himself a Guinness when he heard a couple of the guys behind him say her name, telling her they were glad she'd finally decided to join them. He glanced quickly over his shoulder, and sure enough, there she was, looking damn cute in jeans and a simple, white, button-down blouse. She was with a tall, olive-skinned woman who looked like a kid in a candy store.

His heart sank. He'd come here to unwind with his boys after a rough game, not fend off the publicist from hell. He wished she'd consider where she was and give it a rest for once. She had to know that one mention of PR or Kidco would find him draining his glass and heading back out into the chilly night. He hoped, then, that she had come for the same reason he did, to relax with friends.

He returned to where he was sitting with Abby and Kevin Gill as Janna circulated amongst the other tables, introducing her friend to his players. His guys were gracious, welcoming. It made him feel proud. Of course, the friend was attractive, so it didn't take a rocket scientist to figure out what was up. But the Chapter House tended to be a friendly place, which was why they all hung out there. Ty knew some people might think it was a real hole-in-the-wall, with its crummy old jukebox, dirt-caked windows, sawdust-covered floors and rickety old tables, but to his mind that was part of its charm. The wizened old bartender

had been there forever and had a cache of entertaining
tales about his days in the merchant marines that could
keep you there all night. The atmosphere was low-key and
the clientele were just regular working people, none of
whom cared who the Blades were. It was a well-kept secret, a place where they could drink their beer in peace.
Occasionally fans would show up, but Ty's feeling was
that if they were clever enough to figure out where the
team hung out, then they deserved to share a drink or two
with them.

With the jukebox blasting some old hit from the '60s—
Ty thought maybe it was "American Woman" but he
wasn't sure—Janna and her sidekick eventually found
their way to his table.

"Abby, Kevin, Ty—" Her eyes held his for a split second longer than he would have liked—"I want you to meet
my friend Theresa."

Kevin, ever friendly, raised his mug in salute. "Nice to
meet you."

Ty echoed the sentiment, as did Abby.

"Nice to meet you, too," Theresa replied.

"Would you like to sit down?" Abby offered graciously.

Smiling, Janna and Theresa pulled up two chairs and
sat down. They weren't seated for five seconds before
Michael Dante, the team's third line winger, sauntered
over from the table he was sharing with Blades defenseman Burke Dalton and "Siberian Express," Alexei Lubov.
Dante smiled politely and offered to buy Theresa a drink.
His two front teeth were missing. She smiled back, but declined.

"Just one drink," Dante urged, friendly. "We don't
bite."

"Maybe that's part of the problem," Ty quipped under
his breath. Didn't this Theresa realize that she was surrounded by men who, between them, had more false teeth
than the residents of a nursing home? Janna scowled at
him while Theresa appeared not to have heard. Realizing

that she wasn't going to change her mind, Dante shrugged affably and left. The scene repeated itself when his teammate, Burke Dalton, approached with the same question. This time Theresa accepted, and with a quick glance at Janna to make sure it was okay, followed Dalton back to his table.

"Well, that was interesting," observed Abby.

"That's one word for it," Janna muttered, a small frown creasing her brow.

"Wonder what Burke had that Michael didn't," Kevin mused aloud.

"Teeth," Janna answered grimly, looking nervously in Theresa's direction.

She's worried about having to baby-sit her friend, Ty thought. And now he was worried about having to baby-sit *her,* about sitting here and wanting to make sure she had a good time. *Why the hell did she have to come?*

"Can I get you something to drink?" Ty heard Kevin offering, which annoyed him. He was going to ask the same thing, and now Kevin had beaten him to the punch! *Make up your mind, Gallagher. Do you want her to stay and have a beer with you or do you want her to go?*

Janna looked grateful. "A Bud Light would be fine, thanks Kevin."

"I'll get it." Ty jumped to his feet. He could feel the three of them watching him with raised brows as he pushed back from the table and headed toward the bar, but he didn't care. Ordering Janna a drink would give him time to figure out how he wanted to handle being in a social setting with her. Up until now, he'd been doing a great job of avoiding her, pushing her out of his thoughts. He had to keep a clear head here. He placed his order and surreptitiously glanced back at the table, where she was chatting away with Kevin and Abby. When she was happy, her whole face lit up, the cornflower blue eyes crackling with animation. Those big eyes sometimes had a sense of waiflike vulnerability that made you want to protect her. Which is why he'd jumped on Lubov on the train. Had nothing to do with wanting to ensure Lex kept the hell away from her. It was all about protection. *Yeah, right.*

Order filled, he returned to the table and handed her the beer.

"What do I owe you?" she asked.

Ty waved his hand dismissively. "It's on the house." He took a sip of his Guinness, the full-bodied taste warming his throat and belly. Nothing better than a nice dark beer after a backbreaking night out on the ice. "So what did I miss?"

Kevin rose, extending a hand to his wife. "Abby and I are going to dance. Janna can fill you in."

You're gonna pay for this, Ty's glare told Kevin, whose only response was a huge grin as he gently put his hand in the small of his wife's back and guided her out onto the tiny, makeshift dance floor.

"So," said Ty, edging his chair an inch or two closer to Janna's so he wouldn't have to raise his voice to be heard. "How's your brother?"

The blue eyes registered surprise, then admiration. "He's fine. He talks about what you did for him incessantly."

Ty shrugged, uncomfortable with the praise. "He seemed like a nice kid."

"He is."

Her eyes darted down to the floor, over to the wall, looking anywhere but at him. She was nervous, but for the life of him he couldn't figure out why. Jesus Christ, she'd seen him naked. What could be so hard about talking to him? Worse, it was making him nervous. He took a long pull at his beer, then cocked his head in the direction of Theresa.

"Your friend—is she a puck bunny?"

Janna recoiled, offended. "What? Why? Are you interested?"

Ty laughed, unsure what to make of the testiness in her voice. "No. She's not my type."

"What is your type?" she asked, looking directly at him.

"Well," Ty began slowly, rolling his beer mug between his hands, "I guess that's for me to know and for you to find out." Her glance darted away again then, and he used the awkward pause between them to steer the conversation in a different direction.

"Look, I didn't mean to insult your friend. It's just that when she walked in here, her eyes glazed over like she'd hit the jackpot."

"Theresa's not a puck bunny. She's a hopeless romantic."

"Meaning?"

"She's imagining every guy in this room standing up at the altar in a tux while she glides down the aisle to the strains of 'The Wedding March.' "

Ty laughed. "So she's husband hunting, huh?"

"Continually on the look out for 'The One.' "

"Well, she's sure as hell barking up the wrong tree with that trio. Except maybe for Dante, who she seems to be trying hard to ignore."

"Poor Michael Dante," Janna lamented. "He seems so nice."

"Isn't that what women want?" Ty queried edgily. "A man who's 'nice'?"

"Nice is good. Remembering to wear your bridge in public is even better." They both laughed at that.

"What does she do?" Ty asked, determined to keep the conversation on Theresa.

"She's a publicist at *The Wild and the Free*. We used to work together."

"Ah." He'd go to his grave before he'd tell her that he, like half the guys in the NHL, was totally addicted to that soap. Lots of jocks were. It was a way to pass the time when you on were on the road, stuck in a hotel room with nothing to do. He resisted the urge to ask if the actress who played Carmen was really a bitch and asked another question instead, one which interested him even more. "How did you get into publicity? Was it something you always wanted to do?"

Janna peered down into her drink. When she looked back up at him, he was taken aback to see her eyes were sad. "Actually, what I really wanted to do was start my own business."

"So why didn't you?"

"It's complicated," she replied evasively. "I'm not sure I can explain."

"Try."

Her eyes flashed then, which is what he'd hoped for. He hated the melancholia that had descended upon her so fast. She took another sip of her beer, thoughtful. Her eyes continued to have a hard time meeting his.

"I didn't pursue being an entrepreneur because I didn't have what it took."

"Who told you that?"

No answer.

"C'mon, who told you that?" he repeated. "I want to know."

Still, she kept silent.

"Oh, I see." He leaned back in his chair. "You told yourself that."

That got her attention. Whereas a minute before it seemed as if the tacky picture of dogs playing poker on the opposite wall held more interest for her than his face, now she was glaring at him. "Did you even try to start your own business?" he kept on. "Or did you throw in the towel the first time you had to sit down and write a business plan?"

"I threw in the towel after the hundredth time I sat down to write one, okay?" she snapped.

He ignored her. "Did you really not know what you were doing? Or is that something you've convinced yourself of to help you deal with not hanging in there and going for it?"

Janna looked stunned. "What?"

"C'mon, Janna," he said cajolingly. He leaned forward, elbows on the table, friendly. "Be honest with yourself for one minute. Did you really think you weren't capable of starting up a business?"

She swallowed. "No."

"Then why didn't you try?" He could feel a fit of Captain Gallagher's famous esteem boosting coming on, but couldn't stop himself. He hated seeing her this way. "Because it was too hard? Anything worth having requires a struggle. You know that, right? Christ, you don't give up trying to get me to do Kidco's bidding!"

"That's different," Janna insisted.

"No, it's not. It's the same damn principle of persistence." He paused, carefully measuring out his words. "I really admire the way you do your job, you know."

Janna snorted. "Right."

"I mean it. I may not agree with your reasons for doing it, since you know I think PR is bull, but I respect the way you march into the locker room day after day and tell the team what's what. Not everyone can do that, especially when it comes to hockey players. You should feel proud about how many of the guys have been willing to see things your way and cooperate on the PR stuff. It's a testament to your feistiness and powers of persuasion—powers you could tap into if you decided to start your own business."

Janna mumbled something and looked down. Gazing at her, he felt as if he was actually seeing her for the first time. That tiny terror who relentlessly pursued him around the locker room had been replaced by this delicate woman sitting here beside him, a woman who was afraid to go after what was rightfully hers and soar. He couldn't believe it, which was proof of her steely determination. Apart from the first time they'd met and he'd nearly bitten her head off, he'd never have guessed in a million years that beneath her no-nonsense exterior, there lurked someone with serious esteem problems, someone whom he felt shouldn't have such problems at all.

"Janna." Her head was down again, fascinated by her beer. Carefully, oh so carefully so as not to startle or offend, he put his index finger beneath her chin and gently tilted her head up so he could see her eyes, which were now glistening with liquid. *Shit*. The last thing he'd wanted to do was make her cry. And of course, right on cue, Kevin and Abby were laughing their way back to the table.

"Hey, you two—"

Abby stopped short when she saw the anguished expression on Janna's face and slid immediately into her seat, taking her hand.

"What did you do?" she hissed at Ty. Before Ty could roar back in self-defense, Janna jumped in.

"He didn't do anything," she reassured Abby. "We were discussing something very sad, that's all."

"You sure?" Abby asked suspiciously, her eyes still reprimanding Ty.

"Honestly," said Janna.

Abby relaxed. "All right, then." Her hand slid from Janna's, reaching for her purse. "Kevin and I told the sitter we'd be home by twelve-thirty, so we'd better run." She peered at Janna, concerned. "You sure you're okay?"

"I'm *fine*," Janna insisted.

Abby rose, pointing a finger at Ty. "She's supposed to be having fun, not sitting here crying. Think you can manage that?"

Ty's jaw clenched. "I'll try."

"Good." Abby leaned over, kissing the side of Janna's face. "We'll see you soon."

Again Ty's eyes sought Kevin's as he and his wife drifted from the table, but this time the message in them was different: *Tell your wife I didn't do anything!* Kevin gave a small nod, seeming to understand.

Ty looked back to Janna, who had twisted around in her seat to again check on Theresa, who appeared to be reading palms for some of the guys. At least, that's what Ty thought she was doing. If it was some bizarre courtship ritual, he didn't want to know.

"She having fun?" he asked when Janna turned back around. She nodded. "I'm sorry I made you cry," he murmured.

"No, no, it's okay," she replied with what seemed to him false breeziness. "What you said is the truth, and sometimes, as we all know, the truth hurts."

His voice was a persuasive rumble. "You should do it, Janna. You should decide what kind of business you want to run and give it a try. If you don't, you'll hate yourself."

She glanced away, clearly ill at ease. "That's easy for you to say. You're a leader. A winner. The concept of self doubt is alien to you."

"Yeah, but that doesn't mean I can't sympathize. I can't tell you how many of the guys on the team—guys who have made it into the NHL, for Chrissakes—lack confidence."

"Really?"

"Hell, yeah. But they feel the fear and do it anyway—with a little help from me, of course, and the coaches. We all work hard to help them build up their esteem. And it pays off. But you gotta take that first step off the cliff; you have to have faith, you know what I'm saying?"

She frowned. "Can we change the subject, please? This pep talk is starting to depress me."

"Just trying to help." Since it was clear that any further discussion on the subject was off limits, he stood. "Would you like to dance?" Some slow, R and B tune had just kicked in on the jukebox—Percy Sledge's "When A Man Loves A Woman"? He was so bad with these oldies, and it seemed the perfect deflection.

Janna hesitated a moment, weighing his offer. "No thanks."

Ty was surprised to find himself feeling rejected. "C'mon," he urged. "It's three minutes of your life. It will cheer you up."

"Okay," Janna capitulated, still sounding unsure.

They made their way out to the dance floor, Ty well aware that all his teammates were nudging each other and turning to watch Hatfield dance with McCoy. Jesus, was he gonna catch hell for this on Monday.

Out on the floor, he extended his left hand to her, and she took it gracefully as her other hand came up to rest on his shoulder. He felt awkward putting his hand around her waist, but she didn't resist, so he let it rest there, just above the small of her back. Careful not to bump into the other couples clinging to each other as they shuffled around the floor, he drew her closer. With that, they slowly began swaying in time to the music.

Ty was amazed at how natural it felt to hold her like this, and wondered if she felt the same way. He got his answer when she moved in closer to him, nestling her head on his chest. In contrast to the slow, sensual rhythm of the music, he could now hear his own heart pounding in his ears, rapid-fire and insistent. Could she hear it, too? He breathed slowly, deliberately, trying to keep one step ahead of the slow spread of heat beginning to simmer through his body. She was so tiny, perfect, like a little bird that needed shelter. Who needed him. As if reading his mind, she lifted her head from his chest and gazed up into his eyes. Neither of them said anything. *Maybe,* Ty thought, *because nothing needs to be said*. Or maybe because neither of them had the guts to. She lowered her head again, sighing, and they danced on.

The music ended, and the spell broke. For a split second, neither of them seemed to know what to do or who should do it first. They jerked apart awkwardly, Janna seeming to blink away the dreaminess he swore had been in her eyes only moments before. Regaining her senses, she was all business now.

"I better get Theresa home," she said shakily, "before she proposes to Lex."

Ty nodded, his pulse rate slowly dropping down to normal. "Need a lift?" he asked politely, hoping it wasn't too obvious that he wanted her to say "No."

"We'll just grab a cab." She started moving in the direction of Theresa's table, then spun back around as if she'd forgotten something.

"Thanks for the beer," she said quickly. "And the dance. See you at practice Monday."

"Yup," Ty replied, watching her propel herself toward Theresa like a drowning woman making for a lifeboat. Some line had been crossed tonight and they both knew it. That's why she couldn't get the hell away from him fast enough. She was terrified. Normally, a woman treating him like he'd suddenly contracted a contagious disease would have pissed him off, but not tonight. If he could get away with it, he'd do the same thing, hotfoot it out of there with one of his pals and shove what had just transpired between them deep down into the cracks of memory, where it would never see light again.

In fact, that's what he was going to do anyway.

He went back to his table, chugged down the remains of his beer, and ordered another. Then he joined some of his teammates at another table, and, working harder at it than he ever had in his life, made sure he had a good time.

CHAPTER

05

If it's true that hearing voices is a sign of insanity, then I'm certifiable.

It was the Monday following her weekend shuffle 'round the dance floor, and inner Janna was cursing on an endless loop.

Mistake! Mistake, mistake, MISTAKE!!!! What on earth possessed you to tell Captain Perfect you hadn't followed your entrepreneurial instincts?! Now he knows what a loser you are! Now he thinks you're a quitter! You know how some men sleep with a woman they feel sorry for and call it a "Mercy Fuck"? Well, your dance with Ty Gallagher was a Mercy Dance! He asked you to dance because he felt sorry for you. And who can blame him? You're pathetic. As if a man like him could feel anything for you. God, you are an idiot, you know that? A total idiot.

Theresa's imagined voice then joined with inner Janna's, the two beginning a harmonizing duet of charge and counter charge.

You and Gallagher have chemistry. Can't you see that? When are you going to DUMP that DRAIN on society, Robearr?

Chemistry? Look who's talking! You're a perfect match for Michael Dante but you couldn't see it 'cause you were too busy batting your eyelashes at Lex like some deranged Mae West impersonator! Chemistry? What a stupid soap-opera word. How many insipid press releases did we churn out at The Wild & the Free *gushing about "incredible" or "undeniable" chemistry between two actors who hated each other off the set?! Chemistry, shmemistry!*

Then a third voice chimed in, making it a trio in her head. A deep, rich, confident voice. Ty Gallagher's voice.

You'll hate yourself if you don't start your own business. HEL-LO! I already hate myself about that.

But the voice sounding loudest in her head wasn't inner Janna, or imagined Theresa, or imagined Ty. It was a real voice, complete with New York accent, and it belonged to Lou. Two nights from now was one of the largest fund-raising events in the city, a black-tie dinner to raise money for the United Way. Janna had managed to coax former Blades Captain Roy Duncan, one of the most beloved players in New York hockey history, to attend, which was no small feat. But less than an hour ago, Lou had called her into his office to tell her that Duncan wouldn't be able to make the dinner, because his brother had died in Vancouver. They needed someone else—fast. Someone who was as big a draw as Duncan, so that those who'd paid a helluva lot of money to hobnob with a hockey legend under the guise of a good cause wouldn't be disappointed.

"Get Gallagher," Lou had commanded, while murdering an egg and cheese sandwich. "Do whatever you have to do—beg, cry, sell your firstborn child—I don't care. Just get him."

"I'll try," Janna promised as she tried hard not to cringe at the yellow river of egg yolk cascading down all three of Lou's chins.

"Get him," Lou repeated. "Today. Now. And pass me a napkin on your way out."

So here she was, less than an hour until game time, on her way to try, once again, to sweet talk the world's most uncooperative man into doing the one thing he clearly despised. The timing couldn't have been worse: while the team was usually available to the press on an informal basis around four-thirty P.M. or so while they worked on their sticks and skates, after that it was a closed shop except for the players, coaches and trainers.

And now her.

Maybe, she thought, as she hurried along the labyrinthine concrete hallways beneath the arena, he'd cut her some slack. They'd turned some kind of corner on Saturday night, hadn't they? Maybe he'd have pity on her and agree to help her out just this once.

The locker room door was shut tight. Discreetly, she tried the handle. Locked. Not good. Swallowing, she rapped hard on the door, twice. A second later, the door jerked open just a crack. In the crack stood Ty. He already had his "game face" on. He did not look happy to see her.

"What?" he barked.

"I need to talk to you. It's important."

"Now's not a good time."

The door slammed.

Janna stood there, the old familiar nausea creeping up her throat. She took a deep breath and knocked again. This time the door flew wide open. Behind Ty, Janna could see all the players assembled in a circle. A minute ago Ty had held their rapt attention. Now it was fixed on her.

"When *is* a good time?" she demanded.

"If this is about PR, then the answer is never."

He moved to close the door again but Janna wedged herself between the door frame and the door. "I'm not going anywhere."

Ty chuckled mirthlessly. "Yeah, you are." Gently but

firmly, as if she were light as helium, he picked her up and put her back down in the hallway.

"I'm going to wait right here," she informed him. "Like I said, this is important."

"Suit yourself."

Once again the door closed with a frame-shaking bang. Alone now in the hallway, Janna propped herself up against the cold concrete wall. Why had Lou insisted she talk to him *now*, when the team was trying to concentrate on the upcoming game? It was like deliberately sending a nice, plump lamb into the lair of a vicious, snarling wolf. Ten minutes passed. Fifteen. Half an hour. Janna knew he was taking longer than usual to give his pep talk to torture her. She knew it. Just as she was about to whip out her cell phone and call upstairs to Lou to let him know he should feel free to fire her, the door flew open and Ty stepped out into the hall.

"Well?" He was less than half dressed for the game in boxer shorts, big, thick socks, and the long-sleeve, gray cotton T-shirts issued to the team. His wrists and ankles were taped. His gaze was hard.

"Look, I hate to bother you, but—"

"This is important," he mocked. "What?"

"Wednesday night is one of the biggest black-tie dinners in the city. Roy Duncan was set to go, but his brother died and now he can't make it."

"So?"

"So I need you to fill in for him." Before he could protest, Janna hurried on. "Please. If you do this one thing, I swear to God I will never ask you to do anything again."

Ty blinked, unmoved. "Ask Kevin."

"Kevin isn't you," Janna replied, glancing quickly around the empty hallway to make sure there was no one there to hear. "He's not one of the greatest leaders in sports history. People aren't going to feel they've gotten their money's worth with Kevin."

" 'Their money's worth'?" Ty repeated, his handsome

face distorting with contempt. "What are we, circus performers, there to amuse the rich little donors?"

"You know that's not what I meant."

"Then what did you mean?" Ty shot back, clearly unwilling to let her off the hook.

"Ty, this event raises a lot of money that goes to lots of worthy causes. The United Way is an umbrella organization for groups like Meals on Wheels, Literacy Volunteers. The more high profile people there are at these events, the more people want to attend, and the more money is raised. When word went out that Roy Duncan was going to be there, a lot of plates sold. If the Blades organization doesn't cough up someone comparable in his place, it's going to look really bad. It could hurt our reputation."

"You mean Kidco's reputation," Ty sneered.

Janna said nothing.

"It's not my problem."

"God help me," Janna muttered to herself, her temper starting to simmer. "I'm begging you, okay? Please help me out just this once. *Please*."

"No." His gaze was unyielding. He raked a hand through his blond hair, frustrated. "You know how I feel about this stuff, Janna. Give it up."

"Oh, that's rich," Janna snorted. "The man who told me that persistence is the key to achievement in life is now telling me to give it up! You should be happy I'm hounding you to death like this, Ty! It shows I took what you said to heart."

"This is different."

"My ass it is," Janna snapped. She saw a mild blink of shock shudder across his face and laughed. "What, you've never heard a woman say 'ass' before? I seriously doubt that."

"Say what you want, think what you want, and beg all you want," was Ty's unequivocally cold reply. "But I'm not filling in for Duncan."

"So that's that."

"That's that."

"No PR, ever, no exceptions."

"No PR, ever, no exceptions," he repeated, turning to go.

"You know, you are one hypocritical, heartless bastard," Janna hissed to his departing back.

Ty stopped dead. Janna saw him take a deep, calculated breath before spinning back around to face her. When he did, there were storm clouds brewing in his eyes, black and dangerous.

"What did you say to me?"

"I said you're a hypocritical, heartless bastard," Janna repeated, warming to her topic. He'd thrown the ball back to her, and like it or not, she was going to run with it. "Forget Kidco for a minute, okay, and let's discuss the team. You talk about how important it is to 'give back' to the guys who work so hard for you. You treat them great, making sure everyone's happy, making sure the poor scared rookies fit in so the Blades are just one big, happy, *winning* family. But you know what, Ty? Every one of the guys on this team has a pretty cushy life. There isn't one of them who isn't pulling down at least a six-figure salary.

"Did it ever cross your mind that it might be nice to give something back to the community that makes all that possible? If it weren't for those fans that pay to see you play, you guys would be out of a job! How about giving back to the poor guy who can't read very well, so he goes to Literacy Volunteers, but in the meantime every spare cent he makes at his menial job goes to buying tickets to watch the Blades? Ever think of him? Or the hockey fans stuck in the hospital who can only watch games on TV? Do you have any idea what a difference a visit—one lousy, stinking hour of your life—could make? Your celebrity is a special resource. Why won't you use it? How can you not *care about* what goes on outside this locker room?!"

She reared back slightly, stunned and breathless from her outburst. Meanwhile, Ty stood with his hands on his waist, staring down at the floor. He was breathing hard, waves of resentment zigzagging off him, one after another after another. When he lifted his head, Janna could see he was furious, a vein in his left temple throbbing as he glowered at her.

"You have no idea what the hell you're talking about. Not only that, but what I choose to do, or not to do, is none of your goddamn business to comment on, never mind judge. I play *my guts out* on the ice for the fans every night. If that's not enough 'giving back' for them—or for you—then that's just too damn bad. You got that?"

"Oh, I've got it, all right," Janna replied bitterly. She straightened, buttoning up her blazer. "Thank you for your time, *Captain* Gallagher. It's certainly been illuminating, as they say."

She spun on her heel and began walking away, head held high. This was the part where he was supposed to come after her and grab her arm and say, "Wait a minute, I didn't mean it, I'll help you, Janna." But it didn't happen. Instead, all she heard was the sound of her own footsteps echoing down the hallway, and the locker room door slamming.

She was halfway back to Lou when she suddenly remembered an item she'd read in "Page Six" of the *Post* the morning before: Wayne and Janet Gretzky were back in New York for a week visiting friends.

"Idiot!" she said to herself as she started to run toward the elevator, laughing.

By the time she reached her desk, she was panting, her fingers fumbling for her Palm Pilot, where she kept every phone number she knew or thought she might need. She and Janet Jones Gretzky were acquaintances. They'd taken a kickboxing class together at the New York Health & Racquet Club when the Gretzkys still lived in New York. Janna had gotten her a cameo on *The Wild and the Free.*

"If you ever need any help with anything," Janet had told her, "don't hesitate to give our publicist a call."

Well, it was time to call in the favor. She found the number and, fingers crossed, dialed the number the wife of the Great One had given her. By the time she hung up the phone, nothing in the world mattered less than Ty Gallagher and his stupid refusal to help her out in a bind. Soaring on feelings of invincibility, she hurried downstairs to the street to hail a cab home.

Damn, I'm good! she said to herself as she hopped into the back of the taxi.

And for the first time in a long time, she actually believed it.

The dinner was being held at Tavern on the Green on Central Park West. The restaurant looked absolutely magical at night, the tiny white lights in the surrounding trees twinkling as limos, taxis, and private cars pulled up one by one to dispense guests who were dressed as if attending a ball. Janna was enchanted, the more so when she was escorted to the banquet room where the party was being held. With its glass walls, high-domed ceiling and shimmering Baccarat chandeliers, this room always reminded her of a wedding cake: light, airy, delicate. She gave herself a minute or two to enjoy her surroundings, listening to the light jazz being played by a young man at a white piano in the corner. Then she helped herself to a flute of champagne offered by a passing waiter and began to work the room.

Thanks to her previous job, she already knew a lot of the people in attendance and made a point of reconnecting with them, especially the magazine editors, to whom she blatantly pitched ideas for pieces on all the young, sexy players. An editor she knew from *Seventeen* seemed interested in a possible photo shoot with Lex or Michael Dante. Janna took her card and promised to call her on Monday. When there was a break in the action, she headed off in the direction of the Bull, who looked to be doing a great job of working the room himself, even if his hand did shoot out every time the waiter carrying the canapé tray breezed by.

"Happy?" she asked him.

"Happy? We've got Wayne freakin' Gretzky here! If I was sure I'd be able to get up again, I'd get down on the floor and kiss your tiny little toes."

She squeezed his arm. "I aim to please."

For forty minutes Janna made the rounds, her confidence genuine. She knew how to do this—knew how to schmooze, how to sell the Blades as a potentially active force in the community without pushing it. As a result, two individuals from two different community programs had agreed to work with the PR office on a charity event. As if that weren't reason enough to celebrate, people were going nuts over the Gretzkys' presence, and Lou hadn't spilled anything down the front of his tux. The only fly in the ointment was her oily coworker, Jack Cowley, who'd been shadowing her ever since he'd arrived. So far, Janna had managed to stay one step ahead of him and avoid contact. But when both Lex and the man she was chatting up from Hockey on the Hudson excused themselves to go the men's room, she was left defenseless and Cowley moved right in.

"Janna." Even the purring way he said her name made all the tiny hairs on her arms stand up on end. "You've been a very hard lady to catch up with."

"I'm working, Jack. You should try it sometime."

He gave a hearty laugh phonier than a WWF match. Oblivious to the hint, his eyes slowly toured her body, making her wish she'd worn a potato sack, and not the tight, midnight blue sheath she relied on whenever she really had to play dress up.

"Look at you," he murmured. "I've always said good things come in small packages."

"Like diamonds and poison?" Janna replied sweetly.

"And such a dark horse, too," he drawled on.

"I don't understand."

"Telling us all that you could get Gretzky but not Gallagher, then getting them both. Nice surprise, Janna. Lou's going to love it."

She turned her head, following Jack's gaze to the front of the banquet room. There, drop-dead handsome in a tux and looking like he owned the room, was Ty Gallagher.

And on his arm was her sister, Skyler.

Pain jackknifed through her but she refused to give in to it. "Listen, Jack, I have some other people I need to talk to," she said hastily, politely pushing past him. The room felt like it was contracting. Ty would be looking for her, she knew he would, if only to say, "Look, I'm here, I did what you asked." *Look, I'm here with your sister. Bastard!*

She drained her champagne glass and reached for another. The temptation to guzzle it down, to anesthetize, was strong. What was that old saying? "Be careful what you wish for because you just might get it?" Well, God knows she'd wanted Ty Gallagher to cooperate and do some PR—but not like this, not with her beautiful, lissome sister in tow. Talk about a swift kick in the head. Ty and Skyler. How could she not know about this? She took another quick sip of bubbly for fortification and decided there was only one way to deal with it, and that was to launch a preemptive strike. She would go to them, endure small talk, and get it over with. Then she'd be free to carry on working the room until dinner was served. As if she could eat now. As if she'd be able to get through the rest of what would now be an absolutely interminable night without crying, vomiting, or both.

They'd spotted her and were moving toward her through a sea of toned, impeccably dressed bodies. The handsome athlete and the gorgeous model. *How predictable,* Janna thought disdainfully. He really was like the rumors said,

going for boobs over brains every time. Not that she gave a
rat's—

"Hey, chickadee." Skyler's voice carried so much genuine affection that for a minute, Janna almost felt guilty for
all the times she wished her sister would suddenly pork up
overnight. Calling on every ounce of control and compo-
sure she had, Janna returned her sister's dazzling smiling
and reached up to kiss her on her flawlessly made up
cheek.

"Hey, Stretch."

She turned her attention to Ty. She had to admit, his expression was priceless. He was damn near slack-jawed
with bafflement, his confused glance ping-ponging from
Janna . . . to Skyler . . . back to Janna. "You two know
each other?"

"We're sisters," Janna answered coolly.

"Can't you tell?" Skyler joked.

"You don't really look much alike," Ty observed carefully.

"No, she's tall and gorgeous and I'm short and plain,"
Janna supplied gaily. Skyler laughed, clueless that she was
the only one doing so. Her laughter seemed loud to Janna.
Everything did. The music, the swirl of voices around
them, all of it deafening. Perhaps she was about to faint.
Meanwhile, Ty's eyes were burning into her retinas. What
was he trying to convey? Embarrassment? An apology?
Well, whatever it was, she didn't care.

Skyler's laughter—loud, endless, cloying—eventually
faded away, leaving a hole in the awkward, hellish moment that Janna didn't have the energy to fill. Nor did Ty:
the slack-jawed expression was gone, replaced by a look
Janna interpreted as plain old discomfort. Skyler, as ever,
was completely oblivious.

"So, what's on the menu?" she asked brightly.

I'm sure you are, thought Janna. She flashed a big
smile. "Don't know, baby sis. But I do know I have to run.

I have a couple more people I have to corral before we sit down to eat. I'll catch up with you later!"

Feigning urgency, she flitted away into the crowd. *Excruciating. That had been excruciating.* Her eyes quickly scanned the room: Lou was with the editor from *Seventeen. Good.* Jack Cowley was staring down the cleavage of some poor unsuspecting woman on the board of Family and Children's Services. *Not good.* She was halfway across the crowded room, nearly home free, when she felt a strong, firm grip on her arm.

"Janna, wait."

Damn! She was close, so close, to escaping. Caught, she turned around to peer up into Ty's face. "Yes?" she asked impatiently.

"Your sister and me—it's not what you think."

"I don't think anything."

"Janna, please. I can tell you're upset."

She thought fast. "I'm upset because you didn't let me know you were coming. If you had, I could have drummed up a lot more publicity for this event. Then again, with Wayne Gretzky in the room, your being here is kind of redundant, know what I mean?"

Ty shook his head affectionately. "You're a pistol, you know that?"

"Yes, well, this little pistol still has some bullets left to shoot before dinner. You and Skyler have fun, okay?"

"Janna." She went to bolt but there was a hint of entreaty in his voice that kept her rooted. "Skyler and I—"

Brrrring.

"Shoot." Eyes rolling in exasperation, Janna impatiently pulled her cell phone out of her purse. "I'll just be a minute," she told Ty, jamming the offending instrument to her ear so she could hear over the din of the buzzing crowd. She'd kill Theresa for this, absolutely *kill her.* "Hello?"

But it wasn't Theresa. It was Wills. Wills hiccuping and

crying and saying Mom was drunk, and Dad was in a rage, and could she come get him, please, could she come now?

"I'm on my way," she told him. "Wait for me in the guest house." Trembling, she folded up the phone and shoved it back into her bag.

"Janna?" Ty asked, concerned.

"I have to go," she mumbled distractedly, starting away from him.

"Is everything all—"

"I have to *go,*" she repeated, calling over her shoulder. She hurried to Lou, explaining there was a family emergency. And then she was gone, out into the night that just an hour before had felt utterly magical, but which now seemed only troubled.

CHAPTER
06

"Jesus Christ, Gallagher. Didn't you have your Wheaties this morning?"

Ty whipped off his helmet and skated toward the bench, the coach's comment ringing in his ears. Though it was only practice, he was off his game: there was no jump in his legs, and his reflexes were a millisecond slower than usual. Driving toward the net, the defense was nailing him every time. They stole the puck from him left and right. They ran him again and again into the boards. Everyone noticed and no one said a word—no one but Coach Matthias, whose job it was *to* say a word, to say lots of words, not all of them nice. Ty supposed he should be grateful for the coach's diplomacy. It could have been worse; he could have told Ty he should be taken out to pasture and shot like an old, unproductive horse, which, right now, is precisely how he felt. Like an old, unproductive, and very distracted horse.

Last night. That was the problem screwing with his concentration. He'd tried to do something nice and it had

blown up in his face. When at the last minute he'd decided
to do Janna a favor after all, he'd just assumed that the
right way to proceed was the way expected of him. Everyone expected high-profile jocks to show up with a model
on their arm and smile for the cameras, right? It was all
part of the game, part of the fantasy. So he'd called up the
model "Skyler M," who had slipped him her number at a
restaurant bar the night before, and asked her if she wanted
to go to this black-tie thing with him. And she, being
someone who lived and breathed for being in the public
eye, jumped at the opportunity. Great. Fine. They were on.
He'd hung up the phone feeling quite pleased with the
prop he'd picked out for himself. A little eye candy never
hurt anyone.

Except Janna.

How was he supposed to know they were sisters?

It wasn't even that which was troubling him, really. It
was his lack of forethought. If he'd really thought this
through, he would have shown up alone. It would have
proved to Janna—after she stopped breathing fire at him—
that when push came to shove, he wasn't just a puck-
shooting automaton obsessed with winning; he was
someone who would do a favor for a friend. Instead, he'd
performed the favor *on his terms,* and in the process . . .
Christ, he didn't even want to think about it. The woman
was clearly upset, and he was the one who upset her. He
knew *why* she was upset, which upset *him.* He felt guilty
she was upset, and now he was going to have to dance
even faster to make amends, because if there was one thing
he couldn't take, it was Janna being upset with him.

All because he'd brought Skyler.

Skyler. Jesus, what a Twinkie. He could hear the wind
whistling around her head, that's how empty the space between her ears was. It blew him away: How could one sister be so sharp and the other be so self-absorbed and
dumb? Yeah, looking at her definitely got him dreaming
from the waist down, he wouldn't lie about that, but all she

talked about was herself, and truth be told, it was a mind numbing bore. Not only that, but the woman was a goddamn human remora fish. He'd gone to give her a small peck on the cheek when the evening was over, and she'd grabbed him and practically sucked his face off. Maybe he was old-fashioned or backward or sexist, but he preferred to be the one who made the first move, if indeed a move was going to be made, which hadn't been his intention, at all.

He'd planned to relate all this to Janna at practice this morning, but there was just one small problem: She wasn't there. Usually he skated out onto the ice, and there she'd be, sitting with the Bull and the beat reporters, shooting the breeze. But today it was just Lou dazzling the troops. Ty waited until practice was done, then collared the neckless Capesi on the way into the locker room.

"Hey."

The Bull turned, surprised. "Nice of you to show last night, Gallagher. Now that you've seen the light, maybe we can get you to do some more stuff."

Ty ignored the irritating comment about "seeing the light"—a tidy euphemism for doing things the Kidco way—and shrugged dismissively. "Yeah, maybe. Where's your henchwoman today?" he asked casually.

"Janna? Something happened with her family, I'm not sure what. That's why she ran out of there in a hurry last night." He reached up and attempted to drape a brotherly arm around Ty's shoulder, dropping his voice conspiratorially. "Look, you're not injured or anything like that, are you?"

"No. Why?"

"'Cause you really sucked out there during practice, and the writers were asking me about it—'Is he hurt?' Yadda yadda."

"What did you tell them?"

"I told them that practice isn't the same as a game, and

everyone's entitled to an off day once in a while, even you. Did I do good?"

Ty patted his shoulder. "You did good. But you can do even better."

"Wha?"

"Give me Janna MacNeil's home address."

Yellow roses. They meant friendship, didn't they? Janna wondered as her fingertips caressed the delicate flower petals before finally setting the vase to rest on the steamer trunk in the living room. So sweet of him to send flowers, although when they first arrived, she had thought— hoped—they were from someone else. But the disappointment she felt evaporated somewhat when she read the card accompanying them:

> *"J—Atta girl—knew you'd nail the captain eventually. Gretzky the cherry on top of the cake. Kidco's thrilled. Congrats on a job well done—Lou."*

Of course, she hated herself for hoping they'd been from Ty. Hating herself was starting to become a full-time occupation, she'd noticed. Time to do something about that.

Sighing, she moved to the bank of windows looking out on the Fifty-ninth Street bridge. Traffic was doing its usual stop-and-start cha cha beneath the gray November sky. Janna thought she detected a few random snowflakes spiraling down to the crowded sidewalk below. When would the first snow fall? Before Thanksgiving? After? She loved watching the snow fall, loved the delicacy of it, like a baby gently closing its eyes. But in Manhattan, the virginal purity of the snow never lasted long. Between the trucks and the soot and the people, it blackened in no time. Janna hated dirty snow. It depressed her. But thinking about it was better than dwelling on . . .

She wondered if it hadn't been a mistake taking the entire day off work. She could just as easily have taken the morning to drive Wills back up to Connecticut in time for school, then gone into the office after lunch. But she was exhausted: She and Wills had been up late talking, after which Janna couldn't fall asleep. At five, tired of lying there with her mind racing, she'd gotten up and baked a batch of lemon poppyseed muffins. "When in doubt, cook" was one of her mottos. Wills and Theresa were both thrilled with the breakfast surprise, and for some reason, baking the muffins made her feel less guilty about bringing Wills back to Connecticut. Right now, she had a chocolate cake cooling, which she was waiting to frost, and she'd bought all the ingredients for moussaka, which she planned to make for dinner for her and Theresa tonight. *Who knows,* she mused, *maybe crises really were blessings in disguise.* After all, if they got her into the kitchen chopping and mixing and grating and measuring, which she loved, how bad could it be?

Answer: pretty bad. She didn't want to think about Wills's face when she'd deposited him at school that morning, knowing that after hockey practice later that day, he'd have to go home—if you could call it that. "Why don't they just get a divorce?" he'd whispered on the drive back. Janna had no answer. It was a question she herself had been asking for as long as she could remember.

At least her father had called late last night to make sure Wills was all right. It was always her father, never her mother. He was always the one who expressed remorse, apologized to the kids, tried to make it up to them. Her mother never did; in fact, her mother's behavior often seemed to imply that the war between her and her husband was somehow *all their fault*. Janna had spent hours assuring Wills of the opposite: that their parents' horrible marriage was *in no way* his fault, that it was their problem. Whether her words sank in, she didn't know. She was just glad he'd been willing to reach out for help when he needed it, and that she was able to get him the hell out of there, even if it was only for one night. Crazy thoughts had ricocheted through her mind while Wills had sat on the couch in the living room crying: *Maybe he should move in here with me. Maybe I could become his guardian.* But even while she thought about it, she knew it would never happen. Her parents would never *let* it happen. In the meantime, she'd do what she could: love her baby brother, be there for him when he needed her, assure him that the roller-coaster ride that was his home life had nothing to do with *him*. Perhaps most significant of all, she could prove to him that one could survive living in that house and come out the other side okay—*okay* being a relative term, of course.

Restless, she went into the kitchen to check on the cooling cake, gingerly resting her palm on top of it. Nope; still too warm to frost. She toyed with the idea of opening the can of frosting and simply spooning it into her mouth for lunch, but decided against it, knowing it would make her nauseous, and she'd had enough nausea over the past twenty-four hours, thank you. Thoughts of being sick to her stomach led inevitably to thoughts of Skyler—or, more specifically, Skyler and Ty.

It occurred to Janna as she'd hurried out of Tavern on the Green that maybe she should alert Skyler that the latest installment of Armageddon had commenced at their parents' home in Connecticut. After all, it was her family, too. Why should Janna be the only one to have her evening ruined? But then Janna realized her evening had already been ruined—by Skyler. Besides, she knew what Skyler's reaction would have been: "Oh." And that would have been it. *Oh.* Because unless something impacted Skyler directly, it simply didn't exist. *Oh.*

Pouring herself another cup of coffee—What was this, three? Four? She'd better watch her stomach—Janna tried to wrap her mind around the Ty/Skyler *thing*. It shouldn't have upset her, but it did. It upset her that she was upset.

She had no right to be. She and Ty Gallagher weren't even *friends*. And she did have a boyfriend, if you counted Robert. So where did she get off thinking she could throw a hissy because one of the hottest bachelors in New York had shown up at a charity event with a major model at his side? Granted, the model was her sister, who also happened to be a major dodo, but still, she had no right.

Or did she? This was where she was getting confused. Ty seemed concerned she was upset, and that wouldn't be the case unless he felt something for her, correct? So what was the deal? He'd rushed over to her pretty darn quickly, too, trying to explain what the situation was with him and Skyler. Now, why would a guy do that, unless he cared? Or . . . unless he thought *she* cared . . . and . . . he was trying to let her down easy?

Oh, God. That was it. Ty knew she was attracted to him, and he didn't want her to be hurt. It had nothing to do with him having any feelings for *her*, it had to do with courtesy. Diplomacy. Pity. *He pities me.*

The thought smarted. It humiliated. And then it got her angry. He pitied her?! Well, she pitied him right back. *Jerk!* She knew he had a brain inside that thick skull, yet he was willing to be led around by his—by—he was willing to settle for a cipher like Skyler. *Dumb jock.* Take away the mega salary and the Hugo Boss threads and all you were left with was a big, dumb, shallow, rowdy jock. He and Skyler deserved each other. Let them go off together and create genetically gifted babies for all she cared. She'd stick with Robert, a man with brains, someone who could appreciate the finer things in life like books and art and music and mooching—no, not mooching, movies, she meant movies. She'd take brains over brawn anytime.

The doorbell buzzed and she jerked in her kitchen chair, startled. Putting down her coffee mug, she started toward the foyer. It must be Theresa, who had no doubt forgotten her keys again and was back to pick up the gym bag she'd left sitting by the front door. Grabbing the bag with one hand, Janna unbolted the three locks with the other and opened the door.

"Forget something?" she teased.

There stood Ty Gallagher in a brown leather bomber jacket, blue jeans and a black crew neck sweater, his blond hair still damp from a shower, hand poised to ring the buzzer again. *Okay, God,* Janna thought miserably. *Could you please just kill me now, so I don't have to face any more humiliation?*

"Ty," she said, struggling to look neutral, while instantly remembering that she was in grungy old sweats, wearing glasses as thick as coke bottles. She tore her glasses off. "What are you doing here?"

"I—why did you just take your glasses off?"

"What?"

"Your glasses." He gestured toward her hand. At least she thought he did, since without her glasses he'd been transformed into a tall, well-built blur. "Why did you take them off?"

"I was reading. I only use them for reading. "

"Oh." He seemed to be looking over her shoulder past her—checking, she thought, to see if Theresa was home. "Can I come in?"

"Sure." She ushered him inside, her mouth beginning to clog with words she wasn't sure she wanted to say. She couldn't believe he'd just shown up, especially when she looked like this. "Don't you believe in calling first?" she asked peevishly, squinting as she thought he peeled off the bomber jacket, carefully placing it over the back of the couch. She detected head movement; he had to be glancing around.

"Nice place."

"Glad you like it. Now tell me why you didn't call."

"I'll tell you when you put your glasses back on."

"I told you, I don't need my glasses except for reading."

"Bull, you're squinting at me like Mr. Magoo. How many fingers am I holding up?"

Janna angrily folded her arms across her chest. "Sorry, I'm not playing this game."

"How many fingers?"

"Fine," Janna huffed. She squinted harder and craned her neck forward. "Two."

"Wrong. Three. Put 'em back on, Janna. They're not as bad as you think."

"That's easy for you to say, you don't wear glasses."

"Yeah, I do. I wear contacts most of the time, just like you. Now put 'em back on."

Sighing, she donned her glasses, the world springing back into Technicolor.

"Better?" he asked.

"Yes," she was forced to admit. "Now tell me why you didn't call."

"Because I thought you might not talk to me." He paused. "That you'd even hang up on me."

Her gaze was steady. "Why would I do that?"

"You were pretty upset last night. I think we need to talk."

"Yes, I think we do," Janna agreed. She was about to ask him if he wanted to follow her into the kitchen when he began moving in that direction himself, his head and shoulders thrown back in a relaxed gait, revealing a man used to assuming he owned whatever space he entered. *Cocky bastard,* Janna thought.

He paused in the entrance to the kitchen, inhaling deeply.

"Mmm, what's that smell?"

"Chocolate cake." Janna squeezed past him. The way the man filled up a doorway! "I'm going to frost it in a few minutes."

"Smells great." He remained in the doorway, taking in the room. "Nice kitchen. Homey." He directed his gaze to where she stood by the counter, once again checking the cake. "You like to cook?"

"Yup."

"Huh," he said thoughtfully.

"What does *that* mean?"

"What does what mean?"

" 'Huh.' What does 'huh' mean?"

"It means," he started slowly, his deep-set brown eyes irresistibly drawn to the bald chocolate cake, "that I never figured you for a cook."

"Huh," Janna repeated back in the same tone. What did he figure her for, a fast food junkie? He'd managed to tear his eyes away from the cake and was now glancing longingly at the coffee machine atop the faded blue Formica counter. "You want a cup?" she offered blandly. *I could spill it on your lap if you'd like.*

He smiled appreciatively. "Coffee would be great."

She could feel his eyes watching her as she padded in her thick, woolly socks across the small, rectangular room, reaching high above her to extract a mug from the cabinet above the stove. She turned to the coffee machine on the counter and began pouring.

"Lou told me there was some family problem last night and that's why you left."

Janna stiffened. *Damn Lou and his big fat mouth.*

"Is everything okay? Your brother?"

"My brother"—she opened the fridge and held a quart of skim milk aloft, to which he nodded yes—"is okay *now*." She poured the milk in his mug then returned the carton to the fridge. "He wasn't last night."

"What happened, if you don't mind me asking."

"I do, actually, but since you seem genuinely concerned, I'll tell you." She handed him his mug on her way back to the kitchen table, sliding into a seat. Ty remained standing, leaning against the doorjamb.

"To make a very long, very boring, very complicated story short, my parents have an awful marriage, and fight quite a lot. Last night was a doozy. Liquor flowing, plates flying . . . you get the picture. Wills called and asked me to get him out of there, which I gladly did. Unfortunately, though, I had to bring him back this morning, so he wouldn't miss school." She took a sip of coffee. "That's it."

"Are *you* okay?"

"I'm fine," said Janna a bit sharper than she would have liked. "I didn't get much sleep last night, but apart from that, I'm okay."

"Family stuff can be rough," Ty observed sympathetically.

"You have a family? I always got the impression you were spawned from a test tube. You never, ever mention them in interviews."

"No reason to," Ty replied. "They've got nothing to do with hockey." He took a quick gulp of coffee. "Wills is lucky to have you."

"Yes, he is. But you didn't come over here to talk to me about Wills."

"Yeah, I did, partially." He sauntered over to the table and slid into the chair opposite her, his large hands clasped around the mug as if for warmth. Janna could see he was tired. "When you weren't at practice this morning, I got worried, especially with the way you ran out of the dinner last night."

"How *was* the dinner last night?" Janna asked facetiously. She knew she was treading on thin ice, but she couldn't help it. The imp of the perverse was now screaming in her ear, goading her on. "You and Skyler have fun? Sky and Ty . . . I wonder if that's what the papers will start calling you. 'Sky and Ty were seen dining at Nobu last night.' 'Look who's sitting courtside at the Knicks game— it's Sky and Ty.' "

"You know, I wish you wouldn't act like that," Ty said quietly. "It's beneath you."

Janna could feel her face burning with humiliation at his rebuke.

"Can we *talk*? Sans the bullshit—the way we did in the bar last week? Is that possible?"

"Sure," Janna murmured, on her guard after being put in her place. "You start."

Ty considered his words carefully. "I meant what I said the other day when you were reading me the riot act outside the locker room. I *do* play my guts out on the ice every night, and in my opinion, that's all I'm required to give, or willing to give."

"But."

"But one of the things you should know about me is that I don't like to let my friends down, especially friends who are downright begging me for my help, the way you were." He took a long, slow sip of coffee. "That's why I showed up last night. Not to throw those pigs at Kidco a bone. I came because I wanted to help you out. Period. End of story."

"And I appreciate that," Janna returned sincerely, feeling let down at his choice of the word *friend*. She rose to get the can of frosting and a spatula from the counter. "But I really do wish you had let me know you were coming so I could have played up the publicity a bit more." She glanced back at him, nearly keeling over from shock when she saw he actually looked contrite.

"Sorry about that."

"Well, I am too." She ripped the lid off the can of frosting and moved back toward the cake, which sat on a cooling rack on the opposite counter. "Maybe next time you'll give me some advance notice."

"Hey, there's not gonna be a next time, remember? You said that if I helped you on this you'd never bug me for anything again."

"I lied." She dug the spatula deep into the rich, gooey frosting and carefully, so as not to rake the top spongy layer off the cake, began frosting. "I have to bug you, you know that," she continued. "It's what Lou hired me to do."

"Right," he said glumly. He rose from the table and came to where Janna was standing. "Need some help?"

"No, thank you. I can manage on my own." She waited for him to sit back down, but he didn't. Though outwardly she felt perfectly in control, in truth his proximity was taking its toll on her, the sheer male warmth coming off him making her feel lightheaded. "So," she asked casually, "how long have you been seeing my sister?"

She glanced up just in time to catch him clenching his jaw.

"I'm not seeing your sister. She gave me her number at some restaurant and I called because I didn't want to walk into the United Way bash alone. End of story."

"So you're just sleeping with her."

"Jesus Christ!" Ty exclaimed, losing his famous temper. "I am not sleeping with her! I don't *want* to sleep with her! I want to sle—"

He stopped. Janna froze, her hand involuntarily tightening around the spatula. She closed her eyes for a moment, swallowing. She could feel her heart banging against her ribs, could feel the charged air in the kitchen swirling around them. For a split second, it seemed as if the room itself were gently vibrating, so intense was the power of the unspoken emotions between them. She waited for Ty to speak, longed for him to either leave or grab her and turn her around to him. But he did neither. Instead, he reached out, and gently prying the spatula from her hand, laid it down on the counter.

"You've got frosting on your finger," he said quietly.

Janna forced her eyes open and made herself turn to him. Their eyes locked as Ty reached out for her hand and slowly, deliberately, took the offending chocolate coated index finger into his mouth and gently began sucking. Janna drew a sharp breath. *What was he doing?* She watched, fascinated, as he took each of her remaining fingers into his mouth, kissing, licking, sucking them in turn, his actions tender yet provocative, her body beginning to tremble ever so slightly as the pleasure of it snaked its way through her system like fine brandy, heated but mellow.

Warmth began percolating deep within her—slow, honeylike. No one had ever done this to her before. No one had ever done something so simple that aroused in her such feelings of want.

"Ty." Her body was humming with energy now, an energy born of equal parts fear and desire. Feeling weak, she gripped the kitchen counter. "I think—"

"I know." He opened her hand and kissed her palm deeply. "I should leave. But I'm not going to. I want you, Janna."

Her legs nearly gave way then. To hear those words actually spoken—words she'd fantasized about, words she was convinced this man would never, ever speak about her—made her head swim. She leaned against the counter with a half gasp of disbelief.

"Janna? You okay?"

She nodded, unable to speak, though a low, feral moan escaped from the confines of her throat. Hearing it, concern faded from his eyes, and in its place came blind, reckless arousal, her moan the sign of acquiescence he'd clearly been waiting for. He whipped off her glasses and crushing her to him, covered her mouth with his, his kisses desperate, ravenous. Janna felt her grip on the counter slipping, saw a million blazing colors explode behind the closed lids of her eyes as they nipped excitedly at each others lips, body pushing into body in an animal longing to meld, to become. My God, how she longed to have this man. *Here. Now.* Longed to feel those hard, rippled muscles of his burning beneath the touch of her fingers. Wave upon wave of restless desire surged through her as he roughly explored the terrain of her body with his hands, her own hands groping, wanting, grasping. Clinging to each other, they staggered their way toward the white refrigerator. Ty had her up against it now, and lifting her ever so slightly, pinned her with his body.

"Janna," he murmured into her throat, his mouth fevered as he showered the tender skin there with hot, swift kisses. Greed for him overtook her, and she clutched at him, her fingers twining through his blond hair, her moans matching the demands of his mouth, goading him on to explore her further, lift her higher.

His hands, which he'd cupped around her buttocks, slid silently to the waistband of her sweats. And then, in one swift movement, he yanked them and her panties down. Janna gasped loudly, the shock of it shivering straight through her, making her giddy. Her garments pooled around her ankles, she eagerly kicked herself free of them. Grabbing his face, she kissed him with an abandon so ferocious his breathing became ragged and strained. *Yes,* was all Janna could think. *Yes. Now. Please.*

Reading her mind, he tore his mouth from her flesh. "Wrap your legs around me," he whispered urgently.

Shuddering with anticipation, she slowly slid her left leg up along his denimed thigh. She saw his eyes glaze over, felt him struggling for control in the wake of this simple yet effective form of caress. Pleased, she repeated the motion on the right, encircling his waist with her legs. "Don't worry," he promised as his hand slowly moved to cup her between her legs, "I won't let you fall."

Yet that's exactly what she was doing—falling through clouds, through wet forests, through depths of deep azure ocean as his fingers reached down between the cleft of her thighs and expertly began teasing her. Good, so good, the layers of desire building, her body arching and tightening as her eyes fluttered closed and her nails sunk deep into the hard flesh of his shoulders.

"God," she half sobbed, breath clogging her lungs. She could feel herself going slick and wet beneath his touch, her body going taut as a bow as he continued stroking deeply, taking his time.

"I can tell you're really hating this," he teased.

"Despise it."

"Tough," he growled, pushing his erection hard against her.

Another gasp escaped her throat, this one of a woman swept close to the brink. The need to touch him in return, to feel that broad expanse of perfectly sculpted flesh that was his chest, overwhelmed her. She released her hands from the golden tangle of his hair and yanking his sweater free from where it was tucked into his jeans, shoved her hands up beneath it, palms flat to his chest. His skin was burning, the iron muscles hard, almost steeled. Janna reveled in teasing him, felt icy hot pinpricks of delight hiss through her as his shallow breathing filled her ears the longer she kneaded and stroked. Her hands continued their roaming, fingertips occasionally dipping below the waistband of his briefs to lightly brush and tease the flesh below.

These small, feathery movements brought forth a savage male groan of appreciation. Janna could feel his desire to possess her rip through him. Wanting to match her, or perhaps surpass her, his fingers between her legs began moving faster. Janna's sense of herself began melting as he brought her ever closer to toppling off the edge of the known universe. Her world faded to white mist; there was only this, now, the all-consuming drive to devour and be devoured in return. She rocked against him, arched, stretched, reaching with her body, so close, almost there. . . .

"Tell me what you want," he growled.

"You," she gasped. "You deep inside me. You."

He unzipped his jeans and freed himself. They were both on the verge now, the frenzied need between them almost unbearable. She opened her eyes briefly to address the inevitable question in his, whispered to him she was on the pill, closed them again. His hands came to her hips, and then he lowered her, slowly and with great care, down onto his erection.

The perfection of the fit startled her. Blood roared through Janna's head as he began moving her up and down on him, her own hips pumping wildly, driving him on, wild desperation tearing through her.

"Now," she cried out hungrily. "Now. *Now!*"

Ty groaned, and dropping to his knees with her still wrapped around him like a second skin, laid her down on the tiled floor of the kitchen. His head came up once, looking into her eyes to double-check this was what she truly wanted. And when he saw she meant what she said, he plunged—hard, deep, burying himself within her just as Janna demanded, her own shocked cries of mind-lashing pleasure ringing in her ears as he hammered her again and again until she peaked, senses crackling and sizzling. Never had a man driven her to the extreme edge like this before. Never had she been so willing to blindly follow the map of her own desire.

Mind still reeling, she reached up and linked her fingers through his, folded their joined hands into fists. "Now you," she commanded. A wave of appreciation swept over his face as he smiled down at her languidly. Then he was off, eyes closed and body working, dipping in and out of her with expert, rhythmic strokes that began coming faster and faster. Janna arched to meet him each time, tightened the grip of herself around him in a delirious dance that could only end one way. Finally he came, the explosive release of his climax sending a long, shuddering sigh through his solid body, and through Janna who lay quivering beneath him, grateful, sated, and utterly amazed at what had just transpired.

CHAPTER

07

The silence of the kitchen sang in Janna's ears, though it had only been a few seconds since she and Ty finished their lovemaking. Lying beside him, holding his hand while they both regained their breath, it occurred to Janna that if anyone walked in right now, what they'd see would be two sweaty, panting adults stretched out on a white tiled floor, staring up at a ceiling fan—which needed dusting—with their pants off. The image made her giggle, provoking an uneasy look from Ty, whom, she thought, probably wondered if his prowess was the source of her amusement.

"What?" he asked.

"I hope we're not on *Candid Camera*, because this is one image I would not want beamed out into millions of living rooms."

Ty chuckled appreciatively and pulled up his trousers, prompting Janna to locate her sweats and do the same. Erogenous zones now safely covered, he rolled onto his side toward her, his head resting on his open palm as he propped himself up on one elbow, his free hand gently grazing her cheek.

"That was amazing."

Janna sighed. "I know." She turned to look at him. "Did you mean what you said a few minutes ago? About wanting me? Or is that something you say to—"

His fingers stilled her lips before she could finish. "I meant it. Why do you think I went after you at the gala last night? I didn't want you to think I was seriously involved with your sister."

"Because you knew I had a crush on you and you didn't want me to be hurt, or because you had a crush on me and thought it might ruin your chances with me if I thought you were seeing Skyler?"

"Grown men don't *get* crushes, okay?"

"Just answer the question, Gallagher."

His gaze was frank. "Both." He paused. "But . . ."

Here it comes, Janna thought. *The part where he thanks me for a great time and then runs out the door.* She steeled herself, turning her whole body toward him so they were facing one another. Jesus, he was gorgeous. The temptation just to touch his face, to run her fingers over his eyelids and lips to make sure he was real bones and blood and muscle, and not an apparition borne of her long held hunger for him, was strong. She couldn't believe she'd kissed that sensual, determined mouth, couldn't believe she'd been held against that rock-hard body. Nervously, almost tentatively, she reached out to caress his face, relieved when he momentarily let his eyes drift shut in response, clearly enjoying the sensation.

"I didn't come here with the express purpose of seducing you, you know," he murmured quietly.

"I know that," Janna replied, pushing a hank of damp hair off his forehead. A small white scar ran parallel to his hairline, another war wound earned on the ice, no doubt. She found it infinitely sexy.

"But now that it's happened," Ty continued, eyes opening to search hers, "I wouldn't mind if it happened again."

"Me, neither."

"There's just one hitch."

Janna took a deep breath, held it. "What's that?"

He hesitated. "I'm not looking for a serious relationship in my life right now."

"Neither am I."

"Really?"

"Why are you surprised?"

"I don't know, I guess I just assumed . . ."

"Well, don't."

"All right." He began playing with her hair, twirling and untwirling a lock around his index finger. "So you're fine with keeping things casual?"

"Well, it depends. Define casual."

"Casual as in the occasional dinner and—"

"Sex."

"Right."

Janna shrugged. "Sounds good to me."

Ty looked mildly skeptical. "Yeah?"

"Am I missing something here?"

He shook his head as if to clear it. "No, I just . . . I guess I *am* a little surprised, okay? Usually, women like you—real women, you know, with brains and looks and the whole package—want something more."

Janna leaned forward and playfully nipped his lower lip. "Maybe I'm not like other women."

"You got that right," he agreed.

"There's one other thing I just thought of."

"What?" Ty sounded cautious.

"I think we ought to be discreet about this."

"I agree," said Ty.

"The last thing I need is people insinuating I've whored myself just to get you to do what Kidco wants."

"I'm not doing what Kidco wants," Ty reminded her.

Janna ignored him. "And the last thing *you* need is people thinking you're using me just to get *out* of doing what Kidco wants."

"Uh huh."

"So," Janna continued, "we really need to be careful how we behave around each other. We can't afford to give anything away."

"We won't," Ty said confidently, enfolding her in his arms. "You're driving your point home excessively, you know."

"I know. I do that." *I could die here,* Janna thought, *and not regret a thing.* She snuggled close to him, basking in the moment, dreamily content.

"Janna?"

"Mmm?"

"Do you think it would be possible for me to get a piece of that cake when you finish frosting it?"

"*That's* what this is all about! You seduced me so you could get some cake!" She narrowed her eyes with mock suspicion. "Or maybe you thought this would get you off the hook with Kidco."

If the thought hadn't occurred to Ty before, it did now. "Does it?" he asked hopefully.

"Nope. Is that how you think it works? You screw the publicist and she'll stop doing the corporation's bidding?"

"Don't say 'screw.' It sounds crude, it doesn't suit you."

Janna raised her eyebrows. "Tell me more about myself, Captain Gallagher."

He kissed her forehead. "What would you like to know?"

Before Janna could answer, there was the heart-stopping sound of multiple locks springing back, followed by the front door opening. They both froze, staring at each other in wide-eyed horror. Dreading what she'd see but unable to stop herself, Janna gingerly lifted her head, peering over the ridge of Ty's body into the hallway.

There stood Theresa, pop-eyed. For a split second, the two roommates simply *looked* at each other. Then, because she couldn't bear the tension and didn't know what else to do, Janna waved, offering up a feeble smile. Theresa's response was to excitedly mouth "OH. MY. GOD," give a huge thumbs-up, scoop up her gym bag, and flee the apartment.

Ty sat up. "I guess she wasn't in the mood for cake."

"I'm never going to hear the end of this." Janna sighed. "She's going to want to know every blessed detail."

Ty rose to his feet, extending a hand to Janna to help her up. "And what will you tell her?"

"Every blessed detail."

Ty flashed a seductive smile. "Don't tell her *everything*. Some things are private. Wouldn't you agree?"

Janna nodded, a haze of weakness for him filling her head.

"Now about that cake . . ."

Tonight would be the gabfest to end all gabfests. Janna knew that the minute it hit six P.M., Theresa would bolt out of work, hail the first cab she could find, and race back to their apartment. In anticipation, she had chilled a bottle of Bordeaux, tossed a salad, and had already put the moussaka in the oven to bake.

After Ty left, she spent the afternoon floating in a mild dream state, her mind endlessly replaying what had happened while she analyzed it all, dissecting sentences, parsing emotions, scanning lines for missed meanings, inflection, nuance. Was it possible he had slept with her sister but lied? Was it possible that a man like Ty Gallagher, who could have any woman he wanted, would really want *her*? Had she agreed too readily to keep things casual? On and on her second-guessing went, until finally, having so ruined the buzz of having been with him, she sought respite in a shower and a nap. It helped; she awoke feeling fortified, ready to field the endless barrage of questions Theresa would be firing at her.

As if on cue, Theresa came barreling through the door, breathless. "I swear to God, I almost had to throw some poor schmuck under a bus to get a cab!"

Janna watched from where she sat curled up on the living room couch as Theresa quickly unbuttoned her coat, hung it in the hall closet, hustled into the kitchen, and came back bearing two glasses of wine. Usually, Theresa changed out of her work clothes immediately before settling down to relax. The fact she went straight for the vino indicated just how newsworthy she considered her tryst with the captain to be.

"Okay. Here's some wine. Spill. Dinner smells great, by the way."

Janna took a tiny sip of wine, deciding to be devilish. "Let me finish watching the news first."

Theresa snatched the remote off the steamer trunk and switched the TV off. "It's on again at eleven." She turned to Janna. "Well?"

Smiling happily, Janna proceeded to tell Theresa everything—well, almost everything. When she was done, she sat back, letting Theresa take it all in, awaiting her friend's pronouncement. At first, Theresa said nothing. Then she got up and began pacing, her footsteps silent on the Oriental rug.

"Let me make sure I'm getting this straight," she said very seriously. Between the pacing and Theresa's tone, Janna felt like she was in a courtroom drama. "You agreed to keep it casual."

"Right."

"So am I correct in assuming you're finally going to ditch that drain on humanity, Robert?"

The question seriously shocked Janna. "Of course I am! I would never sleep with two men at the same time! That's so sleazy."

"And what about Ty?" Theresa stopped moving, planting herself right in front of Janna. "Is he planning on sleeping only with you?"

Heat flashed up Janna's neck to her face. "I—assume so," she replied, flustered. She hadn't even thought of that.

"You assume but you don't know," resumed Theresa, Perry Mason–style.

"Theresa, what was I supposed to say?" Janna's eyes began following her friend as she resumed her pacing. She was beginning to feel incredibly stupid.

"How about, 'Are you planning to continue to sleep with other people, Ty?' " Theresa's expression was resolute. "You have a right to know, Janna."

"I know, I know, I know," Janna replied, feeling harangued. She sipped her wine. "I guess I was just so—I don't know—*stunned* by what happened I didn't think to ask that."

"Well, the next time you two decide to christen a kitchen floor, I think you should." She perched on the arm of the couch. "Guys are different creatures, Janna. Their definition of 'casual' and our definition of 'casual' are radically different."

"Really?" Janna replied sarcastically. "I had no idea. Tell me more about relationships, Miss Twelve Years in Catholic School."

Theresa pulled a face. "Look, I'm not trying to piss in your Cheerios, okay? I just don't want you to get hurt."

"How can I get hurt?" Janna asked plaintively. "We *both* agreed to keep it casual."

"Yeah, but you're lying." Before Janna could protest, Theresa was off again. "I *know* you, MacNeil. I know when you really like someone, and you really like this guy."

"So?" Janna sniffed defensively.

"So given the choice, you'd really rather have a *relationship,* but since Captain Kitchen Sex wants to keep it casual, you've agreed, because having something with him is better than nothing."

"Sister, you are *so* wrong," Janna insisted. "For one thing, I don't think Ty Gallagher and I could *have* a relationship: The man lives, eats and breathes hockey. It would never work outside the bedroom. For another thing, I don't want to jeopardize this gig with Kidco. They're paying me a lot of money, you know. I really have to make sure that work remains my priority. I know you don't believe me, but a casual fling with Ty Gallagher suits me just fine. I've got enough on my plate without having to worry about keeping some guy happy."

"Hhmmph," Theresa harrumphed, clearly not buying it. "You want to believe that, that's fine. But don't come crying to me when you find out he's shooting his puck into some other woman's net."

Janna cringed. "Oh, that was bad. Bad, bad, bad."

"Cut me some slack, I had an awful day at work." Carefully holding her glass aloft, Theresa let herself tumble sideways off the arm of the couch onto one of the cushions.

"Speaking of which," said Janna, "I need to talk to you about something business-related."

"And that would be?"

"Do you think you could arrange for one of my guys to do a cameo on *The Wild and the Free*?"

Theresa blanched. "A cameo? What are you, nuts? These guys aren't actors, they can't speak lines."

"It'll be three lines max, Theresa. You know that."

Theresa paused, thinking. "What about Lubov?"

"Lubov?!" Janna exclaimed. "As you know, he can barely speak English."

"I bet I can teach him," Theresa purred.

"Your obsession with Lex is becoming unhealthy, you know."

"I've told you repeatedly that I want to go on a date with him but you refuse to listen."

"Hey, you had your chance at the Chapter House," Janna pointed out.

"Hardly!" Theresa retorted. "That toothless *gavone* Michael Dante wouldn't let either of us get a word in edgewise!"

Janna remained unmoved, so Theresa put on her best let's-make-a-deal smile. She began massaging a crick in her neck. "If you won't help me, then I just don't know if I'll be able to help you."

Janna clucked her tongue. "Fine, I'll tell Lex you're interested *if* you get me the cameo. We'll go down to the locker room before the game Friday night, okay? After that, you're on your own."

Theresa leaned forward eagerly. "You'll butter him up beforehand, though, right? Let him know it was really him I wanted to talk to that night at the bar, etcetera, etcetera."

"Sure. Fine. Whatever," Janna agreed, too tired to argue.

Theresa smiled. "What would I do without you, Jans?"

"Gee, I don't know, Ter. What would you do?"

"Starve. Be bored. Have no way to get into hockey games for free." She reached out and tweaked Janna's cheek. "You're the best, MacNeil. Who knows? Maybe you and me and Lex and the captain can go out for a *casual* dinner one night."

"Right, and maybe my boss is going to go veggie and start running five miles a day. C'mon, let's go check that moussaka. I'm starved."

Chanting "You can do this" was usually her work mantra. *This* morning, however, Janna was trying to fortify herself in order to break up with Robert. They were meeting for coffee at the Happy Fork Diner. No Starbucks for Robert the artiste, no sir, God forbid. He'd nearly bitten her head off when she even dared to suggest it, spewing something about Corporate America, how they force you to say "tall" when you really want "small," pesticide-coated arabica beans and God only knows what else. Once, his vehement politics would have had her swooning, he was just *sooo* committed. Now it drove her to the point of coma, she was so bored. She let him pick the place, she picked the time, and they left it at that.

She'd never broken up with someone before, at least not someone with whom she'd been involved for three years running. Granted, she had been the one to pull the plug on her relationship with Tony Alhandro in college, but that didn't count, because it was college, and anyone who claimed to be a Marxist while owning a gold Amex card courtesy of Mummy and Daddy deserved to be dumped anyway. But still, it did make Janna wonder why, up until now, she always found herself attracted to these lefty, artist-types. Could it have to do with deliberately choosing men who were different from her driven, working-class father? Or did she subconsciously pick men she could feel superior to economically? Maybe there wasn't a grand reason behind it at all. Maybe she was, as Theresa so delicately put it once, a "freak magnet." But if that were true, how did one explain the appearance of Ty Gallagher on the radar screen?

She pushed through the heavy swinging doors of the diner, grateful for the rush of warmth immediately enveloping her, and the fact that Robert wasn't there yet. It was cold outside, the morning forecast calling for possible flurries. Spotting a booth in the back, she hurried toward it, quickly slipping off her trench coat and sliding onto the maroon Naugahyde bench.

Within seconds a dark, heavyset man with a distinct unibrow appeared and grunted what sounded to her like "Coffee?" Janna nodded and he plodded away, returning a minute later with a sloshing cup of viscous black liquid and a menu the size of a small headstone. Janna told him she was expecting someone else and would wait to order. His response was to hurl some sugar packets down on the table and trudge over to the next booth. Janna sipped the contents of her cup, which had spilled over onto the saucer. *Oh. Yuck. This might have been coffee yesterday,* she thought disgustedly, *but today it's diesel oil.* After she was done breaking up with Robert, she *would* head over to Starbucks for a double cappuccino, no two ways about it. There were some things a body simply couldn't do without.

Perusing the menu, she kept one eye cocked on the door. The diner was loud and crowded. The mousy-looking guy in the booth behind Janna was screaming into his cell phone about "the operation not being successful." In the booth across from her, an older couple were eating dry English muffins and reading the *Post*.

Just when she was on the verge of developing extensive biographies of her fellow diners to entertain herself, Robert came in. Janna felt her guts plummet to her feet. He ambled toward the table, his secondhand overcoat swimming on his licorice-thin body, his black beret tilted at what he probably thought was a rakish angle. Mortification seized her. Was this really the man she'd been seen around town with for the past three years? What had she been *thinking*?

"Ma cherie." He leaned down and planted a chaste, affectionate kiss on her cheek before hanging up his coat, the strong scent of cigarettes wafting from him, the result of the *très expensive* Galoises he insisted on smoking. He didn't have money for a decent coat, but he'd spend money on imported French cigarettes. Amazing.

He slid into the opposite side of the booth from Janna and craned his head around, searching for the waiter. *"Garçon,* a cup of coffee, please," he called out.

"Can you cut the Chevalier imitation for just one minute?" she asked, irritated.

"Someone seems cranky this morning."

"Someone is."

Amazingly, the waiter appeared within seconds with a cup of coffee for Robert.

"Ah, *merci*." He smiled at Janna, a clueless smile she wished she could rake off his face. "Are you ready to order, my sweet?"

Janna shot him a look that could curdle cream and glanced up at the waiter. "I'll have a chocolate chip muffin, please," she said politely, handing back the oversized menu.

"And I'll have a croissant," said Robert pleasantly. The waiter disappeared. "So, what's on your mind?" Sympathy lined his face. "You look tired."

"I am. I've been working really hard." Just seeing him sitting there, so unsuspecting, filled her with guilt. "You look tired, too," she observed, stalling.

"I was burning the midnight oil. You know me, I work best at night, as is the case with many artists. But"—his face broke into a self-satisfied grin as he reached into his back pocket and he pulled out a folded wad of papers—"the lack of sleep paid off. I wrote three new poems, which I intend to read at the Poetry Slam tonight. In fact, one of them is about you, it's called 'Angel in Practical Shoes, A Canto.' Want to hear it?"

"No, I don't." She'd heard his poetry before, and admittedly, it wasn't that bad. But this was neither the time nor place for him to recite a poem about *her*, especially in light of what she was about to do. In the meantime, she had begun shredding the napkin in her lap. She hesitated, looking for the right words. Then she realized: there were no right words. No matter what she said, he'd be upset. Better to just get it over with.

"Look, Robert, I don't think we should see each other anymore."

"Um, okay," he managed after a considerable pause, looking and sounding confused. "Can I ask why?"

"It's just not working for me, all right?" Shred, shred, shred. "I think you're a great guy, it's just time for me—for both of us—to move on. You know?"

You're so right, Janna wanted him to say. But he didn't. Instead, the color drained from his face and his eyes looked sad as he asked in a beaten voice, "Did I do something to offend or upset you? Because if I did—"

"You didn't do anything," Janna jumped in to assure him. "It's me, all right?" Shred, shred, shred. *Spout another cliche why don't you?* "It's me."

Glassy-eyed, he appeared not to be listening. "Have you found someone else?"

"Of course not, don't be silly." She wished she could tell him the truth, but she was afraid: Robert was an intense guy. Janna could imagine him intensely stalking her if he found out about her and Ty.

"You're just unhappy," he said woodenly.

"Yes."

Looking numb, he slipped his papers back into the rear pocket of his jeans. Then, without any warning, he hung his head and began to cry. Out of the corner of her eye, Janna could see the old couple at the next booth discreetly peering at him over their newspapers.

"Robert," she implored frantically, "get a grip, will, you please?"

"Mon dieu, how can this be happening?" he wept. He raised his teary face to Janna. "You're my muse! Without you my creative impulse will die, it will wither on the vine!"

And then you'll get a real job, Janna thought. Instead she said, "That's not true, and you know it. You'll still be able to write."

"Ability is one thing, desire another," was his bitter response. "Without you, I won't *want* to write."

Janna was silent. This could go on forever, him pointing out how she was ruining his life and her insisting that really, she wasn't, even though it was possible she was. He'd grown up poor, he'd chosen a profession where he'd no doubt remain poor, his mother was the poster girl for Thorazine, and now his girlfriend was dumping him. The impulse to completely contradict herself and take him back was strong, but Janna squelched it, reminding herself that pity was a poor basis for a relationship. It had to end here, now. She kept quiet.

Robert's face, which had been contorted in agony, now shone with incredulous anger. "You don't care, do you? You don't care if you kill my creative spirit."

Janna thought a moment. She knew the right answer. "Not really."

"I knew it! I knew you'd turn into one of *them* eventually."

"One of them?"

"It's finally happened, hasn't it? You've utterly and completely sold out."

"Pretty much," Janna agreed.

"You'll regret this, *ma petite belle*." He rose, wrestling his coat on. "You'll rue the day you let me go; but what's more, you'll curse the morning you arise and realize you've no heart left, that you're just a willing cog in *their* machine."

With that he stormed out of the diner, leaving Janna, as always, to foot the bill.

At work later, she knew she should feel relieved about cutting the cord with Robert, but she didn't. Instead, she felt self-conscious and nervous, as if she were walking around wearing a huge sandwich board that proclaimed, "I'm sleeping with Ty Gallagher." She knew this was ridiculous, but she couldn't help it. It was a variation of her impostor fear. Walking past the secretary into Lou's office, Janna thought, *She knows*. Sitting down opposite Jack Cowley in Lou's office and having to endure his false grin revealing tiny, pearly teeth better suited to a doll, she thought, *He knows*. Smiling shyly at Lou as he waddled past her and ruffled her hair saying "Hiya, kid," she thought, *He knows*.

In her paranoid frame of mind, they all knew, and they all thought—what? That it was a joke? A one off? That she was a slut? She was being crazy, and she knew it. She had to stop. If she was this paranoid one day after the main event, what the hell would she be like after she and Ty started fooling around regularly? Convinced everyone was watching them do it through the windows?

She sat back against the crinkling leather of the couch, waiting for Lou to get organized. This usually involved him taking two or three slurps of coffee, severing an egg and cheese sandwich by cramming half into his mouth, and rustling a few papers. The process always fascinated Janna, mainly because it never varied. Jack Cowley, on the other hand, always seemed to avert his gaze from Lou whenever possible, clearly disgusted by whatever Lou did. *It must really frost his uptight little butt to have to work for a guy like Lou,* Janna mused. The thought gave her perverse pleasure.

"All right, ladies and germs, here's the latest. As you know, we got three road trips next week: Minnesota, Vancouver, and Calgary. Jack, you'll be with me as usual." Lou looked to Janna. "As for you, Missymiss, tell Big Lou what's on your plate this week."

Janna peered down at the notes on her lap. "In addition to handling that visit by Dobler to the Kid's Hospital, I'm going to be on hand when the writer from that women's mag interviews the Gills on . . . what is it, Thursday? I'll be there for the photo shoot, too. Let's see, what else . . . I spoke with the editor I know at *Seventeen*. She definitely wants to do a shoot with both Lex and Dante, maybe a group shoot with a bunch of the other hot, young, single guys."

Lou pounded a squishy, exultant fist on the desk. "Yees! Penetration into the teen market! I knew there was a reason I loved you."

Even though Jack was glowering at her, Janna's pride still swelled under Lou's praise. It felt good to know she was doing her job well; it made her feel that maybe she *did* deserve the incredible salary she was pulling down. Maybe she *was* competent enough to strike out on her own after all.

"Now." Lou's voice turned serious as he made the other half of his sandwich disappear. He picked up a sheet of paper from his desk. "This just came down from Corporate this morning, and you, Janna Banana, are gonna hate it, because I, being the Grand Poobah, am going to be exercising my executive privilege and make *you* deal with it."

Janna's heart sank. "What?"

"Corporate's feeling better about the guys getting involved in the charity stuff and all that jazz. It's a step in the right direction. And they're thrilled with that idea you came up with that all the guys have to wear suits and ties when they show up for away games." Janna felt another rush of pleasure at being rewarded shoot through her. "But it's still not enough."

Janna's head dropped back. "Let me guess," she said to the ceiling. "They want to enforce a curfew on the road."

"No, but that's a great idea." Lou grabbed a pencil and began scribbling. "What they want is for the guys to wear jackets and ties on game night both home *and* away."

Janna lifted her head. "Home?" she echoed. "Lou, most of these guys are coming directly from their apartments. They don't want to have to dress up. It makes sense when they're out of town, representing the team, but to have to do it here—"

"I agree with you," Lou cut in. "But this is what they want. They want *all* of 'em to do it, or else."

"Or else what?"

"Or else they're gonna be fined two hundred cannolis every time they don't."

"You have *got* to be kidding me." She could already imagine what would happen when she hit the guys with this one: mutiny in the locker room, and it would be her walking the plank. "Lou, c'mon. They'll never go for this, they're going to freak out. Can't you talk to Corporate and tell them this is completely unrealistic?"

"I tried, doll face, believe me. They won't listen. They want what they want when they want it."

"Personally, I don't think it's such a bad idea," Jack Cowley drawled. Janna and Lou turned to him simultaneously. "Kidco's right. The way some of these goons come slouching into the locker room before a game, they look like they just rolled out of bed. Especially Gallagher."

"That is not true and you know it," said Janna, trying very hard not to sound defensive. "They come in sweats, jeans, khakis . . . they're *athletes,* for God's sake. Not male models."

"They're professional athletes," Cowley rebutted, "who should look professional. Draping these apes in Armani may not *make* them gentlemen, but at least they'll *look* like gentlemen."

"Apes?" Janna repeated angrily. *Ty Gallagher is not an ape, you effete jackass.* "How can you—"

"Whoa, whoa, time out, boys and girls," Lou calmly intervened. He regarded Jack coldly. "Cowley, I know you'd rather be doing PR for some A-list actor than a bunch of guys you think have the collective IQ of a footstool, but keep your personal feelings to yourself, *capisce*? It doesn't exactly fill me with confidence in your abilities to hear you calling them apes." He turned to Janna, his expression softening. "As for you, I know the guys are gonna bust your chops on this, but I also know you can handle it. Anyone who can get that hardhead Gallagher to put on a tux and show up at a benefit knows how to work this crew. I have no doubt that come Friday, every one of those boys is gonna show up before the game looking like a million bucks."

"Right," Janna agreed tepidly. *A million bucks.* That was roughly the amount she'd have to wave in Ty's face to get him to comply. Oh, this was going to be ugly. Mean, bad, and ugly. She should never have taken this job. She should never have gotten involved with Ty. But since she had, she had no choice but to do Kidco's bidding, and hope that her personal relationship with the captain gave her some extra, invisible clout. Heart heavy and fingers crossed, she left the meeting.

CHAPTER

08

Anger. Incredulity. Scorn. Shock. Depressed resignation. These were the emotions Janna saw flash across the team's faces while she explained Kidco's new dress policy to them. She was careful to avoid Ty's eyes, knowing damn well that of all the players, he was the most outraged. Yet he didn't curse, protest, or outright refuse. He simply listened until she was done speaking, then spit on the floor in disgust and walked away, his feelings on the issue made crystal clear.

Janna waited to speak with him until most of the team had cleared out, and he had gone into the players' lounge. She was relieved to see there were only two or three other players in there, teammates who were showered and changed, and getting ready to leave. Ty was sitting on one of the couches in chinos and a button-down denim shirt, thumbing through the sports pages of the *Daily News*. A carton of orange juice sat on the floor beside him. Anxious, Janna gingerly sat down. The pressure of another body on the couch made him glance up; when he saw it was her, he closed the paper, regarding her with unabashed disbelief.

"They've got to be kidding. Tell me it's a joke."

"Ty—"

"It was bad enough being told we have to get dressed up when we're on the road. Whoever came up with that idea should be taken out and shot."

Janna blinked.

"But this is too much. What's next? Telling us where to live, what to eat, what to watch on TV? Who the *hell* do they think they are?"

"The owners of the team," Janna replied softly. "Whether it's right or not, they see you guys as employees, pure and simple."

"Yeah?" Ty's voice was defiant. "Well, they can fine this employee all they want; I am *not* being told what to wear, and before you even ask it, *no,* I will not try to convince any of my guys to toe the line. It's every man for himself on this one."

Janna's heart sank. "Great."

"C'mon, Janna." His eyes quickly darted around the room to see if any of his cohorts were listening. Both of them had stiffened considerably since she'd sat down, almost as if they were trying to overcompensate for their familiarity with one another. "This is bullshit, you know it is. It's a totally unreasonable demand."

"I agree," Janna admitted. "And I told Lou so. Lou agrees, too, and he told Corporate so. They don't care. This is what they want. It all comes down to image."

"Screw them and their image," Ty fired back stubbornly. The last of the other players said good-bye as he left the room. Ty waved and continued, "Here's the thing: I wouldn't have any objection to playing it their way if I got the feeling they respected the team, or even gave a damn about the sport. But they don't. We're just a marketing tool for them."

"This is the way professional sports is now, Ty. You know that."

He reached down for his juice carton, and tilting his head back, drank deeply. "Doesn't mean I have to like it. Doesn't mean I have to do what they say, either." His eyes traveled a slow, straight line from the top of her head down to her feet, pausing to linger at her breasts, her hips. "Lookin' good today, Miz MacNeil," he murmured appreciatively.

Janna gritted her teeth. "Don't."

"Don't what?" Ty teased quietly.

"You know what." Janna felt her face going hot.

"No, I don't," Ty insisted, moving an inch or two closer to her and discreetly pressing his knee against hers, bone touching bone, heat matching heat.

Janna closed her eyes.

"What's wrong?" Ty half whispered. "Don't like to live dangerously?"

Janna's eyes sprang open as she edged her body away from his. "No, I don't," she hissed under her breath, "and neither should you. You better watch yourself."

"Meaning?" His eyes followed two teammates as they walked past the doorway, waving good-bye. "Catch you tonight, guys." He turned back to Janna. "You were saying?"

"If you keep being difficult, Corporate's going to come down on you with everything they've got. That's the way they work."

"Do you know this for a fact, or are you just assuming it?"

"I'm just assuming it. But it's worth thinking about, don't you think?"

"Nope. You forget: I brought the Cup to the city last year, and we're going to repeat this year. Corporate won't do anything to me."

"Except bleed your team dry in fines," Janna pointed out. She felt guilty thinking it, but the bottom line was, the more obstinate he was, the harder it made her job. "Ty, please. Do what Kidco wants, okay? Wear the suit and tie."

His hooded gaze turned seductive. "What will you do for me if I do?"

"What do you want me to do?" Janna flirted back. She realized her heart rate seemed to have tripled in under a minute.

"How about coming home with me after the game Friday night?"

"It's a possibility."

He reached forward, his hand lightly grazing her thigh. "Anything I can do to convince you?"

"Uh, Ty?"

Janna thought her heart would shoot straight out of her chest at the sound of Kevin Gill's voice behind them. She and Ty jumped apart guiltily, even though there was no way Kevin could have seen Ty's hand quietly withdraw from her leg from where he stood. Still, this was not good, not good at all. There was no way her nerves would be able to take this kind of delicious, close-to the-edge flirting. It was fun, okay, but not worth it, definitely not worth it.

"Hey, Kev." Ty's voice was smooth as he turned to look at his friend, standing in the doorway to the lounge. "What's up?"

It alarmed Janna to see Kevin looking befuddled. "Tubs wanted to know if you and I could stick around and review some video of the last game with him. You got some time?"

"Sure."

That was Janna's cue. She rose, making a great show of gathering all her papers together. "I hope you change your mind," she said to Ty in what she hoped was a cold voice.

"Don't bet on it," Ty called after her combatively as she moved to leave the room.

"Hello, Kevin," Janna said, smiling, as she passed him.

Kevin gave a friendly nod. "Janna."

Ty watched as his best friend deliberately waited until Janna had departed the lounge before joining him on the couch. *Shoot,* Ty thought. *Busted.*

Working hard to suppress a smile, Kevin said, "So, how's it going, pal?"

"It's going great. You?"

"Great, great." Curiosity danced all over Kevin's face. "So what's up between you and Janna, huh?"

"Nothing." Ty struggled to remain stone-faced. "Why?"

"Oh, man, don't bullshit me. I've known you too long, and the vibe in here was just too weird." He picked up the paper and began casually perusing it. "You guys seeing each other?"

"In a way."

Kevin slowly put the paper down. "What does that mean?" Before Ty could formulate an answer, Kevin came up with his own. "Oh, Christ. Don't tell me you're playing with her."

Ty stared at him, offended. "I'm not 'playing' with her." He glanced around again, even though the place was empty, save for the two of them. "We're casually dating, okay? And that's between you, me, and the walls."

"Casually dating?" Kevin looked distressed. "What does that mean? You're screwing her, no strings attached?"

Ty couldn't believe what he was hearing. "You really think I'm a jerk, don't you?"

"Not at all," Kevin insisted. "I just know where your head is at right now as far as women are concerned."

"Yeah, and that's where Janna's head is at as far as men are concerned. She wants to keep it casual, too."

Kevin looked dubious. "She told you that?"

"No, I'm making it up. *Yes,* she told me that." He reached down and finished his juice. "Why are you getting so bent out of shape over this?"

"Because this isn't some bimbo you bang a few times and send on her way. This is an intelligent, interesting, nice woman."

"I *know* that," was Ty's irritated response. Why the hell was Kevin lecturing him?

"Well, I just want you to know that if you hurt this intelligent, interesting, nice woman, your ass will be grass, my friend."

"Whoa." What was this? Now his best friend was threatening him? "What the hell is going on here, Kev? Care to fill me in?"

"I like Janna. Abby and I both do. That night at the bar, we could tell something was happening between you two, or was about to."

"So?"

"If you weren't concentrating on winning the Cup again, you'd see that this is a woman who could make you—"

"Halt. Stop. Time out. We are not going down this road. I want it casual. Janna wants it casual. End of story. I don't want to hear this."

Kevin rose. "Because it's true?"

"Because it's none of your concern." He could feel his shoulders knotting with tension and stood up, grimacing. "C'mon, we better get to Tubs's office, he's probably throwing a fit by now."

"I meant what I said," Kevin reiterated as the two headed out of the players' lounge. "Hurt that woman and you die."

"Got it," Ty bit out. He didn't like being told what to do. Hated even more being told what *not* to do, especially by someone so close to him. But he'd gotten the message, loud and clear. Whether or not it was heeded, however, was strictly up to Janna.

"Stay."

"I can't. I promised Theresa I'd come home tonight so she can tell me all about her date with Lex."

"You can hear about it tomorrow. Stay."

Janna sighed, closing her eyes. The thought was tempting. Snuggled beneath a thick, downy comforter with Ty's body possessively wrapped around her, the last thing on earth she wanted to do was drag herself out of his king-size bed and trudge back out into the arctic night, cabbing it alone back to her place. It was a little after one A.M. Theresa might not even be home yet. She could always leave a message on their answering machine, swearing she'd be home first thing in the morning, couldn't she? Theresa would understand.

Her hand darted out from beneath the covers to reach for the phone, but just as quickly she retracted it. No, Theresa would not understand. Theresa was Sicilian, and claimed that when you made a promise to a Sicilian, you'd better keep it or else. If she wasn't home waiting for her, or if she stayed with Ty, Theresa would be very pissed. Home it was.

She snuggled closer to Ty. Five more minutes in his embrace and then she'd get up. Just five more minutes. His breathing was relaxed, the feel of his arms around her the most natural thing in the world. And the sex that had preceded it—Mother of God. They said practice makes perfect. She didn't want to think about how many women before her Ty had "practiced" with, but she was certainly glad to be the current beneficiary of it. The man knew how to please a woman, knew the delights of long, slow, bring-you-right-to-the-edge foreplay followed by a dazzling display of building to climax that left her feeling she might lose consciousness. The irony was that she had feared he might be awful in bed: quick, selfish, and clueless as so many men, so many athletes, reputedly were, the deliciously frenzied incident in her kitchen an aberration. But he was anything but.

Drowsily, she lifted her head and peered across the room to his open bedroom door. She could see the trail of clothing they'd left snaking down the hallway to the edge of the bed in their eagerness to come together. Janna was glad she'd decided to go home with him after all. Initially, she wasn't going to; the Blades had been beaten badly on home ice, and Ty's impassioned post-game postmortem could be heard through the closed door of the locker room. It wasn't pretty. She wasn't so sure his black mood would lift once he left Met Gar.

Not only that, but the cloak-and-dagger logistics involved in getting to his place were slightly off-putting. First Ty had to come up with an excuse for why he wouldn't be going to the Chapter House with his teammates, which is what they always did after a losing game. Then there was the issue of transportation: so as not to invoke suspicion, they took separate cabs, Janna's arriving ten minutes earlier than Ty's. The watchdog doorman of his building wouldn't let her wait for him in the plush lobby, so she was forced to stand outside on the sidewalk, stamping her feet to keep the cold at bay. By the time his cab rolled up, she was sure she'd lost her nose to frostbite, and her own mood had soured considerably.

Thankfully, he had brandy in his apartment to warm her up, though not much else. The apartment made her think of a high-tech monk's cell. It was spare yet modern, a wide screen TV dominating one wall, a state-of-the-art entertainment system encased in black lacquer claiming another. There were no personal touches to be found: no pictures of friends and family, no display case full of trophies and Stanley Cup rings to admire. The entire feeling of the place was rather impersonal. It needed a human touch—a woman's touch, though as soon as Janna had that thought, she knew she'd never give it voice. When she questioned him about the austerity of the place and its lack of warmth, Ty just shrugged.

"I guess I don't really think of it so much as 'home' as a place to sleep, or rest before games," he admitted.

So where was home, she asked him.

"The ice."

She should have known.

Her five minutes were up. Tenderly kissing his collar-bone, she gently disentangled herself from him.

"I really do have to go."

He went to kiss her but Janna sat up.

"I have to go, Ty," she repeated, though it was the last thing she wanted to do. *"Really."*

Ty sighed, resigned. "Shall I call you a car?"

Janna smiled appreciatively. "That would be nice."

Leaning over, he playfully nipped her hip where she was sitting on the edge of the bed. "Would you like a play-mate in the shower?"

Just picturing it made Janna's blood begin to stir anew. "I would, but I'd better not, or I'll never get out of here."

"That's the general idea."

"You're a wicked man, Captain Gallagher." She glanced back towards the ribbon of strewn clothing stretching out beyond the door. "Could you do me a favor? Could you gather up my clothes while I'm in the bathroom and put them on the bed?"

"Your wish is my command."

"Mmm," Janna purred. "I'll keep that in mind for next time."

Next time. **Bundled** up in the back of a Lincoln Town Car as it glided down the near silent streets, Janna felt a warm, confident glow as she thought about the next time she and Ty would be together. He had been the perfect gen-tleman, escorting her downstairs to meet the car, instructing the driver on where to go and charging the ride to his ac-count, before his lips brushed tenderly against hers in farewell. None of which she had expected somehow, but all of which she enjoyed. Paranoia had gripped her when they stepped out of his building onto the sidewalk together; after all, you never knew who might be around, especially in midtown, where Ty had—insanely, in Janna's opinion—chosen to live. But the lateness of the hour worked in their

favor; no one seemed to take any notice of them at all. Then
again, this was New York. Nine times out of ten, no one noticed anyone else anyway.

She watched the world rush by outside her window, the
late night bar and club patrons spilling out onto the wide
sidewalks, laughing and talking. And it hit her: the blush
of heat beginning to flicker deep within her was happiness.
She mouthed the word to herself: *happiness*. At first the
sensation surprised her. Yet the more she thought about it,
the more it frightened her. It implied a depth of feeling not
consonant with the concept of "casual." Casual meant fun,
it meant fluff, it meant easygoing. Relaxed. Well, her body
was certainly relaxed, but her mind wasn't, and neither
was her heart. This thing, this small seed of happiness taking root, felt untamed, like it had a life of its own. It was
one thing to be happy over the quality of the sex, quite another to be happy because of who she was having it with.
*Attraction, not emotion. That's the key. Attraction not emo-
tion, attraction not emotion, attraction not emotion* . . .

The car came to a halt outside her building and Janna
made her way inside, stopping to chat with the overnight
doorman who pretended to be watching the building's
video monitors, but was really absorbed in an infomercial
on a tiny TV.

Riding the elevator up to her apartment, Janna's sense
of curiosity began to peak. She wondered how Theresa's
night out with Lex the Wonder Boy had gone. They
seemed to hit it off in the locker room when she'd reintro-
duced them, and by the time the Blades had skated out
onto the ice, they'd already made plans to go for dinner at
a tiny Ukrainian restaurant Lex frequented. Janna hoped it
had gone well for Theresa's sake, as well as her own, especially after all the nagging she'd had to endure.

She opened the door to their apartment and stepped
inside. The living room was pitch black. Had Theresa
already gone to bed? She paused; it was then she heard the
sound of sniffling coming from the direction of the sofa.

"Theresa?"

The sniffling stopped, but the room remained dark. Alarmed, Janna felt for the light switch and turned it on. Light flooded the room, and there on the couch sat Theresa in her bathrobe, arms locked tightly around her waist as if trying to hold her guts in. Her eyes were swollen and blotchy from crying, her left cheek bruised.

"Oh my God." Janna rushed to her side. "What happened?"

Theresa mumbled incoherently and shook her head.

"Theresa, talk to me. *Theresa.*"

Still she said nothing. Unsure of what to do, Janna put an arm around her and began stroking her friend's hair. Theresa stiffened beneath her touch. Panic mounting, Janna took her hands away but remained beside her. "Terry, please, tell me what happened. Whatever it is, I can help. Please."

As if in a fog, Theresa slowly turned to face her. The anguish in her friend's eyes brought Janna's heart to her throat, the pain reflected there was so intense. She waited. Theresa just kept staring. Then, without a word, she curled up and put her head in Janna's lap. Neither moved. Neither spoke. The minutes passed, Janna literally sitting on her hands after Theresa's previous rebuff, feeling useless. When Theresa finally did speak, it was just one sentence, uttered in a voice so dead it gave Janna the chills.

"Lubov tried to rape me."

CHAPTER
09

The story came out in fits and starts, punctuated by choking sobs. A not-so-simple story of a casual dinner gone awry, of an invitation to come up for a nightcap that was a pretense for violence.

Hearing Theresa stutter it out, Janna could picture the scene perfectly: Her friend and Lubov mellow after a few drinks each, Theresa agreeing to go back to his place for one more. Lubov moving in for a kiss. Theresa succumbing. Then panic setting in as he refused to heed the word *No* as his hands groped and roamed and squeezed, as he pinned her down with his body and stuck his hand up her skirt, yanking, tugging, not letting go. Theresa struggling, Theresa yelling, Theresa getting backhanded across the face, Theresa biting. The shock of her bite stunning Lubov long enough for her to jerk her knee up to his groin. Then him crumpling off her yowling "You bitch, you bitch, you whore." Theresa running. Theresa alone in a cab weeping. Theresa at home frantically brushing her teeth, desperate to erase the bitter taste of wine and forced kisses from her mouth. Theresa in the shower scrubbing the invisible filth of him off her, no penetration but violation, feeling soiled, frightened, like she couldn't breathe, like maybe this was her fault.

As the story came out, Janna's mind raced: *Not Theresa's fault . . . My fault . . . Should never have introduced them. . . . Should have known better. . . . Should not have cut Lubov slack on the train. . . . Should have taken it seriously. . . . My fault . . . My fault . . . My fault.*

During the telling, Janna held her friend, gently rocking her. "It's okay," she whispered, smoothing her unruly hair. "It's okay."

"I wish I were dead," Theresa sobbed.

"No, you don't. You're just upset right now, and you have every right to be."

Theresa whispered something in response, curling up even deeper into Janna's lap.

"What, Terry, honey?"

"I want that bastard to pay."

"Oh, believe me, he will. Why don't you put some clothes on and we'll go down to the police station." A thought struck her, and she hesitated. "Theresa, are you sure there was no—you know—"

Theresa stiffened. "I'm sure."

"Okay," Janna said slowly, figuring it out as she spoke, "so we can skip going to the emergency room. Though your face—"

"No," Theresa said frantically.

"But what if there are some internal injuries—"

"No. There's nothing. No examinations! I don't want anyone touching me I don't—"

"Sshh, sssh, it's okay," Janna soothed, clutching her tighter. "It's okay." Close to tears now herself, she struggled to think straight. Her gut instinct was to find a gun and kill Lubov for doing this, the sick son of a bitch. Her own body began shaking with outrage. *Pay for this?* Pay *was not the word for what was going to happen to that ar-*

rogant little pig. But right now, it was Theresa she needed to focus on, Theresa who required her energy and attention. There would be time to worry about retribution later.

She lightly touched Theresa's cheek. "Are you up to going to the police to file a report?"

"Yes," Theresa whispered.

"Good." Again Janna hesitated. "I hate to ask this, but did he . . . tear your clothing at all? Because if he did, we might want to bring that with us to the cops as possible evidence."

"No," Theresa replied numbly. "No ripped clothing."

Goddamn, Janna thought. *It's going to be her word against his. No, wait . . .*

"Did you draw blood when you bit him?"

"I don't know."

Damn.

"Janna, please stop asking all these questions," Theresa begged.

"Honey," Janna said gently, "what the police will be asking you is going to be ten times worse. You know that, right?"

Theresa didn't respond.

"So you better be sure you're up to dealing with this."

"I will be," Theresa said woodenly. "Because I want that piece of shit to pay." She looked up into Janna's eyes. "I'm sorry now I bugged you so much about him, Janna."

Janna began to cry. "Don't you apologize for anything! I'm the one who's sorry. If I'd known he was like this, I swear to God, Theresa, I would never have introduced you. You're my best friend, I would never have put you in danger like this."

"I know that," Theresa choked, then burst into a small hiccuping laugh. "Jesus, will you look at the two of us? We're a good pair."

"The best pair," Janna sniffled, wiping at her eyes.

"I'm going to go get dressed," Theresa announced, sitting up. She shuffled listlessly towards her bedroom. "It's time to make sure he never tries to do this to anyone else."

Later, after a few numb, awful days passed, and she had helped Theresa hire one of New York's top female attorneys—something dawned on Janna. The repercussions of this case extended to *her*. She was a publicist for the New York Blades. This was a PR nightmare, precisely the kind Kidco hired her to handle. The day Theresa's attorney held a press conference and went public with the case against Lubov, Janna seriously considered calling in sick for the rest of the week. She didn't know how the hell she was going to be able to walk into the Blades' locker room without spitting in Lex's face. Worse, she didn't know how the hell she was going to be able to walk into Lou's office and be expected to take part in plans for damage control. Lubov had attacked her best friend. How on earth was she supposed to turn around and work on saving this guy's image, or the image of the team? She couldn't. It was absurd, impossible. It was also her job.

Walking into Met Gar, she felt as if she were moving under water. All of her actions felt labored, as though performed against a great wall of invisible resistance. She had deliberately avoided looking at the morning papers and listening to the news, knowing full well what she'd read and see. She could already imagine the talking heads on all the various sports channels discussing the case, mentioning fresh-faced little Lex Lubov in the same breath as Mike Tyson. Janna's spirits rallied momentarily as she recalled that Tyson's case had resulted in conviction. Hopefully, it would be the same with Lubov.

She entered the PR office and was immediately accosted by her assistant, Sophie, who looked frantic.

"Janna, the phones are ringing off the hook about this Lubov thing. What do you want me to—"

"Not now, Sophie. Not until I've talked to Lou."

She waved her off and walked on. She was still far down the hall from Lou's office but already she could hear his voice, roiled and intense, ricocheting down the corridor. *Welcome to hell,* she thought, wordlessly slumping past Lou's secretary, whose switchboard was lit up like a Christmas tree. *I don't want to go in there. You have to go in there.* She entered Lou's office.

"Janna, Jesus Christ, where the hell have you been? Cowley and I have been on pins and needles waiting for you to get here!"

"There was a delay on the subway," Janna lied, peeling off her coat. Not really looking at either of them, she took up her usual seat on the couch opposite Cowley.

"You see this?"

Janna glanced up to see Lou holding that day's edition of the *New York Sentinel.* Splashed across the front cover was a huge picture of Lubov with a headline in all caps that screamed, RUSSKY RAPIST? Sickened, Janna nodded and averted her gaze, wishing to God she could just vanish—poof!—in a ball of white smoke, never to be seen or heard from again.

"Look at this." Lou snatched up a crumpled bunch of pink "While You Were Out" messages, letting them fall to his desk like confetti. "*Seventeen* pulled out of the photo shoot. *New York* pulled out of an article *and* a shoot. Bauer Skates is killing their endorsement deal with him. The Sports Chick on WJOX doesn't want to interview him. *ESPN* magazine isn't sure whether they're going to put him on their January cover. You know what this is? A fucking, unmitigated nightmare." He dropped down into his seat behind his desk, cradling his head in hands. "Corporate is going ballistic. They want this fixed, and fast."

"What do they suggest we *do*?" Jack Cowley asked in frustration.

Janna had a few choice ideas but kept them to herself.

Lou lifted his head. "First thing? We go down and talk to the team and make sure we're all on the same page with this. We tell them we don't want any of them to comment on this in public at all, unless it's to say Lex is their teammate, and they stand by him and his story one hundred percent."

"What if his story is a lie?" Janna asked quietly.

"What if it is?" Lou shot back. "We can't be bothered with that shit right now! Our primary job is to make sure this doesn't impact the Blades' ability to sell tickets, period. You got a problem with that?"

"No," Janna managed in a barely audible voice.

"Good, because I'm depending on you here, Janna. I know you dealt with shit like this when you were with the network. Now. What do you think we should do next?"

Janna was silent. There was a buzz in her head, getting louder and louder.

"Janna?"

She licked her lips, trying to compose her thoughts. Lou seemed far away, like she was viewing him through the wrong end of a telescope. *Is this how people feel before they faint?* she wondered. She hoped not. "Next we should . . . um . . . issue a statement to the press, and—"

"Right, right," Lou cut in impatiently, "telling them the same thing we told the team, that we stand by Lubov one hundred percent. I'll write that up. In the meantime, I want you to talk to the guys, Janna."

God, no. Please, no. "Lou," Janna said, rubbing her forehead in an effort to silence the buzzing, "could Jack do it instead? I'm not feeling too well today."

"I got something else planned for Jack," was Lou's dismissive reply.

"Can't wait to hear this," Jack deadpanned.

Lou ignored him. "Like I said a minute ago, Corporate is going crazy over this. Lubov's the one they've been on us to push as 'the next big thing,' as you both know. Now something like this comes along and they're panicking. They want us to fight fire with fire."

Janna tensed. "What does that mean?"

"Jack, I want you to dig up everything you can on this bitch, Theresa, whatever the hell her name is. Where she's worked, who she's fucked, where she hangs, the whole shebang. The idea is to discredit her, make her look like the gold diggin' whore she probably is." He shook his head disgustedly. "These women, they come on to these famous jocks like gangbusters, and then when the guy turns around and tries to give her what she's been teasin' him for, they scream rape. Who the hell are they kidding? They know these guys are likely to settle out of court; that's why they do it. They just want the fucking money."

"That's not true," said Janna.

Lou gave a curt laugh. "Oh, it's not? No offense, but when did you turn into Gloria Steinem? Believe me, pussycat, I've been in the business a lot longer than you have. I know a cocktease when I see one, but more importantly, I know a cocktease who smells cash. This bitch smells cash."

"She's not a whore, Lou!" Janna snapped. "The woman was attacked!"

"How can you be so sure?" Jack Cowley demanded, clearly siding with Lou.

"Because she's my roommate!"

Silence filled the room, awful, pregnant, and ominous. The buzzing in Janna's head stopped, and she closed her eyes, waiting—for the dismissal, for the shouting. Instead, Lou said to her in a voice so calm it was terrible, "Could you repeat that, please?"

"She's my roommate," Janna repeated. "Theresa is my roommate."

"Jesus, Mary and Saint Joseph." Lou struggled out from behind his desk and approached Janna, one hand gripping his chest as if in cardiac distress. "You're shitting me, right? Please tell me you're shitting me."

Janna stared down at the carpet.

"Holy Mother of God, what did I ever do to deserve this?" Dazed, Lou slowly began circling his office. "Okay

Okay. Janna?" Wincing, Janna slowly lifted her eyes to meet his. "I want you to listen to me very carefully, okay, hon? If you ever—*ever*—introduce one of your girlfriends to any of the players again, I will fire you. You got that, sweetie?" Janna nodded dumbly. "The same holds true for you: If I *ever* find you're mixing business with pleasure, *you are outta here*. Am I making myself clear?"

"Yes," Janna whispered.

"Good. Terrif. Glad we understand each other." He circled back to his desk and heaved himself back into his chair. "Just when I think things couldn't get any worse . . ."

"Actually, I think things might be getting considerably better, and soon," Jack Cowley offered cryptically. He'd been deep in thought throughout Lou's speech to Janna, and now had the look of a man who'd had an epiphany.

"Care to elaborate?" Lou pressed.

"Well, rather than wringing your hands over Janna's connection to the . . . defendant"—he flashed Janna an overly polite smile that made her skin crawl— "let's use it."

"How?"

"We have Janna persuade her to drop the suit completely."

"What?!!" Janna squawked.

Lou was nodding his head slowly, taking it all in. "More, I want to hear more."

"Janna talks her into dropping the suit by pointing out how her name will be dragged through the mud, and how she's not likely to get much money from it anyhow. Lubov's good name is restored, we don't have a PR nightmare on our hands, and everyone goes on with their lives. It's a quick, painless solution, and it's exactly what Corporate wants."

"Except I won't do it," Janna retorted.

"Why not?" Cowley asked. "Are you one hundred percent sure things happened the way your friend said they did? Were you *there*?"

"No, I wasn't *there*," she replied vehemently. "But I saw the condition Theresa was in afterwards. She was a mess. Her cheek was bruised. She wouldn't lie about something like this."

"You're sure?" Cowley asked again.

"Doll face, listen." Lou's tone was coaxing. "I can see you care about your friend deeply. Don't you realize the pain you'll be saving her if you talk her into forgetting this whole thing? You'll be doing her a favor."

"Oh, really?" Janna's tone was curt. "And what about the next woman Lubov attacks? Will I be doing her a favor, too?" She crossed her arms in front of her chest. "I'm not doing it, Lou."

"So you want her life to be a living hell?" Jack Cowley asked. "You want her to go through all this public humiliation and pain."

"Of course I don't!" Janna shouted in frustration. God, she hated his weasly guts. "But I don't think it's right to try to talk Theresa out of this just to make our lives easier. If I thought it possible she was exaggerating or didn't understand what bringing charges against him entailed, then maybe I'd think about dissuading her from going forward with this. But I know Theresa. If she said this happened, it did. And I am not selling her out."

"Aren't you noble," Cowley sniffed sarcastically under his breath.

"Go to hell," Janna snapped. She turned to Lou. "Up until now I've done everything you've asked, and more. But please don't ask me to do this. Please."

Lou sighed. "Go down to the locker room, then, and tell 'em Corporate loves and supports Lubov. Tell 'em to keep their mouths shut and not to talk to the press. When you're done with that, set up a press conference for late this afternoon. See if you can get Gallagher to sit there with you. It'll look good if the public sees the team's captain standing by one of his players."

Janna blanched. "You want *me* to do the press conference?"

"Goddamn right I want you to do the press conference. Having a woman come out there to say Kidco supports Lubov is the best PR move we can make."

"But—"

"It's your job, MacNeil," Lou growled. "No buts."

Janna rose unsteadily as the feeling of being underwater returned. "Then I guess I better go do it."

The cold metal wall of the bathroom stall felt soothing against her cheek. She had fled to the Ladies Room as soon as the press conference ended, wanting nothing more than to hide. She knew now that if she ever had to switch careers, she could probably make it as an actress. She'd given two Academy Award–caliber performances today: one in front of the media minutes before, the other in the locker room earlier in the day, both involving carefully crafted scripts. Pretending. And for Janna, outright lying, because she didn't support Lex, she didn't stand behind him, she wanted him to rot in jail, to suffer, to pay. And as good as her performance in the locker room was, she knew damn well that every player in there aware of her relationship to Theresa *had* to know she didn't believe a word coming out of her own mouth.

She wondered about that. Wondered how they viewed her in light of it. Did they see her as a hypocrite? Someone just doing her job? Did they think she was a traitor as far as Theresa was concerned? Or did they stupidly, mistakenly, think *she* thought Lubov *was* innocent? The thought killed her, that anyone could think she, of all people, didn't believe Theresa's story. *How many of them believed it?* she wondered. Ty did, she was pretty sure of that. Kevin Gill, too, although she hadn't had a chance to speak with either of them. But the rest of the team? She wasn't so sure. She'd caught some of the sympathetic glances the guys

shot Lubov while she was speaking. She also noticed how
a few them walked past him and squeezed his shoulder in a
gesture of unmistakable solidarity. It had made Janna sick
when she'd seen that. Made her sick even to be in the same
room with Lubov. Her impulse had been to stare him
down, challenge him, but she couldn't. Her actions had to
match her words as much as possible. And so, she simply
avoided eye contact with him even while she acted her
guts out for the rest of the team, carefully meeting the gaze
of each and every one of them as she always did, her voice
strong and unwavering. She could honestly say she hated
her job today, and the place it had brought her to. She had
no integrity.

The word made her laugh, a hollow sound that echoed
off the tiled walls of the empty bathroom. Integrity. What
planet was *she* on?! Doing PR could be the antithesis of
having integrity, especially if you believed the age-old
adage that there was no such thing as bad publicity. Plastic
surgery, public drunkenness, divorce, adultery, attempted
rape—all of it was grist for the PR mill. So what if the
actor in question purchased five thousand dollars worth of
crack from an undercover cop, or the rising young hockey
star sexually assaulted a woman? As long as the PR machine ensured that their actions didn't aversely affect their
ability to make money at the box office or for their em-
ployers, what did it matter? The offense was incidental;
what was important was remaining in the public eye. That
was the career path she'd chosen to pursue.

She exited the stall and went to the nearest sink, damp-
ening a paper towel that she pressed to the back of her
neck. Not surprisingly, her skin felt clammy, almost as if
she was coming down with a flu. She glanced at her face
in the mirror. She looked pale and tired, like she'd been
through an ordeal, which of course she had. *Poor little me,*
she mocked her reflection. It crossed Janna's mind that
when she got home, she would have to let Theresa know
that she gave a press conference, if her lawyer hadn't told

her already. *Great.* She knew Theresa would understand she'd been forced to do it, but she could also imagine Theresa telling her that if the situation were reversed, *she* would have quit. *Maybe that's what I should do,* Janna thought. *Quit.*

The door to the Ladies Room quietly creaked open. Janna looked in the mirror; reflected there was the image of Lex Lubov creeping inside. She whirled to face him.

"What the hell do you think you're doing?" Fear overtook her in the form of a cold sweat. Did anyone else know she was in here?

"Janna, please, I must speak with you."

"Give me one good reason why I should listen to *anything* that comes out of your lying mouth."

"Because I am human being, human being like you." He held his hands out in front of him in supplication. "Please, two minutes."

Janna's eyes traveled the length of his arms, to the bandage carefully wrapped around his right hand. The buzzing in her head started again, low but insistent. "What happened to your hand, Alexei?"

His eyes briefly flickered down to his wound, then back up to her face. "I hurt in practice."

"Liar."

"Janna, please."

"What?"

"Your friend, what she say is not true, it did not happen that way."

"Oh?" Janna could barely keep the contempt out of her voice. "What happened?"

"Your friend, she want to have fun very badly. Very much, she was saying, 'Kiss me, touch me.' So I kiss, I touch."

"And then she asked you to stop, but you wouldn't."

"No. *No.* I keep on and she saying, 'More, more,' so I give her more and then I am stopping because I am respecting her and she goes crazy, she is mad I am not loving her, she goes crazy on me. I swear to you this is the truth."

Janna was incredulous. "You expect me to believe this? You expect me to believe *you* and not her? Why would I do that?"

"Because I am telling the truth!" he exclaimed. His face was turning red with obvious frustration. "Why you do not believe me?!"

"*Why?!* Because I know for a fact you're lying, Lex!! I live with Theresa! I saw the shape she was in after she managed to get the hell out of your apartment! You tried to rape her!"

Lex was stubbornly shaking his head. "No. No. I did not do this thing. No."

"Yes! You! Did!" Janna yelled. She took a deep breath, trying to regain control of herself. "Fine, let's say you didn't, Lex. Why come to me? What do you want from me?"

"Talk to that girl, tell her not to do this thing."

"What? Haul your ass into court? Forget it."

"This could hurt my career!"

"You should have thought of that before you attacked an innocent woman."

"Tell her," Lex demanded. "She will listen to you. Tell her."

"No!"

Janna had had enough. She picked up her briefcase, and moved to walk out the door. But Lex blocked her way.

"Get the hell out of my way, Lex."

"Tell her not to do this thing!" he repeated angrily. Glaring, he grabbed Janna's arm. "Tell her, goddammit!"

Livid, Janna twisted out of his grasp. "If you ever lay a hand on me again, you SOB, you're going to have another assault case on your hands, you got it?!"

With that, Lex laughed. A low, threatening laugh. "Fine. Go back to your whore friend. Tell her she will be sorry, eh? She will not succeed! I am great hockey player! I have many friends, lots of money! She will not succeed! Tell her! Or else!"

Janna responded with a laugh that was just as ominous, if not more so. "You stupid, little jackass! Don't you *dare* threaten me! Don't you understand what I *do* for a living? One phone call from me to the newspapers and your career is sunk! Or don't you realize that?"

"You would not do such a thing."

"Try me," Janna growled. "Now *get out of my way* unless you want to wake up tomorrow morning to headlines about your embarrassing drug problem!"

"But that is a lie!"

"Just like your saying you didn't hurt Theresa," Janna countered sweetly, pushing past him.

She started down the hall; a second later, she heard the bathroom door swing open. She glanced over her shoulder just in time to see Lubov storming away in the opposite direction. It wasn't until he was well out of sight that she realized she was shaking. Tears of relief formed in her eyes, and she let her briefcase drop to the ground as she leaned up against the wall, breathless. The confrontation with Lubov terrified her, but she'd risen to the occasion and held her own. She had, as Ty had said to her that night in the Chapter House, felt the fear and did it anyway. And that made her feel proud.

Even so, she couldn't help thinking about Theresa, who also knew what it was like to fight her way out from under Lubov's glare. Theresa who'd had to struggle beneath those hands. . . . She had to find Ty, make him realize what an animal they were dealing with here.

She had to find Ty.

CHAPTER

10

"Can you believe that?!"

Ty was lying on the couch staring at Janna, who stood halfway across his immense living room glaring at him, nostrils flaring, steam coming from her small, perfectly shaped ears. For the past ten minutes, she'd been raving—no, ranting, raving implied lunacy whereas ranting implied seething anger, so he'd go with ranting—about Lubov.

It had been one helluva day, right from the moment he woke up to see that disgusting headline in the paper. Practice was a bust, which he knew it would be; the whole team understood what was about to go down and no one could concentrate worth a damn. Before he'd even had a chance to talk to them, Janna had come from Corporate and given her little speech, which ticked him off but he let it go, because after all this was a "crisis," right?

Next thing he knew, he was sitting next to her at a press conference feeling like a total schmuck because he'd been told not to say anything, just sit there in a supporting role. He'd complied, but before he could grab a minute to talk to Janna she'd disappeared, only to reappear ten minutes later when he was in Coach Matthias's office with a look in her eyes that screamed "I need to talk to you *now*." He raised his left hand in the "Gimme five" gesture, and as soon as he wrapped up with Tubs, he had tracked her down in the players' lounge, where she'd growled at him that they couldn't talk there.

And so, two separate cab rides later, here they were at his place, with him lying on the couch trying to listen while resting after a physically punishing game the night before, and her ranting.

"Just try to relax, all right?" He tried to keep his voice calm without being patronizing. Janna's blue eyes flared again as if she were gearing up for a rebuttal, but then her shoulders seemed to drop in what he took to be sheer physical exhaustion. She sunk down into one of the huge, overstuffed armchairs opposite the couch, her small stocking-clad feet dangling over one of the plump arms, business suit be damned.

Ty laid his head back down and sighed, amazed that this was the same woman who less than two hours before had been the very picture of crisp, corporate professionalism. Watching her in the locker room as she addressed his team about how Kidco was behind Alexei, he'd been awestruck at how in control she was, especially in light of the subject matter. He knew that deep down she had to be choking on every word. But you'd have never known it to see her: her voice was steady, her face a mask of perfect neutrality. It had impressed him. No one knew better than he did what it was to rise to the occasion to get a job done, especially when every fiber in your body railed against it.

He flicked his eyes to hers, aware of her watching him. Her gaze was expectant. She wanted a response to the tale she had just laid bare for him, starting with the night she'd come back from his place to find Theresa a devastated mess, to Lubov cornering her in the bathroom earlier in the day. That part of the story had provoked a fury in him so

deep he dreamed of breaking Lubov's neck at the next
practice. Yet he was reluctant to get into it with her for reasons he thought should be obvious to both of them.

"What would you like me to say?" he asked.

Janna just stared. "Hel-*lo*, have you heard a word I've
said?!"

"Of course I have."

"So doesn't it bother you that he grabbed me?" she demanded. She was in terrier mode; she wasn't going to let it
go. He braced himself.

"Of course it bothers me. But—"

"But what?" she snapped, cutting him off. She was
glowering at him now. Ty fought to stay detached.

"You yourself said Lubov was harmless that time he
was bothering you on the train."

"Obviously I was *wrong!"*

She was squinting at him, hard, and had crossed her
arms in a gesture of obvious displeasure. Clearly he'd said
the wrong thing. In this situation, however, he knew everything he said was going to be the wrong thing, which is
why he hadn't wanted to go down this road in the first
place. He opened his mouth to tell her so, but was seized
with a fierce back spasm. He hated admitting it, but he was
more beat up than he thought, and the older he got, the
longer it seemed to take him to recuperate from physical
punishment—not that anyone on the team or coaching staff
knew. Riding the wave of pain, he gritted his teeth until it
passed. Janna, meanwhile, remained silent. He didn't expect sympathy from her, but for Chrissakes, an "Are you
okay?" would have been nice.

"Don't mind me, I'm just dying here."

"Oh, you're fine." Janna waved her hand dismissively.
She was peering at him now as if he were some revolting
specimen beneath a microscope. "You believe him, don't
you?" Her voice was chilly with disbelief. "You believe
Lubov."

"I'm not sure what to believe," Ty replied cautiously. That was the truth. But not the one she wanted to hear.

"How can you say that?!"

Ty sighed heavily. There was no avoiding it. Time to dive into the shark tank. "No offense, Janna, but I remember how Theresa behaved that night you brought her to the Chapter House with you. She was coming on to my guys."

"What?!!" Her voice was shrill enough to pierce an eardrum. "She was not coming on to them! She was flirting with them! There's a huge difference!" A sitting duck, he watched as her anger continued to gather force. "What are you insinuating, Ty? That Theresa is a 'bad girl' who 'brought it on herself' or 'asked for it'? That her behavior in the bar that night somehow proves Lubov is telling the truth?"

"All I'm saying is it lends a little more credence to Lex's side of the story," he said carefully.

"Oh my God."

Ty involuntarily tensed as he watched the blood slowly drain from Janna's face.

"You do believe him. Admit it. You believe him."

He wasn't sure which he wanted to silence more: the pain in his back, or the voice in his head which longed to tell her to let this conversation go for now, because he was in no goddamn mood for it, and her shrillness was making it even worse. Irritated, he came back with, "Don't put words in my mouth. I already told you, I don't know what to believe." His hand went to his lower back as he slowly began massaging the muscle, his gaze contemplating the ceiling. "To be honest, worrying about who's telling the truth isn't really my main concern right now."

"Oh? And what is?"

"How this lawsuit might affect team performance and morale. I don't give a rat's ass if the charges against Lubov are true or not. What's most important to me, as captain, is making sure it doesn't interfere with my guys giving one hundred percent, especially Lubov. If he's distracted, it hurts the team, which hurts our run at the Cup. It's not acceptable."

There was a long, shocked pause. "I can't believe you're saying this. I can't believe all you care about is the team!"

He jerked his head to look her way. "That's my job, Janna—just like your job was to get out there today in front of the guys and the press and lie your little heart out on Kidco's behalf, saying *you* support Lex." Her expression told him she had registered his comment like a slap. "I'm just doing what I'm paid to do. Like you."

"So it doesn't bother you that you might be covering for a rapist and helping advance his career," Janna said hotly.

"No more than it bothers you," Ty shot back, irked she was getting sanctimonious on him.

"I'm a publicist, Ty, I don't have a choice. You do."

"Fine." He was on the verge of seriously losing his temper now. "Then I choose to turn a blind eye to Lex's possible guilt and to focus instead on what has been, and always will be, my number one priority: winning the Stanley Cup."

Janna twitched with rage. "So that's it. He's not going to be reprimanded, he's not going to be ostracized, it's all going to be business as usual."

"Yes, ma'am, it is. I imagine that's how it's going to be on your end as well, no?" Janna was silent. "Look, let's stop talking about this, okay?"

"Good idea."

She rose. Ty watched as she marched over to the coat closet in his marble-lined foyer and fetched her coat.

"What are you doing?"

"Leaving."

"What the hell for? I thought we were ordering in Japanese."

"I changed my mind."

"Why?" With great effort, he forced himself to sit up. "Because I won't hang Lex out to dry?"

"Because I could lose my job if anyone finds out we're together, and it's not worth it." She donned her coat and slipped her heels back on. "Plus I don't know if I can be with someone who puts winning at sports ahead of—"

"Integrity?" Ty interjected angrily.

"That," Janna agreed primly. "And—"

"Whoa, wait a minute here." The anger he'd been holding at bay couldn't be contained any longer. "You're saying I have to have integrity when it comes to Lubov, but you don't?" A dark chuckle escaped him. "No offense, sweetheart, but that's bullshit."

"Don't call me sweetheart. It's offensive."

"Not as offensive as your double standard."

"I'm going."

"For good?"

"Yes, for good. I don't think this casual, clandestine fling thing is working, do you?"

Ty shrugged diffidently. "I thought it was working fine, but hey, you wanna pull the plug because I refuse to do my job the way you think I should, you go right ahead. I might be a lot of things, but whipped ain't one of 'em." He reached for the phone on the end table. "Shall I call you a car?"

"I'll get a cab, thank you."

"Well, I guess that's that, then." The irrationality of what she was doing knocked him for a loop, but he'd be damned if he'd let it show. "If you can stand my presence three seconds longer, allow me to say that professionally at least, I hope we're able to maintain the same warm, close relationship we've always had."

"You bet."

With that she turned and walked to his front door, the click, click, click of her heels on the black marble floor sounding harsh to his ears. There was a brief pause, a resounding slam, then silence. *So, that was it. Hasta la vista. Finito. Revert to former adversarial status.* Thoroughly exhausted, he settled back down on the couch and closed his eyes.

"What the hell just happened here?" he said aloud to the empty living room. He knew the answer: Janna had just had a major meltdown. *Face it,* he thought, *women are nuts. Ergo, Janna is nuts. Christ Jesus.* Well, maybe it was a godsend she pulled the plug, even though he did think it was a bit of an overreaction. He needed this kind of moody, crazy behavior like he needed a hole in the head. Better to go back to anonymous bimbos, no strings attached. That was a much better plan of action. But if that was the case, why did he feel as if his guts had been clawed out? And worse, why was he missing her already?

Okay, Janna asked herself, as she fought her way through the densely packed crowds that made Manhattan's sidewalks a holiday hell, how stupid was it to break up with Ty three weeks before Christmas? Maybe breaking up was the wrong turn of phrase, since they weren't really "going out." But still, how dumb was it to ditch the best lover you'd ever had in your life at this time of year? Talk about guaranteeing a textbook case of the holiday blues.

She tried to like Christmas, really she did. Tried to convince herself that elves were cute, and carols fun to sing, and trees a thrill to decorate. But it never worked. For as long as she could remember, Christmas meant only one thing: family discord.

Oh, her folks would always try to put a good face on it. The house would be decorated perfectly, with pine garland circling the gleaming banisters, candles flickering in every window, and the biggest, most perfect Scotch pine in the world dominating the den while a roaring fire blazed in the big stone fireplace. On Christmas Eve, her parents held a huge open house party for family, friends, and business associates. The house would ring with conversation and laughter as toasts were drunk way into the morning hours, after which a staff, hired for the event, would clean up so the family could toddle off to bed, sweet dreams of a hangover cure dancing in both her parents' heads. If Janna and her siblings were lucky, the fireworks between them wouldn't start until dinner was served later in the day. Actually, there had been a few years where they'd erupted while opening presents, but that was a long time ago. Even so, eruption was inevitable.

Demoralized just thinking about it, she ducked into a Starbuck's to get some coffee to warm her bones. Starbuck's always made her think about Robert. She wondered how he was doing. Maybe she would call him, just to touch base, say hi. Just to avoid being alone. God, she was pathetic.

The long line snaking up to the counter was at a virtual standstill, giving her more than enough time to indulge in her latest obsession, replaying her last scene with Ty. Maybe she'd been overly emotional; maybe she had acted hastily, crazily, in flouncing out the door after telling him they were history. But what did he expect? He just lay there on the couch like a lummox while she clued him in to what was really going on, and then, as if that wasn't bad enough, he had the sheer gall to suggest Lubov might not be lying. And worse, that he didn't care if he was, that the only thing that mattered was the Stanley Cup! Just thinking about it now had her harumphing and snorting all over again, causing people on the line to stare. But really, what was wrong with him?

And then there was that line of his about her double standard and about being whipped! It made her teeth grind. No, she was right to nip their little liaison in the bud.

But that didn't mean she didn't still want him.

She hated her job now, hated having to see that creep Lubov every day. She shuddered with anger. How she longed to smack that perpetual smirk from his lips. She couldn't stand him thinking—and acting—like he'd gotten away with something.

Then there was Lou, on her butt every hour of every day about trying to get Theresa to drop the suit. She knew he didn't mean to be putting excess pressure on her, but that's how she was experiencing it. Last but not least, there was the torture of being around Ty.

They barely made eye contact, and when they did, the look was guarded and hard. Conversation was cursory, strictly business. Sometimes she would steal a glance at him and think, *I know every inch of that man. I know the arch of his back, how he likes to be kissed. I know the feel of his body moving inside mine*. It depressed her. That was part of another lifetime, the one that existed before the lawsuit. Sometimes she caught herself wondering what would have happened if Lubov hadn't attacked Theresa. Would she and Ty have continued to keep things casual? Or would he have eventually realized there was more to life than the obsession to win, allowing their liaison to evolve into something deeper, a real "relationship"?

But Lubov *had* attacked Theresa, and things were what they were. He was the captain, she was the publicist. He cared about the team's performance, she cared about the team's image, and never, she mused bitterly, the twain shall meet. Queasiness took hold as she realized Lou planned on going over the details of the Blades' upcoming Christmas party with her when she arrived at the office. The last thing on earth she wanted to deal with was being at the same party as Ty Gallagher. And Lex Lubov. Left to her own devices she wouldn't even show up, but in this case she had no choice. All the big kahunas from Kidco would be there, and she'd have to smile and circulate and jump up and down for them saying, "See? See how presentable the team looks? See how hard I'm working? See?" Just imagining it made her brain constrict.

She finally made it to the counter, placed her order and received her tall latte, and ventured back out into the New

York cold, unable to tear her mind from work. That was all she had now: work, and her friendship with Theresa. Maybe it was all she'd ever had.

"Tight-fisted bastids" Lou had muttered when Janna helped him squeeze into a Santa suit that seemed in serious danger of splitting at the seams. He had tried to cajole her into dressing as an elf to assist him in handing out gifts, at this, the cheapest of all Christmas parties, but she would have none of it. The last thing on earth she wanted to face was Ty Gallagher seeing her in lime green tights and pointy yellow shoes.

Now she was trapped, listening politely while some big Muckymuck from Kidco bored her with the details of his three million dollar home. *Must be nice,* she thought sourly. She resisted the urge to point out how interesting it was that he made enough money to construct his own personal Xanadu off the New Jersey Turnpike, yet Kidco was so damn cheap they wouldn't spring for a hotel banquet room for this Christmas party. Officially, the word was that it was being held at Met Gar so that the "players could skate with their kids." *Tight-fisted bastids* was more accurate.

Managing to extricate herself from the three-million-dollar windbag, she moved to the Plexiglas, nursing a glass of punch. Kids as young as two years old were being pulled around the ice on tiny, gleaming skates by their hockey-playing fathers, while older kids whipped around the ice as if it were their birthright, which she supposed it was. Even some of the wives were out there skating, helping to complete the happy family picture, which pinched at Janna like a too tight shoe. Jealous, that was what she was. Jealous to see how happy they were. Jealous they had each other while she had no one.

As discreetly as she could, she kept an eye on Ty while he circled the rink with the Gill boys, who were clearly enamored of their strapping "uncle." All three of them were laughing riotously at some private joke, the children basking in the glow of the captain's undivided attention. An unbidden thought popped into Janna's mind: *What a good father he'd make.* Horrified, she killed the idea immediately, focusing instead on his attire. He was casually dressed in jeans, a black turtleneck, and a red ski sweater with a black snowflake pattern across the chest, looking every inch the rugged male she knew him to be. As if he knew he was being watched, his eyes flitted to hers as he skated past. For a split second Janna thought he might smile at her, but no, his face gave away about as much as a sphinx. Aggravated at herself for giving a damn, she went to refill her punch glass.

"Hey, Janna. Happy holidays."

Smiling, Janna turned at the sound of Abby Gill's voice.

"Hi, Abby. How's it going?" Janna aimed her punch glass in the direction of the rink. "I'm surprised you're not out there skating."

Abby leaned towards Janna conspiratorially. "Want to know a secret? I can't skate. Kevin's been offering to teach me for years, but I'm too frightened. I'm convinced I'll fall and break my neck."

"I know what you mean," Janna said. She raised her cup of punch, and they clinked in a friendly toast.

"You all set for Christmas?" Abby asked. "What are your plans?"

"I'll be at my folks in Connecticut. You?"

"Kevin and I are going to stay in New York. Kevin's folks might come in. And Ty will be with us, as always."

Janna nodded, as if she knew all about Ty's spending Christmas with the Gills, which of course she didn't.

"All done shopping?" Abby continued chattily.

"I try to finish by Thanksgiving," Janna confessed. "I'm totally anal retentive."

Abby's eyes lit up as she leaned in even closer to dish. "What did you get Ty?"

Janna stiffened. "I don't understand."

"Oh, God." Mortification transformed Abby's normally placid face. "I wasn't supposed to know, was I?" She touched Janna's shoulder. "Kevin told me, but I swear I haven't said a word to anyone, nor will I."

"It's okay," Janna assured her, even though it wasn't. "It's over."

"Oh." Now Abby looked genuinely upset. "I'm sorry."

"Don't be," Janna said curtly. "It was just sex. No big deal."

"Janna," Abby replied as she looked her straight in the eye, "it's never 'just sex.' "

Shouts of "Mommy, look!" diverted Abby's attention, providing Janna with the perfect opportunity to excuse herself, which she did. So the Gills knew about her and Ty. She wasn't sure why, but it embarrassed her, especially since she had no idea in what context Ty had presented the relationship. Judging from Abby's reaction, she assumed Ty hadn't gone to Kevin and declared, "I'm doing the publicist." But what *had* he said? She hated that she didn't know. That she would never know.

When Corporate determined the players had had enough time on the ice with their offspring, everyone was herded into Met Gar's in-house restaurant, The Grill, to chat and mingle before a late lunch was served. Janna was dismayed to see that a dais had been set up at the front of the cozy, publike room for the Kidco execs. The message was clear: We're royalty and we're in charge. They had already been "receiving" players and their families down by the ice, and had, Janna noticed, made a special effort to talk to Lex, which set her teeth on edge. Predictably, Ty had ignored them and seemed in fact to go out of his way not to pay them any homage at all, heading straight for the ice as soon as he arrived and lingering on it for as long as possible until it was time to go to the restaurant. Unfortunately for Janna, Lou had noticed too; before he had a chance to bug her about it, she promised him she'd talk to Ty, which she was now on her way to do, if only to get it over with.

She made her way to where he stood at the long, polished maple bar with Kevin, reaching up to tap him on the shoulder.

"Excuse me, but I need to speak with you a moment."

Ty turned, surprised. Janna caught him giving her a quick once over and was glad she'd dressed for the occasion: black leather pants, boots, and a lilac colored cashmere V-neck that made the blue of her eyes really pop. But the happy smile that had been on his face a second before was now a frown.

"What is it?" he asked.

"Kidco Corporate would like to meet you."

He leaned casually against the bar. "I'm right here. Tell 'em to come on over."

"Don't be deliberately difficult. You know it doesn't work that way."

"And you know I don't give a damn how it works. I thought this was a party."

"It is."

"Then why are you on my ass?" Ty inquired sweetly. "Don't you ever take a day off?"

"Don't you?"

"Touché." Ty raised his beer glass in salute to her. "Tell

you what. When I'm done with this beer, I'll go over and kiss their rings. Will that make you happy?"

"Do what you want," Janna replied disgustedly. "It's your career."

She was about to walk away when out of the corner of her eye, more vivid than a nightmare, she saw Robert coming toward her. *Oh, this was just the icing on the cake, thank you very much.* In a moment of weakness, she had called him and they had agreed to get together for coffee after the party. So what on earth was he doing here now? She steeled herself, trying hard not to notice the who-the-hell-is-this-loser? look forming on Ty's face.

"Mon cherie." Robert went to reach for Janna's hand but she quickly jerked it out of range. "I tried calling you on your cell phone but you weren't picking up."

"Hi, I'm Ty Gallagher," Ty said, putting out his hand to shake Robert's. His voice was super-friendly, and there was a wicked glint in his eye that made Janna long to kill him. "And you are—?"

"Robert Turner." The superiority in his voice was unmistakable, as was the faint touch of a French accent.

"Pleased to meet you, Robert. You a friend of Janna's?"

"I'm her boyfriend."

"Ex-boyfriend," Janna corrected sharply.

Robert gave an arrogant sniff. "A mere technicality."

"Ex-boyfriend," Ty repeated thoughtfully, his eyes deliberately seeking Janna's. Seeing the mockery there, she imagined poking them out. "That's interesting," Ty continued.

"Is it?" Robert replied coldly. "Why?"

Ty pondered the question. "Oh, I don't know," he finally said with a sigh. "I guess I just pictured Janna with someone a bit more masculine, you know?"

Janna gave him a withering look before turning her attention to Robert. "What are you doing here?" she asked him calmly. "I thought we agreed we'd meet at five."

She watched with embarrassment as Robert made a

great show of turning his back to Ty before speaking. "As I said, *ma petite belle*, I tried to reach you on the cell phone but you weren't picking up. I can't make it. The editor at *Anarchy Now!!* wants a small piece from me by tomorrow and I'm afraid I'm going to have to work on it." He bowed deeply. "*Desolé*. I am sorry."

"No offense, but what's with the French phrases, pal?"

Janna clenched her fists. Ty wasn't going to be happy until he'd completely and utterly humiliated her, was he? Seeing that Robert had no intention of turning around to acknowledge him, Ty shifted his position so that he now stood beside her, staring down at Robert as if he were some sort of freak, his question hanging in the air.

Robert put a hand to his chest. "I'm French in my heart." His eyes took in Ty contemptuously. "I doubt someone like you would understand."

Ty nodded sadly. "*Oui, c'est pas vrai.* We Neanderthal athletes rarely do." He held out a fist for Robert. "If you look hard enough, you can see where my knuckles scrape the floor." His eyes darted towards the bar. "Right, Kev?"

Kevin turned away, obviously suppressing laughter. Ty ducked his head and stared down hard into his beer, clearly doing the same. Furious now, Janna grabbed Robert by his ragged coat sleeve and dragged him out of the party.

"My dear," he said sympathetically when they were out in the hall, "I didn't realize the goons you had to deal with on a daily basis. You poor thing."

"Don't ever bother me while I'm working," Janna hissed, poking him in the chest. "Ever. Ever. Ever."

Robert shrunk from her. "But—"

"Ever!" Janna barked one final time before storming back into the restaurant. *Stay calm,* she told herself. She didn't dare glance over at the bar, even though she damn well knew Ty's eyes were glued to her; she could just feel it. She did a quick survey of her surroundings. Most people were at tables, talking. Others stood, drinks in hand, chatting and laughing. Janna groaned inwardly. That was an-

other "thing" she was supposed to be keeping an eye on—
making sure none of the players had too much to drink.
Well, too late. She could already tell a handful of them
were well on their way to tossing a few sheets to the wind,
and she didn't care. This was a party, for God's sake. If
Kidco couldn't excuse these guys letting their hair down at
their own damn Christmas party, then they really were the
minions of Satan Ty always accused them of being. Maybe
getting drunk wasn't such a bad idea.

Of course, that meant venturing over to the bar, where
Ty and Kevin were now holding court, a group of younger
players splayed in a semicircle around them, their gaze rapt
as the captain and his sidekick prattled on about God knows
what, probably the first time one of them had their teeth
knocked out with a hockey stick or something equally riv-
eting. Stealthy as a cat, Janna edged her way to the far end
of the bar, sure she had managed to arrive undetected. But
she was wrong. She had no sooner placed her order for a
gin and tonic than Ty sidled up to her.

"What do you want?" Janna asked, deliberately staring
straight ahead.

"I want to know why you looked so shocked when I
spoke French."

"You never mentioned it."

"I never had to. You can't be in the NHL for as long as I
have and not speak some French."

"Fascinating."

Ty leaned over, elbows on the bar, so they were eye
level. "I can't believe you went out with that guy," he murmured. "No wonder you were so desperate to hook up with
me."

Janna's head whipped around. "I beg your pardon?"

"You heard me. My sainted old granny has more testos-
terone than that guy."

Janna's teeth clenched. "I hate you, you know that?
Hate, hate, hate."

"Hey, Cap, Janna, Merry Christmas!"

Janna and Ty turned around just in time to see Michael Dante striding toward them with a sprig of mistletoe. Earlier in the evening, he'd politely inquired after Theresa, which both touched and impressed Janna. If only Theresa had given *him* the time of day rather than the Siberian Express . . . well, too late now.

"C'mon, you two." He shook the mistletoe over their heads. "Time to bury the hatchet you've been chucking back and forth at each other since September. We're all part of the Blades family, right?"

Janna's eyes narrowed in warning as she regarded her companion. "Don't you da—"

Too late. In one swift motion Ty had grabbed her and their lips were fused in a kiss so deep, so hard, that Janna had to remind herself to breathe. The taste of beer mingling with mutual desire overwhelmed her, warmth climbing through her like the sun. *Yes,* she longed to sigh. *Yeess.* But just as she allowed herself to relax into his arms, longing for it to go on, he ended the kiss, gently pushing her away.

"Thought you might need a reminder of what you're missing," he whispered, and turning with what she thought was a mildly triumphant smile, returned to his teammates at the end of the bar, who stood hooting and cheering like the yahoos they were.

Except Kevin Gill. His expression seemed to be one of pity—not for her, but for Ty. Perhaps for both of them. Unable to bear his gaze, Janna looked away, and taking her gin and tonic from the bartender, went in search of a place where she could quietly fade away without too much fuss.

Christmas Eve. Janna was in her old childhood bedroom. Downstairs, merriment and good cheer were prevailing quite loudly, nearly drowning out the strains of *A Bing Crosby Christmas* which her father insisted on playing at their open house for as long as she could remember. She had put in her face time, greeting her parents' friends and making small talk with her father's most important clients. It dawned on her, as she watched her infinitely charming, cocktail-driven mother circulate among the guests, making sure everyone was happy and well watered, that this is where she herself had acquired her ability to work a room. It was genetic.

After she was sure she had been seen by all, she made a small plate of hors d'oeuvres, poured herself a well-deserved glass of champagne, and crept upstairs to her old boudoir, fully intending to reappear after she'd had a small taste of peace and quiet.

The room hadn't changed since she'd last occupied it as a teenager: same canopy bed with matching dresser and armoire, same plush white carpet. The back of her door was still covered with a collage of Playbills from Broadway shows she had attended, and the plump, pink silk divan she used to carelessly toss her clothing over still sat in the corner by the built-in bookcases. This was the room in which she used to dream. How fitting, then, that sitting here now on her marshmallow soft bed, her thoughts strayed to Ty.

She was angry with him for oh-so-many reasons: his stance—non-stance—on Lubov; his refusal to give two minutes of time to the men who signed his checks; his kissing her at the party. She shouldn't have let him do it. Instead, she should have made a great show of pushing him away. Everyone around them thought his grabbing her was a joke, but they both knew better. He said he wanted to show her what she was missing. Did that mean he was missing it, too? Or was he just trying to get under her skin?

She used to scoff at friends who claimed to miss their lovers to the point of actually aching. Now she knew they weren't exaggerating. She ached for him, ached so badly that she fantasized about putting anger aside and confessing to him she didn't care where he stood on the Lubov case, she simply couldn't go one more day without feeling his body next to hers. After the Christmas party, she had picked up the phone at least half a dozen times, but each time she chickened out. The prospect of rejection was too devastating to contemplate, the depth of her own need a source of shame and weakness to her.

Miserable, she drank deeply from her flute of champagne. She wished Theresa were here. Janna had invited her, but apparently, not being with the family on Christmas Eve was tantamount to treason among the Falconetti clan, and she'd had to decline. *Theresa is doing pretty well considering,* Janna thought. She suffered from sporadic panic attacks and nightmares now, but her therapy really seemed to be helping, and she was as determined as ever to take the Lubov case to the bitter end if need be. Were she in that position, Janna didn't know if she'd be keeping it together as well. She decided to call the Falconetti house to wish them a Merry Christmas, but just as she picked up the phone on her nightstand, there was a small knock on the door, and Wills popped his head in.

"Hiding?"

"For a bit." Janna replaced the phone and patted the space beside her on the bed. Wills entered, quietly closing the door behind him. He was flushed and bright-eyed, making him look younger than his twelve years.

"Have you been sneaking sips of dad's 'Hop, Skip, and Go Naked' punch?" Janna questioned suspiciously.

"Mom let me have a glass," he replied defensively, flopping down beside her. "Whazzup?" he asked as if she were one of his school friends.

"Things are fine. How about you?"

"Okay. I'm kinda—"

He began coughing, a deep, rattling cough that he'd been battling all day. Janna gently patted him on the back until he returned to himself.

"Should I get you some water?" she asked.

Wills shook his head no.

"That cough sounds awful," Janna noted with concern.

"It's just a cough," Wills pointed out testily. "It's not a big deal."

"If you say so. But you sound like a dying goose."

Wills made a face and plucked a pig in the blanket from her paper plate. "How are the Blades?"

"Fine."

"How's Ty Gallagher?"

A big fat jerk. Janna reached for a cracker slathered with brie and took a bite. "He's okay."

"Skyler says he's gay."

Cracker crumbs flew indelicately from Janna's mouth as she choked. "What?" she barely managed to croak as she wiped them away.

"Sky says he's gay. She said they went on a date, and he would barely even kiss her when most guys fall at her feet and are all over her. She said it's obvious he's gay."

"I see." Janna bit her lip, barely able to contain her laughter. *Oh, boy, baby sister, are you ever wrong on that score.* It made her happy to realize Ty had been telling the truth when he claimed he hadn't slept with Skyler—though why it should matter to her now, she didn't know. "What do you think?" she asked Wills.

Wills shrugged. "I don't think he is."

"How come?"

"'Cause that time you took me to the rink? He kept checking out your boobs."

"Wills!" Janna exclaimed, mortified.

"Well, it's true," Wills protested. He crammed another pig in a blanket in his mouth. "It doesn't matter what he is, anyway. He's just great."

"Yes, he is," Janna agreed quietly, suddenly filled with sadness. Obviously, she was having a minor nervous breakdown. One minute she was about to bust a gut laughing at Skyler's assumption that lack of attraction to her equaled homosexuality, the next she was about to weep. And why? Because she'd killed a casual sexual relationship with a big dumb jock that never would have gone anywhere anyway? *Puh-lease.* She had an extreme case of the holiday blues, that's all. Another glass of champagne and she'd find herself sobbing to "Have Yourself A Merry Little Christmas."

"Whatcha lookin' so serious for, squirt?" Wills grabbed her in an affectionate headlock and gave her a noogie.

"Don't *you* call *me* squirt," Janna warned with mock seriousness, backing out of his headlock and retaliating by mussing his hair, which she knew he hated. "What do you say you and I go back downstairs?"

"It's boring down there," Wills lamented. "Plus Dad won't take off the CD by that dead guy."

"So we'll sneak into the kitchen and steal some cookies. You know Mom won't be putting them out until the bitter end."

"I thought you wanted to hide."

Janna shrugged, moving toward the door. "Can't hide from yourself."

"Huh?"

"Never mind. Let's go downstairs."

CHAPTER

12

New Year's Eve. Was there any night more laden with expectation?

Slumped on his couch channel surfing, Ty wondered just how he was going to ring out the old and bring in the new. It was the first time in years a game wasn't scheduled, and he didn't quite know what to do with himself. He was used to being out there on the ice, in front of an unusually tanked up and rambunctious crowd.

Afterward, he'd attend a small party with the coaches, players, trainers and their wives and girlfriends. Or, if the game were away, he'd board a chartered plane bound for home, the "party" taking place as players roamed the aircraft's aisles drinking champagne from clear plastic cups and toasting each other. But instead he was here, all alone. On the biggest night to party in the greatest party city in the world, his plans consisted of—what? Lumbering into the kitchen for another Perrier? *Christ.*

Truth be told, he had been invited to a bunch of parties. Some of the guys were going for a quiet dinner in Brooklyn at Dante's, the restaurant Michael Dante's family owned, and others were having casual get-togethers in the city, but he needed a little break from the boys, especially after being on the road with them the past week. He'd gotten a few invites to some swanky "do's", too—a couple of them being thrown by folks he didn't know from Adam, but who knew an A-list guest when they saw one. But he was in no mood to do the monkey-suit routine.

That left a standing invitation to go out for a nice dinner with Kevin and Abby, but having just spent Christmas with them, he didn't want to wear out his welcome. Christmas had been great, it always was, but this year he had felt somewhat awkward being there, like he didn't belong. Christmas was a time for families, and much as he and Kevin were like brothers, the fact remained that the Gills were one unit. He was good old "Uncle Ty," the bachelor. The same role he'd played for years. Maybe that's why this Christmas had left him feeling depressed. It was the first time he really had a sense of what he might be missing by making hockey his first love rather than a real, flesh and blood woman.

Which meant he had to rustle up *something* to do tonight or else he'd wind up on the ledge. No way was he going to sit home alone like some pathetic, lonely loser. He reached for his address book and flipped it open. The first name and number that he saw was Linda B.

Linda B . . . He wracked his brains . . . Who was Linda B? He looked down to check his notes beside her name. "Likes limos," was all it said. So much for Linda B.

Next up was Christie. That was it, just Christie. Ty paused thoughtfully. He remembered Christie, all right. Who wouldn't? Perfect body, long dark hair, a real she-devil. *Mmm, Christie.* Maybe he'd call her. But first he'd examine his other options.

Denise Duncan . . . didn't remember her and there were no notes. . . . Elul. Elul? He squinted at his own scrawly handwriting. "Israeli belly dancer. Talks a lot." *Sorry, Elul.*

Tonight is not your lucky night. Francois . . ."Thin, French, a biter." Ty shuddered and crossed Francois from his book, wondering why he'd even included her in the first place. If he remembered correctly, he'd spent the week after Francois looking like he'd been attacked by a cheetah.

He sighed, and started thumbing through the book at random. He was about to give up when it fell open to a particular page. Ty looked down at the name and number written there, and a slow smile spread across his face. Of course. That's whom he'd call. He knew she probably wasn't even home, but what the hell? What was life without risk? And if she was home and said yes, well, he knew just what they'd do for fun.

"You're pathetic. Completely and *utterly* pathetic." Theresa tsked.

Janna turned the volume of the TV up one notch louder. It was New Year's Eve, and Theresa was going out dancing with her brother Phil and a bunch of his friends. They had invited Janna, but she had declined, on the grounds she couldn't dance worth a damn. Really, she just wanted to hole up in the apartment and torture herself, imagining which supermodel Ty was wining and dining over a romantic, candlelit dinner.

"I'm sorry, I can't let you do this." Theresa grabbed the remote and pointing it at the TV like a weapon, turned it off.

Janna sighed. "Theresa."

"You don't think it's pathetic lying alone on the couch on New Year's Eve, watching *The Way We Were*?"

"I watch it every year," Janna protested.

"Not alone on New Year's Eve you don't." She tried wheedling. "C'mon, Jan."

"Theresa, I told you. I'm just not in the mood to go out partying, okay?" She burrowed deeper beneath the comforter tucked under her chin and stared her friend down. "Now please give me back the remote."

Theresa reluctantly handed it over. "I'm not in the mood either. But I'm going. This is all about that lunkhead, isn't it?"

"Lunkhead?"

"Gallagher."

Janna switched the TV back on. "What about him?"

"You're pining for him."

"I don't pine, Theresa."

"Fine. Then you're moping." She slipped on heels that had her towering over Janna like a building. "How do I look?"

Janna grinned up at her. "Great."

"I can tell Phil to wait if you want to get dressed real quick and put on some makeup. He won't mind."

"No, thank you." She craned her neck to look past Theresa. "Now could you please move? Hubbell and Katie are about to meet for the first time."

Theresa groaned in frustration and snatched up her beaded purse from the steamer trunk. "You are the most stubborn woman I've ever met." She leaned down and gave Janna a quick peck on the cheek. "Remember, I'm crashing at my parents' house."

"Have a great time."

"You, too," Theresa called as she hurried toward the door. "Don't eat too many Ring Dings."

"I won't," Janna promised.

She hit "pause" and watched Theresa go. When she heard all three locks on the door click into place, she settled back down and relaxed. Okay, so maybe she was pathetic. But so what? She could have done worse: she could have accepted Robert's invitation to attend an all-night reading of the poems of Leonard Nimoy. Besides, what was wrong with being alone on New Year's Eve? She hated all that false, manufactured gaiety, the pressure to

have a good time. Having a good time should come natu-
rally, it shouldn't be an obligation.

She turned her attention to her supplies on the steamer
trunk/coffee table. Ring Dings, Krispy Kremes, Diet Coke.
A copy of *Ghost* in case she wanted more tear-jerking
amour after Redford and Streisand. *Theresa doesn't know
what she's talking about. Pathetic? Club Janna is the place
to be, baby.*

She plumped the pillows behind her, tore open the bag
of Doritos, and hit "play." No sooner had she made herself
comfortable in optimal reclining-cum-dining mode than
the phone rang. To pick up or not to pick up? A creature of
habit, she picked up.

"Hello?"

There was a split second of hesitation on the other end.
"Janna? It's Ty."

Oh. My. God.

"Ty," Janna replied, hoping the mild squeak she'd just
heard in her own voice wasn't detectable on the other end
of the phone. "What's up?"

"Go to your living room window and pull back the curtains."

"What?" Drunk, he had to be drunk. And it wasn't even
midnight yet.

"Just do what I say," Ty urged. "Go to the window."

"Is this some kind of joke?" She had visions of opening
her curtains to find herself being mooned by the Blades.

"It's not a joke," Ty assured her. "Just do it, okay? Trust
me."

"Okay," Janna replied reluctantly. She sat up, Doritos
scattering, and with the comforter still wrapped around
her, went to the huge bank of windows facing the street
and pulled back the curtains. Down below, she saw a cab
parked in front of a phone booth. In the phone booth, waving up at her, was Ty.

"What the—?"

"Get dressed. No need for anything fancy, jeans and a sweater will do."

"Ty—"

"Don't bother with makeup, either, you don't need it. Meet me down here in five minutes."

She was about to agree when it dawned on her that he'd shown up just assuming she had nothing else going on, like she was some kind of wallflower-loser. Well, she'd show him.

"I'm sorry, I have other plans."

There was a split second of stunned silence before he replied. "Then why are you in sweats with a comforter wrapped around your shoulders?"

"Because my date and I are having a nice, cozy New Year's Eve at home. In fact, he should be here any minute."

"Really? Well, I'll just wait here outside your building and check him out when the doorman lets him in." He hung up the phone.

"Shit!" Janna yelled, backing away from the curtains and slamming down the phone. Why couldn't she live on a higher floor? He had seen her sweats! Now what? She stormed back to the couch, flinging herself onto it. When the phone rang again, as she knew it would, she was not going to pick it up, she was not. Five minutes passed. Ten. Finally it rang. Taking a deep, steadying breath, she picked it up.

"So where's your Mystery Date?"

"He just called to say he can't make it. He has the flu. Can I help you with something?"

"I told you. Get dressed and meet me downstairs in five minutes. I have a surprise for you."

"I need ten minutes at least."

"Fine, ten." She could practically hear him frowning. Meanwhile, her head was swimming.

"No offense, but how did you know I'd be home?"

"I didn't. I took a chance. You know the old saying: Who dares, wins. See you in ten." He hung up.

Stunned, Janna put the phone back in its cradle. She didn't know what to do. Didn't know what to think. She felt numb and excited and scared all at the same time. In a state of shock, she moved to her bedroom to get dressed. Jeans and a sweater, he'd said. That she could do. But no makeup? Forget it. She never went anywhere without at least a little mascara and lipstick, and tonight was no exception. Tonight was New Year's Eve—one, she had a feeling, she would never forget.

Anxiety took hold as she followed Ty through the players' entrance to Met Gar. All the way over in the cab, she'd been unable to get him to confess what he was up to or where they were going. "It's a surprise," was all he'd say, but she noticed his gym bag was sitting quietly at his feet. She noticed, too, how handsome he looked, his strong jaw host to the faintest hint of a five o'clock shadow, his blonde hair just the tiniest bit mussed, the way she liked it. She thought he might have cologne on, but wasn't sure. His natural scent was clean and vaguely citrusy, his skin tangy. *Tangy skin,* she said to herself derisively. *Get a grip*.

When the cab had pulled up in front of the arena, she didn't know what to think. The first thing that flashed across her mind was that he was bringing her to some private party for the players, the thought of which left her completely unnerved. She spent five days a week surrounded by the Blades and their personnel. Why on earth would Ty think she'd want to spend her free time with them as well?

Her next thought was that perhaps he'd sustained a blow to the head at the game against Chicago the night before—a game that she had made a point of not watching—and had gone totally psycho, his gym bag hiding a machete with which he planned to slice and dice her in the locker room. But his mood didn't seem particularly dark; in fact, he seemed to be happy, his big, bad secret making his handsome face glow with delight.

"Care to tell me what we're doing here?" she questioned as he led her through the bowels of the building.

"You'll see." They passed the Blades' locker room, the coaches' office, and were halfway up the carpeted ramp the players used to get on and off the ice when Janna halted.

"I'm not taking another step until you tell me what's going on."

"You really want to know?"

"I really want to know."

"I'm going to teach you how to skate."

Janna just stared at him. "I don't own skates."

"Don't worry. It's been taken care of." He bent over and unzipping his gym bag, pulled out a pair of size six skates which he dangled in front of her face, smiling devilishly. "Shall we?"

Janna hesitated. "Look, this is a wonderful surprise, but I can't learn to skate. Not tonight."

"Why?"

"Because I just can't," she said peevishly. "I'm tired."

Ty scratched philosophically at the stubble on his chin. "You're just afraid of falling on your ass in front of me."

"I am not."

"Yes, you are."

"No, I am not," Janna insisted indignantly.

"Then prove it. Come sit on the players' bench with me and put your skates on."

"Fine," Janna muttered, following him up the rest of the ramp and out to the bench.

Eerie . . . that was the feeling within the empty arena. Row upon row of empty seats surrounding them, and the silent, smooth ice . . . Janna felt as if she were violating some sacred space. Not so Ty; he sat down on the bench and laced up his skates one, two, three. *What clout,* Janna marveled to herself, *to be able to pick up the phone and say you wanted the rink at Met Gar for your own private use and presto! It was done. Talk about impressive.*

Skates on, Ty stood before her. He clucked his tongue disapprovingly. "You're not doing a very good job lacing up."

"How did you know what shoe size I was?"

Ty shrugged. "I looked in your shoes once when you were in the bathroom at my apartment." He knelt before her and slipping one skate on her foot, began lacing her up. Janna could feel her defenses melting.

"Why did you call me?" she asked softly.

Ty's hands stopped moving, and he looked up into her face. "Because you're the person I wanted to spend New Year's Eve with."

Janna nodded with understanding. That was it; no more needed to be said. She watched as he lowered his head and resumed fitting her skates to her feet. When he was through, he stood up again, and offering her his hand, helped her up off the bench.

"How do they feel. Too tight?"

"I don't know. How are they supposed to feel?"

"Stiff. You want ankle support."

Janna looked down at her feet, flexing them. "I guess they're okay." She hoped her face didn't betray how vulnerable she was feeling, knowing humiliation was right around the corner.

"Ready?" he asked, smiling.

"No."

"C'mon." Still holding her hand, they took a few careful steps away from the bench and out onto the ice. Janna instinctively reached out for the boards.

"This wasn't a very good idea."

"Listen. Keep your legs locked, and let me take your hands so I can pull you around, give you a sense of what it feels like. Then, when you're ready, I'll show you how to skate."

Janna clung to the boards. "If I let go, I'll fall."

"Not if you give me both your hands. Trust me." He gently took her hands in his. "Legs locked?" Janna nodded, terrified. "Here we go."

Skating backward, he slowly began to pull her around the ice.

"See?" he said. "It's not so bad."

"Not for you. I feel like an idiot."

"Don't. This is how everyone starts."

"Even you?" she asked skeptically.

"Even me." Gliding, he continued leading her. "Like it?" he asked hopefully.

"I guess," Janna replied nervously. She was more focused on the ease with which he could skate backward than the actual sensation of moving across the ice. "You make it look so easy."

"It is, eventually. Everything is."

"Everything?"

His eyes caught hers. "Everything," he repeated. "Things can be as hard, or as easy, as you make them."

Janna blushed. "I see."

"I know you do."

They circled the ice two, three, four times. Janna began relaxing a little, allowing herself to enjoy the feeling of sliding smoothly across the rink's glassy surface. "Having fun?" Ty asked. Janna nodded. He slowed to a stop. "Ready to try it out for yourself?"

Janna felt her stomach contract. "I guess."

"Okay. Watch me." He skated away from her slowly. "See how I push off with each foot? Push, glide. Push, glide." He circled back to her. "Let's try it. I'll hold you so you don't fall."

"Push, glide," Janna repeated to herself as Ty stood slightly behind her, his hands around her waist.

"Ready when you are."

"Okay."

Slowly, tentatively, she pushed off with her right foot.

The front of the skate dug into the ice, and she would have gone sprawling were Ty not holding on to her.

"You okay?" Ty asked.

"Yes," Janna snapped, embarrassed.

"You pushed down. Just push forward."

"Okay," Janna huffed. Careful, she pushed off with her right foot . . . then her left. Her right foot . . . then her left.

"You're doing great," Ty told her.

Janna's face lit up. "Really?"

"Yup. Keep it going."

"This is fun," she admitted giddily.

"Just wait until I let you go."

Janna panicked. "Don't," she begged. "Not yet."

"Don't worry," Ty assured her. "I'm right here."

Gradually, almost imperceptibly, he let one hand slip from her waist while tightening his hold with the other. Eventually, they were skating side by side.

"You're holding me up," Janna accused.

"Bull. You're skating."

"When are you going to let go?"

"I don't know."

Maybe never, Janna found herself wishing.

"Just concentrate on keeping moving."

And so she did. Around and around they went, Janna gaining in confidence. Though she knew she would never experience the exhilaration hockey players felt as they sped around the ice—fast, powerful, aggressive—even this small, stumbling taste was enough to help her appreciate why he loved it so. She glanced up at Ty; he looked content. Janna hoped it had something to do with being with her.

They were on their seventh lap when Ty finally slipped his remaining hand from around her waist. It took a split second for Janna to process she was skating without him. Once she did, she tumbled to the ice.

"Shoot." Ty skated back to her, helping her to her feet

"At least you didn't fall on your face," he chuckled, looking at her damp behind.

Janna was too mortified to respond.

"This time, I'm going to hold you, but when I let you go, keep skating. Just do it—don't think about yourself doing it. Got it?"

Janna shot him a look. "Aye, aye, Captain."

"Here we go."

Side by side again, they took off skating. Janna was a nervous wreck, only half listening to the small talk Ty was making. Her whole body—cold butt included—was tensed in preparation of his letting go of her. But when it happened, she followed his instructions and just kept moving. Amazingly enough, she found she was skating on her own.

"You've got it!" Ty called.

I've got it, Janna thought excitedly, and promptly fell again. "Don't help me," she called out to him. "I want to get up on my own."

Shaky, she rose, reaching out to the boards with one hand for support. Ty stood far down ice from her.

"C'mon," he coaxed. "Skate to me."

Janna shook her head. "You're too far away."

"Give up now and I kick your icy butt. That's a promise."

Sucking in her breath, Janna cursed him and with great determination, pushed off the boards. She nearly fell immediately, but regained her balance and through sheer force of will remained upright, working her way toward him in slow, choppy fashion.

"That's it," he enthused. He clapped, holding out his arms. "C'mon, Blue Eyes. Almost there."

Haltingly, Janna skated the final few feet toward him. When she was close enough for him to touch, he guided her into the safety of his arms.

"I knew you could do it," he said proudly, enfolding her in an embrace. "I knew . . ."

He stopped, his gaze gentle as he looked down into her

face. Then his mouth was on hers, the kiss sweet and tender, her own lips responding in kind as he drew her in closer, almost as if he wished their bodies could meld together right there on the ice.

"What do you say we continue our New Year's Eve celebration back at my apartment?" he whispered in her ear seductively.

"How about mine?"

"Why yours?"

"I've got Ring Dings and donuts and Diet Coke."

"Well, in that case," he replied, kissing her nose, "your place it is."

CHAPTER

13

His instinct was to devour, possess. To take what was his and find quick release for the ache building within him. And yet, gazing at her tenderly as she stood beside the sleigh bed in her tiny bedroom lighting a candle, he was overwhelmed with a sense of wanting to know every inch of her. He imagined his mouth lingering on the pearl white skin at the nape of her neck, could almost feel the enticing firmness of her small, sexy breasts as he cupped them in his hands. Such sensations could not, should not, be rushed. And so, despite the hot-blooded voice in his head feverishly urging him on, he determined instead to devour her slowly.

Candle lit, she turned to him. The flickering light shimmered gold and danced off the blond of her hair, creating an effect almost halolike. Silently, Ty reached out and put his hands on her shoulders, pleased with the mild shiver that ran through her as he slowly slid his hands down the length of her arms, his fingers reaching for hers. Head cocked, she looked as if she might be getting ready to ask

him a question. But no; it was more an anticipatory move
as she stood on tiptoes and kissed him full on the mouth,
the mere taste of her reminding him to take his time.

There was hunger in her kiss, and urgency. If he followed her lead, they'd be tearing their clothes off and div-
ing for each other within seconds. He had to slow her
down, make her see that their coming together would be
worth the wait.

Gently withdrawing his mouth from hers, he kept hold
of her hand and sat down on the bed. She did the same. He
could hear her breath hitching as he folded her back like an
empty dress, a languid, contented smile playing across her
beautiful face. Moved, he reached out and caressed the
softness of her cheek.

Holding her gaze, basking in the quiet happiness he saw
reflected there, he gently moved on top of her. Janna gave
a small purr as he pressed his body against hers. Ty
watched as she deliberately arched her hips against his, a
challenge. Aroused, he buried his face in the sweetness of
her neck and throat, his lips teasing, skimming, never resting. Janna moaned, her body twisting slightly beneath
his—restless, tormented. At last she reached for his head,
her hands grabbing his hair.

"Ty," she whispered. He lifted his head from his teasing
to lay eyes upon her again. "I want you so badly."

"Soon," he promised, the ache within him spiking. Sliding down her body, he put his hands to her breasts, touching, caressing, taking his time, making sure he'd memorized
the feel of her, the curve of her. Her response told him sub-
mission was imminent: Janna's head fell back as if she
were offering him the purity of her throat as a sacrifice.

Head reeling, he again chose to feast there, careful as he
sunk his teeth into her warm, soft flesh. When she cried
out, her naked arousal drove him damn close to the brink,
but he was determined not to surrender control, not yet.
Rolling off her, he calmly undid the buttons of the vel-
veteen shirt she was wearing, revealing a black lace bra

underneath. He saw Janna tense in sweet anticipation of his undoing the clasps at the back and freeing her. But instead, he left the bra on, his mouth closing over the lace covering her right nipple, small sparks of pleasure shooting through him as she gasped.

"Please, Ty, now," she begged.

"Soon," he repeated gruffly, wondering how much longer he'd be able to hold off. He pulled her so she was sitting upright, sliding her shirt from her shoulders. And then, planting a series of delicate butterfly kisses across her collarbone, he finally unfastened the bra and gently removed it. "You're beautiful," he murmured, kissing the cleft between her breasts.

Tears glistened in Janna's eyes. "No one's ever told me that before," she whispered, sounding as if she were trying to catch hold of her own breath.

"Then no one's ever really seen you before."

He moved to kiss her breasts, but she stopped him, just for a moment, to take the reins herself. He watched her careful concentration as she tugged off his sweater and the turtleneck beneath. Pleasure pumped through him as he wondered what she might do. Touch him? Kiss him? Lick him? He closed his eyes. A second later, he felt a burning sensation as her palms began stroking his chest, white hot, the need within him driving him over the precipice of reason into passion.

Grabbing her they fell back on the bed, mouth seeking mouth, flesh seeking flesh, his hands moving faster now, but still not rushing, still taking her in. He was determined to memorize it all: the sweet curve of her ribs, the gentle rocking motion of her hips, the way her skin seemed to rise in temperature beneath his touch. And the taste of her, too, *God, yes*. Sweet yet salty. The taste of a woman who hungers and is not afraid to show it. The taste alone was enough to drive him headlong into oblivion.

Lower and lower he explored with both hands and mouth, pausing only to tear away her jeans and panties.

Janna's eyes fluttered closed as her body trembled. Sliding off the bed, Ty knelt on the floor before her. Ankles, calves, knees and shins—how often they were neglected, and how soft hers were. He stroked and kissed them, his lips and fingertips entranced with their silkiness. And then there were her inner thighs—couldn't forget those. He leaned forward, kissing, nipping, while Janna begged him with her body to go on. And so, not wanting to disappoint, he parted her legs and put his mouth to the slick, wet heat.

She came all at once, in a flood, her body quivering violently as her voice cried out for release. It was more than his heated blood could take. Rising, he tore off the rest of his clothing and slid deep inside her, both their bodies shuddering with recognition and surprise as she wrapped her legs tight around his waist, the fit exquisite.

The ocher glow of the candlelight, the musky scent of mutual desire, even the delicacy of the snow that had begun falling outside—all conspired to make his heart soar with the need to complete her, to close the circle. He sought out her hands, and twining fingers, they began moving together slowly, their ease that of lovers who can choose to linger, or jump start the tempo and succumb to wild pleasure. Ty let her decide, holding on and on until her frenzied cries of "Now! Now!" let him know his own time had come. Taking a deep breath, he plunged, senses exploding as he finally, joyfully, emptied himself into her.

She was afraid to drift off to sleep. She was certain that if she did, she would wake up to find herself drooling on the couch, the evening nothing but a dream. She reached out and touched Ty's hip to reassure herself. He responded by rolling toward her side of the bed, his expression dreamy.

"Hi," he whispered sleepily, reaching for her.

"Hi. Did I wake you?"

"Nah, I was just dozing." He lifted his head, peering around the darkened room. "What time is it?"

"About three."

"Mmm."

He lay back down, eyes drifting shut once again. Janna wondered if he was a heavy sleeper. She had no way of knowing, since they'd never spent an entire night together.

"Ty?"

"Mmm?"

"Will you stay the rest of the night?"

"Of course." He dozily kissed the top of her head.

"Good." Janna nestled deeper in his arms. The candle had long since sputtered out, but even so the room seemed cast in a pale silver glow, the result, she thought, of the snow falling outside.

"I wonder how many inches we'll wind up getting," she wondered aloud.

Ty yawned. "Maybe there'll be a blizzard."

"And then you guys won't have to fly to Ottawa on Monday."

Ty groaned. "I don't want to think about that."

Janna traced a lazy pattern on his chest with her finger. "What do you want to think about?"

He opened his eyes. "Truth be told? Food. I'm starving."

"Me, too," she confessed with relief. She was glad to know she wasn't the only one whose stomach was crying out in desperation. She sat up. "What should I make us?"

"Nothing. It's three in the morning. I say we have a junk food feast right here in the bedroom. Where are those goodies you lured me here with?"

"I thought athletes didn't eat junk food," Janna teased.

"This one eats what he damn well pleases. Bring it on."

Laughing, Janna rose and slipped on her robe before heading out into the living room. All her goodies were just where she'd left them. She gathered an armful, and returned to Ty, who had sat up and put the bedside light on.

"Why do I feel like there's something vaguely decadent about this?" he asked as Janna spread the junk food out on the comforter before rejoining him in bed.

"Decadent would be smearing a Ring Ding on your chest and licking it off. This is merely fun."

"Ah." He reached for the bag of Doritos and shook some chips into his hand. "Where's your roommate?" he asked casually.

It hadn't crossed Janna's mind that in bringing him back here the subject of Theresa, and all it entailed, might come up. But now it had.

"She went out dancing with her brother." She watched Ty's eyes for any sign of disapproval, registering relief when she saw none. "She's staying at her folks tonight."

Ty just nodded.

"I think we need to talk about this—you know, the whole Theresa and Lubov thing."

Ty's expression turned guarded. "Okay."

"I was wrong to storm out of your apartment the way I did," Janna admitted. "I was also wrong to hold you to a double standard." She sighed deeply as she began unwrapping her Ring Ding. "I think the best way for you and me to deal with the situation is not to discuss it at all, since it's something we're never going to see eye to eye on."

"You sure you can do that?" Ty questioned.

"I can try." She bit into her treat. "Mmm, this is good."

"The Coke is warm, though. Oh, well." He munched away happily on his Doritos.

"There's something else I think we should talk about," Janna continued.

"Yeah?"

She hesitated. "Us."

Ty looked unfazed. "What about us?"

Janna suddenly felt shy. "Are we the same us as we were before—you know, casual?"

Ty shrugged. "I don't see why not."

Janna closed her eyes for a moment so he couldn't see the disappointment there.

"Good," she lied. What else could she do? He didn't want a relationship. She'd take what she could get, despite her growing feelings for him. She would just have to work at keeping her emotions in check, is all. She opened her eyes. "We'll have to continue keeping it secret, though. Lou said if he ever found out I was 'consorting' with any of the players, he'd fire me on the spot."

"It's better to keep it secret anyway. Like we discussed when we first started, you don't want Kidco thinking you're whoring yourself to get what you want PR-wise, and I don't want them thinking I'm sleeping with you just to get out of doing stuff."

"Speaking of which—"

"Don't." His eyes darkened. "You already know my answer."

"I wasn't talking about that." She finished her Ring Ding. "You really should toe the line a bit more with Corporate. They were very unhappy about you ignoring them at the Christmas party."

Ty gave a small snort of displeasure. "Too bad. They can kiss my ass."

"It wouldn't hurt to kiss theirs just once."

"Maybe I would if we were in a slump. But we're twenty-four, twelve and three right now, Janna. Do you have any idea how amazing those stats are? We keep focused, and we will bring the Cup back to New York this year. In the meantime, every game has been sold out, meaning the boys at Kidco get to bask in our reflected glory. We're nothing more than a way for them to keep their name in front of the public."

"Why do you think they bought the team in the first place, Ty? It's all part of a marketing strategy, a way to grab the eighteen–to–thirty-five male demo they've been missing. "

"*Exactly,* and that's all they care about: demos and

branding and making sure everyone on the planet knows the name Kidco," Ty retorted. "Not the players. Not the art of the game. Not the integrity of it. Not—"

Janna stuffed a tortilla chip in his mouth. "Enough. I get your point. Clearly this is another topic we would do well to avoid whenever possible."

"Agreed," Ty mumbled as he chewed. He gave her a heavy-lidded look. "I kinda liked that," he murmured.

"What?"

"The way you took control and jammed the chip in my mouth. It was kinda sexy."

"Really?" A frisson of warmth shuddered through her. "I'll have to keep that in mind."

"I have a better idea. Why don't we finish eating and continue celebrating the New Year?"

"A grand idea," Janna agreed, licking chocolate crumbs from her fingers. "Shall we?"

The buzzing woke her. Thinking it was the phone, she reached out to answer it. Ty muttered that it was the doorman calling, and her foggy brain was then able to process the need to get out of bed. She staggered to the intercom, bleary-eyed, and pressed the button to speak.

"Yes, Jimmy?"

"Uh, sorry to disturb you so early in the morning, Miss MacNeil, but there's a little boy down here named Wills who says he's your brother."

Janna was instantly, jarringly, awake. "Oh my God. Send him up."

She hurried back to the bedroom for her robe, glancing at the bedside clock. Six o'clock in the morning New Year's Day and Wills was here. A shudder passed through her as her mind raced with all the possible reasons for his appearance. *God, please help me to keep calm,* she prayed. *Please*.

She quietly closed the bedroom door on Ty, who ap

peared to have fallen back asleep, and waited for her doorbell to ring. When it did, her hands were shaking so badly she had a difficult time undoing all the locks and opening it. But open it she eventually did, to the heart-wrenching sight of her little brother, face smeared with tears, standing alone in the hallway.

"I'm sorry," he choked, "but I couldn't think of anywhere else to go."

"Don't be silly." She pulled him inside and hugged him to her tight, her own tears threatening when Wills began sobbing against her chest.

"I hate them!" he wailed. "I hate living there!"

"Sshh, it's okay, everything is going to be okay." Still holding on to him, she closed the door and steered the two of them into the living room, onto the couch. With the sleeve of her bathrobe, she wiped his tears away. "Tell me what happened."

He hiccuped. "Mom and Dad went out for New Year's Eve. Mom got totally wasted and when they came home they started to fight. They were breaking plates and shit, I couldn't sleep. I—"

He stopped dead. Janna followed his line of sight and turned to see Ty walking towards them, clad only in his jeans. His hair was a tousled mess, and it was clear he was struggling to wake up. Wills was going to want to know what the captain of the New York Blades was doing coming out of his sister's bedroom. She could worry about that later.

"It's okay. You can talk in front of Ty."

Hesitant, Wills waited until Ty situated himself on the other side of Janna before continuing. "Mom came up to my room and sat on the end of my bed and wouldn't shut up." His breath caught. "She said she'd never loved Dad, and if she hadn't gotten pregnant with me she would have left years ago and all this other stuff." He stifled a sob. "Finally she left and I ran downstairs and took some money from her purse and caught a cab to the train station. And here I am."

"Oh, honey." He looked so small sitting there, a lost, scared little boy. "I'm so sorry." She brushed the hair out of his eyes. "So they don't know you're here?"

"No, and I don't want you to tell them!"

"Sweetie, I have to."

"They're probably not even awake," Wills snorted.

"Then I'll wake them up. Why don't you sit here with Ty, and I'll go give them a call. When I'm done, I'll make us all pancakes for breakfast, okay?"

"Okay," Wills sniffled.

Janna left, leaving Ty alone with her brother. Ty leaned towards him, a look of unmistakable sympathy on his face.

"You okay?"

Wills gave a barely perceptible nod.

"Want anything to drink? A glass of water? Some juice?"

"No, thanks," Wills said in a small voice.

"You know, the same thing used to happen in my family."

Wills eyed him suspiciously. "What thing?"

"My old man used to get toasted and wreck the house."

A look somewhere between disbelief and relief crossed Wills's face. "Really?"

"Oh, yeah. It was a Friday night ritual. He'd get off work, hit the bar with his cronies, then come home three sheets to the wind. Then he'd keep me and my mother up all night babbling about how no one loved or appreciated him, and how crappy his life was because of us . . ." Ty shook his head. "I bet you think it's your fault, right?"

Wills looked down at his feet.

"I bet you think that it's something you're doing, that if you get great grades in school, or really kick ass out on the ice, that they'll love you and things will change. That's what I thought. That's why I became such a good hockey player. To please my old man. He'd wanted to play, but couldn't, so I thought I'd do it for him. I thought it would make him happy if I were great on the ice. That it would make him stop hitting my mom and getting drunk. But you know what? It didn't. Because what was going on really had nothing to do with me, and it wasn't my fault, just like the situation with your parents isn't your fault."

Wills peered back up at him, shy. "So how did you, like, deal with it?"

"I slept over my friends' houses a lot, that was one thing. And when I was old enough to get the hell out of there, I did." He paused. "I also talked to people when I needed to get it off my chest, the way we're doing now."

"Does your dad still drink?" Wills asked.

Ty shrugged. "I don't know. I haven't talked to him in years. But you know what? Any time you feel like talking about this stuff, you can call me, okay? I'll give you my home number and my cell phone number."

Wills was wide-eyed. "You would really do that?"

"To help a brother-in-arms? Sure. But let's keep it between us, okay? I don't want your sister knowing what a softie I am."

"I won't say anything, I swear." He peered at Ty curiously. "Are you and Janna in love?"

Oh, shit, thought Ty. What the hell was he supposed to say? If he told the kid that the only thing he loved was hockey, he'd be sending the wrong message about sex and commitment. On the other hand, if he lied and said yes, God only knew what would follow from that. He settled for the vague catchall, "We're very good friends," and rising from the couch, tilted his head in the direction of the kitchen.

"You hungry?"

"Yeah," Wills said.

"Me, too. Whaddaya say we give your sister a head start on making those pancakes?"

When Wills dutifully followed without asking any more

personal questions, Ty felt as if he'd dodged the biggest bullet of his life.

Heading to Lou's office for the first PR meeting of the new year, Janna's mind was elsewhere. As she expected would be the case, both her parents had been remorseful about what had transpired on New Year's Eve. Even her mother had seemed willing to take responsibility for her actions for the first time. She vowed to cut back on her drinking, and swore she'd seek marital counseling. So did her father.

"I'll believe it when I see it" was Janna's take, but she kept her opinion quiet, since, being their child herself, there was a secret part of her that longed to believe what they were saying. She had left them with a warning: If something like this happened again, she was going to arrange for Wills to come live with her. Judging by the way they bowed and scraped as she made her way out to her car, she had the feeling her words had finally gotten through.

None of this would have happened, though, if it weren't for Ty. It was he who managed to talk Wills into returning to Connecticut. On the ride home, Wills casually boasted that the great Ty Gallagher had given him his number *and* his cell phone number, so he could call *anytime* to "vent." It had taken every ounce of self-control Janna had not to pick up her own cell phone and tell Ty she loved him. This absolute proof that he was a good man with a good heart pushed her simmering feelings over the line from lover to keeper. The only thing that kept her from calling was not knowing if he felt the same.

She reached Lou's door. Was it was possible for him to have added another chin in the three days since she'd seen him last? The thick rolls of wattle beneath his neck were made worse today by a too tight collar that made his flesh bulge and his face red. The man was a heart attack waiting to happen! Since November, Janna was the one driving the two of them back and forth to practice every day. Not just because Lou had trouble maneuvering his bulk behind the steering wheel of his Beamer, but because Janna was afraid one day he'd have a coronary on the parkway and they'd both be history. Volunteering to drive seemed the best solution; she knew there was no way he'd even think of dieting.

"How was your New Year's, doll?" Lou asked, ripping apart a muffin the size of an infant's head. They were waiting for Jack Cowley to show up.

"Good," Janna answered.

"Whatcha do?"

Janna stifled a Cheshire cat grin. "Rented a bunch of videos and stayed home. Nice and quiet, you know. You?"

"Me and the wife hit an all-you-can-eat buffet at the Ponderosa, then came home and watched the ball drop on TV." He stifled a burp. "Same old, same old."

"Sounds like fun." Janna smiled, but it was short-lived as Jack Cowley swept into the room just then. Ever since Theresa had decided to go after Lubov, things between her and Cowley had been more strained than usual, especially since Jack seemed to take such pleasure out of digging up dirt on Theresa. Janna had taken to ignoring him every time he passed her in the hall, waving a folder and murmuring, "Your virginal little friend's lawyer better be *good*." It was so counterproductive, so combative. Lou, bless his fat head, seemed oblivious to the tension.

"Hey, hey, Jackie boy," Lou crowed. "How was your New Year's Eve?"

Jack sniffed. "Passable." Unwinding his silk scarf from around his neck, he carefully folded his Burberry over the back of the couch, opposite Janna.

"Whatcha do?" Lou asked, while Janna pretended to be fascinated by the picture of Lou with Wayne Gretzky hanging directly over Jack's head.

"My girlfriend and I cooked a simple meal at home, and repaired to bed early."

Lou chuckled. "In other words—"

Jack cut him dead. "Right."

Janna took her eyes from the picture to see Jack gazing at her, an expression of utter disgust for Lou mottling his face. *Effete snob,* Janna thought. And who on earth would ever go out with him?

"Awright, time to get down to it." Lou glanced at Jack. "First order of business. How you doing getting info on, er—"

"Theresa Falconetti," Jack replied, somehow managing to make it sound like an obscenity. "Great."

"Whatcha got?" Lou asked.

Cowley leveled Janna with a patronizing stare. "Did you know your little friend dated one of the New York Jets while she was in college, as well as two daytime stars in the past two years?"

"So?"

"So she's obviously a starfucker with a 'thing' for jocks and actors."

"I once dated a waiter," Janna shot back. "Does that make me obsessed with food?"

"Depends how you spin it, doesn't it, dear?" Cowley returned sweetly. He turned to Lou. "You want me to plant this?"

Lou barely nodded yes, avoiding Janna's eye.

"Done," Cowley declared triumphantly.

Janna flashed him a murderous look, which he responded to with an oily smile. Lou, meanwhile, looked like he was suffering from indigestion. When he looked to Janna, his expression was almost hesitant. "Doll, I hate to ask this again, but for your pal's sake, have you given any more thought into talking her into dropping the suit?"

"We've been over this repeatedly, Lou. I am not going to talk Theresa out of this."

"Awright, awright," said Lou, backing off. "It's her funeral."

"You mean Lubov's," Janna murmured under her breath. Neither man appeared to hear.

"Next order of business is the road trip. We got Ottawa, Montreal, Edmonton, Washington, Vancouver and Calgary," recited Lou, counting off the venues on his fingers. "Six cities, two weeks. It's gonna be a bitch, as always. MacNeil, you're coming along with me."

Janna blinked. "But—Jack usually goes with you. I mean—"

Lou blinked back. "There a problem?"

"No, not at all." Janna didn't dare look at Cowley, even though she could feel his resentment zeroing in on her like a laser beam. It was becoming all too clear which of them Lou thought worked the hardest.

"Any particular reason for the switch?" Cowley asked flatly.

"Not really. I just thought I'd mix things up a bit, see how it goes. Besides, it'll be nice not to have to share a hotel room with you. That teeth clicking thing you do in your sleep drives me bats."

Janna's face creased with alarm. "This doesn't mean you and I are sharing a room, does it, Lou?"

"Not to worry, baby doll, you'll have your own. Now, let's talk beat writers."

The meeting went on for another forty-five minutes. Afterwards, Janna forced herself to stop by Jack Cowley's office. With everything else going on between them, the last thing she wanted was him thinking she had anything to do with Lou's decision to take her on the road trip instead of him.

"Jack?"

He looked up quickly, hitting a button on his keyboard o his computer screen went blank. *Dirt on Theresa,* Janna ought.

"Look, I want you to know that Lou's decision to take me on the road was totally his own. I—"

"No offense, but I really don't care," Jack snapped. "It's clear you're Lou's little pet, and why not? I'd be his pet, too, if I ran around behind him perpetually kissing his fat ass the way you do." Janna's mouth fell open. "But let's get one thing straight. You and I might share the same job title, but I'm the one who's really second in command here, and I intend to hold on to that position until that sack of lard keels over dead and his job is mine. Until then, I think you'd be wise to remember your place on the PR totem pole. Because I have no intention of letting anything—or anyone—get in my way. *Capisce?*"

"Oh, I *capisce* all right."

Janna headed back to her own office and sat down, stunned. The viciousness, the paranoia . . . clearly Jack Cowley was an insecure man. Vicious and insecure. She should feel sorry for him. But she didn't.

She felt afraid.

CHAPTER
14

Being on the road with the Blades made Janna long for her days as a publicist for *The Wild and the Free.* At least back then, travel usually meant hopping a jet to an exotic location shoot in Florida or Hawaii, even Italy. But here she was, in the dead of January in western Canada, of all places, with a bunch of hockey players and their attendant personnel. The word *exotic* wasn't quite applicable.

It was grueling, and except when she and Lou were working, boring. Much of the time was spent on private planes or buses. Usually she curled up with a book when they were in transit. But concentration was difficult: the players insisted on watching *Slapshot* over and over again, shouting out their favorite lines à la *The Rocky Horror Picture Show.* She knew it was a cult film among players and fans, but still, hearing the same dialogue repeated endlessly truly tested her nerves, which were stretched to the limit anyway.

She'd never accompanied Lou on a prolonged road trip before and was anxious about doing a good job. Every

time they went to meet and grease the local press, she
found herself doing her old *You can do this* chant in her
head. Worse, they were in daily contact with Jack Cowley,
whose hatred of her crackled down the phone lines every
time she had to speak with him. She had the sense he was
just waiting for her to stumble and it unnerved her, even
while making her even more determined to prove to Lou
he hadn't made a mistake in bringing her. The result was
an over-zealousness on her part that prompted Lou to take
her aside four days into the trip and say, "You're allowed
to enjoy yourself, you know."

Which she tried to do, but it was hard, especially with
the Lubov case dogging them everywhere they went. She
was the one who always addressed the issue with the local
media, and she inevitably came away feeling exhausted
and shaken. Lubov himself had taken to staring her down
every time their paths crossed, his mocking gaze meant as
a challenge, one she refused to rise to. To the extent that
she could, she ignored him, but it wasn't always easy.
Once or twice he had deliberately sat across the aisle from
her on the plane or bus, making comments under his breath
in Russian that were no doubt meant to disturb.

Her one comfort was that none of this was going unno-
ticed by Ty, who said nothing but was quietly taking it all
in. Watching him on the road was an education. As was the
case back home, he commanded his players' respect with
authority and dignity. When one of the younger players
missed a plane after a night of carousing, Ty immediately
implemented an eleven P.M. curfew for the road, making
sure the players adhered to it by doing a room check each
night like the jail warden some of them no doubt thought
he was. For once, he was doing something Kidco could be
happy about.

She had been unprepared, though, for the extent to
which his fame followed him outside of New York.
Canada was hockey country, and Ty Gallagher was their
Messiah. Everywhere they went, the team was met by a

large legion of fans. Ty couldn't walk through a hotel lobby without being accosted for an autograph or being asked to pose for a picture. He had taken to ordering room service every night rather than venturing out to a restaurant with Kevin and risk having his meal interrupted repeatedly. And the women . . . God, how Janna hated the women, the way they undressed him with their eyes, ditzy little puck bunnies who thought a Wonderbra coupled with a recitation of his career stats might gain them access to hockey's most eligible bachelor. Little did they know.

Not that she and Ty were in any way obvious. They'd both agreed that delicious as it was seeing each other clandestinely, to attempt anything on the road was suicide. That didn't mean there weren't stolen moments: a longing glance here, a hand discreetly brushing a backside there. One afternoon when Janna had to bring an interview request to Ty and Kevin's room, Ty had risen from his bed and crushed her to him, his kiss fierce and desperate. It had been a wonderful surprise, but curled up alone every night in her hotel room, Janna found herself counting the days until they were back in Manhattan and could really have some fun.

Calgary was the final game of the road trip. There was a blinding snow, and Janna couldn't believe their pilot had chosen to fly, but he did. After a nerve-wracking flight, the Blades' entourage landed with high spirits and weary bodies. They had humiliated Ottawa and been slaughtered by Montreal, bouncing back to rout both Edmonton and Vancouver. They arrived at their Calgary hotel at close to nine P.M. An early morning practice was already scheduled for seven the next day, which the PR team would have to attend as well.

Despite the late hour, Janna and Lou repaired to the hotel's restaurant to go over interview requests and grab a bite to eat. While there, Lou met up with an old friend who'd worked PR with him back when Lou could still see his feet. He joined them for dinner, he and Lou swapping nostalgic tales to which Janna felt obliged to sit and listen.

It was quarter past eleven before there was finally a lull in the conversation where she was able to excuse herself for the night. She hustled out of the restaurant and into the lobby, which remained filled with fans. It was there she spotted Lubov, chatting with two young and giddy-looking girls. She quickly averted her gaze, but it was too late. Their eyes had met and he was now excusing himself from the girls' company and moving towards her rapidly.

"Janna."

She pretended not to hear him and strode purposefully toward the huge bank of elevators opposite the lush plants and tasteful chintz furniture of the lobby. Fighting off a tremble, she pushed a button for the third floor, but the damn elevator was taking its sweet time. Lubov was now beside her.

"Janna, I wish to speak with you."

Janna said nothing.

"Janna—"

The elevator doors opened and Janna stepped inside. As quickly as she could, she pressed the button to close the doors. No matter—Lubov was physically holding the doors of the elevator apart and had slipped inside. They were alone now, the smell of booze seeping off him like cheap cologne.

"Your friend, it is saying in the papers now she is a big whore, no?"

Janna took a deep breath. The urge to shout was overwhelming.

"Why do you hate me so much, eh?"

"I would think that's pretty obvious."

"No, no, you hate me before your friend do this to me. Why?"

"You're out past curfew, Alexei, and you're drunk. You

better get to your room before Captain Gallagher finds you."

"You didn't answer my question."

The elevator doors opened on the third floor.

"I'm not going to," Janna replied, feeling genuinely nervous as he followed her out of the elevator. "You're on the wrong floor, Alexei."

"No," he insisted, "is right floor. I am going to stay on this floor until you speak to me."

Janna began briskly walking toward her room. "Leave me alone or I'll call security."

Lubov laughed. "Yes, call them, tell them lies like your whore friend. You think anyone will believe you?"

Janna remained silent. She was close to her room now, but there was no way she was going to risk opening the door with him baiting her. She stopped in the middle of the hall.

"What do you want?"

"To tell you your friend is a liar," he said, weaving on his feet.

"You already told me that before Christmas."

"To ask why you never wanted to go with me. All the women want, yet you? No. I am so nice to you on the train that time, and you do nothing. I don't like that."

"Too bad."

He took a step toward her. "I'm thinking you're very pretty, Janna."

"Janna? Lex? What the hell is going on?"

At the sound of Ty's voice, Janna's heart, which had been creeping up her throat, plummeted back down to her chest where it belonged. *Thank God*, she thought gratefully. *Thank God*.

Lubov staggered back, turning to face Ty and Kevin Gill, who was accompanying him on his rounds.

"It's past curfew, Lubov," said Kevin. "What are you doing out here?"

"Janna invited me to her room, she say she want to speak with me," he lied in a pleading voice.

"Bullshit," said Ty. His eyes darted to Janna.

"Is true," Lubov insisted.

"How much have you had to drink, Alex?" asked Kevin. Lubov shrugged. "You realize you're gonna be fined, right?"

"So?" Lubov sneered. "I'm rich."

Ty and Kevin exchanged troubled glances. "What are you doing on this floor?" Kevin asked again. "You're up on the fifth."

"I told you—"

"Can the cock-and-bull story," Ty growled. "What the hell are you doing here?"

"I came for the very beautiful Janna," Lubov purred drunkenly. "Look at her. Look at that hot little ass." He groped drunkenly toward her breasts. "And those ti—"

Boom! He was down on the carpet, Ty's fist connecting with his jaw before he even knew what hit him. Janna watched, frozen, as Ty picked him up by the collar and pinning him against the wall, held him there.

"If I ever—ever—hear you talk to or about a woman that way, if you ever lay another hand on a woman without her consent, I will make your life such a misery you'll wish you were back in Mother Russia standing in the goddamn bread line. Are we clear?"

Eyes rolling up in his head, Lubov barely managed a dazed nod. When Ty released him, he slid down the wall like a limp rag doll.

"Get up," Kevin barked. When Lubov didn't move, Kevin moved to help him. Lubov twisted out of his grasp, muttering. He maneuvered himself onto all fours, then slowly, unsteadily, rose to his feet. When he was upright, Kevin grabbed him and began pulling him toward the elevator.

"I'll see to it that our star Russian player gets back to

his room safe and sound," he called to Ty and Janna. As the elevator doors opened, he pushed Lubov inside.

Alone now with Ty in the silent hallway, Janna exhaled deeply. Her lungs hurt. She felt as if she'd been holding her breath a long time. She looked up at him. His face was ashen.

"You okay?" he asked. Janna nodded. He glanced up and down the hall, and seeing it was safe, drew her to him for a quick embrace, tenderly kissing the top of her head.

"I'm so sorry you had to see that," he said, releasing her. A look of pain flitted across his handsome face.

"I'm glad you guys showed up when you did. God only knows what would have happened."

"Something's got be done about him," he said half aloud. "He keeps on this way, and something else is going to happen. We've all worked too hard to let a scum like Lubov destroy our equilibrium and put team morale in jeopardy." He shook his head in disgust. "I should have taken care of this earlier."

"What are you going to do?"

"No need to worry about that right now. In the meantime, if that sleaze comes within a foot of you when I'm not around, you let me know."

With that he walked her to her hotel room, and stealing a quick kiss, said goodnight.

"*I don't understand,*" Theresa said to Janna. "Why does Ty want to talk to me?"

The two women were bundled in the back of a cab on their way to Ty's apartment, the foreign-born cab driver clearly unfamiliar with driving on ice as the cab fishtailed erratically down Seventh Avenue. Despite the foot of snow that had been dumped on the city, the sidewalks of midtown were still three deep with tourists.

The team had flown back into town three days earlier, their road trip a triumph. Though there were still three and

a half months left in the official season before Playoffs
began, buzz was strong that the Blades were going to repeat and win the Cup. Lou had warned Janna that if she
thought she was busy now, just wait until the Playoffs
began. Janna welcomed the challenge, especially if it
meant more time out of the office and away from the poi-
sonous Jack Cowley.

As promised, he'd planted the item about Theresa's
"appetite for athletes and actors" a few days after she and
Lou had left for the road. Though Theresa's attorney was
quick to respond, the damage was done, sowing more
seeds of doubt about Theresa's character. It killed Janna
that all the bad press about Theresa was being floated by
her office. Luckily, Theresa understood that Janna had
nothing to do with it and further, that she could in no way
control it. Were it otherwise, their friendship would be in
serious jeopardy. As it was, Janna found herself apologizing to Theresa constantly, unable to shake her own feelings
of guilt by association.

When Ty had asked if she could bring Theresa by so he
could talk to her about something, she was skeptical.

"You're not going to ask her to drop the suit, are you?"

Ty had been typically stone-faced, repeating his request.
She ran it by Theresa, who was dubious at first, but in the
end acquiesced to Janna, who thought it was worth hearing
him out, even if she herself was in the dark about the pre-
cise subject matter. Obviously, it was related to Lubov.

Their cab literally slid to a halt a few feet past Ty's
apartment building, and Janna and Theresa scrambled out
of the back, eager for terra firma. Ty's building loomed
high above them, a black glass monolith, delicate yet im-
posing. Braced against the biting cold, they hustled inside,
the doorman greeting Janna with a knowing nod as he
phoned upstairs to Ty. Theresa was impressed.

"His lobby's the size of our whole apartment," she marveled as the quick moving, silent elevator sped upwards.

Janna nodded. "I know."

"What does he pay a month in rent?"

"If I told you, you would drop dead." The elevator doors snapped back at the Fifty-second floor.

"Try me," urged Theresa, following Janna out into the long, silent hall.

"Twelve thousand a month."

Theresa whistled through her teeth. "That is one rich boyfriend you have there."

"He's not my boyfriend."

"Right."

They had come to Ty's door and Janna rang the bell. A minute later, a small, dimpled Spanish woman in jeans and a Yankees sweatshirt opened the door.

"Hello, Miss Janna. Come in, come in."

Janna and Theresa stepped over the threshold and into the marble foyer. "Inez, I want you to meet my friend Theresa. Theresa, this is Inez, Ty's personal assistant."

Inez chuckled. "I am his housekeeper." She extended a hand to Theresa. "Very pleased to meet you."

Moving to the coat closet, she took both women's coats from them and hung them up, gesturing for them to remove their boots as well. Struggling out of her boots, Janna could see Theresa was agog at the sheer size of Ty's apartment, her gaze traveling in circles around and around the immense, glass-walled living room.

"This place is amazing," she murmured to Janna as they followed Inez towards the couch.

"I know."

"A little cold, though. Talk him into getting some plants or something." They sat down.

"What can I get you ladies?" Inez was asking. "There is coffee, tea, brandy, hot chocolate. Senor Gallagher is just getting out of the Jacuzzi, his back is very bad. He'll be with you in a minute."

"Coffee would be fine for me, Inez," said Janna.

"Me, too," Theresa chimed in.

Janna rose. "Let me get it, Inez. Please." She hated being waited on.

"It's no problem. I will get you your drinks, then I'll be going. Tell Senor Gallagher there is a pan of lasagna in the refrigerator for him, and soup in the freezer. There are also cookies in the cabinet if you want a treat with your coffee."

Janna and Theresa both nodded. Neither of them said anything while Inez prepared their coffee. Theresa was still taken with the size of Ty's apartment, while Janna preferred to wait until Inez left to speak freely. Within seconds of her departure, Ty came out of the bedroom in sweats and a T-shirt, his gait stiff, a faint grimace on his face.

"Jacuzzi didn't help?" Janna asked, concerned.

"Not really. I have painkillers but I hate taking them, since they make me nauseous as hell." He went to Janna, planting a quick kiss on her mouth before turning to Theresa and extending his hand. "Glad you could come."

"Let's just say I'm intrigued," Theresa replied politely.

"Ty, why don't you sit down and I'll get you some coffee?" Janna offered. "You're walking like Frankenstein."

"Thanks." He carefully sank down in the overstuffed leather chair opposite the couch while Janna went into the kitchen. She thought she detected a slight tension between Theresa and Ty, mainly on Theresa's part. Perhaps she didn't trust Ty because he was Lubov's teammate. Or maybe it had more to do with a sense of loyalty; she was Janna's friend and was wary about him hurting her. Whatever it was, Janna hoped it dissipated soon.

She brought the coffee out to Ty, resuming her seat on the couch next to Theresa. "Inez says to tell you there's lasagna in the fridge and soup in the freezer."

"Did she leave me any Girl Scout cookies? She better have."

"Cookies are in the cabinet," Janna soothed. "Does anyone want some?" No one did. Ty took a sip of coffee, the oversized mug clasped between his large, rough hands. "I want to talk to you about Lubov," he began.

Theresa and Janna held their breath.

"Up until now, I've given Lubov the benefit of the doubt." His gaze landed squarely on Theresa. "I don't mean that as any disrespect to you. It just means that as his captain, my job has been to stand behind him and support him. That's what teammates do for one another, especially when something like this happens." Distress overtook his face. "I no longer feel I can support Alexei."

"Why?" asked Theresa.

His glance shot quickly to Janna. "I've seen him harass other women."

"And so?" Theresa prompted, still guarded.

"So I intend to do something about it. But first, I think you should drop the lawsuit against him."

"Forget it."

Ty remained calm. "Theresa, let me explain something to you. I've been a professional athlete for a very long time, all right? I've seen this happen before. The plaintiff rarely wins. If she does, it's only because she's got witnesses and rock solid proof to back her up. You don't have either." He took another sip of coffee. "The other thing you don't have is unlimited financial resources. Lubov does. He could tie this up for years and bankrupt you in the process. Is that what you want?"

"I'd rather go bankrupt than let him get away with what he did."

"He won't get away with it. He'll pay. That's what I'm trying to tell you."

"How?" Janna demanded. "What's going to happen to him?"

"I'm going to set him straight."

Theresa chuckled in disbelief. "And what does that mean? You're going to beat him up? What?"

"I'm going to hit him where it hurts: with his team-mates."

Janna and Theresa stared at him blankly.

"I don't understand," said Theresa.

"How do I explain this without sounding like a bad comic book?" Ty paused, struggling for the right words. "Hockey players are like warriors, okay? There's a bond between us, a code of honor, if you will. If one of the warriors lets his team down by breaking the code, he pays a price. That price is the shame of bringing dishonor on his brothers, a shame that results in being shunned by the people who mean the most to him, his teammates." Janna and Theresa both listened intently. "Up until now, Lubov hasn't had to worry at all about what the team thinks about the lawsuit, because the word we got from Corporate was to basically keep our mouths shut about it in public.

"But that doesn't mean we have to keep quiet in private. If I, as captain, go into that locker room and tell them that what Lubov did was an unacceptable disgrace, I guarantee you he will never harass another woman again. That's what you want, isn't it?"

"I want justice," Theresa replied in a quivering voice. She was struggling hard to hold back tears. Janna put a protective arm around her shoulders.

"You'll get justice. But not through the courts, trust me. You go through the legal system, and all that's going to happen is he's going to win and you're going to crawl away broken and poor, your reputation in the trash can."

"But if I drop the suit, won't people think I'm guilty?"

"Dropping the suit doesn't mean dropping the ball. Settle out of court and bleed the bastard for as much as you can get. I'll take care of the rest."

"Why?" Theresa sounded leery. "Why do you want to do this?"

"Because I should have done it right from the start. It makes me sick to think I have someone like that on my team, and I cannot, will not, let a cancer like that go unchecked. If it does, Christ only knows what will happen to the next woman who tells him no, and I don't want that on my conscience." He paused, letting what he'd said sink in. "Finally, I need to make sure all my guys are on the same page or this could wind up hurting us at precisely the time we need to be the most focused. Does that answer your question?"

Theresa nodded reluctantly. She turned to Janna, her expression agonized. "What do you think I should do, Jan? Be honest."

Janna reached for her coffee cup to buy herself some time. Ever since Theresa had brought suit against Lubov, Janna had tried to temper Theresa's quest for justice by pointing out that her chances of winning were slim. Even Theresa's lawyer agreed, and had in fact been pressing her for a huge out-of-court settlement for some time. But Theresa would not—or could not—hear them. Settling out of court seemed to her tantamount to admitting defeat, and to some extent, Janna agreed with her. On the other hand, something was better than nothing, which was probably exactly what Theresa would get if she forced the issue to go to trial and lost.

"I think Ty's right," Janna said quietly. "It would be one thing if there was irrefutable evidence proving Lubov's guilt, but there isn't. There's just your word against his. I think if it went to trial, you'd lose, and Lubov would walk away feeling invincible. It would allow him to keep on harassing women with impunity, because he'd know that all he'd have to do is throw gobs of money at a team of lawyers every time he got in trouble." She squeezed Theresa's shoulder. "Settle out of court and let Ty take care of the rest."

Theresa looked down at her hands folded primly in her lap, pained. Above her head, Ty's eyes caught Janna's, his expression questioning. Janna gave a small shrug, keeping her arm tight around Theresa, who was clearly struggling with what to do. Janna gave her a lot of credit. It couldn't be easy to come here, without knowing why you were being summoned in the first place, and be told by someone

you didn't really know, and possibly didn't even like, that
you didn't have a chance in hell of winning your lawsuit.
Not only had Theresa agreed to come, but she'd also listened to Ty with an open mind. It was a testament to
Theresa's strength of character and her desire to do the
right thing. Janna admired her for it.

The pregnant silence in the immense room seemed to
stretch out for infinity, the only sound Ty's coffee mug hitting the glass coffee table when he set it down. Finally,
Theresa raised her head.

"When would you speak with the team?" she asked.

"Tomorrow," Ty said without hesitation. "I can call a
special team meeting tomorrow."

Theresa looked to Janna, then back again to Ty.

"Do it," she said.

CHAPTER 15

Ty didn't care if some of his guys had been out on the town the night before, or if others were looking forward to stretching out in the sweet bosom of their family with bagels and coffee while reading the *Sunday Times*. The choice of the day and the hour had been deliberate, another of his devices for testing team loyalty. And when Ty said eight, he didn't mean eight-ish. He meant eight.

He'd called Kevin the night before, relaying the details of his discussion with Janna and Theresa. Kevin was behind him one hundred percent. In fact, Kevin, being an old-fashioned western Canadian whose sense of morality was rigidly defined, seemed even more incensed with Lubov than he was. Hell, if *Kevin* was gritting his teeth and calling Lubov every obscenity in the book, then Ty was certain the baby-faced Russian bastard deserved what was coming.

Adrenaline pounding, he arrived in the locker room at seven-thirty, followed by Kevin a few minutes later. Silently, they sat on the wooden bench in front of their

lockers, watching as the rest of the team dribbled through
the door. Some were sleepy and resentful, others wide
awake and chipper. All brought with them a sense of anxious anticipation that made the room feel electric. When
Lubov sauntered in, his smug face hidden behind mirrored
sunglasses, Ty politely asked him to remove them, explaining he wanted to be able to see all the players' eyes when
he spoke. Lubov reluctantly complied, the defiance on his
face rapidly fading as Ty and Kevin's unyielding stares
followed him all the way to his locker.

At precisely eight, Ty stood and surveyed the room.
Satisfied all were present, he locked the door. The tension
ratcheted up a notch. It was Sunday, after all, no coaches
or trainers around. Locking the door was an unmistakable
sign that he meant business. With all eyes on him, he returned to the space in front of his own locker, where he remained standing.

Slowly, one by one, he made eye contact with each of
the players. A few guys looked away, unable to bear the
scrutiny. Others gave him a feeble smile, unsure of what
else to do. He saw fear in the eyes of some of his players,
uncertainty, love and respect in the eyes of others. When
he got to Lubov, he stared long and hard, his expression
cold and appraising. Lubov tried at first to hold his gaze,
but couldn't. Clearly uncomfortable, his eyes dropped
down to the floor. Ty continued staring at him. He could
feel the room holding its breath.

"I called you here today because I want to talk to you
about winning the Stanley Cup." A palpable ripple of relief
surged through the overheated room. "When I look around
this locker room, do you know what I see?" Once again,
his eyes checked out every player in the room. "I see two
kinds of players: those who have won the Cup before and
know what it takes, and those who don't." His laserlike
gaze fixed itself on Lubov. "Alex here falls into the latter
category, having joined the Blades just this year. Alex

doesn't know how to win the Stanley Cup. Because if he did, he never would have behaved so stupidly."

Lubov opened his mouth to protest, but Ty silenced him with a look.

"I want to explain something to those of you who've never won the Cup, okay? Winning the Cup is about going to war. It's about blood and guts. When I hear some of you morons complaining about how hard it's getting now that it's crunch time in the regular season, I don't know whether to laugh at your naivete or cry because of your lack of balls. You think it's rough now? Now, before we've hit the Playoffs? Gimme a fucking break."

"Remember Chicago?" Kevin asked quietly at Ty's side, handing him a bottle of water.

"Chicago." He took a sip of the water, taking his sweet time. He wanted them to twitch, to squirm. Wanted them held in absolute thrall. "When we played for St. Louis about a hundred years ago"—that got some laughs—"it was us versus Chicago in the finals. This was in '92. Chicago was a veteran team. They'd won the Cup twice before. It was our first trip to the finals. It came down to game seven, and Chicago won, 3–2, in overtime. After the game, we went over to their locker room to congratulate them, expecting to find the bubbly flowing and the team partying their asses off. You know what we found?"

He paused, waiting, waiting, reeling them in, holding their attention in the palm of his hand.

"We found guys stretched out on the floor, crying, because they were in such physical pain. Guys sitting in the shower, too weak to stand after the war they'd just been through. That's when we understood why Chicago had won three times, why they deserved to win. Because they wanted it more than we did, because they gave more than we gave. They were willing to put the Cup first—before fame, before glory, before everything."

His eyes carefully circled the room again. "For us to win, we have to be like Chicago. We have to be a team in every sense of the word. That means I watch your back and you watch mine. It means if I race into the corner to dig out a puck that's been dumped in, and I find myself getting creamed against the boards, I want to be damn sure that the Blade I centered it to is going to take a hit, too, that I'm not out there all by myself putting my career and health on the line.

"What I'm talking about here is support. It's about each and every one of us being totally and completely committed to the same goal, and to each other. It means that none of you are going to do anything, either on or off the ice, that might fuck up a teammate."

He took another sip from the water bottle, his mouth already parched from talking. Then he turned to Lubov. "Stand up."

Lubov looked bewildered. "What?"

"Stand up," Ty repeated. "Now."

Embarrassed, Lubov slowly rose, glancing around anxiously at the faces of his teammates, all of whom were still as trees in the dead of night. Finally, he raised his eyes to Ty's.

"You've let everyone on this team down. We put our asses on the line out there for you, backing you up in this lawsuit, and you fucked us over." He walked over to Lubov, getting right in his face. "Your story is bullshit and we both know it. We stuck our necks out for you and you let us, because you're a selfish, immature asshole. You stabbed everyone in this room in the back, not only by doing what you did, but by hiding behind our support when you knew you were guilty of what Theresa Falconetti charged you with."

Fury heating his veins, he jerked back from Lubov in an effort to keep from pummeling him. He was glaring now, he could feel it, but he didn't care. "Does anyone else have anything to say to our sexual harasser here?" He waited. He was answered with stunned silence. "Anyone?"

"I do."

Slowly, and with great purpose, Kevin Gill rose and crossed to where Ty stood before Lubov. His normally serene face was turning pink, the veins in his neck cording as he struggled with his rage.

"I'm pissed beyond belief that you didn't give enough of a damn about everyone in this room to think about the repercussions of your actions. But what really makes me sick is what you did to that woman, and God knows how many others before her who may have been too afraid or too embarrassed to speak out. How dare you treat a woman that way?" Quaking with anger, Kevin turned his head and spit on the floor. "You're a scumbag, you know that? And you know what happens in this locker room to scumbags?"

Before Lubov could brace himself, Kevin's left fist connected with his mouth and sent him sprawling. Shock shuddered through the room. The mellow assistant captain never raised his voice off the ice, never mind decking a rookie! No one moved.

Kevin turned his back on Lubov and slowly walked back to his bench.

Gasping, his face fiery red with mortification, Lubov pulled himself back up onto the bench, the back of his right hand pressed to his mouth to staunch the flow of blood. Ty grabbed a clean, white towel and tossed it to him.

"Lex, you're a great hockey player, and we need you. We need you to go to war with us so we can win. But here's the catch. You've got to play by our rules. What that means is that every guy in this room has to know that you're never going to fuck us over like this again. Because if you do, you're the one who's going to be hung out to dry. All it takes is one player on this team letting it slip that we're not gonna back you up on the ice, and soon there will be defensemen going for your knees, and it won't be pretty."

"So . . . so what you do want me to do?" Lubov rasped.

Ty crossed his arms in front of his chest. "Prove yourself to us."

"I—I have been proving," Lubov stammered. "Kidco say—"

"Fuck Kidco!" Ty yelled. "This has nothing to do with them. They're not the ones playing their guts out on the ice every night. This is about *us*, the guys in *this* room, winning the Cup. You're either one of us or you're not. You decide."

"I am one of you," Lubov answered in a barely audible voice.

Ty cupped his ear. "What?"

"I am one of you!!" Lubov shouted, close to tears.

"Good man." The tension in the room broke somewhat as Ty clapped him on the back. "Now here's what you're going to do: You're going to call your lawyers tomorrow, and you're going to tell them you want to settle out of court. And you're going to pay out whatever price Theresa Falconetti's lawyer names." He turned his attention back to the rest of the team. "As for the rest of you mama's boys, this meeting never happened. This story is over—I repeat, over. From now on, you will all live, eat and breathe hockey." He glanced down at the broken man sitting beside him. "That includes you, Lubov. We don't have to like each other. But I want every player in this room to believe that if he sticks his neck out for his teammates on the ice, his teammates will do the same. Am I making myself clear?"

Lubov nodded.

"And the rest of you jerks?" Ty prompted.

The rest of the team nodded, murmuring their assent.

"Good. See you all tomorrow at practice."

Two weeks later, the case was settled out of court for an "undisclosed amount"—undisclosed to the public, at least. Theresa told Janna how much it was. It hadn't been about money in the beginning, and it wasn't about money now. She planned to invest what was left after paying her lawyer's fee, and get on with her life, hopeful that she did the right thing, and that whatever had taken place in the Blades' locker room would stop Alex Lubov from ever traumatizing another woman.

Janna hadn't pressed for details of the meeting, but when she saw Lubov's bruised and swollen mouth at practice the next day, she knew it involved more than talk. Since then, she noticed a subtle change in attitude among the players. They'd always been a dedicated team, even during practice, but now they seemed to share an almost mystical singularity of focus that she couldn't quite put into words. It was like they were possessed, each player feverish to do his part, their dedication fierce, unwavering. When she'd asked both Ty and Lou about it, their answers had been identical, as if the Blades' behavior was self-evident: "They're preparing for the run for the Cup."

The Cup, the Cup, the Cup. Janna made the mistake of playfully admonishing Ty to stop talking about it like it was the Holy Grail and was greeted with a silence so ominous it made the hairs stand up on the back of her neck. The Cup *was* the Grail. The Cup *was* Nirvana. The Cup was going to make her life hell once Playoffs began.

"You're clear, hit the left lane. *Now!"*

Janna clutched the steering wheel hard and flashed Lou a look that could shatter glass, then proceeded to ease carefully into the left lane. Lou's back-seat driving was really pushing her buttons this afternoon. It was bad enough that Mother Nature had dumped another foot of snow on the ground. But his constant instructions were interrupting her flow of thought . . . *Am I imagining it, or does Jack Cowley look at me like he prays for my death? Ty—would there ever be more than great take-out food and even greater sex? Why does it have to snow so much this wint—*

"Hit the gas! Go!"

Lou again. He was going to drive her nuts today! Plus, he had the heat cranked up so high the car was a virtual inferno on wheels. She'd be glad when they got back to Met Gar and she could breathe.

"Lou, can we turn the heat down a bit?"

"Whaddayou, a polar bear? It's freezing in here."

"Just a little bit. Please. I'm getting a headache." Janna reached out and turned the heat down one notch.

Lou frowned. "Fine, make an old man freeze to death."

"You could walk," Janna offered sweetly, imagining Lou's roly-poly body tumbling from the car like a boulder.

"Ha ha," Lou deadpanned. "Hey, look, I meant to tell you how proud I am that you got your pal to drop the suit against Lubov. Corporate is over the moon."

Janna eyed him sideways. "I had nothing to do with that. Theresa decided on her own."

"Yeah, sure." He began rubbing his gloved hands together, the briskness a counterpoint to the steady rhythm of the windshield wipers.

"I'm serious. I had nothing to do with it."

Lou sighed and his hands stopped moving. "Whatever. I just wanted to let you know that I'm meeting with that skinny guy today—what's his name, Sweeney? Feeney? — and I'm gonna suggest to him that we promote you."

Janna nearly skidded off the road. "What?"

Lou leaned forward and casually turned the heat back up. "You've been doing a real bang up job since we hired you, doll face, you gotta know that."

"I know, but a promotion? I mean, to what?"

"Associate Director of PR."

Janna's stomach clenched. "But wouldn't that put me above Jack Cowley?"

"Yeah. So what?"

"Don't you think that's going to upset him?" Janna could already imagine Cowley's reaction—the murderous glare, the not-so-veiled threats.

Lou shrugged philosophically. "Yeah, but it's his own fault. Maybe it'll light a fire under his ass."

Or under my chair, thought Janna.

"I thought you'd be happy about this," Lou continued, sounding disappointed.

"I am," Janna hastened to assure him. Frowning, she eased up on the gas, increasing the distance between herself and the car in front of her, whose driver seemed addicted to riding the brakes for no reason. "I just don't want it to rock the boat, you know? I mean, I've been here less than a year."

"Yeah, and you've handled the Lubov case like a pro, and even got Gallagher to show his ugly mug at a PR event. That ain't peanuts."

"He's not ugly," Janna muttered to herself.

Lou strained to hear. "Huh?"

"I said if we don't turn the heat down I'm going to start hallucinating," she covered quickly, lurching forward and pointedly turning the heat down three notches. "Look, Lou, I'm sorry, but having the heat on too high is making me sleepy. If you're really that cold you can have my beret—it's on the back seat."

Lou grumbled something unintelligible and stuck his hands deep in his coat pockets, sulking. Glancing in the rearview mirror, Janna saw a black Range Rover gaining on her, brights flashing for her to get out of the way. It was Ty. Mr. Big Shot in his SUV, barreling down the road like it wasn't slick with snow and he was Mario Andretti. *Macho idiot.* She eased back into the right lane.

"Whatcha do that for?" Lou complained.

"Because Ty Gallagher is going to blow past us in about five seconds, that's why." She counted. *One, two, three, four, five.* As if on cue, Ty honked, giving them a friendly wave as he tore past them.

"Crazy bastard," Lou said admiringly. "None of those ⌐ays can drive, you ever notice that?" Janna barely nodded, all her concentration fixed on the weather outside, which was worsening.

"Can I let you in on a little secret?"

Janna gritted her teeth, bracing herself for another driving directive. "What?"

"Between you and me, I think Gallagher's having some serious back trouble. You see him at practice? He seemed a little stiff. And the minute he got off the ice, he was on that trainer's table getting his muscles kneaded."

Janna sighed. "If he's not a hundred percent, then we have to make sure the press has no idea."

"Exactamundo. We don't want to go into the Playoffs with the other team knowing there's a problem—they'll be on him faster than white on rice, literally trying to hit him exactly where he's hurting. "

"I'm sure he's fine. Or will be. But until then, I'll keep all reporters out of the locker room after practice, even the beat reporters. Okay?"

"That's what I wanted to hear. The other thing is, you really gotta push him into doing some stuff, especially with the Playoffs coming up. Sports radio, stuff like that."

"Sports radio won't be a problem," Janna assured him. "Neither will that photo spread for *Sports Illustrated* on 'The Greatest Leaders in Team Sports'—I think. However, there's no way he'll take part in that Bachelor Auction to raise money for heart disease. I've run that by him twice and he just doesn't want to know."

"Maybe he's got some little chippie stashed away somewhere he doesn't want to upset."

"Maybe." *Chippie? Do people still use that word? Is that what I am, a chippie?* The windshield was beginning to fog, so she turned the car defroster up. *Chippie . . . she'd have to remember to tell that one to Ty.*

Sighing to himself, Lou pulled a handful of Tootsie Rolls out of his coat pocket and offered one to Janna. "You haven't asked whether your promotion entails a raise."

Janna mindlessly took the Tootsie Roll, but when sh

saw the wrapper was coated in lint, she discreetly let it drop to the floor. "I was waiting for you to say something."

"I think I can get you a raise," Lou said confidently. "It may not be much, but I'll do what I can."

"You'd better! I'm worth it, dammit!" Janna joked.

"No argument here, sweetie pie. No argument here."

CHAPTER

16

What was the saying? *April is the cruelest month?* Ty snorted to himself. *What a load of bull that was!* It was only the beginning of March, and already he was feeling that to get through the weeks ahead—roughly one month until the Playoffs—he was going to have to pull the will to win out from way deep inside.

He hated admitting it, but when he was younger, the hunger for victory had been enough. It carried him through pain, injury, bad press, the 1001 petty locker room dramas that took place every day. But now that he was older—not old, old*er*—it was getting harder to ignore the ligaments and tendons that wouldn't behave, the players' constant need for him to hear their thoughts and opinions, the back muscles that spontaneously spasmed. He'd get through it, he always did, but in the meantime he was really going to have to put a brave face on it. If any of his guys suspected his bones were aching, or that he occasionally felt mentally fatigued, it could throw a cog in their finely tuned machine.

Goddamn, they were hot right now! Downright super-natural! Everyone on the ice doing their part, hearts and minds tuned to one thing, and one thing only. . . . If it played out the way he thought it might, they could wind up playing Boston in the first round. What a bitch that would be. The Blades were punchers, but Boston was renowned for punching right back. And for playing the neutral zone trap, a system he hated. Round one would be a real fight to the death, no two ways about it. But if the Blades won, if they made it to round two and maintained the same drive and perseverance they were showing now, then he knew they'd go on to win the Cup. Knew it. And then Kidco could really kiss his ass—after renegotiating his contract for another three-year stint. At several million dollars higher.

He checked his Rolex. Ten to nine, he'd be right on time. Tubs had asked him to stop by before practice, which was odd. Usually, they shot the breeze after practice was over. Tubs relied on him to give the lowdown on where the players' heads were at, and they discussed strategy, line changes and possible last minute trades. They were a good match, he and Tubs. He'd dealt with coaches in the past who were threatened by his power as captain, coaches who refused to listen to him on issues of personnel and strategy because he was a player. But Tubs wasn't like that. Tubs trusted him and valued his opinion. In turn, he was loyal to Tubs, refusing to brook criticism of him from the players, never disputing Tubs in public, even on issues they dis-agreed on.

On automatic pilot, Ty headed straight into the locker room to change and lace up before he realized his mistake. He shook his head and walked back down the photo-lined hall towards Tubs's office. He had to admit, he felt a little tired today. He had spent a good part of the night before trying out positions from the *Kama Sutra* with Janna. They killed themselves laughing when things didn't quite work out thanks to his failing knees or her fear of passing out if her head was upside down. But when it did work . . . just thinking about it made him hot all over again. He'd had more than his share of women, but this one . . . this one knew how to keep him coming back for more. And it wasn't just the sex, although he didn't want to dwell on that too much. The important thing was, he hadn't had this much fun off the ice since . . . shoot, he'd never had this much fun off the ice. *And fun is what it's all about with Janna,* he told himself. *Remember that.*

As usual, the door to the coach's office was closed. Ty knocked once and went in. Tubs was standing in the middle of the room in his usual uniform, khakis and a white tennis shirt, reviewing a video of the game against Dallas from the night before. Hearing Ty enter, he paused the video and got them both bottles of Gatorade from the small fridge beside his desk.

"What's up?" Ty asked, accepting the Gatorade while clearing away a mountain of papers and equipment so he could sit down on the beat up couch across from Tubs's desk.

"Couple of things." Tubs sat and swung his short, chunky legs up on the desk. His body had earned him his nickname way back when he was a hockey player himself. "How you feeling?"

"Fine. Why?"

"Don't bullshit me, Ty. I've been watching that hit you took from Porter over and over again on video. He hurt you bad, didn't he?"

Ty grinned. "I've been hurt worse."

"How bad is it? Tell the truth."

"We might need to freeze the shoulder Thursday night, I don't know," he replied, massaging the area in question. "Is that what you wanted to talk about?"

"In a way."

Ty's ears pricked up cautiously. "Yeah?"

Tubs sighed—not a good sign. "I can't afford not to have you in the Playoffs."

Ty laughed. "No kidding." Not to be too modest, but there was no way the team could win without him, and everyone knew it. He was about to tell Tubs so, but the look of worry on the coach's face precluded it. "What else?" he prompted.

"I've been thinking of resting you the next month. Shave a few minutes off your ice time each game."

"That's ridiculous," Ty scoffed. "I'm fine."

"You're thirty-three, and you've got guys ten years younger than you trying to destroy you every minute you're out there."

Ty allowed himself a small, self-congratulatory smile. "Too bad they're not doing such a good job of it."

"Oh, no?"

Tubs picked up the remote from his desk, rewound the video, and hit "play." Ty watched his own feet leave the ice as Greg Porter, a gorilla-sized defenseman for Dallas, smashed him into the boards, his left shoulder jamming up into his ear. He watched his own eyes glaze over with pain for a split second before grimacing and skating, semi-hunched, back to the bench, where one of the trainers began working on him immediately. Seeing it annoyed him.

"Turn it off."

Tubs complied.

"I'm still not getting your point."

"My point is the less chance they have to mess you up, the better the chances of you kicking ass in the Playoffs."

Ty slowly lowered the bottle he had just put to his lips, not bothering to drink. "Are you benching me?"

"Just on Thursday. I want to see how it goes."

"'How it goes'?" Ty echoed incredulously. "Are you out of your mind? This is not the time to experiment. You and I both know that. You bench me, and they're going to think I'm injured. They think I'm injured and then they're really going to go for me, try to take me out for the rest of the season." He shook his head. "Don't do it, Tubs. It's a mistake."

"It's one game."

"One game is all it takes."

Tubs hesitated. "You've been a little off your game, Ty."

Ty lurched forward. "What?"

"Just a little," Tubs amended, swinging his legs back under the desk. "Not enough for anyone but me to notice, maybe, but you are."

"Explain."

"Your skating hasn't been as sharp as usual. Your stick handling's been a little sloppy." He peered at Ty with brotherly concern. "Everything okay?"

"Everything's fine," Ty insisted.

"Anything distracting you? Girlfriend trouble?"

"I don't have a girlfriend," was Ty's terse reply. *Janna,* he thought. *This is all because of Janna.* Because of her his concentration was off. He wasn't eating, breathing, dreaming the Cup.

"Well, I don't know what it is, then," Tubs was saying, "but I really think you should try to be more in tune with what's up with you. Because we don't want it to turn into a real problem."

"No, of course not." His eyes held his coach's. "Don't bench me Thursday. I'm telling you, it's a major tactical error. Trust me."

Tubs seemed to be considering it.

"Who would you put on the line with Kevin and Lonnie if you sat me out?"

"Lubov."

"Lubov!" Ty exclaimed. Talk about adding insult to injury. "That line'll never mesh." He shook his head despairingly. "If you're going to be stupid enough to bench me, then put Deans in with Kev and Lon. It's a better fit."

"Maybe." Tubs tapped a pencil on the edge of his desk,

thinking. "You really think it's a green light to beat on you if I sit you out?"

"Jesus Christ, you know it is. Look, I told you. I'm fine. If you want, I'll rest more when we're not playing, okay? I'll take naps, I'll sip warm milk, I'll go to bed at nine. Shaving a few minutes off my ice time from here until the Playoffs is acceptable. Benching me is not."

"You sure there's nothing distracting you?"

"I'm sure," Ty swore.

But there was, he knew there was. And he had to figure out what he was going to do about it.

Someone was dead.

That was the first thought that sprang to Janna's mind as she emerged from the velvet fog of sleep to the phone ringing. Early morning phone calls, late night phone calls, both meant only one thing. Bad news. It was five A.M. *Please don't let it be Daddy or Wills,* she prayed, squinting against the brightness of her bedside lamp as she turned it on, bracing herself.

"Hello?"

"Janna? It's Jack Cowley."

Jack Cowley? At this hour?

"Lou's had a heart attack. He's in Columbia Presbyterian."

Janna closed her eyes. "Oh my God." The shock brought her body instantly, jerkily, awake. "What happened?"

"He was watching TV with his wife, complaining of heartburn after supper, which apparently was nothing unusual. About an hour later, he rose to get a snack from the kitchen and collapsed, saying that he felt like his chest was being crushed. His wife called nine-one-one. The paramedics got there in time to save him, but the damage to his heart is massive. He might be in the hospital awhile."

"Oh my God," Janna repeated numbly. She could see it all. Lou in a ratty old bathrobe, leaning back in a comfy, reclining chair, pounding his chest while he crabbed about Lily's spaghetti sauce being too acidic. Then waddling off to the kitchen at a commercial break to get some ice cream, only to be seized with the sensation of his rib cage cracking apart. The fear he must have felt, the panic as he wondered if this was it, the end. She gave herself a small shake to force the vision away. "When did you find out?"

There was a small, almost infinitesimal pause on the other end of the phone. "Lily called me at around midnight, actually."

"And you're just getting around to calling me now?!"

"I've been in the office all night taking care of things," said Jack coolly. "Now that Lou's going to be out of action for a while—"

"You thought you'd just move into his office and take over," Janna finished for him. "You must be so disappointed he didn't die."

Cowley ignored the barb. "You might want to come in, since you're clearly going to be doing my job for a while in addition to your own."

"You seem to forget I'm your superior now, Jack."

"And you seem to forget I've worked PR for the Blades years longer than you have. I think experience trumps job title in this case, don't you? So come on down. I need to show you the ropes."

"Go hang yourself with them. It's Sunday. The only place I'm going is to the hospital to visit Lou, unless someone from Corporate calls me to do otherwise. Anything else?"

"Nothing that I can think of," Jack replied with false pleasantness. "Send him my love, won't you? I don't know if I'll be able to get there."

"Send it yourself." She slammed down the phone. *JERK!!!*

God, she hated that . . . creature. The thought of him going to Lou's office in the middle of the night and rifling through Lou's things, thinking he could fill Lou's shoes, made her nuts, even more nuts than knowing that Cowley was probably right. She probably *was* going to have to take orders from that oily, unctuous, awful, megalomaniac swine. The fact he didn't phone her as soon as he got the news rankled her, too. Waiting to call was a deliberate slap in the face.

She slid back down and pulled her comforter up to her neck, then over her head, thinking, *I could hide here and fall asleep. When I wake up, I will deal with it then.* She closed her eyes, opening them again less than a minute later. Forget it, she was too wired. She would get up, put on coffee, and watch bad infomercials on early morning TV until the paper came. Then she'd read until it was time for visiting hours at the hospital.

As she padded out to the kitchen, her mind raced. *If Ty were here, this wouldn't have happened. It only happened because we haven't gotten together for a while for Chinese food and sex. It's an omen. It's . . .*

Ridiculous. Since when was she superstitious? Ty was the superstitious one, always having to lace up his left skate before his right, always having the same dinner before a game—pasta with grilled veggies. A lot of the guys had quirks like that, she'd noticed. Kevin Gill had a statue of the Virgin Mary he kept in his locker that he kissed. Lonnie Campbell always tucked in the back left side of his uniform. Defenseman Wally Manzourek kept a rabbit's foot on the team's bench in the arena. Some guys were even known to stop shaving during the Playoffs. Thankfully, Ty wasn't one of them.

The kitchen was chilly. Even though it was already April, the mornings were still cool. Setting up the coffee as quietly as she could, so as not to wake Theresa, her mind remained on Ty. He seemed squirrelly lately, like he just wanted to be alone. She knew he was preoccupied with the upcoming Playoffs, so she had given him a wide berth. There were only three games left in the regular season. Three games left until they'd begin seriously bumping heads again over PR. He'd already told her he wouldn't talk to anyone but the beat reporters during the Playoffs. Meanwhile, interview requests were pouring in faster than she could keep up with them, especially since the leadership piece in *Sports Illustrated*. She'd need to ask Lou—

Lou. She sat down at the kitchen table, clearing her seed catalogs out of the way to make room for her coffee mug. The last thing on earth she wanted to face was the sight of him helpless in a hospital bed, surrounded by beeping machines and a tangled highway of tubes. But she had no choice; this was one of those situations where like it or not, you have to do the right thing. With that thought in mind, she sipped at her coffee, and waited for dawn to come.

"Are you family?"

The thin, tired looking woman behind the nurses' station in the Intensive Care Unit peered up at Janna suspiciously.

"I'm Louis Capesi's daughter," Janna replied smoothly. The woman, distracted by the computer screen in front of her, didn't answer immediately. When she did, her tone was perfunctory.

"He's at the end of the hall, room 515. No more than fifteen minutes, please."

Janna nodded and started off in the direction that she was pointed in, the clacking of her clogs against the highly polished floor embarrassingly loud to her own ears, especially when compared with the silent steps of the staff hustling past in rubber soles. She hated hospitals. It didn't matter that Lou was in one of the finest cardiac care units in the country. From the moment she'd stepped inside and passed through the first set of automated double doors in the lobby, she'd been overwhelmed with anxiety. It was the smell: cold, sterile, designed to mask fear and sickness and death. She should have brought him some of the fragrant lavender she'd grown in her little garden.

The door to Lou's room was open. Not knowing what to expect, she hesitated before stepping inside. There was Lou propped in a hospital bed, eyes closed, his pallor glowing ghostly green beneath the thin strip of neon lighting above his bed. Despite his girth, he seemed dwarfed by the equipment surrounding him. A heart monitor beeped out its monotone song, while another machine whose function Janna wasn't sure of pinged away in frantic counterpoint. An IV pole pumped what she assumed to be glucose into his pudgy, hairy arm. Tubes thin as spaghetti fed Lou oxygen through the nose while others crisscrossed his chest. Her eyes filled, and she looked down to the floor, composing herself. Should Lou awaken, she didn't want him to see her crying.

Pulling up a chair, she sat down beside him and put her hand on top of his. His skin was cold. It alarmed her. Was his skin supposed to be this cold? She wondered if she should call a nurse. Lou stirred, blinking. His eyes opened. He seemed to take a minute to adjust to his surroundings. When he realized Janna was beside him, he gave a trace of a smile.

"Hey, doll face." His voice was barely a whisper.

"You don't have to talk," Janna murmured to him, slowly massaging his hand in an effort to warm it up.

"I want to."

Janna threw him a look of warning. "Lou, I don't want you wearing yourself out."

"Hey," he wheezed, "who's the boss here?"

"Right now, I am." She reached up, tenderly touching his cheek. "Close your eyes if you want."

He nodded, eyes closed. "Doctor says . . . my love affair with cheeseburgers is over."

"You got that right."

The small, piggy eyes opened up again. "I'm sorry about this."

"Don't be ridiculous." Lou's hand was beginning to warm a bit. Janna started rubbing a bit more briskly now.

Lou sighed. "I feel bad about leaving you alone with Cowley."

"I can handle Jack, " Janna assured him.

A half smile settled on Lou's lips. "The real question is whether Cowley will be able to handle you."

Janna smiled, taking it as a compliment. "Is there anyone you want me to call?" she asked. "Anything you need taken care of that you might have forgotten to mention to Lily?"

Lou shook his head no. "It was nice of you to come."

"You're my friend, Lou. I love you."

"I love you, too, sweetcakes." His eyes shut again as he sank deeper into the pillows. "If I die—"

"You're not going to die. Granted, you did come close, but they got to you in time, thank God." She raised his now warm hand to her mouth and kissed it.

"When I thought I was going to die . . . when I was lying there on the kitchen floor . . . I told Lily I loved her. I realized that was the most important thing, that she knew that. 'Cause you never know. . . ."

"Sshhh, enough. Enough talking now. Rest."

She sat with him, waiting for him to drift back to sleep. A nurse came into the room with two more bouquets of flowers. The room was full to overflowing. Lou really was loved. When Janna was satisfied he was resting comfortably, she rose, kissed his forehead, and left, stopping back at the nurses' station.

"I was wondering if you could give me an update on my father's condition," she said politely to the same nurse she'd spoken with earlier.

"What do you want to know?"

"Is he out of the woods yet?"

"He's still in critical condition."

"Which means what?"

The nurse looked impatient. "That we're doing all we can, but in the meantime, we have to keep an eye on him to make sure he doesn't go into cardiac arrest again."

I see," said Janna in a small voice. "Thank you."

Numb, she made her way down the silent corridor toward the elevators. Anguish squeezed at her heart like pincers. She couldn't bear the thought of Lou dead. She imagined him lying on the kitchen floor looking up into Lily's frightened face, telling her that he loved her. This time she let the tears come. *All of* us, she thought bleakly, *truly are alone unless we reach out, connect, say what's in our hearts*. The simple truth of this overwhelmed her. Outside on the sidewalk, she hailed a cab. When the driver asked her where she wanted to go, she gave him Ty's address.

CHAPTER

17

Ty wasn't big on surprises. So when the weekend doorman buzzed to let him know Janna was downstairs, he felt annoyed. What was she doing stopping by unannounced? He had a game tomorrow, an important game.

Resigned to the intrusion, he told the doorman to send her up. His eyes did a quick tour of the living room. It was untidy, but not a total disaster. Inez had been down with the flu since Thursday, and rather than have someone fill in for her, he'd decided to just let it go. Newspapers had piled up, cast-off clothing draped the back of the couch, and half-empty coffee mugs littered the table. No big deal. Janna wasn't exactly Martha Stewart herself.

The doorbell rang and he let her in. He could see right away that something was wrong. Her eyes were swollen from crying. He pulled her inside, worried.

"What's the matter?"

Janna's lower lip began quivering. "It's Lou," she managed to get out before tears overtook her. "He's had a heart attack. He's in the hospital."

"Oh, baby." He folded her in his arms. "I'm so sorry."

Janna murmured something, but he couldn't make it out because she was speaking right into his chest. Her grip on him got tighter, as if she was afraid to let him go. He tightened his squeeze around her, too, to reassure her.

"Just let it out, honey," he soothed, stroking her hair. "It's okay."

She followed his advice and let go, sob after sob shaking her small body. He was flattered she'd come to him, but he felt like a bit of dolt just standing there holding her, his mind a total blank as to what to say in comfort. Perhaps just holding her was enough for now. If she wanted to talk, she would.

He thought back to the last time he'd seen Lou, after Friday night's murderous game against Tampa Bay. Capesi had respected his wish to deal only with beat reporters, and had barred everyone else from the locker room while the players showered and changed. He appreciated that, same as he appreciated Lou's talent for matching the right player with the right interviewer or photographer. None of his guys had ever come back from a photo shoot or an event arranged by Lou and complained. The same held true for Janna. It was touch and go in the beginning when she was new, but now she was as good as her boss. Except when it came to him, of course. Him she still hounded. Probably so Capesi didn't have to.

He resolved to call a bunch of the guys after Janna left to arrange a visit to Lou before the game tomorrow. That would cheer him up. He wasn't surprised the Bull had keeled, and he doubted any of the guys would be, either. He felt guilty now, thinking about the times they'd all poked fun at Lou behind his back. To a bunch of jocks in peak condition, Lou's physical appearance, eating habits and reckless disregard of exercise was horrifying. Even ow, just thinking about it, Ty felt uneasy. How could any- e let themselves get that way, put their health at risk? He didn't get it. Still, he would never wish a heart attack on the guy. This was bad news, no doubt about it.

Janna gently broke from his embrace. She seemed calmer. "I'm sorry," she apologized, sniffling. "I was just at the hospital and when I left, the only person I wanted to see was you."

"It's okay." He reached out and brushed the tears from her cheeks. "Do you want to come in for a minute?"

"Sure."

Ty could sense she was slightly miffed as he led her toward the couch. Was she upset he'd only asked her to come in for a minute? He hoped not. Because much as he wanted to comfort her, there was no way he was going to let this impromptu visit get out of hand. He was of the old school—sex prior to playing a game saps a player of focus and vitality. Maybe some jocks could handle two athletic events in a row, but he wasn't one of them. Especially since his talk with Tubs. Taking her coat, he draped it over the arm of a chair before dropping down on the sofa beside her.

Janna looked around, still sniffling. "Where's Inez?"

"She's been sick."

"I can tell." She reached out for one of the coffee mugs on the table and peered inside. Disgusted, she put it back down. "Why don't you let me wash these for you?"

"No thanks."

"But—"

"No."

The last thing on earth he wanted her doing was his dishes. It was simply too intimate, too domestic. It meant too much symbolically. If he let her do the dishes, next she'd be offering to do laundry, and before he knew it he'd be married with three kids and a house in Westchester. No, no dishwashing, not now, not ever.

"You're upset I just showed up, aren't you?" She was trying to read his face, a slightly wounded expression on her own.

"I'm not upset," Ty maintained carefully.

"You're annoyed."

He decided to be honest with her. "Yeah, I am. But considering the circumstances, I understand."

Janna's eyes began watering again. "He's really bad," she whispered. "He's in critical condition."

Oh, no, please don't cry again, Ty begged silently. *Jesus.* Could he be a more selfish bastard? Here she was in the midst of a crisis and all he could think about was how uncomfortable all this was making him.

Ashamed, he slid closer to her and put a consoling arm around her shoulder.

"What did they say?" he coaxed.

"That they're trying to prevent another heart attack."

Ty shook his head. "Poor Bull. Can't say I'm surprised, though."

"Me, either."

"How is this going to affect you at work?"

"Oh, work's just going to be great," she said bitterly. "I'm going to have to kowtow to Jack Cowley until Lou comes back."

"I thought you were above Cowley now."

"Technically, but he has seniority since he's been there longer."

"Don't worry, Lou will be back soon." He pulled her closer to him and kissed the top of her head, relishing the smell of her hair. It reminded him of apples, crisp and fresh. Pure. He inhaled again, then forced himself to stop, knowing that if he lingered a second or two longer, he might want more. Janna seemed to sense this; turning in the crook of his arm, she leaned in to kiss the side of his face.

Ty closed his eyes. "Don't."

"Why not?" she teased, beginning to run her fingers through his hair. "You know you want me to."

Yeah, I do, I want you to right here on the couch, and
then I want you right there on the rug, and . . .

"Ty—?" Her voice was a coquettish murmur.

"I can't." He opened his eyes and as politely as he could, slid down the couch away from her. "Don't torture me, Janna."

"It's only torture because of your stupid rule about no sex before a game," she snorted.

"A rule I'd like you to respect."

"You're the one who started it by rubbing your face in my hair!"

Ty raised his hands in a gesture of surrender. "You're right, I started it. I take full and complete blame."

Janna slid towards him. "So let's finish it," she purred.

"Janna." His voice was heavy with frustration as he dealt with the sexual tension beginning to build in him. "Look, I would love to make love to you right now, okay? But I can't. Tomorrow is too important a game. I need to rest." He paused. "You understand, right?"

"I understand."

But the disappointment on her face said otherwise. Feeling badly, he took her hands in his. "I'll make it up to you." He showered her knuckles with kisses. "Okay?"

Her features softened in surrender. "Okay."

"Good." He reached to tuck a stray piece of hair behind her ear. "You all right now?"

"I'm fine." Her face bunched up in concentration. "I just . . . Lou told me about how he was lying on the floor and Lily was standing over him and he thought he was going to die and so . . ." She waved a deprecating hand. "Never mind."

"What?"

"It's not important," she said, quickly rising. She reached for her coat. "I guess I should go."

"Are you sure you don't want some coffee or something?" he offered lamely. "I could make some."

"Ty." Her voice was slightly scornful. "I know you really don't want me to stay, and I know why. Believe me, I can handle it. I'm a big girl. Besides," she deadpanned she glanced down disdainfully at the coffee table, "I don't think you have any clean mugs."

Ty ducked his head, embarrassed. "Yeah, well, let me at least have the doorman call you a cab. I'll walk you down to the lobby."

"Promise me you'll tidy this up before Inez comes back so she doesn't have a heart attack, too."

"I promise."

Cab called, they talked about the Playoffs for a few minutes before taking the elevator down together.

"I assume I'll see you at practice tomorrow?" he asked.

"Of course. I'll be the one walking ten paces behind Jack Cowley, bearing his crown on a velvet pillow."

Ty laughed. "That'll be the day." Lobby empty, he planted a soft, caring kiss on her lips, heat ricocheting through him when her mouth parted slightly beneath his and their tongues furtively met. "Call me if you need to talk," he offered.

"I will."

She hurried toward the door as he began to walk away.

"Ty?"

He turned.

"I love you," she called, bolting out of the lobby and into the waiting cab.

Immobilized, he stood watching the cab as it pulled away from the curb. Inside him, a solid wall of resistance sprang up, separating his heart from his head. The wall was there to make sure his gut response of, "Me, too," never reached full cognizance. It was self-preservation, pure and simple. He couldn't afford to love this woman, not now, not when victory was so close he could almost feel the cold, shining silver of the Cup in his grasp.

Why did she have to say that to him? That, of all things?

*   *   *

"Hoist 'em high, boys, c'mon! To victory!"

Claps, cheers and hoots rumbled through the Chapter House. Everyone in the Blades organization raised yet another toast to the team. They'd just won themselves home-ice advantage in the first round of the Playoffs, in a fight-to-the-finish against North Carolina. Scanning the crowded room, Janna was filled with a profound respect for the players, who looked exhausted yet elated. These men had worked hard during the regular season, and it had paid off.

But her respect didn't mean she wouldn't still get in their faces if need be. Aware that there were a few journalists in the room, she pulled aside the notorious twosome Guy LaTemp and Barry Fontaine, whose foul language and bending of the elbow were bordering on the troublesome.

"Guys? Let's watch the drinking and the language, okay?"

"C'mon, Janna, lighten up," said LaTemp.

"This is a party!" said Fontaine.

"I know that," she said patiently. "All I'm asking is that you don't get trashed and say or do anything that might embarrass the team. In case you haven't noticed, there are some folks from the press here. The last thing we need is one of them reporting that the two of you still haven't gotten your act together since the strip club incident."

Mention of their earlier indiscretion seemed to sober them up considerably.

"Fine," LaTemp muttered. "We'll *behave*."

"No problem," Fontaine echoed.

"Thanks, guys."

She'd come close to missing this celebration. Jack Cowley had taken Kidco's choosing her as the interim head of PR hard. The last thing she wanted to do was spend any out-of-the-office time with him—especially at a victory party. Kidco's decision had been a shock to her, too. She'd thought for sure Cowley's seniority guaranteed he'd be chosen to act in Lou's stead. She'd even considered telling Corporate to give it to him. Not because he deserved it—everyone knew she worked ten times harder than he did—but because at first the offer to fill Lou's shoes sent all her old demons of insecurity howling to the fore. She was convinced she wasn't up to the task and would screw up big time. In the end, though, the thought of taking orders from Jack Cowley far outweighed the terror of stepping up to the plate.

Scanning the crowd again, she was pleasantly surprised to see that the sore loser wasn't present. It looked like Cowley had opted to skip this party. That was fine by her. Of course, she would have to talk to him about his absence, a dreaded task. Well, that would be tomorrow. Tonight, she could relax—while still keeping an eye on the team, as always.

Ty seemed happily buzzed, his third Chivas going down smooth and effortless. Given the choice, she knew he would have preferred to just crawl home and get some much-needed sleep. But his teammates needed the release of a celebration, and they deserved it—within reason. Raising his glass for the first toast, he'd congratulated them even while cautioning them not to get too far ahead of themselves, reminding them that the hardest part of the battle still lay ahead.

In the dim, smoky light of the bar, Janna was overwhelmed with a rush of tenderness for him, despite the fact that ever since she'd told him she loved him, he'd been even more reserved. Not quite aloof, but more self-contained, if that made any sense. She hoped it was the game preoccupying him, not what she'd said. Sometimes she drove herself crazy trying to second-guess him. If Ty was upset by what she said, wouldn't he have told her? Answer: yes. Therefore, he wasn't upset.

A top-heavy waitress swirled by, with another platter of buffalo chicken wings. The din of conversation filling the bar was so loud it was difficult to make out the music being played, though Janna could feel the backbeat of the bass and drums pounding up through the floor beneath her feet. Ty took another long pull of his scotch, and cupping his hands to his mouth to be heard, leaned toward her.

"Wanna dance?"

Janna's eyes flicked to the crowded dance floor, where bodies were packed tight. The thought was tempting, but she was just too damn tired. She shook her head no.

"Aw, c'mon," said Ty.

"Only if you'll do that shirtless photo shoot for *Cosmo*," she parried loudly. She could barely hear herself think.

Ty frowned. "I'm an athlete, not a pinup boy."

"You could be both."

"No, thank you."

She shrugged, and took another sip of her Sea Breeze. Corporate was hot to push the players as sex symbols, seeing a vast, untapped female market. Some of the younger, single guys had agreed to a cheesecake shoot. Others, notably Ty and Kevin Gill, had refused and would undoubtedly continue to do so. Janna couldn't blame them; deep down, she thought it was demeaning, too. But if it was what the Big Boys in Corporate wanted . . .

"C'mon." Ty drained his glass and stood up, one hand firmly gripping Janna's elbow. "One dance."

"Fine," Janna capitulated. She was too tired to argue with him, especially since she'd never seen him with a snootful before. Besides, it would be a chance to feel that body of his against her.

She rose and let him lead her through the dense throng of bodies, recalling the first time they had danced together in this very bar the previous fall. Ty's teammates had been near apoplectic with shock at seeing their captain dance with his number one, off-ice nemesis. Things had certainly changed since then. No one seemed to be paying them the least bit of attention. Best of all, the awkwardness that had plagued them that first time was gone, replaced by a sense of ease borne of their standing intimacy with one another.

wonder if anyone knows, thought Janna. *I wonder if anyone can tell just by looking at us that we're lovers.*

Troubled by the thought, she tried to keep a pleasant, noncommittal expression on her face, but it was difficult. Whenever Ty touched her, the world fell away, leaving nothing but the two of them and the moment. That was the feeling she had now, the sense that they were the only two people in the room. If she closed her eyes and succumbed to it, she'd be finished. She forced conversation instead.

"Do you remember the first time we danced?" she asked, standing on tiptoes so he could hear her. Ty gave a tired smile as he nodded and pulled her closer, his hand slipping dangerously low on her back, almost to the point of cupping her rear. Drink had emboldened him. She flashed a quick look of warning. Frowning with dismay, Ty returned his hand to the small of her back.

"That first time we were here, you told me I should go after what I wanted," Janna continued. "Do you still think that?"

"It depends," he replied.

"On?"

His eyes met hers. "What it is you're going after." His voice was cajoling as he leaned down to put his mouth right to her ear. "Let's not ruin tonight with serious talk, all right?"

Janna's breath caught. "All right." The feeling of his lips brushing against her ear filled her with blossoming desire. He must have sensed this, because his mouth remained there, his hand exerting the slightest pressure to her back as he spoke again.

"If I don't have some real contact with you soon, I'm going to explode. Meet me in the courtyard behind the bar in five minutes."

She looked up at him like he was nuts. "You're kidding, right?"

"No one goes in the courtyard, believe me."

"Except the staff," she felt compelled to point out.

"What are you going to do, throw me down on a sack of potatoes?"

"Just trust me on this, okay?" He moved to leave the dance floor. "Five minutes," he mouthed.

Janna watched as he stopped to chat with two of his teammates before calling over the buxom waitress who'd been serving them. The next thing she knew, he was following the woman through the swinging doors of the kitchen.

This is too risky, she thought nervously. *But very exciting.* A faint thrumming had begun deep in her core—tantalizing and insistent. She casually edged her way back to the bar, completely convinced all eyes were on her and that an entourage would be following her into the kitchen. The next three minutes or so passed slower than Lou doing a fifty-yard dash. When the full five minutes were finally up, she sidled into the kitchen, where she found Ty standing next to the waitress, watching as she busily laid out carrots and celery on a tray.

"That's it," he was saying as he nodded encouragingly. "More carrots. The guys really like the carrots with the buffalo wings." He fixed the waitress with a desperate look. "Is there any place to grab a smoke around here? My friend and I have been jonesing for a cigarette all night."

The waitress, who in Janna's estimation wore too much eyeshadow and not enough of a smile, jerked her head toward the back of the kitchen. "Courtyard. That's where we go to smoke. It's supposed to be staff only, but I'll make an exception for you," she said suggestively, shooting a deadly look Janna's way.

"Thank you," Ty replied graciously. Janna followed him out to the dark, brick courtyard, ignoring the waitress's eyes burning a hole in her back.

The night air was cool and clear, carrying the faintest hint of spring and April showers, which had been abundant. A breeze picked up, sending dead leaves swirling around their feet as they walked to the far side of the courtyard. Janna paused a moment to listen to the sounds of the city: conversation, traffic, distant music, the rush of wind, all of it melding together at once into one beautiful, metropolitan chord she never tired of.

"I hope the guys enjoy the extra carrots," Ty cracked as he guided Janna toward the wall and wrapped his arms around her.

"You've had too much to drink," she replied. The brick felt cold against her back. "You realize that, don't you? You would never do anything like this if you were sober."

He nuzzled her neck. "Would you prefer we go back inside?"

"No," she admitted, looping her arms around his neck. "But I'm nervous."

"You worry too much, you know that?" He kissed her forehead. "Let's just have fun."

Fun. Pain corkscrewed through Janna's heart as he dipped his mouth to hers and kissed her deeply. To him this was fun. To her it was love. She knew she'd broken the rules by letting her emotions move beyond the casual, but still, couldn't he throw her a bone? At least acknowledge what she'd said to him in the lobby that day? Even if only to say, "Thanks, I'm flattered, but I don't feel the same." His silence on the subject hurt deeply. Then again, she hadn't exactly given him a chance to answer, had she, blurting the words out over her shoulder while she hopped in the cab? Hadn't that been deliberate, a way to avoid rejection? As their kiss deepened and his hand skillfully crept up beneath her skirt, warming her thighs with his touch, Janna once again found herself thinking that if this was all he could give, she would take it, because this was better than nothing.

She tried to relax, to enjoy the crystalline pressure building within her as he caressed her body. But when another gust of wind sent some leaves dancing, she tensed.

"What?" Ty murmured.

"Nothing," she assured him.

But there was something. Still locked in Ty's embrace, she sensed movement in the darkness, heard the faint crunching of leaves as if someone were tiptoeing and didn't want to make too much noise crushing them underfoot. The hairs on the back of her neck stood on end.

"Someone's watching," she whispered, indelicately pushing him away.

"You're nuts," said Ty, craning his neck to look behind them. "There's nobody here."

She peered out beyond his shoulder into the darkness of the courtyard, trying to see . . . what? Maybe Ty was right. Maybe her imagination was playing tricks on her.

"I think we should go back inside," she said uneasily.

"In a minute," was Ty's unperturbed response. He gathered her up in his arms again. "I don't think you've been kissed enough."

His kiss was unabashedly tender and loving, so much so that Janna willingly put aside her fears of being observed and allowed herself to be carried away, eyes closed and body languid. But then she heard it. The careful, quiet closing of the screen door leading back into the kitchen. Her eyes sprang open; the courtyard was empty.

Whoever had been watching them was gone.

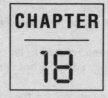

CHAPTER

18

Rather than question Cowley in the office, Janna decided to express her displeasure about his shirking the party over a nice lunch. Hopefully, he would see her invitation as a gesture of goodwill, indicating they both needed to rise to the occasion and work together while Lou was recovering.

She'd chosen a restaurant called Bella's on Sixty-sixth and Central Park West, a favorite from her days at the soap. It was a large, multileveled space serving upscale Italian food, its main clientele actors and staff from the nearby television complex. She and Theresa referred to it as "Little Versailles" since it was all marble, mirrors, gilt and glass. Some of the actors who dined there would stare at their own image multiplied many times over. It was an egotist's dream. Janna had no doubt Jack Cowley would feel right at home.

They began their meal by politely going over business, Cowley ordering two martinis in a row, while Janna sipped

Pellegrino and waited for the right time to bring up the party issue.

"You know," she began, gently putting her water glass down, "I really think the two of us have been doing a great job since Lou's been out."

"But—?" Cowley's tone was sarcastic. "There is a but coming, isn't there?"

"Yes, there is." Janna refused to be cowed. "You should have been at the victory party Saturday night."

"Because—?"

"Because it shows support for the team, and that's part of our job, whether you like it or not. Why weren't you there?"

"Honestly?" Cowley ran a thin finger around the rim of his martini glass. "Because I'd rather have a colonoscopy than whoop it up with the goon squad."

"Those 'goons' are your job." Janna reached for a piece of foccacia and dipped it in the shallow bowl of olive oil at the center of the table. "Don't do it again, okay?"

"Is that a command?"

"It's a request."

"You're the boss," Cowley replied, carefully plucking the green olive from his martini glass. He held it up, examining it as if it were a precious jewel. "But not for long."

"I beg your pardon?"

"How long have you been screwing Gallagher, if you don't mind me asking? Weeks? Months?" His lips curled into a reptilian smile as he popped the olive into his mouth.

She did her best not to react visibly, but her body betrayed her and mortification heated her cheeks. If she tried to deny it, Cowley would just laugh.

"That's none of your business," she replied tersely. She lifted her water glass to her lips, nervous she might choke, or worse, break the stem of the glass, she was gripping it so tightly.

"Oh, but it is. Correct me if I'm wrong, but I could

swear Lou warned you that if you ever dated anyone on the team, you'd be history. Am I wrong?"

A swarm of bees seemed to have taken up residence in her skull, buzzing all at once, drowning out her ability to reason and focus. "How did you find out?" she asked faintly. Her voice sounded distant to her ears.

A look of perverse pleasure overtook Cowley's face. "Let's just say a little Russian bird told me."

Lubov. In the courtyard. That's who'd been watching them! Payback time for both her and Ty. *Stupid. Stupid and careless.* She should never have agreed to go out in that courtyard with him, never. He was buzzed and horny, not thinking straight. But she was sober. No excuse. And now . . .

"The way I see it, you have two options. You can remain interim head of PR, in which case I will tell Lou and Corporate that you're having an affair with the captain and they will fire you. Or, you can go to Corporate, tell them you're not quite up to the responsibility of filling in for Lou, and step down—recommending me in your place, of course."

Janna stared hard at the bread plate before her. "If I do that," she asked slowly, "how do I know you still won't turn around and tell Lou about me and Ty?"

Cowley's eyes lit up as he smacked the table with delight. "Damn, I hadn't thought of that! Thanks for suggesting it."

"You bastard," Janna hissed. "You wouldn't dare."

"Give me one reason not to."

"I could deny it. Lou would believe me before he'd believe you."

"Do you really want to butt heads with me on this, Janna?" Cowley asked condescendingly. "You saw how much I was able to dig up on your little friend, Theresa. Do you really want me to do the same to you? Have you thought about how much it might upset Lou to see pictures of you and Gallagher *inflagrante delicto*, taken at night

with a telephoto lens? Why, it could cause another heart
attack."

"You're sick, you know that?"

"No, I just want what's rightfully mine, that's all."

Janna put a sweating palm to her forehead. The bees
were getting louder. "I need time to think about this."

Cowley pushed up the sleeve of his jacket and lifted his
wrist eye level, the better to read his watch. "You have
thirty seconds."

"I mean it, Jack," Janna snapped.

"Fine. If you need a day or two to think about the exact
words you're going to use when you tell Corporate you're
stepping down, I'll allow it."

Janna reached for more water, wishing now that she'd
ordered something stronger. "If I do what you want," she
said carefully, working hard to keep her hand from shaking, "do you promise you won't say a word to Lou about
my personal life?"

"Can't stand the thought of the old man knowing you're
a puck bunny just like the rest of them, can you?"

"Answer me." The thought of somehow disappointing
Lou was too much to bear.

Cowley smirked. "Perhaps we could work something
out."

"I want a guarantee."

"There are no guarantees in life, Miss MacNeil. Hasn't
anyone ever told you that?"

Janna stared at him. He stared back. She could sit like
this forever if she needed to.

Finally, it was Cowley who broke eye contact.

"All right," he said with a phony sigh. "*If* you do as I
ask, I won't tell Lou about your tawdry liaison with Gallagher. But—and now it's my turn for a 'but,' Janna dear—
I meant what I said a few months back. If you get in my
way again, or persist in trying to outshine me, I will destroy you. Understood?"

Janna nodded tersely.

"Good. Shall we order lunch, then?"

The next morning, Janna took a personal day and drove up to her parents' house. The garden she and her father so carefully cultivated each year was where she did her best thinking, and she needed to be there. Needed to get her hands in the dirt and pull and trim and cut. Next week, when the Playoffs started, she'd barely have time to breathe, never mind take a day off to safeguard her mental health.

As expected, there was no one home. Her father was off at work, Wills was at school, and her mother was out on a standing breakfast date, which would no doubt be followed by a standing tennis date, a standing lunch date, and a standing shopping date. With any luck, she'd be able to work in the garden undisturbed until Wills bopped home from school around three or so.

She parked the car at the end of the long, circular drive, going first to inspect the scalloped beds of heart-leafed brunera, and then to the azalea bushes in front of the house. Both plants boasted tiny, green buds struggling to debut, though it would be at least another three weeks or so before the azalea, with its brilliant fuschia glow, began to bloom. Her mood lightened as she noticed that her father had already done the work of raking out the beds and putting down some Milorganite, a fertilizer that doubled as a deer deterrent. *So much for the front*, she thought, heading around to the back.

The flower beds surrounding the vast patio had yet to be raked, so she would deal with those first. She walked down the sloping back lawn to her father's shed and fetched her old gardening gloves, as well as a pair of shears and the tiny, plastic green rake he had taught her to use as a little girl. Then she trudged back up the slope and painstakingly began raking the first bed, careful not to damage the new shoots coming up. She was still wrestling with her decision: tell Jack Cowley to take a flying hike, or step down.

The way she saw it, she was in a no-win situation. If she refused to step down, Cowley would tell Corporate about her and Ty, and her reputation would be shot, her credibility questioned. She might even get fired. Plus, there was the issue of the media. If she remained in Lou's position for the time being, was she prepared for the blitz of attention that would surround her and Ty once Cowley went blabbing to the press? For a few days at least, it would be a nightmare. She knew she'd be able to handle it. But would Ty?

Her other option, bowing to Cowley's threat, was tantamount to committing career suicide. It didn't take brains to see that backing out of a promotion, even a temporary one, was not a good career move. Corporate would think she was weak, that she couldn't handle the pressure, that she wasn't the "go-getter" Lou had been raving to them about. It was likely she would never be promoted again, and could even find herself demoted. Stepping down was the coward's way out.

What if she went to Corporate and told them outright that Cowley was threatening her, she wondered, as she moved to rake the next bed. Would they believe her? Or would she be labeled a "trouble" employee? The whole situation made her furious. She deserved to be the one filling in for Lou! She'd busted her butt all year long, and she was great at what she did. That's why they'd hired her in the first place—hired *her*, specifically, to spruce up the team's image. And she'd done it, too, done it fast and done it well. And to think all that hard work might come to naught because she and Ty had been stupid and indiscreet.

She put the rake aside, and dropping to her knees on the moist grass, took up the shears and began cutting back the dead peonies and English daisies. She should probably never have gotten involved with Ty. She remembered telling Theresa, way back in the fall when she and Ty had first started fooling around, that she wanted to keep things casual because she needed to keep focused on her career. And what had Theresa's response been? That she was a liar and wanted a relationship with him. Just like Theresa to know her better than she knew herself.

Now look where she was. Because of her "relationship" with Ty, all that famous drive and focus she supposedly possessed was in potential jeopardy. But that wasn't even the worst of it. The worst of it was that she'd fallen in love with the man, and as far as she could tell, that wasn't going to come to anything, either. The tiny blue flowers of the forget-me-nots before her became blurry as tears filled her eyes. She was smart, funny, intelligent, sexy, or at least did a damn good job pretending to be. Why hadn't he fallen in love with her?

If she had a brain in her head—and given her current circumstances, she wasn't so sure she did—she would end things between them, immediately. What was the point? She was never going to get what she wanted from him, and it was now abundantly clear that their arrangement complicated things far more than she ever could have imagined. Ending things would allow her to rededicate herself to her career. It would free her up to find someone who would love her the way she deserved to be loved.

But then she tried to imagine what it would be like never to be held in Ty's arms again, or watch his eyes crinkle up with laughter, or talk to him about the corny old movies they both loved to rent and desolation overwhelmed her. There was no way she could pull the plug on seeing him. She didn't care how irrational it was. So what if their arrangement wasn't everything she wanted right now, she reasoned, pulling off her gardening gloves to touch the withering hyacinths. Maybe the longer she and Ty were together, the more he'd begin to see that she was the right one. Or maybe she was a prime example of a woman desperately grasping at straws. Again, she didn't care. Pitiful as it was, she would take what she could get for now, at least in her personal life.

But as for her professional life? Well, that was another matter. The more she thought it about it, the more she realized she would never be able to live with it if she let herself be bullied by Jack Cowley and his stupid threats. Might she lose her job? Yes. But it was a risk she had to take. Jack had the dirt, but she had the proven track record. Ty was always telling her to believe in herself, to stop the negative self-talk in her head and take to heart the words of the sign he kept up above his locker which read "Who dares, wins."

Well, this time she was going to dare to fight back.

She found Cowley in Lou's office, sitting in Lou's chair, his feet on Lou's now tidy desk, reading an issue of *Smart Money*. The look of triumph in his eyes made what she was about to say even more delicious.

"What are you doing in here, Jack?"

"Getting used to sitting in the Fat Man's chair. I take it you're here to tell me you're stepping down from the interim position?"

"Actually, Jack, I'm here to tell you the opposite. So I suggest you get out of the chair so that I can get down to work."

"I did make it clear what would happen if you didn't see things my way, didn't I?"

"You'd tattle on me to Lou and Corporate. Yeah, you made that clear. Go ahead. I'll be shocked if they give a damn."

Cowley laughed snidely. "Pretty sure of yourself, aren't you?"

"I work hard, and I get results. Oh, and I'm smart. That's why Lou promoted me, made *me* the Associate PR director, not *you*. Or haven't you figured that out yet?"

Cowley stared at her. "You little bitch."

"Actually, Jack, I'm a pretty big bitch. Now get out of the chair."

"Wait'll you see what I plant in the press about you and Gallagher," he hissed, reluctantly rising. "You'll be finished. Your reputation will be toast."

"Take your best shot—after you brief the beat reporters at the rink, that is."

"You'll regret this," he spat as he strode toward the office door.

"We'll see." Janna sat down in Lou's chair as the door slammed.

Well. That was painless. And—shockingly—not nausea inducing! Was it possible that she was finally breaking free of impostor syndrome? Happiness poured through her and she spun around and around in the chair, giggling like a little girl. She'd stood up for herself! She felt proud. Strong. Is this how truly confident people felt all the time? People like Ty? Because if it was, it was wonderful, she never wanted the feeling to end.

"You did it," she whispered aloud. She finally believed in herself. Lou believed in her, too. And Corporate. And Ty. Especially Ty. She would have to thank him for this, thank him for helping her to see just how capable she was.

God, she felt invincible!

She took a deep breath, forcing her lofty thoughts back down to earth. Ty. She was going to have to warn him of what was about to come down, media-wise. Cowley would do his worst, and paint their liaison as sordid, of that she had no doubt. Her intention was to "No comment" her way through it until the noise died down, but she needed to know how Ty intended to handle it. Perhaps, she thought, they could discuss it over a very private, romantic dinner later that evening.

*　　　*　　　*

"I can't see you anymore. I'm sorry."

Ty held his breath, watching as Janna's mouth, which had been gabbing a mile a minute about how they should deal with that weasel Jack Cowley, began to tremble. Then she caught herself and forced her expression back to neutral. The minute he'd set foot in her apartment, he knew that it was going to be harder than he had imagined to say what needed to be said. The lights were down low, and she'd put a mellow, jazzy CD on the stereo. A beautiful table for two was set, complete with two long, glowing, white tapers and a small vase of fresh cut flowers. The aromatic odor of some spicy chicken dish filled the air, and Janna—well, Janna was a sight to behold, her bright, blue eyes luminous, her blonde hair shining like honeyed wheat, every curve of her small, lithe body outlined in the black linen sheath she wore. Seeing her, he wondered if he wasn't making the biggest mistake of his life.

He'd toyed with the idea of waiting until they had finished dinner, but that seemed especially cruel: eating the wonderful meal she'd prepared for him, then turning around and dumping her. Better to do it up front, and get it over with. Then he could leave, take a walk outside to clear his head, and she could do whatever it was women did after a break up.

He said his simple, two sentence piece then waited for a response, but his statement just hung in the air, a storm cloud threatening the room. Janna was mannequin-still, her back ramrod straight while her small, delicate hands sat folded primly in her lap. Was she angry? Devastated? He couldn't tell.

"Janna?"

"I heard you." Her voice was curt. "Is this because Cowley leaked the relationship to the press and you don't want to deal with it?"

"No, it's because seeing you distracts me and I need to put every ounce of attention I have into winning the Cup."

Oh, I understand, he wanted her to say, nodding her head sympathetically. But she didn't. Instead she just kept staring at him. Uncomfortable, he tried to backpedal. "It's not you, it's me."

"And other assorted clichés."

What could he say to that? She was right, it was a cliché. But it was also the truth. They sat in grim silence, and Ty found himself almost wishing she would weep, demand he go, anything. He was feeling like a total creep sitting there, his own words sounding like complete and utter bullshit to him, which was no doubt how they sounded to her.

"So let me ask you something," she said suddenly, breaking the spell.

Ty braced himself for the breakdown that seemed inevitable.

"You say you have to concentrate on the Playoffs. Does that mean you planned on dumping me all along when the Playoffs rolled around?"

"Janna, we both went into this agreeing it was just a casual thing—"

"Answer me." Her voice was sharp. "Were you planning to dump me before the Playoffs all along?"

"Quit saying 'dump,' it sounds so—"

"Honest?"

"Cruel," Ty provided softly. "And the last thing I ever wanted to be to you was cruel."

Janna leaned forward. "You still haven't answered my question."

Ty hesitated. "I didn't plan on us continuing into the Playoffs," he reluctantly admitted. "I didn't plan on us lasting beyond a few months, to be honest."

"I see."

Tiny, so tiny, her voice had become. Worse than the silence, her tiny voice. God, what a bastard he was. If only she knew it was an act of self-preservation. That the last thing on earth he wanted was this, what was happening now. But he couldn't tell her. That would be like asking a hurricane to hit your house. The steel wall separating his emotion from reason was up, it couldn't be scaled, and he was not going to even try.

He stole a glance at her. Her pain was so real it felt as if it had taken form, as if another person sat there on the couch between them. A person he desperately wished he wasn't responsible for.

"I can't be distracted," he said again, feeling a profound need to explain further, even though he knew words might make it worse. "I enjoy being with you, you know I do, but my first mistress has been and always will be hockey. You knew that when we got together, Janna."

"I didn't know there was a predetermined expiration date when you planned to discard me."

"Then that's my fault," Ty said apologetically. "I guess I should have made that clearer."

"I guess so," she said, turning away.

Now, he thought. *Now she'll ask me to go. Please ask me to go, Janna. This is excruciating.*

"I'm sorry," he murmured, because he couldn't think of anything else to say. Janna said nothing.

He rose. "I guess I'd better get going."

"One thing." She turned back, zeroing in on his face. The anguish and desperation in her eyes were enough to force his guilty eyes to the floor.

"What?"

"Do I mean anything to you? Anything?"

Ty cleared his throat uncomfortably. "Of course you do. You're a good friend."

"Friends don't sleep together, Ty. Lovers do. Partners do."

She had him there. He paused, waiting for her to ask the question he didn't want to answer.

"That day in the lobby, when I told you how I felt? How come you've never mentioned it?"

"Janna," he said quickly, "this type of discussion

doesn't do either of us any good. Let's just end things here, okay?"

"Why, are you afraid to talk about it?" There was anger in her voice.

"No."

"Then what's the problem? I want an answer, Ty. How come you never acknowledged what I said to you?"

"Just let it go."

He moved to leave, but the mounting fury in her gaze pinned him to the spot.

"Hold on a minute. You got to say your piece, now I want to say mine."

"Okay," Ty said carefully.

"Sit down."

He sat down.

"You're a hypocrite," Janna began. "You tell your players, like you told me, not to be afraid, to reach for the brass ring, to take risks, rise to the challenge, but do you? No. You stick to what you know you're good at. When there's a chance to take a risk by having a real, loving, adult relationship, are you willing to try it? Of course not. And you know why? Because you're scared."

He couldn't help but laugh when he heard that. "No offense, Janna, but I've never been scared of anything in my goddamn life."

"Except intimacy and vulnerability. You're scared you'll be terrible at it, aren't you? Scared you'll be rejected, or find out that there's more to life than chasing a goddamn sports trophy. So you avoid the risk to avoid the pain. You lead a shallow, pathetic, one-dimensional life."

"If I'm so pathetic and one-dimensional," Ty countered angrily, "why the hell did you want anything to do with me? Why did you say you loved me?"

"Because I saw there was more to you than your effing obsession to win, and I hoped—God how I hoped!—that I might be able to make you see that! But obviously I ⌐ouldn't!"

Furious himself now, he stood, struggling into the jacket he'd slung over the back of the couch. "I think I've had enough of being psychoanalyzed for one evening, thank you very much. I'll take your advice in dealing with the media vultures and do the "No comment" dance. In the meantime, it would mean a lot to me if we could keep it civil at work."

"That won't be a problem."

"Good."

"One more thing," Janna said lightly.

"What?" Ty snapped.

"For your sake, I hope you learn one day to practice what you preach, at least where your personal life is concerned. Because if you don't? You are going to wind up a sad, lonely, old man. And I for one would hate to see it happen."

With that, she rose and went into the kitchen. Ty heard her turn the faucet on and begin to rinse dishes. The urge to run in there and yell a few choice words at her was strong.

Instead, he left the apartment, quietly closing the door behind him.

Riding the elevator back down to the lobby, he found himself continuing the fight in his head. *Janna doesn't know what the* hell *she's talking about! The Cup is emotional fulfillment, it's the ultimate risk! She has mistaken dedication and drive for lack of emotional depth. What the hell does she know?*

The elevator doors opened, and he sighed. Well, it was done. Now he could concentrate on the Playoffs. Raising his hand in a farewell gesture to her doorman, he escaped back out into the New York night.

CHAPTER

19

The Blades won the Eastern Conference Quarter Final against Boston in a four-game sweep and then triumphed in a brutal seven-game battle against Philly in the Eastern Conference Semifinal. Now they were poised to take on Pittsburgh for the final round of the series. Whoever won would go on to battle LA for the Stanley Cup.

Not that Janna cared.

It was six weeks since Ty's KO punch had left her reeling. Oh, she put a brave face on it, and continued working her butt off, despite the stress of having to work with Jerk Cowley, who had succeeded—but only temporarily—in turning her life into a media hell. And she still attended practice and games as usual, shepherding the press through the process of covering a team that had little time for chatting to a clamoring media, especially Ty, though to his credit, he did speak with the regular New York beat reporters he knew and trusted.

But inside, she was crumbling. Having to see Ty daily, to be reduced to perfunctory greetings and clipped conversation, was pure emotional torture. Each time their eyes met and he averted his, a small piece of her withered inside. With each day that passed, it seemed harder and harder to get up in the morning, harder and harder to feel that it was worth the effort. All she wanted to do was sleep, cry, and eat.

The day after the Blades had clinched the series against Philly, a Wednesday, the stress of all the balls she was juggling finally caught up with her and she called in sick to work. She simply couldn't handle going in. When Thursday rolled around and she awoke with the same feeling of depression and dread, she called in sick again. By the end of the day, she knew she'd do the same on Friday; after all, what was the point of going in for just one day?

She spent Friday as she'd spent the two previous days, lounging around the apartment in sweats, eating the cookies and brownies she'd baked for herself. She must have put on seven pounds in the past month and a half. When Theresa came home early from work, and found her curled up watching *Oprah* with tears cascading down her face and a half empty tray of blondies in front of her, she knew she was in trouble.

"Guess what?" Theresa announced brightly, picking up a blondie and taking a bite as she turned off the TV. "You're going to cut this out or else I'm dragging you to a shrink."

"I'm fine," Janna said listlessly.

"Right. That's why you've blown off work for three days and are lying here sobbing."

"I'm premenstrual."

"If that's the case, you've been pre-menstrual for six weeks. Should I call the Guinness Book of World Records?"

"Very funny." She sat up, wiping her eyes.

"He's not worth it, Janna," Theresa said gently. "Can't you see that?"

"I know he's not." She reached for a Kleenex from the box on the table and honked loudly. "But I just can't shake

the feeling . . ." She shook her head, eyes watering, unable
to continue.

"What?"

"That we had something real. Something beyond sex."
She pounded the arm of the sofa. "And it pisses me off that
he couldn't see that!"

"It doesn't matter. I know that's not what you want to
hear, but it's true. It doesn't matter if you were the world's
next Romeo and Juliet. He ended it. It's over."

"But why?" Janna asked plaintively. "Why didn't he
want me? Am I so awful?"

"You said it yourself: he's a shallow, one-dimensional
moron who's terrified of intimacy." She handed Janna another tissue to tend to her dripping nose. "You have to pretend he's like all those arrogant, boneheaded jocks in high
school you hated so much."

"It's not that easy."

"I know it's not," Theresa agreed, opening the shades,
"but I think it would help." Brilliant May sunshine sliced
through the windows.

"The problem is seeing him every day." The sudden
brightness of the room made her blink. "If I didn't have to
face him at work, I think I'd be coping much better. But
between that and having to watch my back with Cowley,
I'm ready to throw in the towel."

"Isn't Lou coming back in two weeks?"

"Supposedly," Janna groused.

"Well, that should help, right?" Theresa plopped down
on the end of the couch, slid out of her heels, and began
massaging her toes. "As for Mr. Gallagher, all you have to
do is get through the next two rounds of Playoffs and the
season is done. You won't have to deal with him all summer."

"That's true," Janna allowed. She snaked a hand out
from beneath the comforter to reach for a blondie, but
Theresa shot her such a look of stern disapproval she

snatched it back. "But I'll still have to deal with him when the season starts up again in the fall."

"You'll be fine by then," Theresa pronounced.

Janna's eyes began watering anew. "What if I'm not?"

"If you're not, they'll find your body floating in the East River because I'll have killed you. Look, things could be worse."

"How?"

"You could still be with Robert."

Janna laughed in spite of herself. "Maybe I'll give him a call." Theresa froze in horror.

"That was a joke, Ter. I think." She sighed. "I just . . . I don't know if I want to do this anymore. It's not just seeing Ty. It's knowing now that if I really put my mind to things, workwise that is, I can achieve what I want. Maybe it's time to take the plunge and start my own business. I don't know." She noticed Theresa beginning to look pensive. "What? What is it?"

Theresa dropped her right foot to the floor and began working the toes of the left. "I wasn't going to say anything to you until I was one hundred percent sure, but since you're in such bad shape, maybe now is the time to bring it up."

"Bring what up?" Janna asked, trying to ignore the blondies crying out to her.

"My settlement money from the Lubov nightmare came in last week."

"And—?"

"I'm thinking of using it to start my own PR firm." She paused dramatically. "And I want you to run it with me."

Janna's stomach dropped. "Are you serious?"

"You know what it's like working for the network. I can't deal with it anymore. Half the actors are dying for personal representation anyway, and you and I both have great contacts. In fact, I bet there are a few Blades who wouldn't mind hiring a personal publicist if it was presented to them right. Not that I would represent them, but maybe you . . ."

Janna began gnawing on the cuticle of her index finger. "Well . . ." she replied tentatively.

"You don't have to think about it now," Theresa assured her. "Wait until the Playoffs are through and you have a bit of distance." She smiled at Janna slyly. "But it would be great to work together again, wouldn't it?"

"It would be a blast," Janna agreed. Only problem was, it would force her to take complete and total responsibility for her own happiness. To fulfill a dream. Could she?

"So." Theresa stood up. "Where would you like to eat dinner?"

Janna groaned. "Theresa . . ."

"I'm not taking no for an answer. I want you to get up, get dressed, put on some makeup, and decide where we're going to eat. I'll be damned if I'm going to let you continue this pity party."

Janna smiled in spite of herself. "You're a good friend, you know that?"

"I try. I just wish there was something more I could do to make you feel better. My great-aunt Josephina knows some old Sicilian curses. Want her to put the evil eye on Gallagher?"

"I think she already has. You've read about how he's playing."

Ty was playing well, but not great. Every sports writer felt compelled to mention it in articles about the team, without exception. Needless to say, Kidco wasn't pleased with the coverage, which amazed Janna. The Blades had just made it into the Eastern Conference Final, for God's sake. What did they want? Perfection? Still, it did give her a perverse thrill of delight that Ty's game wasn't as awesome as it could be. *Loser*, she thought. *That's what you get for throwing what we could have had away.*

"Actually," Theresa reflected, picking up the blondie tray so they were out of Janna's reach, "I think the curses are more for people's livestock—like, 'A hex on your chicken' or 'May your cow drop dead with pox,' that type of thing. Not very effective against professional hockey players."

"No. But thanks for the thought."

"You're welcome. Now get dressed. You're going out whether you like it or not."

> While there's no doubt Captain Ty Gallagher contin-
> ues to lead on and off the ice, his level of play has
> clearly deteriorated from what it was at this time last
> year. Is it age? Battle fatigue? Whatever the source
> of his often uninspired performance, it's certain that
> if he doesn't up the ante in the series against Pitts-
> burgh, the Blades could find their summer vacation
> starting much sooner than expected.

Ty weaved in and out of traffic impatiently. In his mind's eye, he could still see the words that putz wrote in this morning's *Times*. "F.U.!" he shouted out loud, pounding on the steering wheel. "Those who can, do, those who can't become sports writers!" He made a mental note of the putz's name so that later, after practice, he could pull him aside and give him a piece of his mind. *Uninspired my ass,* he thought. *And as for his play deteriorating . . .*

Problem was, the putz was right. His game was slightly sub par, and he knew why, too, and that pissed him off even more. It was Janna.

Try as he might, he couldn't concentrate fully, not with her in his face every morning at practice, and then sitting there in the press box night after night watching him play. His level of play *was* faltering. Sweet God in heaven, couldn't he catch a break? There was serious hockey to play! Playoff hockey. Hockey requiring that he be completely focused and mentally tough. The realization that he was giving 99.9 percent when he should be giving 110 percent ate at him. He didn't know what the hell to do about it.

Tubs cut practice short. They were all exhausted and needed rest. In just three short days, they'd be facing down Pittsburgh on their ice, a distinct disadvantage. Instead of chasing down the putz reporter, Ty looked at the daily injury report compiled by the trainers and the team's sports therapists. Lubov was still listed as "day to day" with an ankle injury. Michael Dante had separated his left shoulder. Two guys had concussions; their toughest defenseman had cracked ribs. Not too bad, really; he'd seen injury rosters ten times worse than this. But what frosted him was that some of the injuries were public knowledge. He'd read about them in this morning's paper, too. Not good. It affected team morale, tainted public perception, and worst of all, told their opponents exactly whom to go after on the ice.

He'd have to talk to Janna—no, Cowley—and let him know that from now on, beat reporters were to be banned from the locker room. That's what Lou would do. Nothing was more important than giving his guys the best chance to win. There was no way that could happen if the press kept running stories about how beat up they were. He shook his head in annoyance as he headed into the showers.

He had just zipped up his gym bag and was resting on the bench before his locker when Kevin appeared, still dressing.

"We still on for lunch?" he asked.

"Of course we are," Ty answered, his words echoing through the empty locker room. He and Kevin were always the last to leave.

Kevin looked down at Ty as he began buttoning up his oxford shirt. "You dumped her, didn't you?"

"Yeah."

"Thought so."

"What?" said Ty sharply.

"I thought so."

"What the hell does that mean?"

"It means I now know why you're not out there playing like you're nineteen years old." He grabbed his jeans from a locker peg and slipping into them, began tucking his shirt into his trousers. "It's because of Janna." His gaze was direct. "You miss her."

"Get a fucking life, will you, please?" Ty scoffed.

"No, you get a fucking life," Kevin retorted. "What the hell is wrong with you, man? She's the best thing that ever happened to you. She made you human."

"Gee, thanks."

"Well, it's true." He shook his head in disbelief. "Why'd you do it?"

Ty ran a weary hand across his eyes. "You know why I did it. Because I can't handle both hockey and a relationship and be at the top of my game."

"Hhmm. Interesting." Kevin moved to the mirror at the end of the row of lockers. "Lemme ask you something. Am I at the top of my game?"

"Without question," said Ty. "But what does that have to do with anything?"

"Well," said Kevin, untangling his black curly hair, "how is it that I manage to have a wife and kids and play great hockey, yet you seem to think they're mutually exclusive?"

"Because you're you, and I'm me. "

"That's a cop-out and you know it."

Ty snorted. "Maybe to you."

"Look, you asshole, not having her in your life is affecting your play! Doesn't that tell you something?"

"Yeah, it tells me I have to concentrate harder on the ice."

"Don't you get it?" asked Kevin. He began stuffing his gym bag. "Your career isn't going to last forever. If you're lucky, you've got six, maybe seven years left. What are you going to do when it's over, Ty? Sit alone and count your Stanley Cup rings? I know this is going to sound like blasphemy, but building a life with someone is more important than winning the Cup. More importantly, it's not impossible to do both."

"It is for me."

"Then with all due respect, you're a loser." Kevin put a foot up on the bench and began lacing up his shoes. "I love you to death, buddy, but if you can't balance having a real relationship with making a run for the Cup, then there's something seriously wrong with you."

"I guess there's something seriously wrong with me," Ty said coolly, though his friend's words smarted. He rose and swung his gym bag up onto his shoulder. "We ready?"

"Yeah, we're ready," Kevin grumbled.

Together they left the locker room.

"Look at this." Standing behind his desk, Lou held up a wilted lettuce leaf for Janna's inspection. "You believe this?" He let the leaf drop back into the foil container of salad before him and picked up a baggie of carrot sticks, waving it. "How 'bout this? Real appetizing, huh?" He released the baggie in disgust. "They expect me to live on goddamn rabbit food now. Unbelievable."

It was so good to have him back, Janna didn't care what he complained about or for how long—she would gladly listen. He was still extremely overweight, but nowhere near the Michelin-esque proportions he'd achieved before the heart attack. A chin or two had actually disappeared, and his shirts were no longer straining at the buttons. In fact, they were loose. Rumor had it that under his doctor's supervision, he was now walking twenty minutes a day on the treadmill. For a man whose previous definition of exercise was opening and closing the refrigerator door, this was monumental. Janna prayed he grew to see that taking care of himself was worth it. The thought of a Lou-less world was too awful to contemplate.

He'd been back for two days, and in that time had resumed absolute and complete control, much to the dismay of Jack Cowley, who took to skulking around the office like a bad cartoon villain. Lou told him to "get a grip or get out," which Janna loved. But she was overcome with trepidation when Lou asked to speak with her privately, the more so when he closed the office door.

"So, what's up?" she asked after he finished crabbing about his heart healthy lunch.

Lou pulled a carrot stick from his bag and sitting down, began munching on it. "I gotta know something, and I promise you, this conversation is between us."

Janna steeled herself. "Okay."

"That stuff about you and Gallagher? Is it true?"

Janna colored, flustered. "It was. It's over now."

"How did the press find out?"

Janna hesitated. "I—"

"It was Cowley, wasn't it?"

Janna kept silent.

"Cowley was pissed they made you interim head so he spilled the beans, didn't he, hoping you'd get the sack? It's okay, you can tell me. I'm not going to go out there and pound his pinhead into dust. I promise."

God, how she longed to spill the whole thing and tell Lou the extent to which Cowley threatened her, but she couldn't, because she didn't want to upset him. She leaned forward, careful not to pop her own buttons. Her pants were too tight, thanks to all those baked goodies she'd been scarfing. She had to get this eating thing under control or come summer, none of her clothes would fit her. She looked at Lou.

"It was Cowley who leaked it to the press," she admitted.

"Sonofa—I knew it. I knew it was killing that weasel that I wrecked his chances of swanning around here like he was king." His gaze turned sympathetic. "Sorry 'bout that, doll."

"Are you upset?" Janna asked timidly. "About me and Gallagher having been involved?"

"Before my heart attack I probably woulda read you the riot act, maybe even fired you if I was worked up enough. Now I don't give a damn who's doing who, as long as people are happy. So in answer to your question, no, it doesn't bother me—though if he hurt you, he's gonna have to pay."

"He didn't hurt me," Janna lied, touched by his concern. "The break up was mutual."

"All right, then."

Janna sank back on the couch, relieved. *Thank God he's fine with all this*, she thought. She watched Lou pretend to enjoy his salad. "You're not going to say anything to Cowley, are you?"

"Nah, not about this. But I am gonna ask what kind of moron he is, letting the press know the injured status of the players. From now on, anyone asks you anything, you know bupkus, okay?"

"I've been 'No comment'-ing my head off all along," Janna reminded him, which was true.

"Good." Frustrated, Lou threw down the plastic fork he'd been using. "I swear to God I am so freakin' starving, I'm gonna gnaw my own leg off." He picked up the phone.

"What are you doing, Lou?"

"Whaddaya think I'm doing? I'm sending Jules out front to get me a Krispy Kreme and a coffee."

"Lou." Janna's voice was reproachful. "Tell her to get you a black coffee and a plain bagel. That's a much better choice."

"BOR-ING."

"Lou!"

"Awright, awright." He ordered what Janna told him to and hung up the phone. "Happy?"

"Very."

"Yeah, well, it's not gonna last long when you see this."

Janna watched as he picked up a curling piece of fax paper from his desk.

"Something you gotta get Gallagher to do, and I mean gotta."

"Lou—"

"Just read it."

He came out from behind his desk to hand the paper to her. It was a letter addressed to Lou from Sandi Rydel, a longtime Blades season ticket holder and president of the Blades Fan Club. She'd been laid off from her job and couldn't afford her tickets to the Stanley Cup Playoffs. She wondered if Lou knew someone who might be interested in buying them through her. That way she could keep dibs on them for the following year when, hopefully, she'd have another job.

Janna put the fax down. "Where does Ty come in?"

"I want you to set up a photo op where he passes the hat around to the players to collect money for Sandi, so she can buy the tickets."

"He won't do it, Lou. Especially not during Playoffs."

"He's gotta do it," Lou insisted. "If he doesn't, Sandy might go boo-hooing to the press that the organization she's dedicated her life to refused to help her, which will make us look like a bunch of greedy, uncaring slobs. Who the hell could say no to an old woman, for Chrissakes?"

"Ty Gallagher."

"He can't be that much of a heartless bastard."

Oh yes, he can, Janna thought. "You should talk to him about it, Lou. The fax is addressed to you."

"But you know how to get him to do stuff, kid."

"Not anymore!"

"Personal stuff aside, you got him to go to that United Way benefit in the fall. I know you can get him to go to this."

Janna sighed, trapped. "I'll try," she said grimly.

"Do more than try. Beg. Cajole. Threaten. Gallagher

knows Sandi, he knows how much this would mean to her. Don't be afraid to put the screws to him and make him feel really guilty."

Oh, I would love to, Janna thought nastily. *More than you know.*

"And if it doesn't work?" she dared to ask.

Lou bit down hard on a carrot. "Then he really is a schmuck."

CHAPTER

20

It wasn't as if she was asking him to pose naked, right? So why did this feel so hard to do? Partly, it was the knowledge that he'd turn her down and she'd have to go slinking back to Lou in defeat. But mostly, she admitted to herself, it was the idea of actually talking to him, of their eyes meeting. She found him channel surfing in the players' lounge.

"I need to talk to you."

"Shoot." His eyes remained glued to the screen.

"Could you possibly turn off the television?" She'd be damned if she'd compete with Jerry Springer.

Ty switched off the TV impatiently. "What's up?"

"This." Janna handed him the fax and watched as he quickly scanned the page, his expression unchanging. He handed it back to her.

"What's this got to do with me?"

Janna hesitated. "Lou thought it might be nice if you passed the hat around to the players and collected money so that Sandi can get her tickets."

Ty remained silent.

"She's sixty-four and worked in the elementary school cafeteria in her neighborhood for forty years, Ty. She was laid off. All it would take is five minutes of your time."

"I don't have five minutes. Especially if there are photographers there."

He folded his arms across his chest in refusal, returning her stare with a hard look of his own. "Look, Janna, I told you way back when you first started out here that I don't do this stuff—"

"But this is an exception," Janna insisted. She rattled the paper without breaking eye contact. "You *know* Sandi. Can't you do it for her?"

"If I do it for Sandi, before you know it I'll have to do it for Al the janitor's cousin with a hernia, and Jim the trainer's brother with back trouble, and everyone else in the Blades orbit."

She rolled her eyes in exasperation. "I understand what you're saying, but don't you think it's better to pick and choose your battles? This is not the case to make your point with." *Besides*, she added silently, *I know you have a heart, Gallagher. Use it.* But Ty was shaking his head.

"Tell Lou forget it, and tell Sandi I'm sorry, but I just can't."

"Why don't *you* tell her?"

"That's your job," Ty replied pointedly. "It did come to the PR office, after all."

Janna tried another tact. "Do you know what kind of a creep you're going to look like if you don't do this, and your hard-heartedness leaks out to the press? Huh?"

"A busy creep, I guess." His gaze was so frosty she wanted to flee. "That's Kidco talking, not you."

"You're right. I already know you're a creep." She saw something flicker in his eyes momentarily—hurt? anger? discomfort? She wasn't sure. But she'd registered some kind of hit, and was glad.

Ty's demeanor turned even more distant. "Let's try and keep this conversation professional, shall we?"

"Certainly."

"What I'm saying is, Kidco doesn't want me to do this because they care about Sandi. They want me to do it so they can send along camera crews and have a heartwarming story about the captain collecting for the poor old woman."

"You're wrong. This is about you doing a personal favor for someone who's been a loyal fan for a long time. Kidco has nothing to do with it. I don't think they even know."

Ty frowned. "I'm not turning Sandi's misfortune into a photo op so those Corporate bastards can feel good about themselves."

"Ty," Janna said through clenched teeth, "how many times do I have to tell you this has nothing to do with Kidco? Look. At. The. Fax. Sandi is appealing to Lou as a *friend*, not as the head of PR. The only reason this is a PR matter is because Sandi has access to Lou."

"Who wants to use it as an excuse for a goddamn photo op," Ty replied angrily.

"So?! What is wrong with letting the public see you have a human side?"

"I thought I didn't have a human side," he said sarcastically.

"And I thought we were keeping this professional."

"If that was the case, you wouldn't be bothering me with this."

Janna's mouth fell open into an indignant "O." "Excuse me? What are you inferring? That I'm intentionally 'bothering' you with this just to make your life difficult?"

"Bingo."

"How dare you!"

"Come off it, Janna. You and I both know you cooked this up as payback for my dumping you. The amazing thing is that you actually thought I might do it."

"Your ego astounds me."

"As does your need for revenge."

She patted his arm consolingly. "I'm not sure how to break this to you, Ty, but I'm well over you. Know why? Because the cookies I ate for breakfast have a deeper emotional life than you. To tell you the truth, I'm glad we're no longer involved." She glared at him. "Now. Are you going to help Sandi out or not?"

"Not."

"Jesus!" She stamped her foot in frustration. "I know, it only serves Kidco, it only makes you a pawn of the big, bad Corporation, I know, I know I know!" She wanted to choke him. "Fine. Have it your way, Ty. I'll go back to Lou and tell him to call Sandi and let her know that the team she's supported her whole life doesn't have five minutes to spare for her."

Ty clicked the TV back on.

"I feel sorry for you, you know that?" Janna concluded. "You're a great hockey player, but boy, when it comes to being a decent human being, you really suck."

With that, she crammed the fax back into the pocket of her blazer and left the lounge.

Wearing his black, wraparound sunglasses and a Yankees baseball cap pulled down low, Ty easily made it to Queens undetected. He took the Number Seven express train to the end of the line in Flushing. Address in hand, he walked past busy shops tended by Koreans and Pakistanis, the latest wave of immigrants to an area that had once been dominated by Italians, Poles and Irish. Ty liked the feel of the place; it had the same pulsating, multiethnic energy of Manhattan, but on a smaller, more manageable scale. He found Sandi's house—a dead ringer for Archie Bunker's, just like every other house in the surrounding area—and rang the bell. A minute later Sandi appeared, wearing an

apron over her Blades jersey and a surprised smile that
made her look at least twenty years younger.

"Ty Gallagher! What a surprise!" She took his arm and
led him inside. "I was just making some rugelach. Do you
want any?"

"Depends on what it is."

"It's a kind of pastry, you'll love it." She led him toward a maroon, sectional couch slipcovered in plastic.
"Here, you sit down. I'll only be a minute."

She disappeared into the kitchen, leaving Ty alone with
the mouthwatering aroma of baking. The room was comfortable, if a little run-down, filled with nicked, old furniture. The faded, floral-wallpapered walls were adorned
with pictures of fair-haired children he guessed were
Sandi's grandkids. He thought about his latest run-in with
his blond nemesis.

Did Janna honestly think he would turn down an old
woman who was practically the team mascot, for Chrissakes? If she knew him at all—and obviously she didn't—
she would have figured out that he would do it like this:
quietly, privately, no camera crews on his tail. But she
didn't know him, or in the very least was incapable of seeing him clearly when she was in publicist mode. Which
was exactly why he didn't tell her the moment he read the
fax that he planned to visit Sandi. He didn't trust her not to
turn it into a media event.

It bugged him that she had again accused him of being
some kind of inadequate human being. Twice in one week
he'd been told he was, in effect, a "loser" off the ice: once
by Kevin, once by Janna. They'd painted him as someone
lacking an inner life, someone devoid of humanity. He
never thought of himself that way; maybe he'd never had
reason to. Yet hearing it twice in one week had to mean he
was doing something wrong, didn't it? But what, exactly?
And how the hell was he supposed to fix it?

He knew what Kevin's answer would be. Kevin would
tell him to get back together with Janna and keep playing

the best hockey he could, period. But Kevin didn't understand. Kevin didn't burn for glory the way he did.

So what? he countered, playing devil's advocate with himself while the sounds of Sandi bustling around the kitchen floated down the dim hallway. *Kevin might not make it into the Hall of Fame, but he has a wife who loves him. His house is filled with kids' laughter. And he's a damn good hockey player. He may not play as well as you, but who's got the happier life, Ty? You or Kevin?*

Just then Sandi appeared, bearing a tray with two coffee mugs and a plate of rugelach, which she shakily put down on the table in front of them.

"How do you want yours?" Ty asked, the plastic slip-cover of the couch crinkling beneath him as he reached forward for the cream and sugar.

"Black is fine."

He handed her a mug and fixed his own coffee before settling back amidst more plastic crinklings. "You know why I'm here, right?"

"That can wait." She motioned excitedly at the plate. "Take one, go on. See if you like it."

Ty perused the plate and reached for one that seemed to be filled with raisins and nuts. Winking at Sandi, he took a bite, then feigned fainting, which delighted her. The rugelach was delicious, it was melt-in-your-mouth good. Perhaps he could entice her into sending him home with a care package.

He held one out to her. "You?"

She shook her head. "Can't. Diabetes. I make them for my husband, Harold."

Ty nodded, and taking a sip of the coffee, returned to the subject at hand. "About the Playoff tickets."

Sandi's face held hope. "Do you know someone who can buy them?"

"They're yours." He fished in the pocket of his denim jacket and pulled out an envelope with the Blades logo on it. "I'm giving you the tickets as a gift."

Her hands flew to her mouth. "Oh, Ty. Oh, God."

"There's just one condition."

"What?" she asked eagerly.

"You don't tell anyone I gave these to you, okay? If anyone asks, they were a gift from Lou."

"A gift from Lou," she repeated to herself. "I can remember that."

"Good." He pressed them into her hand and leaning over, softly kissed her papery white cheek. "Now enjoy them."

They talked hockey for awhile, much to Sandi's delight. Finally, noting the encroaching lateness of the hour, Ty finished off his coffee and stood up.

"I should get going," he said, extending a helping hand to her. Together they walked to her front door.

"I can't thank you enough for the tickets," she said, her voice trembling with emotion.

"Just make sure you're at Met Gar for Game Two," he reminded her. "Remember, you're our good luck charm."

"You boys had better win!"

"We'll win," Ty promised." We'll win in Pittsburgh on Wednesday, too. Don't worry."

"I do worry," she said, pointing an accusatory finger at him. "Something is up with you. I can see it on the ice. You better take care."

"Everything is fine," Ty assured her. He gave her a final hug and started down the front steps, grateful his back was to her so she couldn't see his scowl. *Something's up with me, all right,* he thought grimly. But as for doing something about it—well, there was nothing to be done, at least nothing he cared to think about right now.

Janna spent the rest of her day laying groundwork for the following fall. Though the season was close to over, the PR office stayed open year round. After leaving Armonk and Ty-the-Heartless, she'd met a woman from the New

York Literacy Council for lunch at the Algonquin; the Council was planning a major fundraiser and was interested in having one or more of the players attend to help sell tickets. Following lunch, she'd hustled downtown to meet an editor from *GQ* for coffee at Vesuvio, to pitch him an idea for a profile on Ty. He seemed interested, and agreed to get back to her later in the day with a list of possible writers. All in all, not a bad afternoon. A rough morning, but at least she wouldn't be coming back to Lou completely empty-handed.

She returned to the office to find Lou deep in discussion with Tad Morrison, one of the suits from Corporate. *Listen to you*, she chided herself. *You're starting to sound like Ty.* It was Morrison who had temporarily anointed her interim director of PR in Lou's absence, and to whom she'd had to explain that yes, it was true, she had been seeing Ty Gallagher. Just seeing him again made her flush with remembered embarrassment. Lou gestured for her to come in.

"Janna, you know Mr. Morrison?"

Janna smiled politely, as did Morrison, a hawk-faced, beanpole of a man who rarely smiled for pleasure. She noticed the mood in Lou's office was somber, which was unusual.

"How'd it go?" Lou asked.

Janna defeatedly blew out a puff of air, lifting her bangs. "It's no-go on Sandi Rydel."

"What the hell are you talking about? I just got off the phone with Sandi. She called and thanked me for the Playoff tickets."

Janna was stunned. "You're kidding me."

"Captain Mysterious must have bought them for her and went out to Queens himself to deliver them."

Janna couldn't believe it.

"How do you want to handle this to get some ink?" Lou continued. "Obviously Gallagher doesn't want credit."

"We could send someone over to take a picture of Sandi holding the tickets, and we'll say it was a gift from Kidco,"

Janna suggested. "We'll have her put on a Blades jersey, hat, the whole works. "

Lou beamed proudly, looking at Morrison. "What did I tell you? Does this one have it upstairs or what?" He turned to Janna. "Great idea. I was about to suggest it myself."

"Anything else?" Janna asked, still grappling with the fact that Ty had indeed gone to see Sandi Rydel. Against her will, she felt kindly toward him. *I knew he couldn't be that much of a creep*, she thought. *I knew it.*

Lou took a huge gulp of coffee, casually trying to hide the pizza crust on his desk beneath a pile of papers. "How'd the rest of your stuff go?"

"The Literacy Council is definitely on board, and it looks like *GQ* does want to do a major profile of Gallagher. They talked about interviewing him over the summer so the piece could run in September when the new season starts."

Morrison coughed uncomfortably as he and Lou exchanged glances. An awkward silence seemed to pervade the room, augmenting the already solemn mood. *Uh oh*, Janna thought. *Not good.* She glanced back and forth between the two men.

"What?" she asked.

"Call *GQ* and tell them to put any thoughts of a Gallagher profile on hold right now, will you, doll?"

"Okaaaay," Janna said slowly. "May I ask why?"

"Because—" Lou halted as Morrison half rose out of his seat as if to protest. "Keep your shirt on Tad, okay?" Lou barked impatiently. "You know we can trust her." Morrison looked dubious as he sunk back down onto the couch but made no protest while Lou continued. "You probably know Gallagher's play has been a little off lately."

Janna nodded, not sure she wanted to hear what was coming next.

"Well, coupled with the fact he's such a ball-busting,

uncooperative pill when it comes to PR, Corporate isn't sure if they're going to renew his contract at the end of the season."

"I see," said Janna, suppressing a gasp. She was in shock. Utter and complete shock.

Lou drained his coffee mug. "Needless to say you don't know about this."

"Of course," she assured him.

"From now on," Morrison commanded from the couch, "push the younger players like Lubov and Mitford as much as you can."

"Even if Gallagher's play gets better?" Janna asked politely, nauseated at the thought of having to push Lubov for anything.

Morrison nodded sagely. "We need to focus more on the up-and-coming players, not the players who are in the twilight of their careers."

Ouch, thought Janna. Thank God Ty wasn't here, he'd rip Morrison's head off and use it as a bowling ball. As it was, she was having a hard time listening to this. The instinct to excuse herself was overwhelming; there were so many things she longed to say, so many words dancing on the tip of her tongue that could get her into serious trouble. All she could do was stand there and nod like an idiot, and pray Lou released her from this hell soon. Before the dam broke and she found herself rising to the defense of the man who'd broken her heart, ruined her morning, and who only nine short months ago was the biggest thorn in her side.

"You look green, doll, you okay?"

Lou's words broke the spell. She shook off his question with another smile, this one faker than the last. "I'm fine," she told him. "It's just been a long day."

Lou's laugh was hollow. "Truer words have never been spoken."

"Does Jack know about this?" Janna asked.

"Not yet," Lou replied cryptically, his eyes once again

meeting Morrison's in some secret exchange of knowledge.

Janna's spirits lifted for a moment. Maybe they were going to fire Cowley!

"Anything else?" she asked Lou again.

"Nah, that's it for today." In an unusual gesture of politeness and formality, no doubt done to impress Tad Morrison, Lou walked her to the door of his office, holding it open for her.

"I know it's hard to have info no one else is privy to, but please keep it under your hat," he murmured.

Janna squeezed his hand. "I will," she promised him.

But even then, she knew she was lying.

CHAPTER
21

The game opener of the Conference Finals. The Pittsburgh fans were rabid, and the Blades fans were easily their equals. The excitement and enthusiasm of their cheering was infusing the arena with a wild, ear-splitting energy. Watching Ty fly down the opponent's ice, Janna had a hard time believing Corporate would let him go. He was the consummate athlete, brain and body working in perfect tandem, with an almost uncanny ability to know exactly what needed to be done on the ice. He had tremendous leadership skills; he was caring yet tough, relentless yet inspiring, was unafraid to put himself on the line if it meant the difference between victory and defeat. And yet . . .

He was drawing more penalties in this Playoff series than ever before. Janna knew part of it was deliberate. It was a way to send a message to the opposing team while shaking up his own guys, and it set the tone for the type of play he expected from them: rough, relentless, mean. But part of it was just plain recklessness; at least that's what she'd heard Lou say. Recklessness that the Blades couldn't afford. Lou also claimed Ty's timing was off, that "he wasn't creating as many scoring opportunities." Since Lou loved hockey more than anything on earth, Janna didn't question his observations. She was still enough of a neophyte that many of the nuances of the game escaped her. But she did know one thing. Even on an off day, Ty Gallagher remained one of the most talented hockey players in the history of the game. Didn't he deserve to know, then, what might befall him if he didn't give Kidco a bravura performance?

It was a question that had been eating at her for over two days, ever since Lou and Beanpole Morrison let her in on the big secret. She'd toyed with the idea of talking to Theresa about it, then quickly nixed it. She knew exactly what Theresa's response would be: "Don't say a word to Gallagher! He screwed you over, now it's your turn to screw him over! Keep your mouth shut and let the chips fall where they may!"

It was a point of view Janna understood, since to some extent she felt the same way. The wounded part of her wanted to withhold this vital information from him and watch as maybe, just maybe, he fell on his face. It would be the perfect payback. Yet not telling him seemed so petty, so spiteful. And spite simply wasn't part of her makeup.

She wondered, though, whether telling him would benefit her. She was sure he'd appreciate it, but it wasn't as if helping him out would magically make him decide he wanted to be with her—even though deep in her secret heart of hearts, that was her fantasy. If she told him, would he suspect her motives? Possibly. Probably. Did it matter? She didn't know.

It was only fifteen minutes into the game, but the tone on the ice had already been set, high speed and nasty. Sitting beside Lou in the press box, Janna's eyes followed Ty as he and Kevin raced into Pittsburgh's defensive zone, Kevin dropping the puck to his best friend as two defensemen charged toward him. She watched as Ty held the puck, waiting for their line's other winger, Brad Frechere, to position himself on the right side of the net. A split second later, Ty blasted the puck to Frechere who nonchalantly stuffed it into the opponents' net. The home crowd booed as the goal appeared on the electronic scoreboard high above center ice: New York, 1, Pittsburgh, 0.

Ty's line skated back to the bench as the Lubov line took to the ice. Above the din, Janna could hear Ty's voice ringing out on the bench: "C'mon now, boys! Drop another one in! Don't let up! C'mon!"

That, she thought, *is what I love about him. That drive, that determination. His singularity of purpose.* Granted, that very same trait in him had broken her heart, but viewed objectively, she found it admirable.

She watched his head tilt back as he put a bottle of Gatorade to his lips and drank. Even something as simple as that made her heart do a double take. *What is it with you?* she asked herself. *Why him? Because he's great in bed, and loyal to his friends, and funny. Because he's smart—and stubborn, too, Mother of God is the man stubborn, but that can be an asset. And . . .* her eyes began welling up *. . . because when he was with me, he always made me feel special. Cherished. He listened to me when I talked. He looked at me with admiration. He admitted he was wrong about Lubov. He teased me about my flaws. He was gentle and caring with my brother. He encouraged me to pursue what I love, even though he had no idea whether I was any good at it or not. He simply assumed I was, because it was me. He made me feel alive.*

Through watery eyes, she forced herself to watch the game. *You have to tell him*, she thought. She would wait and see how the next couple of games went. If the Blades didn't win, she'd let him know what he was up against. . . .

This solution satisfied her until a nagging voice in her head asked where she got off playing God. *Either you tell*

him or you don't, she scolded herself. *But you don't play
"Wait and see."* All right, she moaned silently. *I'm going
to keep my mouth shut like Lou asked me to. Whatever
happens, happens.*

Ty slashed one of the Pittsburgh defensemen and
skated, snarling and angry, to the penalty box. His lips
were moving rapidly as he cursed the ref before settling
down to his fate and watching the play from behind Plexiglas. The Blades successfully killed the Pittsburgh power
play and Ty skated back out onto the ice, stopping to say
something to one of the refs before huddling with the third
line which had just taken to the ice. She watched the players' faces while he spoke, saw the reverence and respect
there as well as their eagerness to please him.

That was when it hit her. She *had* to tell him, not because he necessarily deserved to know, not because she
wanted him to love her again, but because it was the right
thing to do for the team. Kidco could bitch all they wanted
about Ty Gallagher being a PR nightmare. But the bottom
line was, he was the heart and soul of the Blades. If they
lost him, they would lose their spirit and will to win. It was
that simple.

She relaxed back in her seat, confident now that she had
made the right decision. She'd wait until the team was settled back at the hotel after the game. Then she'd pay Ty a
visit.

The Blades beat Pittsburgh, 3–2. *Thank God*, thought
Janna, as she silently padded down the carpeted hotel hallway. Had they lost, she knew she'd be facing an absolute
bear. As it was, she had prepared herself for whatever un-
pleasantry he might throw her way: sarcasm, dismay, disbelief—all the various facets of Ty at his worst.

She paused before knocking, pressing her ear to the
door to hear what was going on inside while silently praying that no one walked by and wondered what she was

doing. She could hear Kevin inside laughing, probably in response to something David Letterman was saying on TV; both were addicted to *The Late Show*. She rapped firmly on the door, trying to pretend she didn't hear Ty moan and Kevin curse in response.

"Who is it?" Ty shouted.

"Janna!" she yelled back.

The dead silence that greeted her felt worse than the annoyance she'd heard them express seconds before. She held her breath. *Please God don't let him be too much of a jerk.*

The door yanked open, and there stood Ty, a navy blue towel knotted around his waist and a scowl on his face. Janna's mind flashed back to the first time she'd met him in the Blades' locker room. He'd been wearing nothing but a towel then too, and she'd been just as unnerved as she was now.

"This better be good."

"Actually it's bad," she informed him, pushing the door open wide, "which is why I need to talk to you." Her eyes caught Kevin's, who was stretched out on his side of the room in sweats. She smiled apologetically. "Hi, Kev. Sorry to disturb you guys."

"It's okay," said Kevin, sitting up. "Why don't you come in?"

At his invitation, Janna brushed past Ty, whom she heard release a long-suffering sigh as he closed the door behind them.

"Can I get you something to drink?" Kevin offered, gesturing towards the minibar across the room.

"No thanks." Her eyes stole to Ty, who stood watching her suspiciously, arms folded against his bare chest. He wasn't going to make this easy, that much was clear. She turned her attention back to Kevin. "I need to speak with Ty about something—"

"Whatever you have to say, you can say in front of Kevin," Ty cut in.

But Kevin wasn't having it. "If Janna wants to talk to you privately, Ty," he said as he rose from the bed and headed toward the door, "then I think we need to respect that." He drew Janna into a quick, affectionate hug. "Don't take any bull from this loser, you hear?"

Janna managed a wan smile in response.

"Where are you going?" Ty demanded. He seemed somewhat edgy about his friend leaving.

"Down to Moonie's room, maybe he'll cut me in on the poker game. Give me a call down there when you're done."

"Right," Ty grunted, watching Kevin depart. Forced now to deal with his visitor, he turned to Janna. "You sure you don't want anything to drink?" he asked begrudgingly.

"A Coke would be fine if it's not too much of a problem."

He muttered something to himself, Janna wasn't sure what, and went to the minibar to fetch her a drink. She watched the strong muscles in his back ripple as he strode across the room, her eyes drawn to his broad expanse of shoulder as he pulled the Coke out of the small fridge and poured her soda into a plastic cup.

"What's up?" he asked, walking back toward her with the drink.

Keep your eyes on his face, Janna told herself, *nowhere but his face*. She accepted the drink gratefully.

"Can I sit down?" she asked.

"Is it going to take that long?"

"I'll make it as fast as I can, I promise."

He gestured for her to sit in one of the chairs across from his bed. As she did so, he sat down too, and his towel began to come undone.

"Shoot. Excuse me." He rose, and letting the towel drop to the floor, walked towards the bathroom. Janna felt her entire body flush with unexpected heat and pleasure. Ty naked . . . was he doing this on purpose to torture her? Or was he oblivious in that way athletes were? That had to be it. By the time he emerged from the bathroom a few seconds later wrapped in a terry cloth robe provided by the hotel, her body temperature had returned to normal and she fancied that maybe she'd be able to get through this conversation without her desire for him clouding her ability to string a sentence together.

"Okay," he said, settling back down on the edge of his bed, "what's so important that you have to throw Kevin out of his own hotel room?"

"Kevin offered to leave," she felt compelled to point out. Looking at Ty's face, a face she loved, uneasiness began overtaking her at the thought of being the bearer of bad tidings. She reminded herself that what she had to say was bad only if he chose not to do anything with the information. Still, the idea of actually saying it . . . She stared down into her coke.

"Lou told me something a couple of days ago that I'm not supposed to know."

"What's that?"

Janna lifted her eyes to meet his. "Seems that Corporate isn't happy with your level of play." She hesitated. "They're saying that if you don't improve your game, they're not going to renew your contract at the end of the year."

He stared at her. That was it. Just stared. No visible reaction—that is, until he spoke. His voice was strained. "I see." His jaw clenched. "Lou told you this when?"

"Two days ago. He was in a meeting with Tad Morrison."

"Who the hell is Tad Morrison?" Ty snapped.

"He's one of the bigwigs at Kidco." She paused. "He's literally the one who signs your paycheck," she added softly.

"I see," Ty repeated. Staring off into space, he ran his hand through his hair distractedly before putting his hands into the pockets of his robe and peering down at his bare feet. Janna fought the urge to throw her arms around him and comfort him. She watched him instead. He didn't seem

upset so much as furious. Contained. Like a geyser about
to blow.

"Ty?" she asked. He raised his head to look at her, his
soft brown eyes now hard as stone.

"You realize," he said, "that half the reason they're contemplating this is because I refuse to kiss their asses."

"I know," Janna concurred.

Without thinking, he reached out for her Coke and she
handed it to him. It seemed the most normal thing in the
world, something they had done countless times before.
Except now . . .

He handed the plastic cup back to her. "This is un-
fucking-believable. I bring them the Cup last year, I will
bring it to them again this year, and this is how they repay
me? By not renewing my contract because of a few off
days?"

"It's amazing, I know. I nearly keeled over when Lou
told me."

His gaze pinned her. "Who else knows?"

"As far as I know, just Lou, myself, and Corporate."
She made a sour face. "Jack Cowley has no idea, if that's
what you're asking."

"It is what I'm asking. Cowley's the idiot who was letting the press know about team injuries. What the hell was
he thinking?"

"He wasn't." *He'll get his*, she added hopefully in her
head.

But Ty wasn't listening. He was looking toward the
window, his countenance solemn, his body still. *I should
go now*, Janna thought. But something held her in place.

"Are you going to be all right?" she asked him gently.
There, that was it, the thing that was rooting her. It was
concern. Love.

"I'm fine," he replied curtly. He looked back to her, and
for the first time since they'd ended things, Janna had the
feeling that he was really seeing her. There was a lack of
defensiveness in his posture, a surrender of the many roles

he imposed on himself. Right now, he was just Ty, a man in pain, a man feeling unappreciated.

"Why did you tell me?" he asked quietly. "You could just as easily have kept your mouth shut."

Janna glanced away, embarrassed. "Because it was the right thing to do. If the situation was reversed, I would want to know." He was watching her carefully, she could feel it, his steady gaze heating the side of her face. "I did it for the team, too. Without you, they've got no spiritual core. I didn't want to see that happen."

He responded with silence. When Janna dared to look back at him, he was staring down at the floor again.

"I should go." She put her cup of Coke on the table beside the chair, and rose. Ty did the same. Together they walked to the door.

"I guess I'll see you at practice tomorrow," Janna said lamely.

Ty barely nodded.

She turned to the door, went to open it.

"Janna?"

She closed her eyes for a moment. *Please*, she thought. *Please*. Hand still gripping the doorknob, she turned around to face him.

"Yes?"

"Thank you."

The strain in his voice said it all.

"You're welcome."

He took a step toward her, then halted. She waited, breath held, body poised. *Please Ty*, she silently pleaded, *do what your heart is telling you to do. Build a bridge to me with all the unsaid words here between us, and cross over it. Please.*

But he couldn't, so she did it for him. She went to him, and standing on her tiptoes, softly kissed him on the cheek.

"Try to get some sleep tonight," she urged. Then she was gone, out the door and down the hall, her heart lighter for the gift she felt she'd given him. *I've done what I needed to do*, she told him in her head. *Now it's your turn.*

A man possessed. That's the cliché all the sports writers were using to describe his play through the next three games against Pittsburgh. They'd won the Conference Final in an astounding four-game sweep, and as Ty held the Prince of Wales trophy high above his head on home ice, he lifted his eyes to the skybox where all the Kidco execs sat watching. He made sure he had a big smile plastered on his face that said, "You're thinking of getting rid of me? Just wait until two weeks from now, when I'm skating around the arena holding the Stanley Cup aloft, you SOBs. Then we'll see how quick you are to give me the shaft, when the fans are screaming my name and my face is on the front cover of every newspaper in New York."

He wasn't stupid. This bull about him upping his level of play *or else* was just that—bull. If they truly valued him as a player, they would have come to him and expressed their concern, asking if anything was on his mind and how they could help. The fact they didn't told another story, one that pointed to their fanatical devotion to image as well as their obsession with the bottom line. They wanted to get rid of him because they couldn't control him. Because they knew winning this Cup would coincide with contract negotiations, placing him in prime position to name his price, which they would undoubtedly not want to pay. It didn't matter that he was a marquee player and his presence on the team helped keep the arena filled. All they gave a damn about was payroll and presentation, and as far as they were concerned, he was trouble on both counts, the high-priced captain who refused to spend all his spare time cheerleading for causes handpicked to make Kidco look good.

He'd heard rumblings that the suits were displeased about the role he played when it came to personnel, too. A thumbs-up or -down from him could mean the difference between a player being traded or not, benched or not. They seemed to disregard the fact that Tubs deliberately solicited his input. The Blades GM was threatened by his veto power. "He thinks you're overstepping your bounds," is what Tubs had told him, and they had both marveled over the stupidity of not wanting a captain who'd won three Stanley Cups to give his insights when asked. He liked to think he would have risen to the occasion without Janna's clueing him in to what the bigwigs had in mind, but he wasn't so sure. Her words had literally lit a fire under him, and when he went on the ice for the ensuing three games against Pittsburgh he blazed, fueled by raw adrenaline and an almost unquenchable drive to show the number crunchers what he was made of. That he'd be damned if he'd let them decide his fate.

He couldn't wait for the final round of the Cup finals to begin. If they thought he was a man possessed now, just wait until they saw him at the series opener in sunny LA.

He passed the trophy off to Kevin, whose solemnity now reflected his own. Winning the Prince of Wales was nice, but all it meant was they'd won the first round. In his mind, it almost didn't count. He could see Janna watching him from the press box. Usually it threw him a bit, but tonight he was filled with gratitude. Letting him know what Kidco was planning despite what had gone down between them impressed him to no end. Were the situation reversed, he didn't know whether he would have been so generous. Probably not. In fact, being a major jerk, he probably would have let her twist in the wind. He didn't know. All he knew was that she had driven his desire to win the Cup to the brink. Until she'd told him what was going on behind the scenes, he'd found her presence a distraction. But now he was going to take all that energy he'd been using trying not to think about her, and he was going to use it to drive himself and the Blades forward. And when they won, he would hand the Cup to her, giving proper thanks to the woman who saved his neck.

And then he was going to give Kidco a surprise they'd never, ever forget.

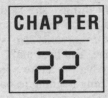

CHAPTER

22

Un.Be.Lievable.

For weeks Janna and Theresa had talked about going to the Angelika to see the late-night screening of *Gone With the Wind*. They were finally here, and of course, right in the middle of the burning of Atlanta, her cell phone rings. Forced to hustle out to the lobby before the other patrons killed her, Janna was now overcome with apprehension. Was it Wills? Had to be. Something awful had happened again. Swallowing hard, she pressed the phone to her ear.

"Hello?"

"Janna? It's Pierre LaRouche."

Pierre LaRouche, the Blades' goalie, calling her cell phone at close to midnight? *Not good, not good at all.*

"Pierre? What's happened?"

"I'm at the police station." There was an uncomfortable pause. "I, uh, got picked up for soliciting a prostitute."

Idiot!!! she longed to yell. *You big, stupid French Canadian idiot!!*

"Have you talked to anyone else?" she asked instead, in

the voice that you use to talk to slow children and dangerous maniacs.

"No—I mean, you said if there was ever trouble we
should call you first, so—"

"You did the right thing," she said quickly. "Tell me
where you're at, and I'll be there as soon as I can. In the
meantime, *don't talk to anyone else*—not your wife, not
one of the guys, no one. You hear me?"

"Uh huh." He gave her the address in a quivering voice.

"Just relax, everything is going to be okay. See you in a
few."

She ended the call and slumped against the lobby wall.
*Oh, this was just perfect, a textbook case of exactly the
kind of publicity the team didn't need. Especially now,
poised on the brink of victory. Now what?*

"Is everything okay?"

Janna looked up to see Theresa striding toward her, a
look of unconcealed alarm on her face.

"A player's in trouble. I can't go into the details right
now. Go back and watch the movie, I'll meet you at home
later."

"Whatever you say, Miss Scarlett." She gave Janna's
arm a reassuring squeeze and disappeared back into the
dark theater.

Unsure of what to do next, Janna began nervously pacing the lobby under the suspicious eye of the theater man-
ager. What did he think she was going to do, stick him up
with a box of Jujubes, steal a tub of buttered popcorn, and
run? She returned his glare and continued wracking her
brain for a course of action. She'd dealt with the police before; that wasn't what worried her. What worried her was
keeping this out of the public eye. If word of this got out, it
could ruin LaRouche's personal life, and put him out of
commission on the ice for the rest of the season, since the
NHL would suspend him, which would certainly affect the
Blades. Not only that, but a situation like this looked really
bad, perpetuating as it did the stereotype of athletes as

sleazes, which, admittedly, some of them were. *Why did he have to do this?*

Feeling as if she might burst right out of her skin, she left the theater and hailed a cab uptown to the police station. The ride seemed to take forever, with traffic grinding to nearly a complete standstill near Broadway and 42nd. Janna was so frustrated she contemplated jumping out and walking the rest of the way, but thought better of it when she caught sight of the dense crowds she'd have to fight through. Her cabby cursed, and she glanced out the window at the car that was trying to cut them off. It had a sticker for the Police Athletic League—PAL—plastered to its rear window. Her mind lurched. The PAL . . . of course! She had a connection at the PAL, a cop named Steve Dalvey. Back when she was at *The Wild and the Free*, she helped raise money for him by arranging a yearly celebrity softball game between cops and soap actors. All of the proceeds went to the inner-city kids PAL helped. Steve had said if she ever needed a favor, she should give him a call. *Well, Steve-a-rino*, she thought, as she frantically rooted through her handbag for her Palm Pilot and her phone, *I hate to bother you this late at night, but the time has come for me to call in my favor.*

Fifteen minutes later, he was walking up the steps of the precinct house to meet her, a burly man with an easygoing demeanor.

"I can't tell you how much I appreciate this," Janna said. "Especially given the time."

"No problem," he assured her, holding the police station door open.

Despite the lateness of the hour, the station was abuzz with activity. A man with a bandaged, bloody head was sitting in one of the orange plastic seats along the wall, pointing and complaining about a drunk in a tattered overcoat who appeared to be asleep on the floor. A domestic dispute between a husband and a wife was being waged at full volume in a far corner, while a hooker with little on besides

pink plastic pants and a bandeau top sat swinging her long
legs and cursing under her breath. The stone-faced female
officer behind the desk was doing her best to ignore all of
them. Thankful this was a side of New York she rarely got
to see, Janna followed Steve Dalvey as he strode up to the
desk and flashed his badge while introducing himself.

"You got a john here, French guy with the name of
LaRouche?"

The officer behind the desk nodded.

"Well, I need to see him and the officer processing the
case."

"Hang on." She dialed the phone in front of her, repeated Steve's request, and a minute later he and Janna
were being led toward the back of the station house, where
they found Pierre and the officer in a large, neon-lit room
filled with endless file cabinets. Pierre was sitting next to a
small metal desk where a paunchy, middle-aged cop sat
typing at a computer. When Pierre saw Janna, he jumped
up and started babbling excitedly in French.

"Sit down, sit down," Janna urged, gently pushing him
back down to his seat. "You don't want to get in any more
trouble."

The cop behind the computer looked up at Janna. "You
the wife?"

Bite your tongue, she thought. "A friend."

Steve showed his badge to the cop, who nodded in
recognition. "I need a favor from you," he said amiably.

"Yeah?" asked the other cop.

"See this guy sitting here? You know who he is, right?"
The other cop nodded. "Treat his case the same way you
treat every other john—process him, fine him, set up a
date for a court appearance, and let him go. Not a word to
the press, TV, sports radio, anyone. Can you do that?"

The cop shrugged. "For you? Sure, no problem."

"Good man." The two shook hands and Steve turned to
Janna. "Let's let Officer Affa finish processing Pierre."

Back out in the waiting room, Janna almost fainted with relief.

"I owe you big time," she said.

"Get outta here. Anything for an old friend. Any chance of arranging a charity ball game between the Blades and the cops?"

"You bet. Just wait until the Playoffs are finished, okay?"

He winked at her. "Deal. I'm gonna take off now, if you don't mind. Will you be okay on your own with this French guy?"

"I'll be fine," she assured him. She gave him a quick hug and watched him go, the man who had just saved Pierre LaRouche's butt and, possibly, the Blades' entire season. Connections. They made the world go round.

Exhausted but elated, she picked a plastic seat far from the hooker and the bleeding man, and waited for Pierre to be released.

"Janna?" Lou poked his head into her office. "Gallagher just called. He said he wants to see you down in the locker room ASAP."

She checked her watch. "Lou, they're in the middle of their pre-game meeting. Are you sure he said he wanted to see me *now*?"

Lou nodded. "He was yelling, doll face. I think there might be a problem."

Making her way down to the Blades' locker room, Janna fought mounting panic. For Ty to summon her during the pre-game prep could only mean one thing: something was very, very wrong. LaRouche again? Why was everything hitting the fan now, when they were so close to the Cup?

Heart in throat, she knocked on the locker room door. She heard Ty's voice shout, "Come in!"

Opening the door, she was completely unprepared for the sight that greeted her. The players stood in a circle, fully dressed. In the center of the room was Pierre LaRouche, holding a huge bouquet of flowers.

"For you," said Pierre, coming forward with his bouquet. "I cannot thank you enough for what you did for me the other night. *Merci.*"

Ty nodded in quiet agreement, his face a mask of reluctant appreciation. "You really came through for the team on this one, Janna," he said. "Thanks."

"Let's hear it for Janna!" said Kevin Gill.

Hoots and hollers ensued. Dazed, she took the bouquet, too overcome to speak. She looked around at the players' faces, remembering how alien she felt among them in the beginning of the season, how worried she was that they would never trust her or perceive her as anything more than a pawn of Kidco. And now . . .

"Thank you," she whispered.

"No, thank you," said Kevin. "We could have had a real disaster on our hands if it wasn't for you. "

"Disaster control is part of my job."

"And getting the team ready to play is mine," Ty cut in. "I hate to cut this short, but we have a hockey game to prepare for, gentlemen." He strode toward the door, opening it for Janna.

"Thanks again, guys," she called over her shoulder. She forced a glance up at Ty. "Win tonight."

"We will," he said, not looking at her.

With that he stepped back in, quietly closing the locker room door behind him. Janna paused a moment, awash in feelings for the men inside she never thought she'd have. Of all her victories so far over the course of the season, this was among the sweetest. Smiling to herself, she started back to her office, proudly carrying the bouquet like the trophy it was.

"*This is so* totally awesome I can't believe it! You rock!"

Wills's delight with the gift she'd just given him—two

tickets to Game Five of the Stanley Cup Playoffs between New York and Los Angeles—made Janna flush with pleasure.

"Just another one of the perks of being the team's publicist," she said, trying to restrain herself, as always, from ruffling his hair. Hugging was still permitted, as was a casual kiss on the cheek now and then. She supposed she should be grateful.

He seemed happy, and for that she was glad. She wondered if Ty had anything to do with it. Wills had let it drop that he had indeed called Ty a few times for advice about the situation at home, and it had been a big help. She wished she could thank him, but she wasn't supposed to know about it. So she contented herself with just being grateful that he was there for Wills and that Wills felt comfortable enough seeking him out. Asking for help, especially when you were a guy, was not the easiest thing in the world to do.

With one week left until the Cup Playoffs began, she had taken advantage of the beautiful June weather to pay this weekend visit to her parents. Ostensibly, the reason for her trip was to give her brother the tickets. But really, she wanted to pick her father's brains about the career issues she was struggling with.

Leaving Wills to his latest video game, she went downstairs and out the front door, stopping short when she found her mother hovering over her father while he knelt by one of the azalea beds, pruning back some of the bushes' lower branches. Her mother rarely took any serious interest in the garden. "Shape them a bit more," her mother was urging, using some vague hand gesture meant to indicate form.

"They're shaped enough," her father replied.

"I like them flatter on top," she complained.

Janna's father rose and handed her mother the pruning shears. "Would you like to do it?"

"You're impossible, you know that?" Courtney Mac-

Neil flicked her long blond hair over her shoulder and waved the shears away, turning to her daughter for confirmation. "Isn't he impossible?"

"Impossible," Janna agreed. She waited for her mother to say something worse about her father—she always said something worse—but this time her mother just turned and strode back into the house, slamming the screen door behind her for good measure. In the world of the MacNeils, this was progress. Janna settled on the brick step, elbows resting on her bare, freckled knees.

"Want some help?"

"No, you just sit here and talk to me. It's been awhile."

"I know." She watched as he returned to the work at hand, an expression of fixed determination on his face. "Dad?"

"Mmm?"

"When you struck out on your own to start MacNeil Builders, were you scared? Were you afraid you might fall on your face?"

"Of course I was. But I was tired of working for other people." He lifted his head to look at her. "Why? Something going on at work?"

"Theresa's going to be starting up her own PR firm and she wants me to work with her," Janna started uneasily.

Her father's face lit up. "That's great, the two of you striking out on your own!"

"The problem is, I'm not sure I want to." She looked down at her sandaled feet, absently chipping away at the polish on her toenails.

"Why's that?"

"Lots of reasons," she replied, hedging. She didn't want to tell him the real reason, that even though she had faith in her abilities, there was still a small kernel of fear deep inside her that made her terrified of going after what she wanted.

"Lots? Well, give me one."

"I like what I'm doing now."

Her father shrugged. "So stay where you are, then," he replied, setting his shears to work again.

"I don't want to do that, either." She paused, feeling embarrassed. "I sound like a whiny jerk, don't I?"

"No, you sound like a young woman who's confused about her career."

"I am," Janna admitted. Her career dissatisfaction had always been like a low-grade fever, annoying, but not debilitating. But watching Ty fight his way back from the doldrums had been inspiring. He clearly loved what he did and was willing to go to the limit to make his dream of winning another Cup come true. It filled her with envy. What was it like to feel that way about what you did with your life? She had no idea. But Ty did, and so did her father, which was why she was here.

"Not to sound like a broken record, but when you struck out on your own, what gave you the confidence to do it? To overcome that fear of failure?"

Putting the pruning shears to rest on the ground, her father carefully stood up and came to sit down on the step beside her. "I'm not sure how to answer that," he began. "All I knew was that if I didn't at least try, I couldn't live with myself. The risk seemed easier to face than settling into a life of compromise." He searched her face. "Is this about your business degree?"

Janna nodded. "A few months back, a . . . friend of mine . . . said the same things to me you're saying now. He gave me a bit of a hard time, implying I threw in the towel too quickly when it came to striking out and starting my own business. He said the only thing that really matters in life is 'going for it,' you know?" She bit her lip. "I think he might be right."

"This 'friend' of yours"—Janna lifted her head at the insinuation in her father's voice—"is he in a position to talk to you like that? Has he pursued *his* dreams?"

"To the exclusion of everything else."

"You don't sound too happy about that," her father noted wryly.

"I'm not, but I really don't want to talk about it, if you don't mind." She flashed her father a quick, apologetic smile.

"Not a problem," he assured her. He squinted into the distance, watching as the small blue and white mail truck stopped at the end of the circular drive to deposit a stack of envelopes into the mailbox. "So, what are you thinking?"

Janna suddenly felt shy. This was her father, a successful, self-made man. What if he scoffed at what she was about to say? Would she be able to recover? Then again, he'd never put her down in her life. Why did she think he would start now?

She closed her eyes and took a deep breath. The air smelled sweetly of flowers and impending summer. "As you know, I make a lot of money. A lot. And I've been socking it away for years. I did the math, and if I match the money Theresa is putting in to start the business, and we both draw minimal salaries for ourselves at the beginning, we could really be a major PR firm right off the bat."

"Sounds like a sound plan to me."

She opened her eyes and turned to him. "Really? You're not just saying that?"

Her father looked dismayed. "Of course I'm not. I've always believed in you, Janna Elizabeth. If you set your sights on this, I have no doubt you can achieve it. But my saying it doesn't mean a damn thing. The person who has to believe it is you."

"I know," Janna muttered. "I just worry about the age thing, you know? I'm thirty. Most entrepreneurs these days seem to be twenty two—"

"Big deal," her father replied dismissively. "Don't hide behind the excuse of your age. Grandma Moses didn't start painting until she was in her eighties. Harlan Sanders didn't start Kentucky Fried Chicken until he was well into his sixties. What's the worst that can happen?"

"I fail. Miserably."

"You're only a failure if you don't give it a shot. That's my opinion, anyway."

"Ty's too."

Her father smiled knowingly. "I thought he might be the 'friend' you were referring to."

"I guess you saw all the stuff that was in the papers."

"It was hard to avoid. Tell me, was the split really mutual?"

"No. He dumped me."

Indignation played across her father's face. "More fool him, then." He pondered his azalea beds. "When would you resign?"

"After the Playoffs. I'd stick around for part of the summer, though, to help my boss train someone else."

He looked at her directly. "Are you sure your wanting to leave has nothing to do with your ex-friend?"

Janna looped her arm through his. "I swear to God, Dad, my wanting to leave Kidco has nothing to do with Ty. Kidco hired me to do a certain job, and I've done it. But I feel the need for something bigger. Something that's really mine."

"Well, in that case, the choice seems obvious." He laced his fingers through hers, holding on tightly. "As far as I know, no one ever went to their grave wishing they'd taken fewer risks in life. Do it, Janna. You'll be amazed at how quickly the universe will catch you if you're willing to fall. Swallow that fear and do it."

CHAPTER

23

"We want the Cup! We want the Cup!"

The cries of Blades fans standing three-deep behind police barricades echoed in Ty's ears as his car pulled into the tunnel beneath Met Gar. It was a beautiful summer day, the late afternoon sun shining, the humidity miraculously minimal. Were the season over, he knew just what he'd be doing: blading around Central Park. Instead, he was on his way inside to play what could be the most important hockey game of his career.

The entire city was in the grip of Blades fever. You could feel it. They were the talk of sports radio, the papers, ESPN. Lou Capesi told him that up in PR, he, Janna and Cowley were fielding hundreds of media requests in anticipation of a Blades victory tonight, many from New York–based programs like *Good Morning America* and *The Daily Show*. To his credit, Lou knew better than to ask him to commit to any media until the Cup was officially theirs. Last year, Ty had agreed to appear on *Good Day New York*. That was it. This year he might be willing to do more. It all depended on his mood as well as who wanted a piece of him.

He hoped they won tonight. Not only because it would be sweet, wrapping up the series in five games, but because his boys were exhausted, their minds and bodies in an extreme state of fatigue. If the fates decreed they had to fly back to LA and battle through a game six or seven, then they'd do it, and they'd win. But for all their sakes, he hoped tonight marked the end of the road.

Inside, the mood was subdued but excited, security guards calling out "Good luck!" to him as he passed, suits he'd never seen before hurrying through the neon-lit corridors in the bowels of the building like they had important business to attend to. *What the hell are they doing down here all of a sudden?* Ty thought resentfully. *Making sure the victory champagne is properly chilled?*

The locker room was a different story. His boys were uncharacteristically quiet as they dressed for the game, barely any small talk between them. Someone had posted an exuberant sign above the doorway declaring, THE CUP IS IN THE HOUSE! but no one seemed to be paying the sign or the sentiment much attention. Ty knew what they were all going through; he was going through it himself, his emotions a strange cocktail of anxiety and determination, seasoned with just a hint of being completely overwhelmed. He knew of teams that didn't say a word to each other as they prepared for what could be their Cup-clinching game; teams who huddled and prayed, or who sat together watching footage of ticker tape parades to get themselves pumped up and inspired. Well, not this team. This team would do what they'd done all season: They would take their cue from him.

"Listen up, guys."

All eyes turned toward where he stood before his locker, the bright blue "C" on his chest standing out in bold relief against the white of his jersey.

"Anyone who has ever put on skates and played hockey has dreamed of the moment we now find ourselves in. There have been players in the NHL—great players—who dedicated their whole lives to this sport and who never

came as close to winning the Stanley Cup as we are now."
He cleared his throat as emotion slowly began building
within him. "If we lose tonight, I know there are some of
you who might not take it so hard. You'll think, 'There's
always next year.' Well, I'm here to tell you that's not
true." He slowly looked around the room. "You may never
come this close to winning the Cup again. All we have is
this moment, right here, right now. This is it.

"Winning tonight will not be a matter of how talented
we are as a team or what skills we as individual players
bring to the ice. Winning tonight will depend on one thing:
how badly we want it. If we want the Cup badly enough,
then come the end of the night, it will be ours. Years from
now, we'll be able to tell our kids and grandkids about this
night. We'll be able to show them our names etched onto
the Cup itself: permanent, lasting proof that we were, right
down to the last man in this room, winners." He picked up
his helmet and strapped it on. "I don't know about you, but
me? I want the Cup so damn bad I can taste it. So let's go
get it. Let's make history."

"Madonn', I can't take this, I'm gonna have another
heart attack right here, I swear to God!"

Janna shot Lou a worried look even though she knew—
she hoped—he was only speaking metaphorically. It was
the last period of the game, six minutes to go, and the
teams were tied. New York had been the first to score three
minutes into the first period, Ty's line charging into LA's
defensive zone like a three-man stampede. Kevin Gill expertly deked the puck past LA's goalie in a move so
smooth it seemed as if the Blades were under no pressure
at all. But LA answered right back three minutes later, and
the tenor of the game was set. The Blades scored a goal
twenty seconds before the first period ended, only to find
themselves caught off guard at the top of the second when
LA came out onto the ice and fired a shot from the blue
line that tied the game 2–2, where it had since remained. A

sense of urgency tinged with desperation hung over the arena as both teams fought for dominance. Janna looked around the stands at the tense, hopeful faces of the fans, some clutching rabbits' feet and horseshoes, others wearing necklaces of garlic to ward off bad luck. Up in the loge seats she could see a huge banner declaring, LIGHTNING CAN STRIKE TWICE! GO BLADES! Like everyone else present, Janna fervently hoped it was true.

Beside her, Wills seemed to hold his breath every time LA skated into the Blades defensive zone. The tension in the house was unbearable, the waiting for someone to score torturous. As the final minutes of the game wound down, Janna sensed all 18,000 Blades fans were desperately hoping their team wasn't scored against—or that the game was forced into overtime. Glued to the action on the ice, she suddenly noticed Coach Matthias whisper something to Ty on the bench. Ty nodded sagely, rose, and went out onto the ice with Kevin Gill, while his line's usual right winger, Brad Frechere, remained seated. Instead of Frechere playing Ty's other wing, it was Alexei Lubov.

Janna turned to Lou. "What's going on?"

"Matthias is trying to shake things up, generate some action," Lou explained.

One minute passed. Two. Janna's mouth felt parched, her heart rate skipping double time beneath her blazer. She watched as Ty drew a defenseman the size of an Amana upright to him, then passed the puck wide to Lubov, who stood alone in the slot not twenty feet from LA's net. Kevin Gill skated to a waiting standstill in front of the goalie, acting as a screen. It worked: Lubov snapped the puck in a low shot against LA's goalie, and the red light above the net went on. Score!! New York was in the lead with only three minutes left of play!

The crowd went crazy, but the roar didn't last half as long as Janna expected. Baffled, she again turned to Lou, whose expression was guarded.

"We still have to work that last three minutes off the

clock, doll. A lot can happen in three minutes. You know that. Break out your rosary beads."

Time suddenly seemed to unfold in extreme slow motion. Wills clutched her arm and was squeezing hard. The entire arena held its breath as LA did their best to ward off defeat. The last few seconds ticked away.

Then the final buzzer sounded, and Met Gar erupted with a deafening roar. The New York Blades had won the Stanley Cup for the second year in row!

"Yeess!!" Janna and Wills were on their feet, hugging, screaming, and clapping along with the rest of the jubilant crowd. Tears streamed down Lou's face as he grabbed her into a fervent embrace.

"That's my girl! I knew you'd tell him!" he cried.

"What?!"

"I knew there was no way you'd let him go down if you knew Kidco was thinking of axing him," Lou shouted in her ear, over the deafening cheers of the crowd.

"You set me up?!"

Lou tweaked her nose. "Bingo."

"You're unbelievable!"

Lou jerked his head in the direction of the ice. "Look down there and tell me it wasn't worth it," he yelled, his voice getting hoarse.

Janna looked down at the ice. Ty was jumping up and down like a little boy, pumping his fist in the air while around him, his teammates wept, laughed, hugged. Their elation was contagious: Janna felt exultant, especially when the Cup was finally brought on to the ice. It was handed to Ty, who promptly passed it on to each of his teammates before taking it back to begin a slow skate around the arena, holding it aloft so the fans could share in the moment of glory as well.

"I want to touch the Cup!" Wills begged.

Janna playfully bumped her shoulder against his. "So get your butt down there, then."

Her eyes followed him as he hurried down to the lowest level of the arena, fighting his way toward the front of the surging crowd. Ty approached, grinning broadly as hands eagerly shot out, a sea of fluttering fingers desperate for contact with the holy of holies. He patiently accommodated them all, a look of warm recognition spreading across his face when he encountered Wills. One minute Ty was saying something to her brother; the next he was lifting his eyes to the press box, seeking her out. They looked at one another; looked into one another. Then Ty continued down the ice.

Smirking, Lou opened his mouth but Janna froze him with a look.

"Don't," she mouthed.

Further commentary was shelved when Lou was tapped on the shoulder by one of the faithful New York beat writers, wanting to know where the victory party was being held.

"The official party for us working stiffs and the team is being held right here at the in-house restaurant, The Grill," Lou replied. "But where the Blades choose to go partying with the Cup afterward is anyone's guess, and nobody's business."

Ty wouldn't have believed it possible, but winning a second Stanley Cup for New York felt even sweeter than winning the first. The repeat performance cemented the team's reputation as a great hockey club. It also all but guaranteed him a place in the Hockey Hall of Fame—not that he was ever really in doubt. He was proud of what the team had accomplished out there on the ice, but even more, he was proud of the men they had become: men who knew the value of loyalty, brotherhood, and perseverance. Even if none of them ever won another Cup in their lives, these traits would always be part of them now, for better or worse. They would always share a special bond.

He and the guys were beyond wiped out by the time they finally made it back into the locker room, but that didn't stop the champagne and beer from flowing, as endless toasts were made. Family and friends all crowded into the small space, while TV cameras and journalists stuck microphones in the players' sweaty faces, asking the same questions repeatedly: How does it feel to win a second Stanley Cup? Were you ever in doubt? How does it feel, how does it feel, how does it feel . . .

Ty, drenched in champagne and close to punch drunk with elation as he headed off to the showers, couldn't resist the obvious reply: "How do you think it feels?! It feels great!"

Because it did. But it would have felt even greater had he been able to share the feeling with the one person who really helped secure the Blades' victory by inspiring him. He tried to catch a minute with her at the "official" party at The Grill, but it was next to impossible. Every time he tried to talk to Janna, someone came up and slapped him on the back, or asked him to pose for a picture, or plied him with a drink, congratulating him. Admittedly, he basked in the attention. Hell, he even shared a few tender moments with the stiffs from Kidco, going so far as posing with them holding the Cup—not because he wanted to, but because he knew it would make Janna's life just a little bit easier. And making her life easier, making it happier, was something he'd spent a great deal of time thinking about lately.

It was close to 3 A.M. before he, Kevin and Abby ducked into the back of the stretch limo that was to take them to the team's private party at Dante's, the restaurant owned by Michael Dante's parents. All of New York seemed to be awake and celebrating, the city's long avenues lined with delirious fans.

"You know, Ty, you could have brought a date to this party," Abby Gill pointed out lightly.

Ty reached forward, patting the Stanley Cup where it sat in the front passenger seat beside the chauffeur. "Got my date right here," he said, hoping Abby took the hint and let it go. He loved her like a sister, but not her meddling. *I know what I'm doing*, he wanted to tell her, *even if you think I don't.*

Outside the restaurant, police barricades kept a few thousand waiting fans at bay. Word had traveled fast that the Blades were in Brooklyn, and the entire block was closed off to traffic—unless you happened to be the driver for the team captain, in which case an exception was made. As the limo pulled up to the restaurant, and Ty and the Gills emerged, the crowd went crazy. Adrenaline surged through Ty as he collected the Cup and held it up for all to see. *This*, he thought, brimming with pride and accomplishment, *is one of those moments you never forget.* The Gills quickly slipped inside, but Ty walked up and down the barricade, allowing the fans their moment with the Cup. He felt it was the least he could do to reward them for their dedication to the team, not to mention the fact they'd waited outside Dante's for hours just for this one moment.

Inside, the Cup was the guest of honor, making the rounds as everyone present took a turn drinking from it. No sooner would it be empty than someone would bring it back to the bar to be refilled. Over the course of the evening, guests broke out into spontaneous song, and the entire restaurant seemed to shake from the pounding of happy feet on the makeshift dance floor. Yet through it all, Ty's pulse beat out one word and one word only.

As the festivities continued, he waited until there was a lull in the partying, and then called for everyone's attention. The room fell still. He took one more sip of Guinness to fortify himself, and then he began to speak. He started by complimenting each of the players by name, as well as everyone else whom he thought had helped contribute to the team's victory, from their crack team of trainers to the lowliest stick boy. He expressed his gratitude and pride. He reminded them of what a rough year it had been, and how they'd weathered the storm together by setting a goal and sticking to it.

And then he stunned them.

"I want to thank every guy I've ever played with in the NHL. I'm a firm believer in going out while you're still on top. For this reason, tonight was the last professional hockey game I'll ever play, and this is the last Stanley Cup I'll ever win. I've decided to retire."

Gasps of disbelief echoed around the room. "Why?" some of his players demanded, their faces pale with astonishment as they tried in vain to hold back tears.

"I've had a great run, but it's time for me to move on and pursue some other dreams I've back-burnered because of"—he shot a quick glance at Kevin—"my fanatical devotion to winning. You know the expression, 'Get a life'? Well, that's what I'm finally going to do, guys. I'm going to get a life."

He reached for his beer, relieved to be finished. The crowd surged toward him, those closest crushing him in a loving embrace. A hundred voices were talking at him at once, but the only one he could make out clearly was in his own head. *There*. He'd done it. He'd said what he needed to say without breaking down. He knew Kidco would be on their knees begging him to stay. He didn't care. He knew that media coverage of him would be especially intense now, but that was okay, too. He would do what needed to be done and say what needed to be said—anything to ensure that his intended departure in no way marred the perfection of what his team had achieved on the ice tonight.

The handshaking, backslapping, and hugging seemed to go on endlessly. Ty felt buoyed up, as if a large burden had been lifted from him. He checked his watch. Six A.M., and the party was still going strong, both inside Dante's and out on the streets. He decided to stay up. There was one more thing he needed to take care of before bringing the Cup home and falling into the deepest, most satisfying sleep of his life. Patient as ever, he waited for the rest of the world's working day to begin.

"My, what glamorous lives we publicists lead."

Janna didn't bother to respond to Jack Cowley's comment, watching instead in horrified fascination as the phones in the PR office continued to light up and ring incessantly. It was the day after the Blades' victory, and while the players and other personnel had the day off to recover from the reverie of the night before, the PR team had no such luck. Their day would be spent in telephone hell, fielding a mind-boggling amount of media requests, questions and offers. Lou had hired two young interns to help out with the deluge, but it seemed to Janna they only made things worse. Each time the phone rang, they asked her whether they should take a message or run it by Lou. She noticed neither of them ever bothered Jack Cowley. Perhaps they knew intuitively that he was an unhelpful creep.

She sighed, trying to clear space on her desk. She'd only been in for fifteen minutes and already the Post-its were piling up. *Good Morning America* wanted Ty. *Live with Regis and Kelly* wanted Lubov. The Mayor's office had called, needing to go over plans for the ticker-tape parade planned for Friday, two days hence. In just two hours the entire team, as well as the coaching staff and GM, were due back at Met Gar to pose on the ice with the Cup for the official team picture. Mild alarm seized Janna as she wondered what to do if some of the players showed up drunk for the photo shoot, or not at all. *That won't happen*, she told herself. *They'll be there*.

Though she hadn't expected it, she'd felt a small surge of delight when she'd come to work to find there were no real messes for her to clean up. None of the guys had gotten into a fight, or taken the Cup to a strip club, or lost it, or done anything questionable with the top prize in sports since she'd seen them last. She allowed herself a moment of pride. Lou had hired her to shore up the Blades' image and help raise them to a higher level of respectability. Judging by the way the team behaved this year compared to last, it seemed all her hard work had paid off. *Maybe I shouldn't resign*, she thought uneasily. *Maybe I should keep working for Lou.*

"Janna?"

For what felt like the hundredth time that morning, one of the interns had called her name. She clenched her teeth.

"Yes?"

"David Letterman's people are on the line," the young woman said breathlessly. "They want to to know if Ty Gallagher and Kevin Gill would be willing to bring the Cup on the show tonight. What should I say?"

"Transfer that call to Lou. Then go down to the Starbucks across the street and get me a tall—no a venti—double mocha latte, okay?" She fished in her purse and handed the girl a ten dollar bill. Then she marched into Lou's office and closed the door.

"Those Twinkies you hired are driving me nuts," she declared.

Lou, in the middle of a phone call, just nodded distractedly. Janna waited for him to hang up the phone. "What did you say?" he asked.

"I said—"

His phone rang again.

"Get it," said Janna, slumping down on his couch. "Just get it."

But he didn't. Instead he directed his secretary to hold his calls for a few minutes.

"Have you talked to Gallagher since the party at The Grill last night?" he asked.

"I didn't even talk to him then. Why? What's up?"

Lou grimaced, scratching the bald spot on top of his head. "That was Jimmy Salo at the *Post*. He heard a rumor about Gallagher and he wants to know if it's true."

Oh, great, thought Janna, preparing herself for the worst. *Here goes my personal life again, splashed all over the gossip pages.*

"What's the rumor?" she asked.

"He said he heard—from very reliable sources—that at the team party last night Gallagher announced he's retiring from hockey."

"Get out of here," Janna scoffed. "His sources are full of it."

"That's what I said, but still, we gotta keep on top of this. Talk to him when he shows up for the shoot."

"Ty Gallagher would never retire from hockey. Hockey is his life."

Lou raised one of his caterpillar-sized eyebrows. "Do I detect some bitterness in your voice, sweetcakes?"

"Not at all," Janna fibbed. "Look, the reason I came in here was to let you know that those interns you hired are useless. They keep asking me questions every three minutes."

"Tell 'em to take messages. Period."

"I thought you told them that already."

"Tell 'em again," said Lou.

"They're not bothering Jack at all," Janna pointed out, miffed.

"That's because I told them not to."

Janna stared at him. "Excuse me?"

"Cowley's history, okay? After all this Stanley Cup hoopla settles down, I'm letting him go. The last thing I want is a backstabbing, power hungry jackass working for me. Besides, the players don't trust him, especially after the injury report fiasco."

"You're really firing him?" Janna tried hard to keep the excitement out of her voice, knowing it was wrong to find delight in someone else's misfortune. Still, if that someone else happened to be Jack Cowley, maybe a touch of glee was permissible.

"It's hasta la vista, Jackie, just like I said." Lou looked amused. "Try not to look so sad, okay? I know this is breaking your heart."

"Completely."

"I'm gonna need your help finding his replacement."

"Sure," Janna replied evenly, feeling like a heel. Should she tell him now, in the midst of all this chaos, that she planned to resign? He'd throw an embolism. Better to wait until things were back to normal. The thought of not working with Lou anymore filled her with sadness. She adored him, bad eating habits and all.

A knock sounded at the door, and Janna turned around, surprised. "Geez, that was fast."

"What was fast?"

"I asked Cindy Lou Who to run across the street and get me a latte."

Lou's eyes lit up. "Did you tell her to get your boss one of those giant chocolate chip cookies as well?"

"No, I did not," Janna replied, "because my boss doesn't eat those anymore, does he?"

"Jesus, Mary and St. Joseph, you're worse than my wife," Lou grumbled. "Come on in!" he shouted.

The door opened to reveal not a coffee-bearing intern, but Ty Gallagher holding the Stanley Cup. Behind him, Janna could see Jack Cowley's smirking face, as well as the stunned face of Lou's secretary and the remaining intern, who looked as though she'd just witnessed the Second Coming.

"Gallagher!" Lou crowed, hitching up his pants as he came out from behind his desk. "Been out all night, eh? You look like six miles of bad road. Your boys behave themselves?"

"As far as I know."

"But not you. You've been a bad boy."

Ty put the Cup down on the floor and looked at Lou questioningly. "What are you talking about?"

Lou looked sly. "You got something you wanna tell Uncle Lou in PR?"

A slow smile spread across Ty's face. "What have you heard?"

"Salo called me not five minutes ago, foaming at the mouth. He says he has it on good authority that you gave the big *arriverderci* speech last night at Dante's. That true?"

Ty's eyes went straight to Janna. "Yup. I'm retiring."

"What are you, out of your mind?" Lou barked. "You're at the top of your game!"

"Which is why I want to retire now." His eyes remained fixed on Janna. "I want to go out on top. Plus there are some other things I'd like to do with my life."

He smiled at Janna then, a happy, weary smile that she returned despite a sudden feeling of shyness in his presence. It was obvious he had indeed been up all night: he was wearing the same khakis and blue oxford shirt as the night before, though his clothing was rumpled now, and his face bore the beginnings of a beard from not having shaved. But his eyes were luminous, not bloodshot, and there was a calmness about him that belied any sense of having struggled to make such a monumental decision. The way he was looking at her—so openly, with such quiet affection, told Janna that Lou wasn't the person he had come to speak with.

The look was lost on the Bull, who was busy looking Ty up and down like a mother inspecting her child before his first day of school. "You're gonna shave and change before the photo session, right?"

"Of course I am." He came toward the couch, lightly resting his hand on Janna's shoulder. Janna swallowed, trying to remain nonchalant, but it was hard. A touch from Ty, any touch, was still like contact with a live wire. She wondered if he knew that.

"Lou, would it be possible for me to have a couple of minutes alone with Janna?" Ty asked politely. "I know it must be nuts in here today, but this really can't wait."

"No problem. I have to hit the can anyway."

Janna tried to ignore the wink Lou gave her as he left the office, quietly closing the door behind him. They were alone now, just she and Ty—and the Cup. She rose and went to inspect the magnificent silver trophy up close. It smelled of booze.

"Show me where your name's been etched on it before," she asked self-consciously.

Ty crouched down, pointing out his name in three different spots.

"Pretty impressive," said Janna. Ty stood, and she could feel him watching her as she distractedly read the hundreds of other names ringing the Cup. "I didn't get a chance to congratulate you at The Grill last night," she began.

"And I didn't get a chance to thank you. If not for you, that Cup wouldn't be sitting in this office right now."

"Yes it would," said Janna, uncomfortable with the credit he was giving her.

"No, it wouldn't," Ty insisted. "Listen to me, Janna. Your telling me what Kidco had planned for me was a wake-up call in a lot of ways." He took her by the shoulders and gently turned her so they were facing one another. "Do you remember telling me way back in the beginning of the season that you would be the pebble in my shoe that I couldn't get rid of, the annoying song lyric I couldn't get out of my head?"

Janna looked down. "Yes."

"Well, you were right. You *are* the song lyric I can't get out of my head. Except the lyrics are those of a love song."

Janna took a shallow breath, wanting to hope, wanting to dream, but still feeling the need to guard herself.

"Are you listening to me?" Ty asked when she didn't respond.

Janna nodded.

"In the past, I've never been able to maintain a relationship and make a run for the Cup. The personal stuff always interfered with the concentration I needed to win, or vice versa. I know there are guys who can balance both— Kevin, for example—but I've never been one of them. So I had to choose. I could either continue dedicating my life to hockey, or I could finish out my career on a high note and pursue a life with the woman of my dreams."

He reached for her hand. "Winning last night was glorious, but it was nowhere near the happiness I felt when you and I were together." He paused, pensive. "I know I hurt you when I ended things. I also lied—to you and to myself. Our relationship was never a casual thing to me, never. But I couldn't admit it, because admitting it meant giving my heart over to you. Look at me, Janna. I'm a jock. I thrive on making myself impervious to pain and vulnerability. But you . . ." He reached out and tenderly touched her cheek. "You really got to me, lady. And it scared the life out of me."

Janna could barely find her voice. "It scared me, too. I'm scared now."

He drew her into a tight, protective embrace. "I know you are, but don't be. I will never, ever hurt you again. I swear it."

Warmth flooded her. It felt so good to be held by him, so right. And yet . . . She drew back just enough to look up into his face. "What happens now?"

"Now I ask you to forgive me for hurting you. I tell you that I love you and hope to God to hear you say you still love me. I tell you that I want to build a life with you."

Tears blurred Janna's vision. "You're sure about this?"

"Absolutely," he assured her, once again pulling her close. "I've accomplished what I set out to achieve. Sure, I could keep playing, maybe even win another Cup, but what would be the point? I want a life, Janna, a real one. And I want it with you."

"Looks like we're both making some career changes," she said.

"What?"

"Don't say anything to anyone, but I'm going to resign soon." She hesitated. "Theresa and I are opening our own PR firm."

"Way to go!" Ty looked delighted. "I'm really glad to hear that."

"We'll see how glad you are when I'm panicking because we don't have enough clients." Her heart gently tapped against her ribs. "Have you thought about what you'll do instead?"

"I don't know. Open a restaurant, I guess," he joked. "Coach. Become a GM. Something will present itself. Maybe I'll just spend hours on end making love to my wife."

Wife. The word made Janna's head snap up in shock. "Is that . . . are you . . . ?"

Ty laughed softly. "Let me do the questioning, okay? Janna MacNeil, will you marry me?"

"Aren't you supposed to kneel?"

Ty shook his head and sighed. "A backbreaker to the end, aren't you? You want me to kneel? Fine, I'll kneel." He knelt down and took her hand. "Janna MacNeil," he repeated reverently, "will you marry me?"

"Mmm . . . yes." She yelped with joy as Ty rose and scooped her up in his arms, spinning her around. "Yes, yes, yeeesss!!!"

"Hey, no funny stuff in my office, ya hear me?"

Janna was still giggling and giddy as Ty put her down at the sound of Lou's voice.

"You kids done yet?"

Janna beamed. "We're done. We—" She looked to Ty, unsure of how much to reveal. "We're—"

"Getting married," Ty announced proudly, squeezing her tight.

Lou rushed towards them, pumping Ty's hand furiously before covering Janna in paternal kisses. "Congratulations! This calls for some *sfogliatelle*, don't you think? Sit tight. I'm gonna use your phone, doll, and order up a big box from a place I know in Little Italy. They're to die for. Won't be a 'mo."

Once again Lou disappeared. Ty and Janna looked at

each other and shrugged. *What was there to say?* Janna thought. That was Lou for you. Leaning in to softly kiss her lips, Ty took her back in his arms, the only place she ever wanted to be.

"So," he said.

"So," Janna echoed, settling back into the exquisite security of his embrace.

"That's that. There's just one more important question I need to ask you."

"What's that?"

"What the hell is *sfogliatelle*?"

Janna laughed. "You got me. But then, you already knew that."

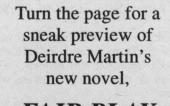

Turn the page for a
sneak preview of
Deirdre Martin's
new novel,

FAIR PLAY

Coming soon!

Theresa Falconetti hated lots of things: waterproof mascara that really wasn't; cheese you could spray from a can; and people who didn't give up their subway seat for the elderly or pregnant, to name a few. But number one on her list was doing something she didn't want to do. That's why Janna MacNeil, the partner with whom she ran her PR firm, was sparing with details about a new potential client.

"It's a restaurant," Janna explained as they shared morning coffee, a mutual addiction.

"A restaurant," Theresa repeated thoughtfully, sinking down into one of the plush leather chairs in Janna's office. She didn't want to think about how much they'd shelled out on furniture. "Since when do we handle restaurants?"

"Since our accountant told me we need to drum up as much business as we can."

Theresa sighed. "Hit me."

"It's a mom and pop place in Brooklyn," Janna began, reading the details from a piece of paper on her oversized desk. "It's got a strong local following, but the new owners, two brothers, want to start pulling in the foodies from Manhattan." She raised her head to look at Theresa. "Are you free this afternoon?"

"I think so."

"Then would you mind going out there and meeting with these guys? I've got to meet with Mike Piazza."

"Mike Piazza? Of the Mets?"

"No, Mike Piazza the *plumber*. Of course Mike Piazza of the Mets."

Theresa sank back in her chair. It always seemed to work out this way: Janna meeting celebrities, Theresa dispatched to check out what was probably a glorified pizzeria. "What time do the Brooklyn brothers want to meet?"

"Around two."

"That's doable. Where's the restaurant?"

"Bensonhurst."

"Really?" Theresa was surprised. She was born and raised in Bensonhurst. She wracked her brain, trying to figure out what family restaurant Janna might be talking about. And then it hit her.

"You're sending me to Dante's, aren't you." she said flatly.

Janna glanced away guiltily. "Yes."

"I don't *believe* you!"

Dante's was the restaurant where the Blades held all their private parties. One of its co-owners was Michael Dante, a third-line winger for the team. He'd made a lasting impression on her two years ago when he asked to buy her drink, failing to realize he didn't have his two front teeth in. At Ty and Janna's wedding, he'd hounded her endlessly to dance. She couldn't stand to be around him—he reminded her of everything she'd like to forget.

"You tricked me," she accused.

"I know," Janna confessed. "But I knew it was the only way to get you to agree. Besides, his brother will be there, too."

"Can't you switch your meeting with Piazza so that *you* can handle it?"

"It's business, Theresa. . . ."

"I really don't want to deal with him."

"I've never understood what you have against Michael. He's a nice guy."

"A nice guy who reminds me of every Italian Brooklyn boy I grew up with and moved to the city to avoid."

Janna gave a small grimace. "Well, try to keep an open mind when you're meeting with them, please. We could really use this account."

"I'll be the consummate professional," Theresa assured her while mentally stockpiling insults to use on Dante if he dared flirt with her. She'd meet with him, fine. They needed the business, so she'd do it.

But she didn't have to like it.

Theresa pushed open the large, carved wooden door to the restaurant and slipped inside, out of the warm September air. The lights and air-conditioning were on, but there was no one behind the long, polished wood bar, and every linen-covered table in the large room was empty. Trying hard to

ignore the bad paintings of Venetian gondoliers and pictures
of local priests gracing the red walls, she loudly called out
"Hello?" A minute later, Michael Dante appeared through
the swinging steel doors of the kitchen. He was scowling,
but upon seeing her, the tension melted from his face and
was replaced by a big smile. *Here it comes*, thought Theresa.

"Theresa. It's great to see you."

Theresa smiled politely. "Nice to see you, too. I see
you're wearing all your teeth today."

"For you, a full mouth," he kidded back. Theresa noticed him subtly checking her out and bristled. *Get over it,
ice boy. It's never going to happen.*

"So . . ." she began, anxious to get the ball rolling so she
could get the hell out as quickly as possible. "Should we
wait for your brother to arrive?"

"That won't be necessary," Michael said stiffly, ushering
her to a table for two. "You want anything to drink? Pellegrino, a glass of wine?"

"Pellegrino would be great," said Theresa, watching his
back as he sauntered away and slipped behind the bar. Objectively speaking, he was not unattractive: black, tousled
hair, tan skin, and green-blue eyes, which seemed to change
color depending upon what he was wearing. A decent body,
too: strong arms and a muscled chest tapering down to a
perfect V at the waist.

Filling two glasses with ice, over which he poured min-
eral water for both of them, Michael tried to hide his disappointment at the change in Theresa's appearance. She was
still gorgeous, but looked nothing like he remembered—or
fantasized about. Clad in black from head to toe, her long,
wavy hair was pulled back in a sleek bun, and her eyes were
obscured by those chic, heavy framed glasses all the hip people seemed to favor nowadays. Her manner was different,
too. Polite, formal. How could this be the same woman who,
just two short years ago, was fun, flirty, and enjoyed cursing
at him in Italian? *Maybe she wasn't The One after all.*

Michael handed Theresa her Pellegrino and slipped into
the chair opposite her. "You look nice today," he noted.

Theresa frowned. "Can we stick to business, please?"

"Sure," he said, seeming to suppress a smile. "My brother and I need your help. We want to turn Dante's into an upscale, Manhattan-style restaurant."

"Okay," Theresa said cautiously, taking out a legal pad and pen. "Tell me what you have in mind."

She listened carefully as he outlined the reinvention he envisioned. Just as she was about to ask him if they planned any renovations, *boom!* one of the kitchen doors flew open and out stormed an older, 1970s version of Michael, pointedly glaring at them as he strode across the restaurant and out the front door.

Theresa turned to Michael questioningly. "Was that—?"

"My brother?" Michael supplied. "Yeah, that was him, all right."

"He doesn't seem very . . . happy."

"He's not. He thinks upgrading the restaurant is a cardinal sin on a par with jarred gravy and *Godfather III*." Michael shook his head dismissively. "Don't worry about him. I've got him covered."

Trying to regroup, Theresa posed the question she'd meant to ask before they'd been interrupted. The answer was they were planning to expand both the dining area and the banquet room within the next couple of months.

"What about decor? What have you got in mind there?"

"I don't know." Michael looked around the restaurant blankly. "Some more paintings, I guess. A couple more pictures."

"If you want to attract a more upscale clientele," Theresa began gently, "the restaurant may need a more . . . polished . . . look."

"Okay." Michael drained his Pellegrino like a man needing fortification for what might come next. "What else?"

"The food has got to be exceptional if you want to draw from the other boroughs."

"It is," he said confidently.

"You're sure it is or you hope it is?"

"It is," he repeated stubbornly. "You know it is. You've eaten here."

"That was over a year ago." *At Ty and Janna's wedding, when you were such a noodge I wanted to shove a square of lasagna down your throat just to get you to shut up and leave me alone.*

"Well, nothing's changed. If anything, the food's gotten better." He jumped up from the table. "Hang on a minute, I want you to taste something." He disappeared into the kitchen, returning a minute later with a small dessert plate that he placed in front of her.

"What's this?" Theresa asked suspiciously, staring down at puffy pancakes drizzled with honey.

"Just try it," Michael urged. "Go on."

Uncomfortable with being watched but trapped, Theresa reached for a fork and cut off a small piece of the pancake, popping it in her mouth. It was good. Okay, it was very good. No, she had to be honest, it was great. If he wasn't there she'd snarf down the whole thing.

"Well?" he asked expectantly.

"BTS," she declared rapturously.

"BTS?"

"Better than sex."

Michael laughed. Now *that* was the Theresa he remembered: blunt, funny, unself-conscious . . . obviously, the girl who haunted his dreams was still in there somewhere, lurking behind the crisp, clipped demeanor.

"Careful. Your roots are showing, and I'm not referring to your hair."

Theresa's eyes narrowed. "What?"

"Your Brooklyn accent," Michael said affectionately. "It was there in full force just a moment ago. As for BTS," he added with a devilish grin, "are you sure about that?"

Theresa's expression darkened. *"Zoccolo! Come sei sciocco,"* she muttered under her breath, just loudly enough for him to hear.

Michael's heart swelled. She'd called him a tasteless clod! In Italian! God, he adored her.